THE DRAGON
AND THE EAGLE

SAM SANSUM

ISBN 978-1-961017-27-6 (Paperback)
ISBN 978-1-961017-28-3 (Ebook)

Inquiries and Book Orders should be addressed to:

Leavitt Peak Press
17901 Pioneer Blvd Ste L #298, Artesia, California 90701
Phone #: 2092191548

ACKNOWLEDGEMENTS

The lady who makes all my books tick.

Using her skills, Katie Hoolahan has once again added her touch as she edited this book.

I believe that together, we have produced a book where the reader will enjoy the adventure and romance which flows throughout.

CONTENTS

Chapter 1: A God Given Right 1

Chapter 2: From Traitor to Patriot 14

Chapter 3: An Unexpected Invitation 26

Chapter 4: The Tuscarora..39

Chapter 5: Turtle Bay 50

Chapter 6: Out of the Frying Pan and into the Fire 62

Chapter 7: The Battle of Lindley's Fort 74

Chapter 8: The Battle of Bennington..........................87

Chapter 9: The Battle of Bemis Heights......................100

Chapter 10: Valley Forge..112

Chapter 11: The Siege of Boonesborough 122

Chapter 12: Philadelphia 135

Chapter 13: The Raid on Unadilla and Ouaquaga 149

Chapter 14: The Battle of Beaufort Or The Battle of Port
            Royal Island. 163

Chapter 15: Oh, Brother..172

Chapter 16: The Battle of Newtown 185

Chapter 17: Where Shall We Go? 197

Chapter 18: A Place To Call Home.................................210

Chapter 19: The Battle of St Louis.................................222

Chapter 20: But Our Country Isn't Free Yet 234

Chapter 21: No one Messes With a Ranger When There
is a Dragon and an Eagle About 247

Chapter 22: The Battle of Cowpens 257

Chapter 23: The Battle of Haw River 268

Chapter 24: The Siege of Augusta 278

Chapter 25: A Second Home 290

Chapter 26: The Battle of Johnstown 302

Chapter 27: Siege of Bryan's Station 310

Chapter 28: Siege of Fort Henry 321

Chapter 29: The Way West: In Search of Our Dreams 328

BLURB

Dafydd Rhees lived in a small village in South Wales with his father, a Welsh methodist minister. His father was killed which led young Dafydd to join the British army and go to fight in the Americas.

A British officer killed his best friend, causing Dafydd to desert the army and eventually join up with a young American woman.

They both had been blessed with the abilities to raise their adrenaline in their bodies. Somewhat like an adrenaline rush. In their case this was far more powerful than the normal person.

They become stronger, faster, more agile. In fact, they both become the ultimate fighter.

They both gained nicknames by those who have seen them in action. Dafydd, becomes known as the Dragon, and Katie, becomes the Eagle. The Bald Eagle of course.

Together they fight to drive the British back across the Atlantic.

We join the story with Dafydd watching helplessly as his father's Church burns. Sadly, his father is believed still inside. With nothing left to keep him in the Village, He joins the British Army.

The book is set at the time of the American war for independence.

Join Dafydd and Katie, in their fight to drive the British out of their country.

This book is filled with historical facts and romance. You will begin to feel that you are with our young heroes as you journey through this book.

INTRODUCTION

It was a cold January evening. I was having a drink with my best friend Arwyn. We had been best friends since we both started school together. Well, it's true, we did start school but sometimes it wasn't always possible for me to attend. We lived in a small village in South Wales. My father was a Welsh methodist minister. His wages depended on how caring his flock were. True, they gave whatever they could but often it was in goods like some apples or vegetables. My brother and I took the same size shoes. Yes, you got it. We went to school on alternate days.

Arwyn and I left school when we were thirteen, seven years ago, but neither of us has had a steady job. Just odd jobs here and there. This beer has seen the last of my money.

"Arwyn, my friend, why can't we get permanent jobs?" I groaned.

"Dafydd, you know jobs go in order. First to the English, then those who are better educated than us. Then it's about who bows and begs for the job. We are none of those." He replied.

"I believe that everyone has a God given right to food in their bellies, a roof over their heads, and a bed to sleep on. And that means also a job, in order to pay for these things." I growled.

"What happened to your girlfriend, the one with the long blond hair?" Arwyn asked.

"She was never my girlfriend. Although I proposed to her once."

Arwyn looked surprised.

"I did not know that; did she turn you down?"

I nodded.

"Of course. The reason was the same as the other girls that I've had a crush on." Their faces ran through my mind. "They all said;

you have no job, no money, and no future. And the thing that hurt the most, was that it was true."

Arwyn stared at me.

I am sorry. I sighed, then suggested that we had better start making our way home.

We were not far from where I lived, when Arwyn shouted.

"Look at that smoke! It's coming from the direction of your dad's church."

We both began to run. Luckily, we could only afford the one tankard. On arrival, the flames were leaping into the sky. The police were there trying to keep the crowd back. I tried to get through but I was stopped.

"You can't get any closer, son. The church has been ablaze for over an hour, it is past saving."

But I continued to push.

"I need to find my father."

The same officer put his arm around my shoulders.

"We have been looking for him since the fire started, it's possible that he was in the church when the fire started."

I broke down crying. Arwyn was there for me as I watched the flames consume the holy building. When the fire was finally put out and we were just left looking over ashes. Arwyn asked me to go home with him. At a time like this he was the kind of friend that I needed. Later that day, the police informed me that they had found my father's body in the ashes. My blood ran cold.

My mother had died giving birth to me. My father did his best to bring me up. Now he has been killed by some evil being who hated the non-conformist church. I had no job, no money and now no family. Was life really worth living?

CHAPTER 1

A GOD GIVEN RIGHT

I was sitting alone, with darkness consuming my thoughts, when Arwyn came running towards me with a massive smile on his face.

"The army is recruiting for the war in the Americas. They have opened up a recruiting office in our village hall. And they are paying one pound and ten shillings a month."

I wasn't sure about this, but I didn't have anyone to leave behind, no family, no job, no relationships. Joining the army would offer regular money, a chance to see other lands and adventure. So I didn't give it any more thought.

"Ok, let's do it my friend."

"Look at those smart uniforms. I wonder if they will impress the girls." Grinned Arwyn.

"I hope they do, otherwise what's the point of joining." We both laughed.

We wandered leisurely down to the village hall.

"The 41st Regiment of foot soldiers." Read Arwyn from the poster on the noticeboard.

"Sounds like a lot of walking, I had been hoping to join the cavalry and get a horse. That would be so much better than walking." I groaned.

"This way General… Sorry, my mistake, that will be next year." Smirked the soldier at the entrance. We both stumbled into the room. A rather short, fat man seemed to be in charge.

"You want to serve your King and country," he said encouragingly, more a statement than a question.

"Yes sir," replied Arwyn in a soldier-like manner.

"And how about you young man?"

I looked him up and down, I feel that I am fairly good at assessing people, I could tell that whatever I asked for he would agree to give to me. That of course would be until I signed the form.

"Will I be a general next year, sir? And does my money get doubled each month, sir?" He stared at me blankly for a while. He could see that I was no fool. Then he smiled.

"I will gladly promise you whatever you want, but we both know that you won't get any of it. What I can offer is, 1 pound and ten shilling a month; a uniform, which if you fail to keep in pristine condition will mean a flogging; a rifle, the same applies to that - and don't lose it, that would result in the firing squad; a sabre; and best of all, 3 good meals a day; not to mention the adventure of travelling and seeing things that you could never even imagine trapped in this quaint little village of yours."

I felt a smile creep up on my face.

"I would be glad to sign then." I said, picking up the pen next to the form.

We both signed and then went to wait with the other new recruits. We were given a uniform. I was lucky mine was a good fit, the one which Arwyn got was a bit large - I had trouble stopping myself from laughing. Next was the real reason I had joined. I had always wanted to learn to fire a rifle.

"Gentlemen, you are all truly honoured. You are about to be given a Ferguson Rifle. It is the first breech loading rifle to be adopted by the military. This rifle can be reloaded while in the prone position. For the information of you ignorant lot, the prone position is lying on your stomach." The officer in charge informed us.

He handed us all a brand-new Ferguson Rifle. It felt good in my hands. I had no idea as to what breech loading meant, but I am sure I would learn soon.

"I hope you like them," smiled the officer. However, you won't be given them until we meet again in Aldershot. So on the way out please return them to the officer."

We were then dismissed. Well, at least from the presence of the officer in charge. A rather tall and loud sergeant then approached us recruits.

"I won't be calling you gentlemen, because I know you aren't. Normally new enlisted men get two months training. I say 'normally' as the British Army is short of men in the Americas. You will receive one week, so learn fast or you will die even faster. Report for training at Aldershot barracks on Monday at 9am sharp."

He then clicked his heels and started to leave.

"Sir, we don't have any money, how will we be able to get to Aldershot?" Asked Arwyn.

"At noon tomorrow there will be transport, make sure you arrive on time as they won't wait for late arrivals." We all began to discuss this with each other.

"That is a bit short notice, sir. We all have so much to do before leaving." I cautioned.

"What if we do arrive late?" Enquired Arwyn.

The sergeant grinned.

"You have just joined a foot soldier regiment, so it will be good for you to have a bit of practice with walking." I stared at him with disdain.

We all began to discuss our concerns with each other, but no amount of complaining would change anything. Arrive late, and we would have a long walk ahead of us.

Arwyn and I arrived just before noon. The others were all there, they were quite excited, discussing their expectations. At exactly 12 o'clock, our transport arrived. It was only then that we realised that John Davis had not arrived yet. We could not leave without him. If he didn't get on these wagons, he would not arrive in Aldershot on time and be charged with desertion.

"I am sorry young man, but my orders are to leave in five minutes' time. If your friend isn't here then, I will have to leave without him." Stated the driver.

Arwyn and I decided to go look for him, and resigned ourselves to finding another way to get to Aldershot if we were unsuccessful. The waggons left on time. We found John ten minutes later.

"Sorry lads, thanks for waiting for me. How are we going to get to Aldershot?" enquired John.

"Do you remember that poster at the pub? Tonight, the British boxing champion will be in the field next to the pub. He is offering £10 to anyone who can stay on their feet against him for six minutes."

Arwyn smiled.

"You are going to beat the British boxing champion?"

I shook my head.

"No, but I sure as hell will try to stay on my feet for the six minutes."

"I think you need to start making plans on how you will get to Aldershot by foot. I have seen him fight before; he can punch nails into a log." A lad at the back of the room stated. The lad with him nodded in agreement. "If you are not at Aldershot on Monday, you will be charged with desertion."

I was at the field early. I wanted to see this man in action. Wow. I'm six feet tall, but the British champion must have been at least six inches taller than me.

It was soon time for the challenge of the evening. He stood there looking like a true champion. The call went out for challengers. There was no response. Eventually they doubled the prize money in order to find a challenger. Two money hungry young men stood up. Both were soon carried off to hospital. Finally, I stood up.

"Make it thirty, and I will accept your challenge." The crowd went silent and they all began to stare at me.

"Come on up. Stay on your feet for six minutes and I will give you forty pounds." He said with a smirk on his face.

I had a strategy. I was faster than him, so the idea was to just keep moving and avoid his punches. Later as I start to slow, I would then cover up and try to soften the blows, but whatever came at me, I had to stay on my feet. As I climbed into the ring, the champion asked me.

"So, why are you going to fight me?" I told the truth. We had to get to Aldershot by Monday. Either I won the Money, or we would all have to walk.

"I like your honesty." The Champion declared.

The bell went. I was moving well, with the champion following me. Two minutes went well, I was still staying away from his fists. About the third minute, he caught me on the side of my head. That hurt. I couldn't afford to catch many of those. I just about kept up my dodging tactic, taking another few glancing blows, but nothing that shook me. By the fifth minute, I was just covering up and taking blows. I was now bleeding badly.

Punches were coming in fast, left and right. With 30 seconds to go, I was still on my feet. Then it came. A haymaker.

His right fist smashed into my jaw and my legs gave way. I woke up maybe half an hour later, still laying in the ring. Arwyn was peering down at me with the biggest grin I've ever seen.

"You won Dafydd!" I was just getting my senses together.

"But I remember losing. He knocked me out." I protested.

"My brave friend. Apparently, you had lasted six minutes. He told me to tell you, you are a brave man."

I was not totally sure as to what was going on. "Well, here is your £40. You can use it to arrange the transport to Aldershot" I shook my head.

"No, you do the arranging." I grunted; I had not fully recovered.

Arwyn hired a farmer to take us to Aldershot. I was a rich man now… well, at least for the time being.

At 9am sharp we were all there, all smart and shiny, wearing our bright red uniforms. The last thing I wanted was an encounter with a whip on my first morning.

"Attention! I am your sergeant major, it will be my duty to get you all ready to fight the Americans. You will undergo two months of training in one week."

What a week! Running; jumping; climbing. I finally learnt how to fire a rifle. I was the best shot of the recruits. It seemed natural to me. We also learnt the basic sabre strokes, which again, I picked up quicker than most.

On Saturday night we were given the night off. Sunday, we had to report to Portsmouth Dockyard. Monday morning, we would all be sailing to the Americas to support the rest of the British Army.

We all went to the local pub, we planned to dance and chat up girls, but in reality we had one pint and went to bed. It had been a *long* week.

It was the first time that Arwyn and I had seen so many ships. They were massive, with many guns on both sides. I silently hoped that we wouldn't be involved in any battles with other ships.

First thing on Monday morning we boarded our ship. We were sailing on The Silver Phantom. We were ordered below deck. This, it seemed, was where us soldiers would live for the journey, while the sailors stayed on deck.

There was not much room below deck, there were not only my mates, but twenty others who were already here when we arrived. It would have been good if we were all friends, but there was a short man who always seemed to have something to sit on - he had his own bodyguard - and a blond-haired man about my height who appeared to think that he was in charge. The penalty for fighting was fifty strokes of the whip. I did not fancy having my back cut to pieces, so I avoided them.

We were about two days out of port, when we were all ordered to go up on deck. There was a hapless sailor tied to a rack. He had probably done some trivial misdemeanour, and now he was going to be used to create discipline on board. *Crack*. The whip whistled through the air and sliced its victims back. Fifty strokes later, he was cut down and his back had salt rubbed into it, to prevent infection. That was so strange, they have his back cut to pieces, then they are concerned that his back may become infected.

A shout rang out and we returned below deck. As I reached the last step, the bodyguard was waiting.

"Watch out, or you will be next." He whispered. The food was mainly stews, which would usually contain either beef or fish, and ship's biscuits. I never got used to them. They are made from wholemeal flour, salt and water and when baked they become very hard, but they are often left until they become stale or soft. You would have to be very hungry to eat them - most were full of weevils or maggots. If they wanted strong, fit, fighting men to arrive in America, you would think that they would have fed us better. Every morning we were let up on deck for exercise. This involved running around the deck five times, with the sailors making rude comments. We were let up ten at a time, but we ran in two shifts of five. While I was waiting for my time to run I got chatting to one of the sailors.

"How long will it take us to reach Boston?" I enquired. He grinned.

"It's not how long, but if we arrive at all."

I stared at him.

"What do you mean?"

He chuckled.

"There are possibilities of hurricanes, pirates, or the worst, disease. If we avoid all of these, we may make land by December."

We sailed on for maybe another four weeks, down in the hold, we had no idea of time. I was glad that the weather had been good. If we had to endure a hurricane, I would not fancy our chances down here.

Then it all happened. We heard our cannons being fired.

"Everyone on deck, and don't forget your rifles!" It was one of our sergeants calling us. We all hurried up the steps. Nothing could have prepared us for what welcomed us. One of our masts had been hit and had crashed down onto the deck. There were dead and injured sailors all over the place. "Line up along the side and shoot as many of them as possible, before they attempt to board our ship." Came the order.

I quickly dropped to one knee and shouldered my rifle. Arwyn followed suit next to me.

"Time to see how much we actually learnt during training." He laughed.

We must have learnt a lot as we hit about twelve of the enemy before they were able to board our ship. I hid my rifle under some oilskins and drew my sabre. I planned to collect it later, the last thing I wanted was a whipping.

The pirates poured over the side onto our ship. Arwyn and I were fighting back-to-back. I suddenly shouted out an order, out of instinct.

"41st regiment to me now!" To my surprise, even the bodyguard joined me. I had gathered our men at the front of our ship. "Line up in three lines of five, I will lead. Let's try and fight our way to the centre of this ship." I cried. "Then we will form a square and either we will all die, or fend off these pirates until they leave."

Together, we slashed left and right, as we slowly cut our way to the centre of our ship. We had lost five men, with four more injured, when we arrived at the centre.

"Well done men, you are brilliant. Bring the injured into the middle of our formation. Then continue to fight as courageously as you have been doing." At first it was fast and bloody, but gradually the enemy fell back, eventually returning to their own ship. We had been joined by the remaining sailors.

"Do any of you know how to fire those cannons?" I pointed to three which were directly in front of the pirate's vessel. Most of the sailors nodded.

"Then go. Now! Fire directly at their ship." I shouted."Being this close to them, you should cause a decent amount of damage."

It worked like a dream. Massive holes were smashed in the side of the ship. They were starting to sink.

"Quick, riflemen, make sure they can't return to our ship as theirs sink." We all rushed to the sides with our rifles, picking off the enemy as the pirate ship sank.

"Sir, there is another British ship on the horizon." shouted the man in the crow's nest.

I laughed.

"Did you hear that Arwyn? I am now a 'sir'."

While we waited for our other ship to arrive, the time was spent tending to the wounded and burying the dead. Well, a sailor's burial - they were slid into the Ocean - but that still counts.

Eventually the other ship arrived and men began to come across to our ship. We formed up in a line and came to attention as their captain began to board.

There he was, all bright and shiny. Wearing his white pants, red jacket with a golden collar and black hat. Let's not forget those medals, there must have been twenty of them. It was a shame that we didn't have any officers to meet him.

I happened to be standing in the centre, so I received his first question.

"Soldier, where is your captain and the other officers?" I was doing my best to stand at attention, but the cut in my side was causing a problem.

"Dead, sir. They are all dead." What else could I say, they were all dead.

He stood for a while taking in the situation.

"As you don't have any officers left, who has taken command?" he asked. Silence hung in the air.

Then the bodyguard began to speak. It was funny, I had never thought of asking his name.

"Sir, the Welshman took command in the absence of any officers." He saluted and stepped back.

"And who is this Welshman?"

Well, there were two of us, but I knew he was talking about me. I stepped forward and saluted.

"Me, sir."

He stared at me for a while before asking his question.

"What is your name? And how long have you been in His Majesty's service?"

I saluted again; I am not sure why.

"My name is Dafydd Rhees. I am not entirely sure how long I have been in the King's service. I know we joined two weeks before we boarded this boat. But I have no way of telling how long we have been at sea. Sir."

He then held out his hand and I shook it.

"Well done man, I will remember your name." He pressed a gold sovereign in my hand. I may have saved his ship, but all he gave me was a gold sovereign. Amazing.

The captain returned to his ship, and sent officers and sailors aboard, to get the ship to its destination.

Our ship eventually docked at New York City. The captain decided to avoid Boston, as there had been riots there.

The captain had sent over to my ship, a newly promoted second lieutenant. He was out to make a name for himself. He would have men whipped for anything, no matter how minor the offence. Before the men disembarked, he ordered an inspection. That would be all of our kit, including, of course, our rifles.

When we first set foot on this ship, there were forty of us. Now there are only thirty. Three of my friends, who had enlisted with Arwyn and I, are now feeding the fish. We saved His Majesty's ship from pirates. And he still wanted to have this inspection.

We all lined up in a straight line. He arrived with his batton under his arm. Slowly he walked up and down the line. Then it happened. He stopped in front of Arwyn.

"This rifle is dirty and there is a dent on the side." That dent came when he hit a pirate who was about to plunge his sword into my chest.

"Before this man leaves the ship, give him fifty lashes."

We were all speechless. How could he order this?

At the time I had not noticed, but many passers-by on the dock had stopped to watch what was about to unfurl.

"Sir, this man damaged his rifle saving my life when we were fighting the pirates to save the ship." I informed him. "Please, rescind your order."

He went red in the face.

"You scum keep talking about saving this ship. Let me get this through your thick skulls. I am in command. What I say goes. I have power over whether you live or die. You are expendable and if you think that saving one ship is anything but your damned duty then you don't deserve to serve." He then drew his pistol, and shot Arwyn in the head. I knelt beside him in shock; tears were running down my cheeks. My best friend was dead. My blood was like ice running through my veins. I rose to my feet and for a second stared at Arwyn's killer. Then I drew my blade and plunged it up to the hilt into his stomach. I withdrew the knife and watched the officer fall to the floor, the shock of what just happened to him painted plainly on his face. As he lay dying in his own blood, I sprinted down the gang-plank and slinked off into the side streets. Many of the spectators that saw what unfolded, helped me in my escape.

The redcoats were after me. I should have thanked the spectators for blocking my pursuers. I had dumped my uniform and stole some clothing. I needed a place to hide until everything calmed down. After evading the soldiers for a couple of hours, I stumbled upon a stable. I say a stable, but there was only one horse. I found some dry straw in the corner. The stable was warm, I was soon asleep, it was probably the first time I had fully fallen asleep since boarding that ship. I later began to wake up. That was such a wonderful sleep. I felt so refreshed. Then the reality of my situation hit me hard, like a punch in the gut. I saw the pistol that was pointing right at me.

"Who are you, and why are you sleeping here?" Demanded a beautiful young woman.

"Is this your stable? It is nice and dry," I quipped.

"It belongs to my parents, and they won't want a tramp like you sleeping here. Leave. Now."

Lucky for me. One of the people with her, had seen me stab the officer.

"Hold on Katie, He could be a friend." He then explained to the young woman what had happened on the ship.

"Hmm, I wonder how much the Redcoats will offer us to turn you in to them?" She joked. "Seriously, it seems to me that you have burnt your bridges with the British. What are your plans now?"

I scratched my head. The thought of what I'd do next hadn't even begun to cross my mind.

"Well… I have no friends or family in Wales now that my father was killed. And I am now a wanted man by the British army. You are right, I have burnt my bridges. If I can avoid the British for a few days, I guess I could head West. That's probably the only way I can get away from the soldiers." She held out her hand.

"Would you like some food?"

I had forgotten the last time I had eaten. My stomach grumbled, as if in protest to how neglected it had been.

"Yes please," I said eagerly, "if it doesn't put you out." I added out of politeness. Then something occurred to me. "If the British see me with you, you will also be arrested."

She laughed.

"They have a lot more things to arrest me for."

She led me out of the stable, and into her house. They must have money, I thought. What a nice place to live.

"First, a bath and a change of clothes." she ordered. She pushed me into a room with a bath, it was already filled with hot water. I undressed then got into the bath. This was the first time that I had ever had a proper bath. I had always bathed in a wooden half barrel, using a jug to pour lukewarm water over myself. To be fully immersed in a tub felt very warm and relaxing. Suddenly the door opened.

"I have brought you some clean clothes to wear." She declared.

Embarrassed, I held my breath and disappeared under the water. When I was running out of breath, I hoped she had gone. I popped my head out of the water.

"She's gone, that's good," I said to myself, relieved. I began to get out of the bath.

"The clothes are over there on the stool. Put them on." I nearly died with shock. I dived down into the bath again.

"It's ok, I have a brother, you have nothing I haven't seen before."

"You may have seen your brother's body, but I am not your brother, please give me some privacy." I was angry.

She just grinned and left the room.

I dried myself and put on the new clothes. Not bad, I thought. Now where were my knife and sword? They were missing.

There was a knock on the door.

"Are you ready? If so, will you join us for dinner?"

Dinner. I began to drool just at the thought of it.

"Yes, I am on my way."

As I opened the bathroom door, she was waiting.

"Wow, I hardly recognised you," she declared.

There were six of us seated at the table. The food was amazing. Roast Venison, Turkey, or Pheasant. Then came the vegetables.

Potatoes, Yams, Cassava, Beans, Okra, Millet, and Pineapples. I cleared my plate well before the others.

"Would you like a second helping?" she enquired. "Yes please," I gratefully accepted.

"Dafydd, true, you can head west into the wilderness. Or you can think about my offer." She began. "People from all over the world are coming here. They want to carve a new life for themselves out of this land. The British only want this country so they can tax us." I knew that was true, all the British colonies were used to finance the treasury. Then she continued "We are fighting to free this land from the British. We are called Patriots. I understand that you handle a blade well and are a good shot with your rifle. Would you be interested in joining us?"

I found myself scratching my head again.

"Can I sleep on it?"

Katie nodded.

"Sleep well, give me your answer over breakfast.

CHAPTER 2

FROM TRAITOR TO PATRIOT

I was trying to open my eyes. I had slept in a real bed for the first time in my life. I didn't want to wake up.

"Breakfast is ready."

I heard from above me. I accomplished my task and saw this angel looking down at me.

"Wake up, we have a busy day ahead." Then the angel began to shake my body back and forth. Eventually I ended up on the floor. My eyes finally began to focus.

"Good morning, Katie." I remarked.

"Get dressed and I will see you downstairs for breakfast." She barked. I guess she hadn't slept as well as I did. I smiled.

I seemed to float down the stairs, following the wonderful smell of food. There it was, nicely laid out on the table. I sat on the spare chair and began to eat. Breakfast was quite simple. It was called Farmer's stew. She had also made Hasty Pudding. The Farmer's stew seemed to be a lucky dip I tasted rabbit and squirrel.

"I presumed that you had a good night's sleep." She was smiling as she spoke. Was this all a dream?

"We just had a visit by the British army, they were looking for someone who fit your description. They also had an invite for a necktie party." She was still grinning, unlike myself.

The events of yesterday finally came back to me in full reality.

"It's ok, they have left. Did you sleep well?" she enquired, for a second time. This time I was able to respond.

"Yes, thank you. So, what are the plans for today?" I asked. "That, Mr Rhees, will depend on your answer to my offer." She was now staring at me.

For a moment, I began to recall a few weeks ago, when we applied to join the British army. He was willing to offer me anything, for us to sign, knowing full well that they were promises that would not come to reality.

"Well, what will I get if I become a Patriot?" Everyone was now laughing.

"First, you will live. You have learnt too much about us to be able to walk out of my house. Second, you will be serving people who want to carve a piece of this land for their families. And third, I can offer you lots of great adventures." She grinned.

With the army looking for me, I had no other option than to join them.

"Well with such an interesting offer, I have no other choice than to become a Patriot." She smiled, then withdrew her hand from under the table, it was holding a Pistol.

"Your wise decision just saved me a bullet," she giggled.

For once in my life, I was speechless.

"I understand that you are a crack shot with that rifle, the officer you killed can vouch for your abilities with a knife. I have also been informed that you are a demon with your sword, and you have good leadership skills." She declared.

I began to wonder how she knew about what happened on the ship.

"If you are wondering why we have an empty chair at the table, I now introduce you to its owner." The door opened, and in walked the bodyguard. Losing my ability to speak was becoming a more regular thing. Katie stood up.

"Let me introduce you to Major John Martin," she had a grin on her face. "I believe that you two have met." She stated.

The bodyguard, John, walked over to me and held out his hand. "I am pleased to meet you again, Welshman," he chuckled.

I stood up and shook his hand.

"What happened to your master?" I enquired.

"He was not my master, but he was a good fighter for our cause. Alas he was killed during our fight with the pirates." He groaned. "But I am sure that you will make a good replacement. You have already earned my trust."

"Forget it, he is mine, I can use his skills." Katie interrupted. The atmosphere was becoming tense.

"Well, seeing as Katie is better looking than John, I will give my skills to her." I said jokingly, trying to ease the tension a little.

She smiled then turned to one of her men.

"John may trust him; my trust has to be earnt. keep an eye on him."

Major Martin wasn't pleased but he did not let it show. He finally sat in his chair.

"Fellow Patriots, I have news for you. On April 19th, the British plan to raid our armoury. We have moved most of our ammunition and will be sending forces to challenge the British. If this turns out to become a battle, then the Battle of Lexington, will be the opening salvo of our war for independence." A massive cheer filled the room. Then Katie began to speak.

"On the 23rd April, we will be attempting to rob the British Armoury in the City Hall.

There are muskets, bayonets and cartridges there, and that is why we will need the Welshman," she advised.

"Ok, he is yours;" John conceded. "I expect at some point we will be fighting alongside each other again. Katie, why do you continue to call him the Welshman?" He asked.

"It's just easier. I always have problems pronouncing these foreign names."

I was beginning to feel that I wasn't even in the room.

"Ok then, I have a better name for him. I watched him smash through an army of pirates. At times I was left to just stand and stare. He fights fiercely, with power and authority, just like the symbol of his country. Let's call him The Dragon. I feel he has earned such a name." Claimed the Major.

Katie was staring at me.

"Ok then, if he is The Dragon, then I must be The Eagle. Would you not say I was powerful and majestic, just like our national bird?"

The major lifted his glass.

"Let's raise our glasses to The Dragon and The Eagle."

The major finally left, he had business elsewhere. Katie, or should I say 'The Eagle', approached me.

"Did you enjoy your bath and a nice sleep?" She enquired.

"Yes, thanks." I replied.

"Well, I suggest that you have another bath soon, and a quick nap." She winked, and started to walk away. I grabbed her arm.

"Why should I bathe early and sleep now?" I was curious.

"Well, Mr Dragon, the British have demanded this house for their commander. They plan to move in tonight." She was strangely cool about this.

"So, Ms Eagle, what are you planning?" I was slowly getting to know this woman a little better. She pulled herself away from my grasp.

"We have work to do elsewhere, but I will leave them a gift to remember me by."

"Chocolates or Flowers?" I asked with a grin.

"I am leaving something to brighten up their evening." Her smile turned downwards as she continued. "My only problem is, I need a volunteer to light the fuse. I am afraid that this volunteer may not manage to escape from the carnage." She admitted.

"You need a Dragon to breathe his flame on the fuse." I said, still smiling.

"No. I won't let you, you will be needed to break into the armoury. I can't risk you getting killed." She cautioned.

"It seems that you have never seen a Dragon in action. Leave this to me. Don't worry, I don't plan to die yet."

Her face changed and she relaxed a little, no longer seeming doubtful about my abilities; she regarded me with a look of respect.

"May I borrow twenty of your men?"

She nodded, although seemed a little suspicious.

"What do you need them for?"

"I did just guarantee that I would not get hurt tonight, however I am a bit rusty, so I just need a little practice." I stated. She gave orders to someone who I had not met before, then left the room. I gave this man my instructions.

I met up with these 20 men later in the largest room of the house. If I was going to avoid capture tonight, I may have to fight a lot of soldiers. I would need to be at my best. At 2pm, I entered the room.

"Ok, these are the rules. You will all have real swords. I will have a wooden sword. There was a loud gasp, and everyone began talking quietly amongst themselves.

"Silence! If I strike anyone with my sword, they are out and must leave the room. Ok?" As far as I could see, everyone nodded. At this point I removed my top. Although it was still January, I knew I would get rather hot during my practice.

I had chosen the largest room in the house. This provided me with room to move about. I was impressed with myself; I had not lost much of my fitness. Gradually, one by one, my opponents left the room, until there were just three remaining. Sweat was dripping from my brow onto my chest, before dripping onto the floor. One went in seconds. The other two managed to avoid me for a while. Suddenly the door flew open. My opponents looked away, and I struck them both.

"Always keep your concentration," I reminded them. A hearty laugh came from the doorway.

"Would The Dragon like to duel with an Eagle?"

"Well, I *thought* I had just earned myself one last bath and a couple of hours sleep." I pleaded with her.

"Come on! First hit is the winner, ok?"

I gave a tired nod. Someone offered her a sword.

"This Eagle has talons." She winked at me.

We circled each other for a couple of minutes. Then The Eagle charged. She was good, almost catching me. Her next attack, I just sidestepped and put my arm around her, pulling her against my chest. At the same time, I hit her sword hard and it fell to the floor.

She began scratching and punching me. I quickly released her. She hurriedly left the room, as she closed the door, she shot me a quick smile. I was beginning to like this woman.

By 5pm everything was set up. The bombs had been planted around the house, with a thin line of gunpowder running between each one of them. The black line had been concealed as much as possible. I gave my rifle to Katie, sorry 'The Eagle'.

"Look after this. I will be collecting it later." I told her.

"Don't forget, you promised not to get killed." I could genuinely feel her concern. I gave a thumbs up as she disappeared out of the door.

At 6pm precisely, soldiers came pouring through the door and began searching the building. I was hidden in the broom cupboard. Typically, the soldiers did not do a thorough search, leaving me safely concealed. I did not plan to take too long before lighting the fuses. I didn't want anyone discovering the powder. It was already dark outside; well, it was January.

By 9pm, most of the officers staying in the house had drunk their glass of claret, and were dosing in their chairs. I slowly opened the door to the cupboard, and stepped out.

I remembered where the line of gunpowder started in this room. The small glow of light coming from the door did not provide much light, but I managed to locate the beginning. The room I had chosen was not one which an officer would frequent. I pulled my flint out of my pocket and quickly lit the powder. I turned towards the door at the same time as a soldier entered. I had no time to waste. I did not want to break my promise to Katie. The soldier died silently, with my sword in his stomach before he had realised I wasn't a friend. I slipped out of the room and crossed the hall. I now only had to pass one more room and I would be away long before the first bomb exploded.

As I passed the room, the front door opened and a sentry entered. For a moment he stood trying to work out who I was. That was his misfortune. He had finished his last guard duty. As he fell forward, he knocked over a small table. This resulted with an officer popping his head out of the room to find out what the noise was. He gave the alarm and about fifteen gentlemen pushed their way out of the room ready to confront me. This wasn't really a fair encounter as most of them were slightly drunk. I had to move fast as I did not want the rest of the house to wake up. Five of them lay dying before they had managed to draw their swords. Soon there was just one left. He decided to make a run for it. I threw my knife. He died at the bottom of the staircase. I turned and sprinted out of the door. I made about four hundred yards before the first bomb exploded. I knew I should have left sooner; I was caught by the blast. I ended up another two hundred yards further forward. The pain was overwhelming, but I couldn't just lay there. I forced myself to stand up and stagger away.

One of the sentries saw me and began aiming his rifle in my direction. I could see him out of the corner of my eye. I had all but resigned myself to breaking my promise to Katie, when he suddenly disappeared out of my vision - a second bomb had gone off.

I was losing blood and feeling very weak. I felt two pairs of strong hands grab hold of my arms and start to drag me away from the building.

"Katie left us here, just in case you had any problems." Despite my pain, I managed to smile before passing out.

A sharp pain through my back brought me to my senses. I was laying on some form of bed, nothing like the one I slept on the night before. I was on my stomach wearing only my underwear.

"Keep still. I am trying to sort your back out." I recognised that voice.

"Well, I kept my promise. I made it back alive." I winced as she touched my back with some sort of salve.

"If I hadn't left Tom and Clancy behind, I doubt very much that you would have kept it." She chuckled. Then she gently slapped my backside.

"That's the best I can do for you. I think you will still be of use at the armoury." Then she laid a blanket over me. I closed my eyes and was soon in dreamland.

The following morning, I woke to a stinging sensation in my back.

"Aha, you're awake at last. Lay still I will take a look at your back."

"Katie, your tenderness overwhelms me." She laughed. Her laughter did not last long, as she spread the ointment over my back.

"Ouch!"

"Be quiet you baby, you only have a few scratches and the burns are minor." She alleged. Eventually she left with a statement, that if I did not get downstairs soon, there would be nothing left for me.

"Such a hard woman," I mumbled.

John, who was waiting to help me dress if I needed it, responded to my mumbling.

"You may think she is hard, but when we brought you here, with so much blood flowing down your back, that 'hard woman' had tears flowing freely down her cheeks until she had stopped the bleeding."

Wow, maybe I had misjudged her. My belly rumbled loudly.

"Come on John, we need to get down to breakfast."

From January to April seemed a long time. We were now living in an abandoned house, much smaller that Katie's house had been. The good thing was that the previous owners left their furniture behind when they fled.

Day after day, we trained hard. We had to be the fittest fighters in George Washington's army. At the end of March, we began to plan the capture of the ammunition from the City Hall. Katie had lent one of her scouts to Major Martin, his main job was to return as quickly as possible with a report at the end of the battle.

Training 24 hours a day isn't ideal, the body needs rest to repair and grow stronger, therefore Katie ordered us to train for three days, then take a day off. During our day off we could relax, enjoy the countryside, and recharge our batteries. It was on one of these days when I saw Katie going for a walk. I decided to follow her. Secretly, of course.

It was now spring; flower buds were opening up into fragrant blossoms. Katie was walking across a large meadow covered in lush grass, still wet with dew. For a second, my mind drifted and I lost sight of her. There she was, just entering the forest at the end of the meadow. As I followed her, I began to see many animals and birds which I had never seen before. Some looked dangerous. Back in Risca, we did not have any dangerous animals.

Well, we had the adder, but few people had ever seen one. This country was so very different from home. I heard a noise coming from some scrubs. I had come to believe that most things in this forest could be dangerous, so I avoided the area. I had no idea where Katie had got to. Suddenly, I stopped in my tracks and ducked behind a tree. What a nightmare, maybe eight hundred yards away I saw a big brown bear. I had heard about these brown bears, but you didn't get many rambling around near Risca. Luckily, I was concealed, but something had aroused it. To my horror, Katie had stumbled upon the bear.

I had been informed that if I ever came face to face with a brown bear, not to try and outrun it. Try to look tougher than the bear was, and maybe it would withdraw. I did not remember the third option, but I didn't put much faith in one and two. Katie had decided to run. How could I help her? It would catch her soon. I think The Dragon will need to show its fangs.

I was now sprinting towards where I anticipated that the bear would catch Katie. The bear knocked her to the ground and was now leaning over her. I was always a fast runner, before the bear could do more harm to her, I was on its back. My left hand was hanging onto its fur, while the other stabbed it multiple times. This lady was strong, she threw me off her back, turned and ran towards me. A shot rang out. The dead bear toppled towards me and I had to dive out of the way being crushed by it.

Katie walked up to me and offered me a hand.

"It looks like I owe you my life," she claimed. After helping me up, she beckoned me to follow her. She pushed her way past various scrubs, until she found what she had been looking for. A pair of baby bears. "The mother bear was protecting her cubs. I made the mistake of not paying attention, now these babies are orphans." She had a very concerned look on her face. "If we leave them here, they will be dead by morning."

"Let's take them back with us." I suggested. She looked at me. I can't quite describe that look, but I think she agreed." We had gained two new recruits and it was bear steaks for dinner.

Not long after we returned, a rider came galloping into the yard. He jumped off at speed then charged into the room.

"War has been declared against Britain."

We had won! Everyone wanted to celebrate the victory, but Katie made us stop.

"I want to be inside the armoury in four days' time."

There were thirty members of Katie's group of Rangers. She sent five of them into the city to gather information about the armoury. The results weren't good. The city hall had been built like a castle, high walls, and plenty of British troops to defend it. Katie knew that she did not have enough men to break in and carry the weapons and cartridges out.

"We will have to get support from the militia. Follow me." she ordered. I looked around; unsure of who she meant.

"Yes, you." She confirmed, turning around to make sure I got up as she walked out the door. This woman didn't really know me, I have never liked being ordered around. She was rushing somewhere, and I was being left in her wake. It turned out that her destination was a pub - The White Stag. She entered and let the door close before I was able to catch up to her. I pushed the door open. During my days of unemployment in Risca, I visited many kinds of pubs. I was curious as to what kind this one was.

Now where did Katie go? I thought as my eyes searched the room. Then I saw her. She was sitting on the knee of a man who resembled a pirate. I was in no hurry to meet her comrades. I just lent against the wall surveying the action.

"Over here, Welshman," she shouted. I ignored her call. I am not sure as to what she was playing at, but for some reason I was not happy about it. "What's the matter, are you shy?" she called out. I now started to become angry, but I managed to compose myself.

Eventually a big, and I mean *big*, man approached me. 'I know who ate all the pies' I thought to myself as he grabbed hold of my collar.

"When Katie calls, you do what she says." I grabbed hold of his right arm. I bent forward and threw him over my shoulder and he came crashing down on a table, spilling two men's drinks. They both went for their swords. They were too slow; my sword was now pointing at one of their throats.

"I told you he was good," said Katie to the man whose lap she was sitting on.

"Shall I send everyone against him? Teach him a lesson?" He asked her.

"Only if you want them all to die. I think we have pushed him far enough; he is like a bomb ready to explode." She then got off the man's lap, and started to walk towards me. I have met many women who have wanted to use men in the past, I couldn't be bothered with them anymore.

I pushed the door open and left. Katie turned to the man.

"I told you not to push him too far." She followed me out of the door in a hurry. It was market day. If I was going to leave Katie's band, as well as being a deserter from the British, I would need to think about what I would do next. So I was just looking at what was for sale, considering my options.

Katie, in her hurry to find me, had forgotten who she was. After turning towards the stalls, she bumped into a soldier.

"Come here woman," he ordered. I looked to see what the noise was about. What a fool, I thought. Well, I had left her now, she would have to fend for herself. "You are coming with me to the guardhouse."

I just could not do it. I had to rescue her, even if it was the last thing I did for her. I came up behind the soldier and pushed my knife close enough so that he felt the point against his back.

"Gently hold the lady's hand, then slowly walk towards that pub. If you do anything stupid, I will ram my knife up to its hilt into your back. Do you understand." He nodded and held Katie's hand.

Katie opened the door and the soldier followed her. Once inside the pub, I hit him over the head. Better to sleep than die, I thought. The man whose lap Katie had been sitting on, came up to me.

"Let me introduce you to each other. This," she said, "is my brother, Richard." I stood there, dumbfounded for a moment. I had never thought of that being their relationship. "And this fiery Welshman is known as The Dragon." We shook hands. "Can I buy you a drink Mr Dragon?" he asked.

"My name is Dafydd, and you had better get a couple of men to remove that soldier." I glanced down at the sleeping man.

"I think that I am beginning to like you," he said with a grin. "Katie is here to raise the militia in this city. I believe you are wanting to break into the city hall." I nodded. "Well, I am the leader of a group of influential men, who are able to raise the militia." Katie came to my rescue.

"Sorry, he wanted to test you, I had to go with it. He is my older brother after all."

"You were nearly without a brother." I smiled. "While I was leaning against the wall, I was planning how I was going to kill him. I had presumed that he had made you sit on his knee." Now she was smiling,

"You were jealous," She smirked. I shook my head.

"I just don't like women being bullied." She was now shaking her head.

"You were jealous." She repeated. I went red in the face.

"Ok, so what if I was?" And then I was off out of the door again.

We met up later back at the house.

"I met up with my brother, as we need him to rouse the people of this city. We don't have enough men to break into the city hall on our own." I was still uncomfortable.

"So why were you sitting on your brother's knee? That's a bit weird." She then seemed to cool down and relax.

"There was a reason for our actions, but I don't know you well enough to tell you yet." She went over to the door and opened it. "But you aren't far away honey." With that she slipped out of the door. Leaving me feeling an odd warmness in my chest.

CHAPTER 3

AN UNEXPECTED INVITATION

Two days to go. We were still waiting for confirmation that Katie's brother had managed to raise the militia.

We were sitting in silence when I heard a coach approaching the house. We were all on high alert, in case the British found our base. We carefully approached the front door of the house. Before us was a very posh coach. It had two black horses. The coach was black with golden wheels and springs. As we stared in its direction, a smartly dressed man stepped out. On seeing Katie loitering in the doorway, he headed towards her. He bowed before her, then gave her a letter. She read the letter while we all stood and stared at her. Then to my surprise, she walked over to me, grabbed my hand, then whispered to me.

"Follow me."

I was still rather stunned as she stepped into the coach, and off it went. Now how was I supposed to follow her? I would need to turn into a real dragon and fly after her.

To my surprise, Richard quickly arrived with a horse, saddled and ready to ride.

"This horse will catch the coach in no time." He stated. I was sure that it could, but there was one teensy little problem. I did not know how to ride it. They say that necessity is the mother of invention, but it would need to be a very special invention to help me here. Somehow, with Richard's help, I clambered into the saddle. I leant forward, grabbing the reins and the horse's neck. Then with the slap on the horse's buttocks from Richard, we were off in pursuit of the coach, with me hanging on for dear life.

When the coach arrived at its destination, we were not far behind. Somehow, I managed to slide off the horse. Then I stood and stared at the building. Katie's house was amazing, but this was something else. Truly a mansion.

The whole building had been painted white. Lots and lots of windows. Four pillars, like the ones in Greece, I noticed the main gate with four guards standing to attention. I felt that it would be a lot better to find another way to enter the building. For me, this was never going to be a problem, I was soon over the wall. Now where to? I thought. It was now dusk, which helped me. I figured that my best way in was via a window.

"Father, why have I been dragged here? I am very busy. The last time we met, I promised never to see you again." Katie's Father was a self-made man. He, like most people in this country, were immigrants. Using his business skills, he had made a fortune, mainly from the British. The last thing he wanted was a war.

"My wayward daughter, I have left you to do your own thing for too long. You are the heir to one of the richest families in the city. It is time for you to stop running around and marry one of the eligible young men that have been vying for your hand."

The Eagle would never have put up with this. She was her own woman, but her father apparently had some power over her. A tall thin woman entered the room.

"Mother, tell father that I am happy as I am, I have no wish to marry anyone, at least at this moment in time." This woman was in no hurry to reply to her daughter. She casually strode up to stand beside her husband.

"Daughter, you are now a woman, no longer a child. As a woman, your duty is to marry a powerful nobleman. Your father and I have worked hard to create our riches. It is now your turn to do your part. You have the choice. Be an adult and marry the man who we have chosen. Or be a child and be cut off from our house and wealth." Katie was shocked. To make things worse, four women appeared and took her away to another room.

I finally found a lower window that had been carelessly left open. It did not take me long to get inside. It was now dark.

I dared not light a candle, that was of course if I could have found one. I stepped out of the room and into a corridor. Which way should I go, left or right? My decision was made for me. Two smartly dressed men were coming towards me. Should I run, or not? The answer was of course quite simple. I had to put them to sleep, before they made a noise. This did not take long, I then dragged them into the nearest room. As I was about to leave, I heard a group of women approaching. I pushed both men under the very large bed, then having no other choice, I joined them.

The door was pushed open and the women entered the room. They lit a few candles, then proceeded to undress one of the women.

"Let go of me!" The woman shouted. I smiled; I knew that voice. I had found The Eagle. I did not have time to mess about. The two men lying beside me would wake up soon. I rolled out from under the bed into the room, at the same time I drew my pistol and pointed it at the ladies.

"Be quiet Ladies. My pistol is inclined to go off all of a sudden." I looked towards the other women who were no longer shouting.

Katie stared at me in disbelief. Then she realised that some of her clothes had been removed, so she quickly grabbed a sheet to cover her modesty.

"It's ok Katie, I have a sister, I have seen it all before." I laughed. Ok, I haven't got a sister, only a brother who lived with our gran, but for all she knew I could have had one.

"Quick Katie, let's get these women gagged and tied up." We made quick work of it. Then Katie, back in her buckskins, led me towards the main hall.

"I'll go in, you follow later," she said. I began to ask her when exactly she wanted me to come in, but she had already gone and closed the door behind her. I guess I would just have to improvise. I peeked through the keyhole of the door to watch what was going on.

I had to admit, this was an amazing place, I doubt if any of King George's castles would be any better. "What are you doing in those old clothes?" asked her mother sternly.

"Too late now my love," her father replied, also visibly annoyed at Katie.

"He is here?" Asked her mother, in shock that her daughter would be presented to her future husband in 'rags'.

Then into the room walked a man in his fifties, wearing a grey wig. The clothes he was wearing… if they were sold, the money would feed a family for a year. He was wearing a tight fitting coat with a band collar, which was covered with silver stars. The waistcoat was shortened to just below the waist; the breeches were longer and tighter; and he was wearing a rather stiff stock, instead of a cravat. He walked up to Katie, then walked around her a few times.

"Yes, she is indeed young and beautiful. As soon as we get rid of those scruffy clothes, and give her a good bath, I am sure she will produce some strong babies for our family."

I was now standing in the doorway, trying to suppress my giggles so as not to make any noise.

"Daughter, this is Lord Rothchild. He had done us the honour of offering to marry you," said her father. The Eagle had landed. I could see she was about to explode.

It was my turn to make my entrance. I walked coolly across the floor, until I came alongside Katie. I held her hand.

"Do you mind? Why are you talking about marrying my wife?" I was speaking in a posh, British voice.

I whispered to Katie.

"Shall I tell them about the baby?"

"Don't push it." she whispered back, with a grin on her face. She then turned to Lord whatever and explained that it was impossible to marry him, but thanked him for coming. Then she faced her parents, I knew what was coming. This was no longer Katie the demure daughter, this was The Eagle in full flight.

"Parents," she began, "you are now aware that I cannot marry any of the men you choose. They may have lots of money and possessions, they may have titles, but this man offers far more. He is willing to give his life for the cause I am fighting for. A country where people are free to live the life they want, without having to get permission from mad king George." I was not sure about the bit where I was willing to give my life, but it was a strong speech. Her parents stood in shock.

I thought her father was going to have a heart attack.

"Remove this man now!" Six servants arrived at the door and started toward me.

"Father, if these men take another step, they will all be dead. My husband is also known as The Dragon, simply because he fights like a dragon. As I can't make the two of you accept my wishes, we will happily leave and I promise I will never see either of you ever again." Her parents began to chat between themselves.

"Evening everyone." It was Richard. "Evening Welshman, have you been getting into trouble again?" He laughed.

I smiled; I loved this man! Well, not as much as his sister. Wait, where did that thought come from?

"Mum, Dad." He went right up to his parents. "As years go by, and you are reading about heroes to your grandchildren, two names will stand out." He turned and pointed towards us. "Your daughter and son-in-law will be heroes of the revolution." He then came down to where I was standing.

"Did you really marry my sister?" he whispered. I shook my head.

"I had to think of something to save her." I muttered. He began to laugh again.

Katie's father sighed, then finally spoke.

"It is true, my daughter, that we tried to make you do what we thought was best for you. We can see that you have grown into an independent woman. No one will bend you to their will, not even us. Therefore, we can do no more than wish you luck in whatever you decide to do. If we can help, let us know.

"Please think of us now and then." begged her mother. Now that was nice, I thought. So, what was all the forcing her to marry about?

I think the Eagle has just won another battle. She ran to her parents and hugged them. Tears began to flow.

"Richard, is there any beer in this place?"

"Follow me." He grinned.

Everything was settled, we were invited to dinner. I thought I had died and gone to heaven. Venison, Beef, Duck, and various game birds. I counted ten different vegetables. There were even four very large pies.

If I was back home, I would have stuffed some of these marvellous foods into my pockets for later. But I am apparently too posh now-a-days to think of doing anything of the sort.

While we were both stuffing our faces, Richard lent over.

"It's all set, the militia will be ready to strike at 6am, well before any British troops will be awake."

Katie found her horse outside the walls, and tied him behind the coach. We both got in the coach and enjoyed a relaxing trip home.

It was very late when we arrived back at the house. As we closed the front door, I asked her a question. I think I may have had a bit too much to drink.

"So, darling, shall I carry you to bed?" A very stern look came upon her face.

"Listen Welshman, don't get carried away, we both know that we are not actually married." I got the message. I took off my racoon hat and bowed. As I backed away from her, I continued to bow. She laughed, then put two fingers to her lips and blew a kiss to me.

As I slipped into my bed, I was convinced that she loved me, she just wasn't ready for me yet.

Yesterday had been a very busy day, I had problems waking up. Of course, maybe it was the beer. Finally, I managed to fall out of bed and stagger down to breakfast.

"What's this, where is our breakfast?"

Everyone was sitting about with long faces.

"Katie is still asleep." For some reason that made me grin.

"Ok, so Katie is having a lay in, so what? Let us make breakfast for her. That will be a nice change." Unbelievable, they were all looking about, not knowing what to say or do. "Ok, I will make breakfast for everyone."

Living with just my dad, who was often at church, I often cooked the meals, cooking for this lot wasn't a problem. I even made a special breakfast for Katie. I took it to her room and knocked on her door. There wasn't any sound. I gently pushed the door open. There she was, looking like a sleeping beauty. I leant over her still carrying the tray of food. Suddenly she woke up and raised her arm. Yes, you got it, egg, sausage, bacon, all over her. She stared at me for a moment. I was thinking about running. Her lips began to widen, then she began to laugh. What a picture. Egg on her forehead, bacon, sausage, and tomatoes lying on her cheeks. Lucky for me, she saw the funny side of it.

As soon as she finally got up and had a bath, we were then able to plan for the raid in the morning.

The plan was this. At 6am, the sentries would be silenced, and gunpowder placed at the main door. The door would be blown to pieces by 6.30am, so that us and the militia could charge into the building.

At the same time, wagons would be drawn up outside the building. We and half the militia would take the ammunition and weapons, and place them in the wagons; while Richard takes the other half of the militia up the stairs to try and remove the remaining soldiers from within the building. If all goes well, the wagons would be away with their cargo by 9am. The transport of the ammunition to the army would be down to us, Katie's men. We had twenty wagons; therefore, most would only have a driver. These single manned vehicles would go first. Those with a shotgun wielding guard, would follow behind.

It all seemed perfect. In theory. But how would it turn out on the day?

At 6am precisely, we were all there as planned.

The weather had changed and it was pouring with rain. I was not sure if the rain would help or hinder us. The skirmishers went out to silence the sentries and the gunpowder had been placed ready for lighting.

Then the first problem occurred. The Gunpowder would not light because of the rain. The lookouts on top of the building were becoming concerned, there were far too many people about so early in the morning. Then it happened, they noticed something was amiss and began firing at the militia. If the front door wasn't broken soon, all hell would break loose.

I noticed some small piles of dry powder, packed against the door, too close to be affected by the rain. If I use my trusted Ferguson rifle, I may be able to set the gunpowder alight. A shout rang out. The local British regiment were rushing from their barracks to try and prevent the militia from stealing the weapons. It was now a race against time.

I loaded my rifle. The first shot was just short, hitting a wet part of the gunpowder, doing nothing. The second hit right on the little mound of dry powder which instantly set alight. The door soon began to burn. Ten minutes later I gave the order.

"Let's go lads!" We smashed away the burnt embers of the door. The men formed a line between the goods and the wagons, everything was passed along this line and loaded in the wagons. Soon the wagons were all full, and the armoury empty. But this was only the beginning. The British army had arrived.

Katie gave orders for her team driving the wagons to depart. And then thanked the militia and ordered them to disappear. Soon the armoury was deserted.

We were lucky, as the soldiers who had come to prevent us taking the weapons were foot soldiers. We were all far away before their cavalry arrived.

Our biggest problem was that heavy loaded wagons don't go very fast and the horses will require a rest now and then. The important objective was to get the weapons to our troops. I shouted for Katie to stop wagons briefly, I needed to talk with her. If we and the non-drivers left the wagons to escape without us, we could set up a trap for our pursuers. So we ordered the non-drivers to alight, leaving the wagons to go on without us. We had stopped near a nasty bend, a narrow path without any oncoming vision. There was a small rock face on one side. We hid ourselves in the shrubs.

It did not take long for the cavalry to arrive. They were going at full pelt. As they turned the corner, we fired and ten soldiers crashed off their horses. Using the breach loading Ferguson, I could load very fast and soon I had shot three more soldiers. I suddenly realised that this was the advance force, those with the fastest horses. Maybe forty horses. I turned to Katie.

"Tell the men to make sure ten of the horses are left alive. We will need them to escape." It soon became ten against twenty. We were no longer shooting; this was now a sword and dagger encounter.

Some of our men had been farmers before joining up with Katie. They were good shots with a rifle but sword play was not their game. There were now more than ten horses wandering about.

"This is not a fight for some of your men. They have no chance against professional soldiers.! I said to Katie, she nodded. "The weapons and ammunition should be safe now. Let these men get the horses and ride after the wagons. After all, we are the soldiers." I advised her. She thought for a while then gave the order for them to catch a horse and follow the wagons. Her men were happy to obey this order. As they disappeared behind the trees.

"Mr Dragon, should we fight back-to-back?"

"Ms Eagle, may I suggest that we use the dragon method?" She looked a bit confused.

"We are outnumbered, twenty against two, with more to follow. Will your Dragon method save us?" She asked.

"Can we give it a go?" I cajoled her.

"Well, we have nothing to lose apart from our lives." She replied. I grabbed her arm, and pulled her alongside me.

"Put your left arm up high, and your right arm behind you." She followed my directions. "Now run as fast as you can." I was off. She didn't hesitate long, before she was after me. I was the fastest runner in our regiment. I was impressed that she wasn't far behind.

Our pursuers were good while riding a horse, but not great runners. We were soon out of their sight. Quickly we dived into the undergrowth, and lay watching them run past us, soon followed by their main regiment. We waited until dusk fell.

"Where to now, General?"

I was thinking about having a couple of hours of sleep here. I found a nice round rock, and laid my head on it, already dozing off. A boot shot forward and kicked me, knocking my head off the stone.

"We don't have any time for that. True, we don't have to find John Martin, as I already have our next orders." I was now lying on my back watching the clouds pass by. "Our next order is to visit the Tuscarora. They are First Nation people, and they are supporting us in our fight against the British."

Now fully awake, thanks to Katie's boot, I began to think about our new orders. I had heard about these 'First Nation' people, commonly known as 'Indians'. I remembered hearing about them on one of the days when I attended school. Apparently, the Queen of Spain paid for an expedition to sail west, hoping to find a quicker route to the Indies. This was a quest born out of faith - no ship has ever sailed west across the Atlantic. Some people still believed that the world was flat, and that eventually their ship would fall off the edge of the earth if you travelled too far. I began to laugh.

"What's so funny?" Katie enquired. "I was just recalling why the natives of this country are called Indians." I explained.

"Why is that?" She asked.

"When the explorers arrived in the West Indies, they believed they had in fact found India. That's why the name West Indies, and the natives were called Indians. Did you not go to school?"

"Of course I did, I just forgot." She looked rather embarrassed.

I thought I would let her off, and I began to ask about the tribe we would be visiting.

"We will be visiting the village of a friend of mine; we have been friends for as long as I can remember. He is a Tuscaroran, his name is Grey Wolf and he is the son of the chief."

As we entered the forest, everything seemed strange. I still recall when Katie was nearly killed by that bear. This forest was inhabited by a far more dangerous animal than a bear. This forest would have humans, who may dislike us.

I hoped that Katie was right, and they were indeed friends. It wasn't long before I could feel eyes staring at us through the trees.

This was a massive forest; I was lost after the first half hour.

"Are you ok?" She enquired.

"We have forest back in my homeland, but none so large as this." I told her. She chuckled.

"Don't worry my Dragon, Katie will look after you." As you can understand, I was not best pleased with that statement.

As we approached the entrance to the village, children ran out to meet us. Katie had brought sweets with her and most of the children ran to her. A couple of children came to me, but they just stood and stared. What could I do? I had not come prepared. I knelt on the leaf covered forest floor, and began to talk with the children in sign language. Back in the village back home, when I was young, I was in a tumbler group. I was always the one who had to hold everyone up. Somehow, I managed to explain what I would like to do with them. The message soon got round their village, even the kids around Katie left her.

I knelt and the children climbed on top of my shoulders. As I was responsible for their safety, I would not let them go more than three high. When they were on my shoulders, I gently stood up. I think every kid in the village was screaming and wanting to be next. A well-built young man approached me.

"Children are easy, how many adults can you carry?"

I let the children gently down.

"I can hold up as many as can climb on my shoulders."

The man called for three of his friends.

"I will climb last; these will climb first."

He pointed to his friends. The first almost jumped up on my shoulders. Gradually the human mountain went higher and higher. This must have been the heaviest I had ever held. Then it was his turn. He stood before me as I sweated.

"Here I go," he warned, and up he went. He was a very good climber. At the top, he shouted down for a child to come and climb on his shoulder. Katie was standing in front of me. I looked at her and shook my head.

"If a child falls from this height, they could die."

A shout from the top, made her begin to lead the child closer to me.

"That's enough, I won't take a chance with children's lives." I then bent forward and the tower of men came tumbling down. I had planned to let them all climb down safely, but I wouldn't risk a child's life. All four men hit the ground. Of course, the higher up the tower, the more chance of a broken bone. Three escaped with minor injuries. The one at the top, cut his arm. He was furious. Despite being in pain, he got up off the ground, drew his Tomahawk and ran towards me. For a moment, I began to believe that this was my last day on earth.

Then a Miracle happened, hundreds of children rushed in front of me, preventing this warrior from getting too close.

"That's enough, Red Dog. Once again, I find you feeding your ego. I have warned you in the past. This man is a guest, and you have attacked him. If it wasn't for the children, he may be dead now." I was impressed, this man oozed authority. "You are now banished, never come here again, or you will be put to death."

Red Dog pulled himself up to his full height.

"I challenge this man, I was the first to see him approaching our village, I claim him for myself. Either he comes with me as my prisoner, or we fight."

Katie, the man who was speaking up for me, and one other, who I deduced may be the Chief, were in discussion. Katie had translated what was happening, before joining the discussion. I had had enough.

"I will fight him!"

"No!" Shouted Katie. "You can't, he is used to their way of fighting. All the aces are in his hand."

What was that? So The Eagle played cards, I made a mental note that I must play her later.

"Katie, I have killed a bear, he is nothing compared to that. Have faith in your Dragon."

We both stood either side of the ring of warriors. In the middle there was a Tomahawk. I had always wanted one of those. At a given signal, we were both supposed to run, the first to the middle would get the weapon.

I am of course very fast and yes, I was able to pick the Tomahawk up with time to spare before he arrived. On seeing this, he called to one of his men, who threw another Tomahawk to him.

We circled each other a few times, then he decided to rush towards me, I sidestepped and stuck my leg out, over he went and his Tomahawk landed a few feet in front of him. Before he could rise to his feet, I was standing with my right foot on top of the Tomahawk.

"Katie, translate this. 'The fight is over, I think it's time for you to get going.'"

He then pulled a knife from his jacket. We both threw our weapons at the same time.

I managed to dodge his knife but he did not manage to avoid my Tomahawk. The two men who had been speaking with Katie, came across to meet me. It turned out that the elder of the two was in fact the Chief, Crazy Buffalo. The younger one was his son, Grey Wolf. It was he who had been friends with Katie since childhood.

Katie arranged a meeting with them, to discuss Major Martin's orders.

"One thing, Welshman, if we ever get separated. Walk due south for two miles and you will come across a small village. There are ten buildings, one is a pub, wait there and I will find you." She smiled.

CHAPTER 4

THE TUSCARORA

Chief Crazy Buffalo, his son Grey Wolf, Katie and myself were all seated in the Chief's longhouse. Sat together, we were waiting for Katie to disclose what her orders from Major Martin were. Eventually she began to speak.

"The New York borderlands are being terrorised by the Mohawks. We are ordered to work with his brothers, the Tuscarora, to form an army and crush the Mohawks." She read. "Signed George Washington. So, my friend, Crazy Buffalo, are you able to support us in this?" Asked Katie. The Chief nodded.

"I will send 6,000 warriors."

"It is May now, when do we plan to launch our attack?" Asked Grey Wolf.

"In the Spring." A new voice had joined the conversation. I put this man about thirty years old. He looked like he had money, and was very self opinionated. Katie looked across the floor.

"Peter!" She cried out. The Blonde-haired man hurried towards her and threw his arms around her waist. For a moment I thought he was going to kiss her, but she pulled away.

"That's enough, we broke up over a year ago." She barked.

"We can't kiss for old times' sake?" he pleaded.

"Peter, we are in the middle of a meeting." She cast a glance in my direction. My eyes were focused on our new guest. Grey Wolf tapped me on my back.

"Don't worry, she only went out with him for a month, then dumped him." he whispered to me.

"Ok my Katie, maybe we can have a drink later." he winked at her.

I had enough. I sprung to my feet and rushed over to him.

"We are in the middle of an important meeting, so can I help you to leave." He was a bit taken aback "Hold on, who are you?" I was about to punch him in the face. Katie intervened.

"I think you had better leave now, before my Welshman makes you regret barging in here. And by the way, no, I won't be having a drink with you." She began to push me back to where I had been sitting.

"Calm down Dafydd," she cajoled. That was the first time she had used my Christian name, it was usually 'Dragon', or 'Welshman'.

"I am not sure why you were so upset? Anyone would think that you were my boyfriend." I stared at her.

"I was annoyed because you are my leader." I mumbled, then went into silent mode.

"Ok, back to the meeting." Declared Grey Wolf.

"So it's the beginning of summer now, do we attack in Autumn, or do we wait until next spring?" she pondered.

"I'll tell you what I think. If we wait until spring, many farmers and their families will be dead. Remember, you never want to be captured by a Mohawk warrior, they are extremely cruel." I didn't let myself think about what they'd do. "Also, I don't trust your Peter, he trades with all the tribes, and most probably the British. I think he heard enough of our conversation, for him to make two and two and conclude what we are planning. If this is true. Then you," I pointed at Katie, "will be sending the Tuscarora warriors into a trap." I then stormed out of the longhouse before anyone could respond.

Crazy Buffalo stood up.

"I think that young man has feelings for you. And I agree with what he said." He cautioned against waiting for too long.

"Grey Wolf, what's up with everyone? Do you really think that Peter can't be trusted?" Enquired Katie. Grey Wolf nodded.

I was now just wandering around the village, trying to cool off. Then I saw him. Peter the wonder man himself. I slipped behind some tree; I did not want him to see me.

I counted twenty men, all with rifles. Horses and pack horses to carry his furs. He was speaking to another white man in German. He was clearly speaking in English when he burst into our meeting.

The British were fighting wars in Europe, and did not have enough soldiers to protect their colonies in America. So, they hired German soldiers. We use Spanish and French soldiers to help our cause. I wondered what he was telling him. After about thirty minutes, the conversation ended and the German mounted his horse and rode off into the forest. Something was wrong. I ran back to Chief Crazy Buffalo, and explained what I had just witnessed. I asked him to send scouts out and find out what the Mohawks were planning. This he agreed to do. I then went looking for Katie. To my surprise, I didn't have to look far. She was in deep conversation with her ex. Lots of giggles and laughter was coming from them. I had warned her about him, but she has chosen to ignore me. Due south for two miles. A nice pub. That would do me fine.

My leader wasn't too good with numbers, it was more like five miles to this pub, but it was worth it. I booked a bed and was soon drinking a nice cool beer. I began to wonder why so few buildings had been built here. If a war party came by, it would not take long to burn this village to the ground. After my third beer, I was walking in the direction of my bed, when a strong hand slapped my back.

I was tired and having a bad day, I did not need a slap on my back. I spun round and was about to punch the owner of the hand.

"Katie, what are you doing here?" I nearly knocked her out. "I looked for you, when I could not find you, I remembered telling you to come here. So, I am here as well." She had a tankard of beer in her hand. "You have the last bed, so I will share it with you." I was too tired to argue, and even if I wanted to do more than sleep I couldn't.

We both collapsed onto the bed and fell asleep as we were. Eventually I woke up to the sun streaming through my window. It did take a while to force my eyes apart. I sat up on the side of the bed, trying to remember what had happened. I jumped at a noise coming from the other side of the bed. Of course, Katie. I had forgotten her.

"I need a drink and some food." She stated. I was still half asleep, but the word food got my attention.

"Me too. Let's go and see what they will serve us." I mumbled. There is nothing like a good cup of coffee to wake me up in the morning. But this wasn't one of them, it was far too strong for me.

"Stop moaning and eat up, we have things to do." I looked at her. #

"The last time I saw you Katie, you were laughing and giggling with your ex - or perhaps he isn't your ex anymore." That was the last word that I spoke before her right hand slapped my face.

"I don't know what your problem is, but don't spy on me." If I hadn't been fully awake, I was now. I was still annoyed with her from yesterday, now this. I stood up, walked out of the door and headed into the forest. I was furious. After about four hundred yards, I sat down. What had I done? I suddenly noticed the silence. A forest is always alive with animal sounds and birds singing - those sounds only become quiet when danger is near.

I heard a twig breaking and quickly laid down in the long grass. I waited patiently for a moment before I saw Indians - but who? The Tuscora or Mohawks? As the last one passed, I slipped through the foliage after them. I needed to find out who they were and how many. I soon found my answer, and it wasn't good. A war party of twenty Mohawks. Well nineteen now - I had removed the one at the back.

Soon I could hear their war cries, and I could see plumes of smoke coming from the direction of the buildings.

My first thought was for Katie. I think I broke all my sprinting records in my run to the pub. As I neared the pub, I dropped to one knee. I fired three shots and three Mohawks went to their happy hunting grounds. Four more decided to attack me. I drew my sword from its scabbard and pulled my tomahawk from my belt. Four more Mohawks died there. I then sprinted to the pub; its front door was already open. When I entered, I saw horror was before me. There lay three men and a woman. This was the lady who had made my breakfast, served me that cool beer, and gave me a bed last night. As I have said before, the Mohawks were cruel. I turned into the dining room; I was greeted with the sight of Katie being dragged towards the back door. I think she had been able to kill the two who were lying on the floor. Two more Mohawk warriors were rushing towards me. Two slashes from my trusted blade, and they joined their friends in the happy hunting grounds. Another two were trying to half carry, half drag Katie out of the back door. I am good at throwing my knife - I used to practise my knife throwing back home. I had recently extended that practice to my shiny new tomahawk. The one with his back to me toppled to the floor. The remaining warrior was now panicking. He was facing me, with his left arm pulling her close to his chest. His right hand was holding a knife pressed against her throat. One mistake by me and she would be dead.

I slowly pulled my knife from my belt. Then tossed it gently into the air, it twisted a few times before the handle fell into my hand. He seemed confused. The look on his face when my knife stuck in his head, was a look of disbelief. Katie was a strong woman but even she was stunned. Slowly it came to her that she was free.

"That's fourteen of them dead, let's get the others." As she rushed past me, she gave me a peck on the cheek.

"Well done." It was now me who was suffering from shock.

We checked the remaining buildings. Katie was the only survivor. The other warriors had fled.

"Why did they build these houses so far from civilization? It was only a question of time before something like this happened."

The two of us buried the bodies, I said a few words over them, which I had heard my father say at funerals in the past. We then returned to tell Crazy Buffalo and Grey Wolf about what had happened.

"I have a question, boss. How come everyone was killed apart from you? You were the only one who they wanted to take with them. That seems pretty strange."

I am sure she was aware of what I was saying.

"I presume you are speculating on what Peter and I talked about yesterday." She stated.

"Katie, your private life belongs to you. But remember that I have warned you about him."

"Have we come up with some agreement as to how we are going to deal with the Mohawks?" Enquired Crazy Buffalo.

I offered my plan.

"There are lots of small collections of settler's homes which are all easy targets for the Mohawk warriors. I think your warriors need to be dispersed to protect each of these. I guarantee that they will all attract raids." I groaned.

As we were all about to leave, some of the scouts arrived back. The main report was about a white captive who was being held at a village about ten miles away. The scouts believed that she was to be sold to the Delaware, as a bride for their chief. They reported that there were about two thousand warriors in the village.

Chief Crazy Buffalo began to stroke his chin. He had promised to lend us 6,000 warriors. But in the village at present, he could only spare less than a thousand. He explained to Katie that in order to provide 6,000 warriors. It would take time. As he would have to bring them from other villages. She thanked him for the warriors he had offered, which turned out to be 800.

"They will be ready in two hours."

"That will be brilliant." She nodded.

"Mr Dragon, have you any ideas for this rescue expedition?" She beseeched.

"Well Ms Eagle, one thing is for sure, as soon as they see any of us approaching the village. The girl will die." I grinned. "I hope that will be of help."

Finally, she noticed my change of character. No longer was I the man who had been so helpful to her in the past.

"You and I need to talk; I have no need for a silly schoolboy's jealousy." She demanded.

That hurt, like a dagger.

In the past, I had left my country, then left the British army. Was I really infused with an American republic? Not really. So, what was I doing here risking my life, fighting under a flag that I didn't care about? I was only really still here because of that cheeky Eagle. I was beginning to think that the Eagle had flown away.

"Wakey wakey, Welshman." She said, bringing my attention back to the room.

"My name is not Welshman. It is Dafydd Rhees." I pronounced in a strong Welsh accent. This seemed to annoy her even more.

"As you are so concerned that the girl will be killed when we attack, I give you the job of rescuing her." She then turned away and walked off.

Grey Wolf had been watching the interaction. He could tell that we both cared for one another. He wasn't sure of what had happened to stir up the water, but he suspected that it was something to do with her ex. He sat down next to where I was standing.

"Dafydd, my friend, come sit beside me."

I knew he was a friend, and a friend was what I needed at present.

"I have known Katie since she was two years old. As children we would play together. There was a time when I had feelings for her myself, but I knew that would not work. We both had other fish to fry. I have two wives now." He laughed. "I believe that you both care for each other. Something is up, which she cannot or will not divulge. I believe that what she said to you hurt her as much as it hurt you, my friend. She needs you now more than ever."

Grey Wolf may be an Indian, living in the midst of a forest, but he must have been a present from God. We hugged.

"I promise I will take care of her, and to figure out what the problem is. Thank you, my friend." I said, standing up, then headed off to find Katie and apologise.

I caught up with her, just as she was telling Chief Crazy Buffalo, that she wanted to cancel the rescue. That did it.

"Katie, we have been given orders to attack the Mohawks, rescuing this young woman is part of our orders. You can't cancel the mission." I demanded.

"Who are you to question my orders? "She shouted.

"I am 50% of this mission, and any orders given to you also apply to me." Tempers were red hot now.

"Stop it, both of you, I want both of you in my longhouse now." Grey Wolf demanded as he approached.

We both stood in his longhouse, like naughty children brought before the headmaster.

"Now Katie, what is going on?" She was standing silently with her head bowed. "Nothing is going on, I thought it best to delay the rescue." Grey Wolf stood watching her body language.

"Katie, I have known you for many years. I know when you are hiding something. So, tell us now." He commanded.

"Not with him here," she muttered. Grey Wolf was not having any of that.

"Katie, tell us both. Now." He would have made a brilliant teacher. Finally, she broke down, tears began to flow. Grey wolf began to move towards her. I raised my hand and shook my head. This is where I come in. I put my arm around her.

"It's ok Katie, just let it out." For about half an hour, tears flowed down her cheeks. Then she finally composed herself a little and began to speak.

"I am sorry, I have let you both down, for personal reasons." Tears began to flow again. "I will resign in the morning and leave." I pulled her to my chest, and held her tight.

"Katie, whatever you have done, I am with you. Please tell us what happened and we can help you sort it out." I whispered. She looked up at me and her crying eased.

"You'd really help me, even though I have been nasty to you?" I grinned.

"When were you nasty to me? I don't remember anything like that." She had an embarrassed look on her face.

"I have been a total fool. I believe that you both saw me speaking with Peter a few days ago," we both nodded. "My brother has been captured bringing me a message. He is being held in another Mohawk Camp. If we rescue the young woman. He will die."

I began to smile. I turned to Grey Wolf.

"You take the girl. I will get Richard." We then grasped each other's hands. "Let's go brother." We nodded to one another.

"Hey, what do I do? "Shouted Katie. We both shrugged our shoulders and made off. "Wait for me Dafydd," she shouted.

"Go with Grey Wolf, you can't come with me, you will get too emotional, and jeopardise the operation." She knew I was right, and went off to find Grey Wolf.

Lucky for me, our scouts were able to deduce where Richard was being held. Also, there were less Mohawks there. I just took a hundred Tuscaroran warriors with me. I saw this as a night mission. We left a couple hours after it became dark. By midnight, we were there and ready to rescue Richard. My warriors quickly removed the guards, one of whom kindly told us which longhouse Richard was being held in. All was going well, we had freed him and had reached the edge of the village, when a warrior awoke, needing to relieve himself. He noticed Tuscaroran warriors running about and sounded the alarm. We all ran into the forest, about ten minutes in front of the pursuing Mohawks. I sent five warriors on ahead with Richard, as the girl could not be freed, until the others were sure that Richard was free. The remaining warriors and I hid among the trees.

As soon as our pursuers arrived, ninety-five arrows were released, plus a bullet from me. That stopped them.

"Come on lads, we have a few miles to go before reaching home."

When we arrived back at the village, Katie and Grey Wolf had long gone. Richard was left behind. He had had a bad time at the hands of his captives.

Katie, the rest of Katie's Rangers and seven hundred Tuscaroran warriors raced to the village where the young woman was being held captive.

They had left just after dawn, by the time they arrived at the village, it would be about noon. At that point her command would be tired and outnumbered by three to one. It would have been far better to have waited for us. I gave everyone a couple of hours rest, before we raced off in pursuit of Katie's squad. My warriors were tired, but we had no time to spare. Katie would need us.

When we arrived, the moon was out. It was a full moon. I was disappointed by that - the whole village was lit up. When we got there, there was no sign of Katie's command - very strange. No sign of any confrontation either.

My original command had been to rescue the woman. This changed when I had to rescue Richard. However, now I had returned, I was back to rescuing the young woman as previously arranged. Thanks Katie, I moaned under my breath.

I took twenty warriors with me. We had first removed most of our clothing, and covered our bodies in mud, also using it to cover the shine of our weapons.

With the full moon, it would be more difficult to camouflage ourselves. My warriors quickly removed all the guards in the near vicinity of the longhouse where the woman was being held. I only carried a knife and my tomahawk. I managed to make an entry into the rear of the longhouse.

Before me stood four Mohawk warriors. Luckily they were more interested in killing me, than sounding the alarm. Two of my warriors entered through the front and in no time the Mohawks were dead.

The girl had been tied and gagged. After signalling for her not to make a sound, I cut her free then we slipped away.

As we were returning, we saw Katie and her warriors marching over the hill. She had hurried off to the village, but on realising her mistake at planning to attack so quickly. She ordered her warriors to stop and rest nearby. They were now ready to rescue the woman. I showed her the girl and reported our actions.

"Let's go home, I am tired." I admitted. Then I collapsed.

I woke to see Katie kneeling next to me.

"What an idiot!" She cried out. "You ran to a Mohawk village and rescued Richard; then ran back to the Tuscaroran village before trying to catch up with me to support me; rescued the woman; then after being stabbed, you managed to return and report to me." She stared at me for a moment. "Are you really a Dragon? Because you seem to have the strength and stamina of one" As she spoke, I could see tears running down her cheek. I reached across and put my arm around her.

"For you my love, I will be anything you want." I hugged her close to me. She breathed out and relaxed into my arms for a moment before pulling away.

"Let me introduce you to Lady Lana Arina Zakharov, grand-daughter of the Russian ambassador to our republic."

A young woman approached my bed - well, a blanket on the floor. She held out her hand.

"Sorry, I can't get up." I began to try and sit up to reach for her hand but my body cried out, so I quickly gave up on that. "Or it appears, even reach your hand."

She smiled. Then knelt and held my hand.

"Thank you for freeing me from those Indians." Then she rose again. "I have an exotic name. I am the granddaughter of Russia's ambassador to your republic. But he and my father were killed when I was captured. Six months before, my mother was killed by General Whitelaw himself, the leader of a group of Mohawks." She bowed her head in silence for a moment. "I am now an orphan lost in a foreign country. The only possessions are the clothes which I am wearing." Katie put her hand on her shoulder.

"Can you fight?" That to most people would seem a strange question. I was well aware why she asked the question.

A strange look came over Lady Lana's face, but she nodded.

"Do you need me to show you?" she asked Katie. Katie smiled.

"Your word is all I require for now. I am in command of a group of fighters named 'Katie's Rangers'. If you have nothing else to do, maybe you would like to join us in our fight against the British." The strange look turned into a big smile that covered her face.

"Do I get a change of clothes, three meals a day, and a rifle?" Katie scratched her chin.

"I think we can just about manage that. We have a nice green uniform." The two women hugged. Looks like we have a new member to the Rangers, I thought.

Crazy Buffalo and Grey Wolf had promised to keep harassing the Mohawks, so Katie believed that it was time to report back to Major Martin. We expected that new orders would be waiting for us. Katie's Rangers had enlisted a new member. And the Rangers had grown to 36 members.

CHAPTER 5

TURTLE BAY

We were all glad to be back at the safe house. We all fell into our chairs and almost immediately fell asleep. It had been a long walk.

I woke up to Katie walking in with a piece of parchment in hand.

"Ok, Katie, what are our new orders?"

She coughed to get everyone's attention. A few that were still dozing jolted awake.

"Listen up. We have been ordered to support the Sons of Liberty. They are planning to capture the British storehouse, at Turtle Bay in New York. They will be led by four of our bravest freedom fighters: John Lamb, Isaac Sears, Alexander McDougall and Marinus Willett." A few murmurs went around the room at the sound of those names. "Their plan is to break into the British storehouse at midnight on July 20th. The plan is to sail from Greenwich in Connecticut, in a sloop - a small sailing boat to those of you landlubbers. They plan to pass through the Hell Gate at twilight, and surprise the guard at midnight." She looked around to make sure everyone had taken that information in. "Our orders are to station ourselves around Turtle Bay. If the sons of Liberty have any problems, then we are to provide covering fire, to support their attack or to support their retreat." Concluded Katie. I could tell that she wasn't happy about something.

"You don't seem very happy. We can always just pretend not to have seen the orders" I grinned. She looked at me with a deadpan stare.

"And I believe you would do that." Some of us feel more of a duty to fight for our country."

"Why are you upset Katie?" I asked.

"I am not upset." She grumbled. "Turtle Bay. Is a small rock-bound cove in the east river. As a child, my family would go there and we would play with the Turtles. They were happy days. Now we are under orders, if necessary, to cover those rocks with blood." I thought I saw the start of a tear for a moment, but as always, The Eagle recovered quickly. Emotions were not to be shown here - that would be a sign of weakness before her men.

"I wonder how many women will be fighting with the sons of liberty." Katie wondered. I decided to continue this line of conversation.

"I thought that women were not allowed to fight on the front lines."

"That's how little you know about women, Welshman," Katie smiled. "They dress in men's clothing."

So, I was back to being 'The Welshman' again. I got up to go and relieve myself.

When I returned, she was all smiles - she had been given lots of congratulations from other officers.

A messenger came in and handed her another parchment. Upon reading it, her mood went suddenly downhill.

"Do we have new orders?" I inquired.

"We will have to be at Turtle Bay by the 19th July. That's over two weeks away. So, spend the time practising. She then turned away and started walking towards the stairs.

"Katie, where will I sleep? I doubt you will want me sleeping with the men." Grinned Lana.

Katie turned around with a stern look on her face.

"First, you will call me 'Captain', and second, you are welcome to sleep wherever you want, but only one woman has a room to her-self, and that is the commanding officer, i.e. me." She then stormed up the stairs. Everyone in the room just stared at her. This was not their captain.

"I will find somewhere for you to sleep later." I advised Lana.

"Dafydd," whispered John Deacon, who was peering over the parchment that Katie had left on the table. "I think I know what is happening with our Katie."

I suggested that we go for a walk. I picked the letter up off the table as I passed. As soon as we were out of the door, I began to read them.

Katie had given us the main gist of the letter, but left out the fact that a 'Captain Morgan' would be visiting us soon. It seemed that he was in command of the Sons of Liberty. He was coming here to make sure we understood his orders correctly. This in itself annoyed me, we were a crack unit - more than capable of under-standing his command.

John called me to hurry up, he had something to say. Dafydd, on our last campaign you met Katie's ex-boyfriend Peter. She was only with him for a month, before she dumped him. This Captain Morgan - yes, he is also Welsh - is another of her ex's, but this time Katie believed that their relationship was the real thing. They had set a date for their marriage, bought the wedding dress and the rings. They even walked up the aisle together, but as the vows were read he turned to her and told her that he could not do it." He let that sink in for a moment. He walked out of the church, leaving Katie broken-hearted. After that her heart has hardened. She set up Katie's Rangers, I think to try and fill the void that he had left."

I scratched my head; I wasn't sure if I liked this man - as he was apparently the reason that Katie was still single - or hate him for hurting her.

"Why do you think he is coming here?" John pointed to the bottom of the letter. I shrugged. "He has obviously been sent here to take command of the Rangers until after the attack on Turtle Bay."

Not only was the appearance of this man going to open old wounds for Katie, but he was going to take command of her Rangers - the thing she had put all her hard work into to help her get over him. No wonder she was upset.

I turned and began running back to the safehouse. I ran up the stairs two steps at a time, then banged on her door.

"Whoever it is, go away." I continued to bang. Eventually she opened the door.

"Oh, it's you, what do you want?" I had to pinch myself, I knew she was only talking to me like this because she was hurt. I pushed the door open wider and entered her room.

"Katie, you are our leader, we will never submit to any other command."

"Stupid man," she replied. "If you choose not to obey a command, you will be shot. And if any of the Rangers disobeys a command, I will be the one to fire the bullet." I stood in disbelief for a moment. Did she really just say that?

"I think you will find that I haven't signed any contract to make me part of your precious Rangers. And I will not serve under an officer who would so readily turn on her own men. When the real Katie returns, I will be in the bar." With that I stormed out of the room and down the stairs.

I walked through the meeting hall, where all the men slept. I made no attempt to be quiet, I was on my way to the bar.

"What's happened Dafydd?" Someone asked as I passed through - I didn't care to note who as I replied without breaking my stride.

"Ask the Eagle, I think she has lost some of her feathers." Then I disappeared into the bar.

Five minutes later Katie descended the stairs.

"Arrest Ranger Rhees! He is deserting." All the Ranger looked at her. John was the first to speak.

"Katie, he never actually signed up for the Rangers, so he can't desert. Not to mention that he is not a man to be taken in easily."

She realised that this was a losing battle, so she turned on John.

"That's 'Captain' to you, not Katie." She told him sternly, before returning upstairs.

I had a few beers and then fell asleep where I was sitting in the bar. I was lucky that this pub appeared to be open 24/7, my only problem was that I was short of money. I may have fought for the rangers, but I had not seen any money yet. I considered asking Katie for my pay the next day.

I was woken early by a lot of noise in the main hall. Then I heard Katie's voice; she was shouting a lot of commands. After an hour or so, some of the men came into the bar to collect breakfast.

"What's all that noise about? You woke me up." I asked, sitting up and rubbing my eyes. John laughed.

"Apparently that Captain Morgan is coming today. Katie wants us all spick and span."

I groaned.

"Ok, ok, just please try and keep the noise down."

John bowed.

"I will do my best sir." He said with a grin, and backed out of the bar. Perhaps today was not the day to be asking for my pay. I managed to get my breakfast for free - the owner's daughter took pity on me. About midday there was suddenly a lot of noise outside. This aroused my curiosity, so I went to the window. There was the new Captain Morgan with four soldiers.

Gosh, Katie must have been hard up, he was short and not very good looking - must have a nice personality to make up for that then. I chuckled. I was going to have some fun today.

This Captain Morgan, sent one of his soldiers into the pub, to tell Katie that he wanted all the Rangers lined up outside for inspection. I heard the orders. This should be good, I thought. The Rangers were not some smart shinny shoe brigade. These boys crawled through bushes, and dragged themselves through mud.

Looking out of the window I watched him walking up and down, demoralising the men. It was time to wish my fellow Welshman good morning.

I walked casually into the area being used for inspection. It did not take long for him to catch the sight of me in the corner of his eye. He quickly turned and pointed at me.

"You there, why are you not on parade?" I yawned and stretched my arms. I then walked up to him.

"Good morning, Taffy, which part of the valleys are you from?"

He turned to the four soldiers who were accompanying him.

"Arrest this insubordinate."

I looked him in the eyes, offended.

"Taffy, I think you should withdraw that order."

I drew my sword and waited. By now all the rangers were leaning on their rifles to watch the coming fight. Even Katie had a glimmer of a smile on her face. The first soldier decided to rush me. A few slashes of our swords and he was disarmed. I pointed my sword towards him and he ran. The remaining three decided to come at me together. A quick sidestep and one was lying on the ground. It was ok, he was still alive - I had only used the flat side of my sword.

"Stop!" the order bellowed out loudly.

Captain Morgan was now in my face.

"You must be this 'Dragon' which I have heard so much about," I nodded. "Let's go to the bar, I need to speak with you." He then turned to Katie and ordered her to take the men into the hall. He would join them later.

Now this was the kind of man I liked to drink with. He insisted on buying the beers.

"I came here to meet you. George Washington has heard about your exploits, and he has sent me here to give you a promotion. Captain Rhees."

I took my time responding to this.

"First, I want to discuss Katie. I understand that you dumped her at her wedding and broke her heart. Since she heard that you were coming here, she has become a completely different person, and I mean for the worst. What do you have to say about this?"

"At the time I was in love with a young Shawnee woman, she was the chief's daughter. Katie was only 18 at the time and we dated for about six months. She was in love with me, but my heart was for the Indian woman, Little Dove. Katie's parents wanted us to marry, I presume you have met them." I nodded. "Well, everyone was against me marrying Little Dove, and I was soon caught in a fast running river to marry Katie. The day came up so quickly I had not had time to collect my thoughts. On the day of the wedding, I finally knew that I could not marry her, despite her being a wonderful woman. So, I walked out."

I pondered this for a couple of minutes.

"What happened to Little Dove? Did you marry her?" He was silent for a minute. Then he spoke. "Two drunken trappers killed her. All they could say was Sorry. But how can those words possibly heal anything? I could see that memories were flooding back to him. I put my hand on his shoulder in comfort. He took a deep breath, gathering himself slightly.

"It's ok, I am now married with two children, a boy and a girl. But you are right, I did hurt Katie, and I should have made an ending to it long before our wedding day. I offered to buy him a beer.

"Shall I arrange for you and Katie to have a chat? Perhaps you can finally put this hurtful event to bed." He nodded.

"How about now?" It was Katie. Apparently, she had been lingering not far away and had heard everything.

"Sounds good to me." Captain Morgan got up and they went for a stroll.

They returned maybe half an hour later. Katie's eyes were red - it looked like there had been a few tears, they both shook hands and parted ways.

"Well lads, looks like I'm finally ready to get back in the dating game." Katie announced with a laugh. "Welshman, you may be a Captain now, but I am still senior to you. So don't go getting any ideas of taking over my command."

A few young men were chatting to each other, with regards' the best way to approach Katie. I strolled across to a large table, then climbed onto it.

"I understand that some of you are considering approaching Katie for a date." The young men nodded to one another. Well, here is a tip, Katie prefers milk chocolate." I took my knife out of my belt and stuck it into the table. "Before you can date Katie, you will have to beat me in a duel."

I could see Katie in the corner of the room, smiling.

"That Welshman is a fine man. You'd do well if you ended up with him." Grinned the Captain. Katie gave a massive smile.

"He is, isn't he? I'm sure I will, I just like to keep him on his toes." She winked and wandered out of the room.

Captain Morgan smiled as she left. It took a few moments before he suddenly realised he had forgotten something.

"Wait! Your role has changed." He said to thin air - Katie had already gone. He turned to me instead. "We don't think that you Rangers will be needed at Turtle Bay. In Katies absence. I will present the latest orders to you, Captain Rhees."

This would be interesting, if I read our new orders out Katie would kill me.

"I will read these orders later when Captain Katie returns." He looked at me, then began to laugh. "I thought you were 'The Dragon'. Are you sure that you are not 'The Chicken'?"

He was well aware where I was coming from. He grabbed my hand with a vice-like grip.

"I will leave things to you then Captain." He gave his personal men some orders and they all were gone within an hour.

It was time for me to have a peep at our new orders. But first I found some similar writing paper. I gave these a front-page title, then began to have a quick look at our orders. I caught a glimpse of the last page, where we were instructed to recruit some fresh members. Before I could see the main part of our orders, Katie had arrived.

"Welshman, let me have a look at our new orders."

"I am sorry," I replied guiltily. "Captain Morgan ordered me to read the orders out before the men." With that I tore up the plan papers which I had put together. "I think I can remember most of them, shall we have a drink while I share the main points of our orders?" I was waiting for her to explode, but nothing happened.

"Mr Dragon, I know you too well. You would never destroy or read anything without showing them to me first. So, let's save some time by giving me the new orders." She sat on the chair at the top of the table and held out her hand. All the men were chuckling. I had no choice but to hand the orders over. She had smashed my feeble attempt to win one over on her. Then to my surprise, she withdrew and left the field to me.

"Captain Rhees, please read these orders out. We are both Captains, so it doesn't really matter which of us reads them." She had let me off, what a wonderful woman. Then she leant forward and whispered in my ear.

"If you think that I have forgiven you… In your dreams."

I stifled a wince and pretended to ignore her.

"We have been ordered to rescue a family that has been taken prisoner by the British. This family are relatives of John Adams, second in command to George Washington. His brother, sister-in-law and three children - a boy and two girls. There is a ransom on their heads for five billion dollars." I waited briefly for the murmur around the room to settle. "They are being held in a wooden fort deep in Mohawk Country. Then after they have been set free, Katie has been ordered to recruit more men. Or women." I added. I dismissed the men and turned to Katie. "This sounds like a big challenge for just 36 Rangers."

"I have been thinking about recruiting for some time. There are several small groups of Patriots locally. Most have five or six fighters. All I would have to do is persuade their leaders to throw in with us." I stared at her for a while.

"Katie, you have built this team. Every one of them are top fighters. They would all willingly give their lives for you. Do you really want to enlist strangers - men who you don't know, or trust?"

She considered my question for a moment before replying.

"You are right, we need to be careful who we allow into our ranks. We must come up with a proper selection process. I'll have a think about how we can do that later though, let's go and rescue this family."

We were all wearing our dark green buckskins, which blended well with the forest.

"I believe that the Mohawks have maybe three hundred warriors. So, we will want to try and avoid them if possible. We can't tell how many British soldiers are in the fort. I have hired some wagons to get us to Mohawk land, but after that it'll be down to us. We can't use the well-worn paths which zig zag through the forest. If we did, I'm sure we wouldn't live long. This will mean us having to make our way off track." Katie explained. "There are five sections in order to complete our orders. Step one, get to the land of the Mohawk. Step two, make our way through the trees to the fort. Step three, free the family. Step four, make our way safely back through the forest with them until we are outside of Mohawk lands."

"Easy!" I exclaimed sarcastically. Then another voice chipped in.

"Why don't you split your company? Let twenty make their way as proposed. Send one back for soldiers. While the other five pretend to be travelling salesmen - it may be dangerous, but if they fall for it. your five men can get into the fort easily." It was Lady Lana.

Katie and I looked at each other.

"It could work." Concluded Katie.

"So the next question would be what to stock the wagon with." Chimed in one of the new lads. "Isn't it normal to sell pots and pans to the Indians?"

I stared at the boy. "If you want to die slowly bent over a fire. I suggest that you leave the pots and pans at home. Perhaps if we take knives and rifles, we will have a small chance of survival." I suggested.

"But sir, if you get caught trading guns to the Indians, you'd be facing the death penalty." The lad stated.

Katie grinned. "Looks like it's a choice between a potential death penalty and almost certain death. I think we'd better take our chances. Although I don't plan on getting caught."

Eventually, we arrived on what was believed as Mohawk land. Twenty-one of the men entered the forest. They had two orders, the first was to stay close to us without being seen. The second was to make sure that they returned alive. We had a cart, where we laid some rifles and knives. Then planks of wood were used to hide them. When all was in place, we then covered them with pots and pans.

The group with the job of meeting the kidnappers was an important one. I had been asked to select Rangers that would most likely be taken before their leaders, rather than be killed on the spot. In the end the team was Katie, John and Thomas Deacon and Lady Lana, plus myself of course. Lady Lana had not been my choice; she had begged me to take her and I could not bring myself to argue against it. Katie declared that she should be the one to do all the talking.

59

"Katie, I understand that as our officer in command, you feel that you should be in charge of the negotiations. But, they will be expecting a man to be the leader, not a woman - women are second class citizens in their world."

For a few minutes everyone could feel the tension. As if I was trying to take control of Katie's Rangers. Of course that was never my intention, what I said was the truth. I was brought up in a Christian household, and I always strived to never lie.

"I understand where you are coming from Dafydd, but I still want to lead the talking." I shrugged my shoulders.

"If that's what you want, then I won't argue." I conceded.

Before we left, I attempted to hide weapons about my person. Of course, as soon as we are stopped, our weapons would be taken from us. I needed to try and keep something to protect us with.

As you probably know, forests are always alive with various sounds; often you may hear the grunting of boars, small creatures rummaging in the underbrush, birds chirping. My brother and I used to play a game where we had to identify the bird which was making the sounds. But something felt very wrong about this forest.

"Dafydd, it's very quiet." Katie spoke before I could bring it up. I looked into her eyes.

"It's been like this for the last mile." Suddenly I noticed a glimmer behind one of the bushes. "It also looks like there are lots of prying eyes popping out from behind the trees." I whispered to her. "I hope you are ready."

We did not have much more time to wait, before many warriors emerged from the trees. They danced around us, trying to make us frightened of them.

"Be strong, face them with courage, and eventually they will play another game." Lady Lana assured us.

As they danced, they removed our weapons. Not bad, I still had two knives and a pistol left after that. A tall warrior walked up to us.

"Who is your leader?" He spoke in perfect English. Katie walked towards him. If he harmed her, I could reach him from where I was and kill him before his warriors brought me down.

"You are traders?" he stated. He then went up to the wagon and began messing about with the pots. Eventually, he pushed the pots away,

"Where is the real merchandise?" He enquired.

"Where are your furs?" Katie retorted. His response surprised even me. He slapped her face hard.

"I have never met a female leader before, trading is a man's game." He then turned to John and his brother.

"Sir," I shouted. I am in charge. If you have lots of quality furs, then I may have some knives for trade."

"I want rifles." He said before the final words had left my lips. "I will pay well in beaver skins. But if you produce some old gun which is more likely to blow up in my face. I will kill you now." I smiled, this was just like being down the market on a Saturday morning.

"I have ten new rifles, plus some knives. For knives I want twenty furs each. For the guns, a thousand furs for each one." There was a lot of grumbling. Then I produced a rifle. I passed it over for him to examine.

"A thousand is too much, I will give you 500 furs for each gun." That's not bad, I thought. I bought the rifles for a hundred dollars each.

"My price is a thousand furs each." I stood firm. Then he turned the table with an offer of 500 furs each, and a safe journey. At that point I knew I had 'lost', so I surrendered and showed him the rifles and knives. He was very pleased.

"Can you get more?" He asked.

"I can, but I will require a thousand furs each." He nodded. Then offered to take us to the fort, with a promise to meet again before we left.

CHAPTER 6

OUT OF THE FRYING PAN
AND INTO THE FIRE

It was a fort unlike any other. We were deep in Indian territory, but the main gate was left wide open. Mohawk warriors were going in and out of the fort without being challenged. The warrior who had been conducting the negotiations turned out to be the son of the Mohawk chief. His name was Thunder Cloud.

On arrival at the main gates, he spoke with Katie and I.

"Why have you come here? I am sure that you would not take such a risk to sell a few rifles." Katie was about to bluff her way out of the situation. But I held up a hand to stop her. I felt that something was off about the way he asked that question.

"I can't lie. What I will tell you is the truth. This may cost us our lives, but this is our story. We are part of a small unit, sent to free a family that is currently being held hostage inside this fort. We are fighting for the independence of this nation from the British. The captives are important people. Five billion dollars is the cost of their freedom."

"Thunder Cloud grinned. It was good that you chose to tell the truth". He then signalled to some warriors in the woods. At his signal, Katie's support Rangers were led out of the trees. He was now laughing.

"Did you think that I was a stupid Indian?" Katie was now staring at me with anger in her eyes. She still believed that I should have made a story up.

"I am an honest man, I hate liars. I knew you were here for more than to trade a few rifles. My warriors captured your men some time ago." He was now staring at Katie; this message was directed at her. I figured I had better try to get her out of the mess, which she had created.

"Thunder Cloud, I told you the truth, because my father always told me that a lie is a point for the Devil. Our cover as traders was only to protect our men and do what is right for our cause and the family we are trying to save."

"My father has decided to support the British, as he feels that they don't want to stay in this country - he believes our lands will be safe. However, personally I think it's too late. Now that people in the East know about this land. They will continue to come in their thousands. The British in the Fort told my father that they will only put a small ransom on the family they hold, maybe a million dollars." He then chuckled to himself. "What use are dollars to us? The point is that they pretend to be friends of my people, but they lie and treat us like children. My father is away and it is I who makes the decisions at the moment." I had respect for this man, what you saw, is what you got.

"Will you return with me and eat with my warriors?"

I nodded. "I would rather eat with your warriors than fight them." I laughed.

All thirty-six Rangers were eating beside some of the Mohawk warriors.

"Where did you learn to speak English?" I asked.

"When I was younger, I went to a missionary school. Now the people there are all dead." That brought about a silence around the table. "I will help you free this family; but this doesn't mean that we agree with you Americans. I simply wish to teach the British a lesson - that we the Mohawk nation are not children."

"We need to be inside the fort before it gets dark."

We spent some time over the meal devising our plan/ The five of us would enter the fort and free the family, then once we were out, the Mohawk warriors would help us escape.

Thunder Cloud went with us to the fort, he then approached the officer in charge, Captain Hawkings. He explained that we had just brought him some rifles, and hoped that we could stay in the fort, until we needed to return.

We shook hands with Thunder Cloud and thanked him for his hospitality. He had assured us that he would take care of the Rangers, so Katie need not worry about them. We each waved to him as we entered the Fort.

Katie, as our leader, spoke with the captain. He was a man of average height, maybe 5"10. He had a large pointed nose, which became the main focal point when talking with him. He offered us two rooms, where we could stay for up to a week. General Whitelaw was away, but he would return soon.

Lady Lana had kept her head down during our encounter with Thunder Cloud and the Mohawk warriors. But on hearing the name General Whitelaw Katie noticed her head raise, and that she began paying close attention to the conversation. Captain Hawkings directed us to our rooms and then left promptly.

"I am going to have a chat with Her Ladyship. I would like you to watch, but not get involved." Katie whispered before walking over to Lady Lana.

"Are you ok? This must be a terrible journey for you." This was Katies opening salvo.

"It's ok, I may be a Lady, but I'm not adverse to a little hardship every once in a while. Plus, in this land, titles mean very little." Explained Lana.

"The family that we are here to rescue - have you met them in the past?" Katie enquired.

"No, never." Lana replied.

"I was told that you volunteered to be part of this campaign, even though it is very dangerous. Is this true?"

Lana had had enough of the questions.

"Katie, why don't you get to the point and stop asking all these questions!" Lady Lana told her sternly. Katie was a bit taken back at this response.

"Ok, why was it so important for you to come with us?" Katie blurted out.

Lana hesitated, as if collecting herself, before answering the question.

"Two months ago, my mother and I were at home, waiting for father to return when General Whitelaw, the commander of this fort, requested to stay with us for a few days. He informed my mother that he had a family in the accompanying coach, who he and his men were protecting. My mother, being a kind woman, welcomed him inside our house. Once inside our house, he shouted orders for everyone in the house to be killed. I was at the top of our stairs when I watched him stab my mother. She fell to the floor with blood flowing from her wound. She looked up and saw me and shouted for me to run and get away from these people. Before my mother's voice had died away, he stabbed her again." Tears began to flow down her cheeks. "I must see that he pays for what he did."

Katie stood face to face with Lana.

"We have a job to do here. Will you try and kill him, even if it jeopardises our mission? Or will rescuing the family come first?"

I was aware that if the reply was the wrong one, Katie would send her away immediately. Finally, Lana responded to her question.

"I will kill him, but not until the family is safe. I promise."

All five of us decided to go for a walk around the fort to scout it out. It was fairly small for a fort, only about five buildings and a stable. At a rough count, there were about 50 soldiers.

"Any thoughts on how we are going to free the family?" Enquired Katie.

"I, for one, do not have a clue." I said honestly. John and his brother offered a couple of options that would never work.

Eventually, we decided to call it a day. And we went to our separate rooms.

At 6am, I awoke to the sound of a cock crowing. "That's an unusual sound in the middle of a forest." I grinned.

Katie and Lana had made some breakfast for us. While we were digesting our meal, there was the sound of horses and bugles.

"That sounds like someone of importance has just arrived." Lana was on her feet and out the door in seconds. Half an hour later she returned. "It's him." She followed that up with a selection of words her parents would not let her use.

"It's ok, he can wait until the family is safe." Lana promised.

There was a knock on the door, I opened it to find the General standing before me. He was tall but rather thin, with snow white hair. Unusual for a man of his age. He did look smart in his red jacket and black trousers.

"Why are you in my room?" he shouted. The captain pushed himself to the front. "I'm so sorry sir, I wasn't aware that you would return so soon. I only let the ladies use your room, the men are staying in the room next door."

General Whitelaw began to stare at Katie and Lana.

"If these two beauties want to share my room, they are welcome to." He grinned.

Lana put her hand on her knife, Katie moved quickly and stood between the General and Lana.

"I thank you for your offer General, but we will move in with our men, we are used to sleeping together on the trail." She explained. For a couple of minutes, the General stood thinking.

"Well, I guess that's settled then. Tonight, we will arrange a dance, of course you are both invited, we don't get many attractive ladies visiting us."

Our leader once again showed her initiative. She put her arm around me. "Thank you for your offer, but my boyfriend and I are wanting to spend the night together after such a long journey." Lana recognised what was happening.

"My lover John and I also had similar plans." John looked a bit surprised as she wrapped her arm around his waist. This visibly annoyed the General.

"Then you had better get yourselves out of my room. Now!"

It was going to be a long night. First there was the sound of someone crashing against the door. Then the door flew open. It was Thunder Cloud. He was either drunk, or at least giving a good impression that he was. Two soldiers followed him into our room.

"You can't come in here" shouted the first soldier.

"I am just delivering some water for my friends." He mumbled in a drunken slur. The second guard grabbed his arm.

Thunder Cloud responded by drawing his knife, on realising that he had increased the stakes, he quickly slid the knife back into his belt. Then continued his impersonation of a drunk. Both the guards working together managed to help him out of our room.

"What was that about?" asked Katie. I was now grinning.

"Did you not notice? He came to give us a message." All four of them were now looking at me with puzzled looks.

"He gave us a message in sign language." Katie was becoming annoyed. "Ok clever man, what is the message?" I began shaking my head. "Our cover is blown. It seems like the General knows why we're here. He has seventy soldiers against our five." For a while there was silence. We could all be shot in the morning.

"Well, it's been nice working with you all, but I won't be here in the morning." They all stared at me. "Stop staring, I am off to empty the bucket."

Each building had a bucket for bodily waste. At present our bucket was empty. I grabbed our bucket, removed the lid. Slipped my pistol, knife and some cartridges in then pulled the lid across the top. I grinned and waved to them as I opened the door.

Both guards queried as to where I was going. I lifted the waste bucket, they both stood back and signalled for me to pass. I carried the bucket to the waste dump. Of course, my bucket was empty, but I still had to pretend to empty it.

If we were going to be arrested in the morning. I had to do something now, in order to free the family. I could see the building where they were being held. Suddenly, an idea came to me. I approached the guards outside the room where they were staying. "I have been sent to change their bucket." I explained while holding my bucket up. They didn't seem certain about this but the one in charge opened the door. I guess, luckily, they hadn't been warned about us.

"Be quick about it." He groaned. I could see the five members of the family, but there were also a couple of other young people - a man and a woman. I wondered who they were. Tomorrow we would be the ones locked up, so I figured that I may as well take a chance now. Two of the four guards had followed me into the room. I swung my bucket. What a shot - it smashed against the forehead of the nearest guard. He fell to the floor without a sound. The other guard drew his sword. I was now holding the bucket with both hands, trying to block his sword cuts. Then help arrived, the young woman tripped him, and as soon as he hit the floor, I grabbed a nearby chair and hit him over the head with it.

I hastily put my finger to my lips to indicate silence. I took out my knife and cut them all free.

"There are still two guards outside the door." I whispered. "If you call them into the room," I explained to the young woman. "Then your friend and I will hit them with chairs." I looked over at her friend and he nodded, picking up a chair.

"Help!" She called. Those guards were so obedient, they rushed in and 'crash' down came the chairs. It worked like a dream, no guards left.

I stuck my head out of the building. The main gate was still open, but there weren't any soldiers anywhere to be seen. All nine of us slipped out of the door. Then, keeping in the shadows, we made our way towards the gate, always expecting the redcoats to attack. Nothing happened. We all made it outside the fort without any issues. I signalled a lone Mohawk warrior who came and collected the prisoners. He would hand them over to Thunder Cloud, who would arrange a safe escort for them.

I explained to them all that we were here to rescue them, but I had to go back for my team who were all in danger. The young man and woman, named Mark and Jean, turned out to be brother and sister. They also wanted to join me in helping Katie and the Rangers.

Mark and Jean hid while I spoke with the two guards outside our door. "I am sorry for being so late, I was told to change the prisoner's bucket." He wasn't interested and opened the door before pushing me inside.

"Katie, give me a hug." I said, grinning.

She looked at me rather surprised.

"Why should I give you a hug?"

"Because the captives are free!"

"What are you talking about?" I still had a big grin on my face.

"I freed the family. There were also two others, siblings named Jean and Mark, who I also freed. They are outside, ready to help us escape.

"So, what's the plan to escape?"

I never had time to form a reply. General Whitelaw and six of his soldiers, with their bayonet's drawn. Rushed into the room. Two of the guards led in Jean and Mark with their hands tied behind their backs.

General Whitelaw was fuming, but he managed to keep control of his anger.

"I understand that you have all had an exciting evening, at my expense." He growled.

Katie was still wondering what I had been up to.

Thomas had always been an impulsive man. At the sight of the British soldiers with their bayonets pointing at him, his blood went to his head. He drew his sword and charged the soldiers. He had no chance and was quickly skewered with a bayonet in his stomach. I was standing next to John and grabbed him just in time to prevent him from joining his brother in death.

Lana stood watching the proceedings, it was not the time to take her revenge yet.

"Take them all down to jail." Whitejaw ordered. "And get rid of this." He kicked Thomas's body. John was now staring directly at this General. I was pretty sure that from that moment, there were two who would be competing to kill him.

"So, what have you been doing over the last hour, to infuriate that General?" Asked Katie. "You were only meant to empty the bucket." She was looking at me with a very stern face.

"Well, you may not have noticed, but the bucket I took with me was empty. It was a nice evening, so I went for a stroll to the building where the family was being held." Katie was now listening intently to my story. "I just happened to be swinging the bucket and accidently knocked a couple of Guards out. Jean and Mark, helped me send the other two guards to dreamland. When all four guards were asleep, I looked outside. No one was about and the main gate was wide open. Luckily, I don't think the guards were warned about us, or they just don't seem to believe in security. Anyway, one of Thunder Cloud's warriors took the family off my hands. Anyway, Mark and Jean wanted to help, so I brought them with me. Now do I get my hug?"

Katies stern face returned.

"I have one man dead and the rest of us are in jail, who knows what horrors are waiting for us in the morning. And you want a hug?" She changed her sitting position. She was now facing in the other direction. Did I hear a giggle? I think I did.

Early the following morning, we were woken by General Whitelaw. I think I will rename him - 'General Loony' seems to fit better. He seemed happier than the night before.

"Good morning, ladies and gentlemen. Last night one of you was very naughty, and my King lost a lot of money. Now when my soldiers misbehave, they get punished."

"So if any of your men murder someone, what would their punishment be?" Lana could not control herself any longer.

He really was in a good mood. He smiled before making his reply.

"That, young lady, would depend on who they killed." Then, still smiling, he issued orders for us to be taken outside.

"The weather is good Katie." She was walking next to me.

"Stuff the weather. Do you have any plans to get us out of this?"

Before I could answer, General Looney came over to speak with Katie.

"There's no point in worrying about plans to escape. I have 70 soldiers, there is no way to escape." He then spoke louder, addressing everyone. "I am going to hold court here in the parade ground. After being judged, the sentences will be carried out. And don't bother getting your hopes up that Thunder Cloud will come to save you. He may give you support outside the fort but he would never come inside and attack my soldiers. Simply put, his father is on the side of the British."

"We are all prisoners of war. The rules are clear. Prisoners should be well treated, until either they are exchanged, or they are freed, when the war ends." Katie knew the rules of war.

General Loony began to laugh again.

"Of course, but here, I use my own rules, which are slightly different." He grinned.

We were all lined up, about 30 yards from a chair he sat down on.

"You four are charged with spying. And you," he pointed at me, "are separately charged with releasing captives." He turned to look at Jean and Mark. "You two are both charged with trying to kill me."

Everyone was found guilty.

"The punishment for spying is twenty lashes of my whip." He then pulled his whip out, and cracked it a few times.

"Sir, please, these are fair skinned ladies. That whip will tear their flesh apart. I volunteer to take their strokes as well as mine."

"Ok, the ladies will still get two strokes each but you and your friend will have 38 strokes each."

Katie and Lana began shouting that it was unfair, that they should have all 20 strokes.

"Stop, ladies, our backs will heal, but your fair skin will never heal properly. Leave it to us."

Katie and Lana were tied by their hands to two poles placed in the middle of the square. Their backs were exposed. Katie took her strokes first. They did not go easy on her, but she made no sound. Next was Lana, she stared at General Loony with burning hatred in her eyes. She gritted her teeth through the lashings and I could've sworn I saw a tear, but again, she kept quiet and refused to give him the pleasure of hearing her scream. It wouldn't be long before she could take her revenge on him.

I was next. After the way the ladies bravely took their strokes, there was no way I would make any sound. John took his strokes as bravely as the rest of us. I was then grabbed by two soldiers.

"The punishment for freeing our captives is that you will run The Gauntlet." General Loony announced. "All my men will be lined up in two lines. You must run the length of the line between them, then return. My soldiers will be issued with knives, and you, of course will be without a weapon."

"Now the last two. The brother and sister. As you tried to kill me, you will both be hanged from the neck until dead." Two portable scaffolds were dragged out. Jean and Mark stood in front of their scaffold. "As soon as the run of the Gauntlet is completed, the hanging will commence."

Talk about out of the frying pan and into the fire.

"He has only just received 38 strokes of the whip! Can't he have a rest before making the run?" Katie protested to the general.

He of course refused to listen to her. Katie was allowed to speak with me before I made the run.

"If I could, I would give you that hug right now. So, I guess you'll just have to survive the run so I can give it to you when you have recovered."

"Katie, I will be back for that hug. Remember who I am? I am The Dragon."

Tactically running down the middle between the two lines of soldiers would be suicide. I would need to attack one side, avoiding the others. The priority would be for me to get a weapon as soon as possible. I was ordered to stand by a line and wait for instruction for me to commence the run. I ignored the instructions and withdrew a hundred yards back. At the signal, I sprinted towards the left side of the soldiers. When I was two feet away I leapt into the air. My feet smashed into the second and third soldiers. Before they could recover, I picked up both of their knives. As I stood up, the next soldier lunged at me with his knife, I side stepped and stabbed him in his stomach. I dislike killing people, but there are times when it is unavoidable. The next two soldiers died as they were too slow.

It was me who was too slow for the next encounter. His knife cut my right side and it was bleeding heavily. I took one more soldier down. Then something hit my head and I fell to the ground. I looked up through a haze. The last thing I saw was a man with a knife leaning over me. Just before I passed out, I think I heard a shot.

I managed to open my eyes.Several people were looking down at me. The light was so bright that I had to shut my eyes again almost immediately. Was I in Heaven? I was fairly sure this wasn't hell. I heard my name being called as I drifted off again. When I came to next, I could see the moon through the window.

"Are you awake Dafydd?" Pleaded Katie.

Once again, I opened my eyes.

"Hi Katie, are you in Heaven as well?" Katie laughed.

"We are both in the fort. While you were attempting to run The Gauntlet, the rest of the Rangers entered the fort and crept up behind the British soldiers. The soldiers, if you remember correctly, only had knives at the time, whereas the Rangers were fully armed and disarmed the British without any problems. Dafydd, you received several cuts, so it will take some time for you to heal. But, we have completed our orders in releasing the family. General Whitelaw has been arrested and will be returning with us."

A couple of days later, I was passed as fit to travel.

"So Katie, it seems as if I've recovered now all fit to travel now!" I called over to her with a grin as I walked towards her.

She laughed, and ran over to give me my well-deserved hug. I winced a little, but it was well worth the small amount of pain.

"Oh sorry! I should've realised you would still be a little tender." She said apologetically.

"I'd trade a little pain for a hug from you any day," I reassured her with a big smile on my face.

The following morning, we started our march back to our headquarters.

CHAPTER 7

THE BATTLE OF LINDLEY'S FORT

I nearly fell off my horse on the way home. Katie had to buy a small horse and cart for me to lay in. It wasn't long before I dozed off on the journey.

"Dafydd, wake up. We're back home now." Whispered Katie.

"We have visitors." I opened my eyes. It was my friend, Major John Martin. "How are you Dafydd? I hear you have been getting into trouble again." He grinned. I held out my hand and then shook his.

"To be honest John, I can't remember how everything ended. I honestly thought that I had been killed."

"Go on Katie, tell them how it ended," suggested John Deacon.

"Well John, it was you who told me why you gave Dafydd the name The Dragon. I had to just take your word for it back then." She began. "He had been sentenced to run the Gauntlet. There were two lines of 35 soldiers with knives. He did not have a weapon and started his run a hundred yards behind the start line.

What happened next became a blur. He sprinted and leapt into the air, landing in the faces of the second and third soldiers on one side. Quickly he picked up their knives and killed the next two soldiers. A soldier not much further up the line grabbed a rifle and hit him on the head, but not before The Dragon had killed ten British

74

soldiers. After knocking him to the ground, the soldier raised the rifle with the intention of killing him." She paused to catch her breath. It was an exciting story. "Everyone, the British soldiers, General Whitelaw and even us, had forgotten Katie's Rangers. Thirty-one of them were staying with the Mohawks. Thunder Cloud had told them what was happening and it was now their hour. They entered the fort silently, then strategically surrounded the British soldiers."

"So the shot I thought I heard was from the Rangers?" I interrupted.

"Yes, that shot killed the soldier and saved your life. Then they quickly captured the soldiers who only had knives. Of course, by then, they were ten of their comrades short."

I noticed the Major staring at me.

"You both have earnt another promotion. John Adams is ecstatic about you freeing his relatives. You have both been promoted to the rank of Colonel."

Major Martin shook my hand and handed me the papers confirming my promotion. Then did the same for Katie.

"Major, as I was promoted first, does this mean that I am senior to Katie?" I smirked. I did not know that she could move so fast. I quickly dived behind the cart for protection but it was a close call.

"Ok, your order for the rest of this year is to rest and recuperate. After the winter break I want you both to recruit and train more Rangers. I want your Rangers, Katie, to include a unit of over a hundred Indian fighters. This war used to be just us versus the British, but the tribes are known to be joining the whites, in an attempt to protect their lands." He informed us. "I want Katies Rangers to meet me in Philadelphia on the 4th of July next year. Where I will give you orders for your next expedition.

Katie and Lana had suffered two strokes of the Whip. They made deep cuts in the girl's backs. They took time to heal, but they did not prevent them from carrying out their normal lives.

John had 38 strokes of that whip. He truly suffered. Twice he had a fever. But when the new year arrived, he was back to his old self. Apart from missing his brother.

I must have appeared to be the weak one of the four. My whip cuts became badly infected and I got a terrible fever. Then there were also the cuts with the knives and a lot of blood lost.

It was the end of winter before I was back to normal. The snow had begun to melt, little streams began to run down the mountain side and buds had begun to appear. There is that certain fresh smell to the spring.

Supported by Katie, I began to run again. By the summer I was back to my best. Katie had done a brilliant job recruiting. We now had 120 Rangers in training.

"Don't forget when we are to meet the General in July." I stated. I then recalled him telling us that we were being trained for Indian fighting. Well, it was better than wearing a blue coat and carrying a bayonet; then slowly walking toward the British guns while they took potshots at us. I could never understand those tactics.

We now had horses, which was much faster than walking. However, that also meant that we had the added pleasure of feeding them and mucking them out. Katie decided to take all her Rangers to our meeting in July. I had this feeling that she may have been showing off a little.

We left our home on the 1st of the month. Katie felt that would give us enough time to get to Philadelphia.

We eventually arrived in the evening the night before. As it was summer, the days were long and warm. We made camp in a large field. It was hard to remember that we were in the middle of a war. That our comrades were dying while we spoke.

"Katie, I think that we all should treasure these moments. I have a feeling that our lives are about to change."

That evening Major John Martin visited us for a while. He congratulated Katie on the size and quality of her Rangers. She had done a great job with recruiting.

"Tomorrow, I want both of you to be with me. Something special is going to happen. After which, your Rangers will be spending the next six months in battle." He then left us to enjoy our evening.

"I told you something like this would happen. If you still had maybe just 50 Rangers, we would still be used as scouts. Now we will really see blood and gore."

She smiled.

"Don't worry, The Eagle will look after you."

She made me laugh. I bent forward and pretended to be a Dragon.

"Come here my tasty Eagle, I am hungry." And I chased her in my dragon form. I caught up with her and pounced to catch her, pushing us both into a nearby haystack. It was quite strange, when I caught her, I went off the idea of eating her.

"It's getting dark Katie; perhaps we should just sleep here? She put her face next to mine. Almost nose to nose. Then she bit my ear and ran off.

It was getting dark, I had lost interest in chasing her, I needed my sleep. I tucked myself up inside the hay. About half an hour later, a warm body came and curled up behind me.

The next morning we both went to find Major Martin. We had managed to get cleaned up and put on our uniforms. We were wearing the dark green buckskins, with the addition of the Colonels pips.

We were introduced to many famous people, including George Washington himself. John Adams was full of praise for us after freeing his family.

We were still wondering what was happening, then it all became clear. Something special was about to happen.

It was July 4th 1776. It was the Declaration of Independence.

The Declaration was signed by all 56 of America's founding fathers. What an amazing day. What an experience.

"Katie, we can tell our children all about this day!" I told her excitedly.

She frowned.

"You can tell your children, but I am not planning on having any."

Before I could respond, The Major arrived.

"I want you to take your Rangers to Lindley's fort, they need help.On the way, check in at Fort Sullivan. It stands near Charleston, they are both in South Carolina." He grinned and added. "Lucky you have horses now. The Fort was built by the British but it's now occupied by our soldiers. They will likely be under attack by the British on land and will have ships in the harbour. Give them a hand if you can, then move on to your main action at Lindley's fort. You will be doing some Indian fighting there. He then saluted and left.

It had been a long day but there were still a few hours left of daylight. Katie felt that we should make full use of the light and get a few hours closer to our next engagement.

We could hear the guns well before we could see the fort. Clouds of smoke hovered over the fortification. The cries of injured men saddened our hearts.

Katie ordered us to refrain from attempting to enter the fort. In order to simply reach Fort Sullivan, we would suffer a massive loss of life. The British had nine man o' war ships anchored in the bay. They were all bombarding the fort. We decided to camp nearby and watch from afar for a couple of days instead.

It was clear that this naval bombardment was having no effect, due to the sandy soil and the spongy nature of the fort's palmetto log construction. The following day, The British withdrew their expedition force to New York.

With the British Navy gone, the Officers in command of Fort Sullivan should have little problem in mopping up what little insurrection they may have left. It was more important that we moved onto our next engagement. As Major Martin had said, this is where our training as Indian fighters would be of most use. It was pouring down with rain, as we moved off towards Lindley's Fort.

Up till now, the tribes had not involved themselves in the war between The Loyalists (loyal to the British) and The Patriots (American revolutionists), but recently they had become concerned. The British were slowly encroaching on their land, increasing the numbers of settlers.

The Cherokee had joined with the Loyalists. The Cherokee went on the warpath on the first of July, burning farms and killing Americans. The settlers took refuge at Lindley's Fort.

We arrived at Lindley's fort in the late evening of the 14th July. The fort was filled with many terrified settlers.

On the morning of the 15th, a joint force of Cherokees and Loyalists adorned with warpaint attacked the fort.

Apparently, they were not aware of our arrival. Facing the crack shots of Katie's Rangers, they were easily repulsed. When they retreated, orders were given to pursue them. Two Loyalists were killed and 13 taken prisoner.

With even more reinforcements arriving, Katie thought that we should leave the fort and challenge the Cherokees in their own backyard. We had better rifles and we had horses. We needed to challenge their war parties and help settlers get to the fort.

We had been given a rough map of where the farms lay. We managed to escort four families to the fort.

Another was under attack when we appeared. We charged down the slope into the house, only to see the remaining member of the family breathing their last breath. At least we were able to bury everyone.

The war parties were not very large, maybe an average of 30. Katie decided to split us into two groups of 60. My group rode west and the other, with Katie leading, went east. It was a sad day to have to say goodbye and let her go in the opposite direction to me.

Early one morning, we had only been riding for about an hour, I heard talking. I ordered everyone to dismount quietly. The horses were tied up and I sent three men out to find out what the sounds were. On return, I was informed that there were eighty Cherokee warriors camped just behind the hill. It looked like two of them had ventured out for a stroll. We quickly dealt with them so they wouldn't carry word of us back to their camp.

We soon found the main entrance to their camp, so I had thirty Rangers stationed on each side of the path a little bit down from it. They would need to take this route in order to leave their camp. They may have started with eighty, but they were lucky to have forty warriors left after we ambushed them. I hoped that Katie was as successful that day as we had been.

It was another month before Katie and the rest of the Rangers returned to our meeting point. She was not the Katie who rode east two months ago. She was visibly distressed.

I think that I understood why. Riding into a settler's farm, just after a visit from the Cherokee can only be described as a horror scene. I had come across this so many times - the smoke still rising from the burning buildings; crops on fire; then the bodies. Who were those poor people who had just been killed? I could never help but ask myself. I, and most of the Rangers have had countless night-mares, dreaming of these scenarios each night.

Katie and most of the Rangers needed rest, and time to forget. It was now late October. It was time to find somewhere for our winter retreat. No one could survive outside, exposed to the elements, during the winter.

We were all riding east back to our headquarters. When one day a messenger caught up with us. We were informed that the British were in control of New York and the surrounding area, which included our old headquarters. The good news was that apparently there was an abandoned school not far away that we were told we could use for the winter. It had previously been used by the British, but they have moved away. I thanked the messenger and asked him to inform Major Martin that I would contact him for fresh orders in the spring.

My scouts returned with good news. The school was indeed abandoned, and it was large enough for all the Rangers. Also, they had made contact with a local doctor who was also a Patriot - he had volunteered to look after our men and women.

I gave orders to send rangers out hunting, we would need lots of dried meat to get us through the winter. Wood had to be collected for the fires and we would need hay to feed our horses during the winter, when the ground would be thick with snow.

Finally, I found time to sit down with Katie. We had a blazing fire, which was creating reflections in the dark room we sat in. We both sat together propped up against the wall. I put my arm around her.

"Dafydd, why do those stupid, selfish, husbands take their wives and children into the wilderness during a war, then build homes where they can all be killed at any time?" I was right, it was the nightmares that were affecting her.

"Katie, I understand what you are saying. A peaceful Indian can put on war paint at any time.

These settlers, many come from bad beginnings. Some are so poor, that they may have stolen a loaf of bread to feed their families and been sentenced to prison. Most, if not all, see this country as a lifeline for them. A chance to build them and their families a new life. To own land of their own."

There was silence for a moment as she began to mull that over.

"Let me tell you about a young Welsh lad." I began. "His mother died giving birth to him. He grew up with just his father and older brother. His brother was sent to live with other relatives as his father could not afford to feed both his sons. His father was a Welsh Methodist preacher, but because some people disagreed with the Welsh Methodists, he was killed. Leaving this lad of 19 all on his own." I took a deep breath, trying not to let the pain of that night return to me at this moment. "He could not get a permanent job; they all went to the English. One day he saw a recruitment poster for the British army, they needed more soldiers for their war in America, so he joined the infantry. There was more than a chance that in the infantry that he would be killed in his first battle. But, just maybe, he might live and build a new life in this Land of America. The settlers must feel the same. Just maybe, they'll get lucky and they won't be attacked, and their farm will be the freedom they have always dreamed of."

Katie was now staring into my eyes.

"I was brought up in a well-off family, I have always had whatever I wanted. I have no idea what being poor is. Or being hungry. Thank you Dafydd, for bringing the real world before my eyes."

Again, silence fell between us and we both stared into the flames as she considered all I had said.

"I am now beginning to understand these settlers who arrived almost every day. They are leaving their old lives behind and grabbing at a dream of a new life, here in this brave new land." Observed Katie. "That young lad sounds like a true dragon to me." She Grinned.

I thanked God; my Katie was back.

"Thank you for taking charge of everything for me. I felt so lost for a while. So, what's going on?" She asked.

I ran her through more of the information than she required. She began to laugh.

"We are in a school, and I have just learnt an important lesson. Thanks, Dafydd."

My heart pounded with love for this woman before me. But she didn't know.

We were brought a bowl of hot stew each with a slice of bread, we sat eating as the flames danced over the logs, limboing lower and lower as the night stretched on. We fell asleep in each other's arms.

"Wake up Dafydd. I want you to take some of our best shots and go hunting."

She really is back. I thought with a smile.

"Ok I will go out into the deep snow; you stay here in the warm." I moaned.

"Catch me a deer and you might just earn another hug." She winked at me.

"If I can shoot a deer out in that snow, I will want a lot more than just a hug!"

She laughed. Now going out into that snow didn't seem that bad. I took ten of my best shots.

I left with Mark and nine others, but somehow we got separated. After an hour ploughing through the snow, I finally came across a large male deer. It was a beautiful animal and I did not want to kill it, but as my father used to tell me "God provided animals for us to eat".

I took aim and killed it with one shot.

I began to fight my way through the snow towards my kill. When out of the trees appeared a young woman with two children, one of them was struggling to wade through the snow, the younger one she was carrying.

"Hey! That's my kill." I shouted. I increased my speed and was getting to the deer before her - she was carrying a young child after all. On reaching the deer, I stood in front of it, protecting my kill from this woman.

On arrival, she tried to push me out of the way. Eventually I took pity on her, and let her get to the deer. For five minutes she tried to tear a piece of the deer off with her bare hands.

I could not watch any longer. I pulled her away from the deer. She was about to protest but stopped when I then knelt down to cut one of the hind legs off. I gave it to the woman. She grasped it with both hands tightly, as if afraid I would try to take it back off her. She said something I didn't understand - I think she was thanking me in her language. By then the older boy had caught up with her. I began to stare at the three of them.

She looked to be in her early twenties. The young girl was maybe four and the boy was just a couple of years older. The snow was too deep for the girl to walk. So, the young woman would have to carry both her daughter and the meat. She would not get far carrying such a load.

I found some rope to tie the deer to my saddle so I could drag it, then mounted my horse and began my journey back home. For some reason, I turned to look behind me. The woman was carrying her daughter in one arm while dragging the meat along in the snow. They were walking towards me. I stopped my horse and dismounted.

"What are you trying to do?" I asked. To my surprise she replied in English.

"Sir, I thank you for the meat. My husband was killed by men wearing green buckskins like what you are wearing. The law of my tribe is that if a husband dies, the wife has to marry a brother of the deceased. My husband's brother is a cruel man, and I knew that he would beat my children. So, I ran away. They will not pursue me. They will say that it is up to the will of the great spirit if we live or die. Please, I believe the spirits have sent you to us. My children will not live long out in the cold like this."

I told her to stand still, while I lifted my rifle and aimed past her. She closed her eyes tight as if I was about to shoot her. I fired then lowered the gun.

"Ok, I will help you. The boy can ride with me, but you must walk with the girl." She was too tired to say anything but "thank you".

She began to usher the boy towards the horse.

"Wait a moment, we have a wolf as well."

I led my horse to where the wolf fell and attached it to another rope on the back of my saddle. I mounted the horse and me and the woman helped the boy up behind me.

"We had better get back to my headquarters before it gets dark, or we will see a lot more of these fellows."

It was slow going, but we arrived back at headquarters just as it had become dark. Katie was waiting at the gate to the compound.

"Correct me if I am wrong, but I don't remember telling you to bring back anything alive."

It had been a long, cold day; I was not in the mood for any clever talking.

I untied the deer and the wolf from my horse, then turned to Jean who had come out to see what meat I had brought home.

"Please find a room for these people, and arrange for their meat to be cooked." Jean took the three of them off into the building. I walked my horse over to where his food would be after I had rubbed him down. I gave him a little extra, he deserved it after such a long, arduous journey carrying all that weight.

Katie was no fool. She could read that it would not be sensible to wind me up today.

"Looks like you have had a hard day. You have done well with the meat!" She tried to encourage me.

It worked a little.

"So, when do I get my reward?"

"Later." She laughed. Then she grabbed my arm, linking it with hers and led me towards our. "Are you going to tell me about the woman and the children?"

"Well, it's a long story and I am so very tired." I pleaded.

"What if I let you lay your head in my arms, would that help you relax and tell me the story?" she grinned.

"Well, it's worth a try." I laughed.

She sat down on the floor and I slowly let my head drop into her arms. I lay there with my eyes closed in contentment for a few moments.

"Her husband was killed by one of our men. Under her tribes' laws, she has to marry his brother. The problem is that her husband's brother is cruel and will beat her children. So, she ran away. I couldn't just leave her and her children out in the snow to die."

"And what will happen in the Spring, when a few hundred Cherokee charge up to our door? Will you hand them over?"

Katie is, at times, a bit more realistic than me.

"We will have to leave here in the early spring, before the red-coats return." I answered.

The door suddenly opened.

"My children are asleep. I have come to thank you both for saving our lives, and maybe to clear a few things up." She stood waiting for our response. Finally, Katie decided to make friends.

She stood up and walked over to the woman, then held out her hand. The woman gave her name as White Eagle, then shook Katies hand.

"As I told him before," she looked at me, "my husband has been killed. But I never told him that I am not a Cherokee. I am in fact a Mohawk. I was kidnapped from my family and sold to the Cherokee. That was when the man who became my husband bought me. He treated me well, but his brother wont. So, I ran away. If you say we can't stay, I will leave with my children in the morning."

Katie was taken aback by such a show of courage.

"You may stay with us, and we will protect you and your children." Promised Katie.

"What about the man, if he disagrees?" replied White Eagle. I had been sitting silently in the corner of the room as if I didn't exist.

"Don't worry about Dafydd, did he not bring you here?" Quipped Katie.

White Eagle let out a massive grin, she finally let herself believe she was truly safe for the time being. I swear she was about to begin literally jumping for joy, she was so relieved that her children were now safe.

"Do you know Thunder Cloud?" I shouted over from the corner of the room. She laughed.

"You could say I know him. He is my brother. How do you know him?"

Katie and I were now both laughing.

"Not so long ago, he saved both our lives."

CHAPTER 8

THE BATTLE OF BENNINGTON

It had been a very cold winter so far. We had enough meat, but in January, another hunt would need to be arranged.

The good news was that all the injuries had healed. Katies rangers now consisted of 90 men and 30 women. Lana, Jean and Mark, along with John Deacon, had all been made officers, they had been given the rank of sergeant.

White Eagle and her children had settled in well. As soon as spring arrived, we would try to get her back to her brother.

"Katie, it will be Christmas soon. Shall we arrange a special day for the 25th?" I suggested.

"Dafydd, that is a brilliant idea! It will take away the boredom for a day." She declared.

"We should organise the programme in secret, along with the other officers." I proposed.

"Or, how about the men organise part of the day, and us ladies organise the rest?" She retorted.

"Now that, Katie, is an even better plan." I said with a grin. "I presume that you will decide who organises what."

She was now looking at me with a beaming smile on her face.

"You know me so well, my dear Dragon." She thought for a moment. "We do have a bit of a problem though, Dafydd. We have Rangers of a 3 to 1 ratio of men and women. They are all fit healthy adults."

I sat on the chair.

"I know what you are about to say. And if this isn't dealt with soon, it will blow up in our faces." I was no longer smiling.

"We could divide the house into, male, female, and married quarters. With strong rules to protect the plan. Otherwise, we may see fighting breaking out within the Rangers." Suggested Katie.

"I think that is a good idea while we are here, but once we leave and are on the road, sleeping in tents, a lot of pre-planning will have to take place." I groaned.

"Ok, let's meet up with our sergeants tomorrow, we can discuss this and I will have a list of jobs to do for our Christmas celebrations." Katie concluded.

I took a deep breath and said what was on my mind.

"Katie, I have a question. We have been together for two years now. I'm fairly sure you know that I have strong feelings for you, but you always seem to avoid getting too close to me. My question is… Can I hope to win your heart one day?"

I bottled it and did not wait for an answer. I just made an excuse that I needed to check the horses, and left the room quickly. To be honest, I felt a little embarrassed.

It was late afternoon, and as it was one of the shortest days of the year, it was getting dark. For some reason the horses were a bit jumpy. We had 130 horses stabled, and five Rangers making sure that they were safe at all times.

I could feel that something was wrong, these horses could sense a threat. I ordered one of the Rangers to run indoors and tell one of the sergeants to bring twenty rangers out quickly. That just left the five of us. We all loaded our rifles and pistols. All 130 horses were in the same stable. I thought this was the best way to protect them. It had meant a lot of moving of the wooden panels, but the final result was safer.

Then it all happened. Wolves!

Somehow, they had dug under part of a wall. We were ready for them. Five Rangers, each with a rifle and a pistol, could and did kill ten wolves. The problem was that this was a large pack. Many more were coming under the wall. I pulled out my knife and the tomahawk that I now carry. It would be easier to defend myself with melee if we got overwhelmed. I quickly killed one wolf by splitting its skull with the tomahawk. But a second one had pounced on me as I did so and was now on top of me.

I was lying on the floor of the stable with the wolf straining to bite my throat. I was trying to keep its fangs away from my neck with my right hand, which held the tomahawk. I quickly brought up my left hand with the knife, and stuck it into the wolf's belly. This wolf was rather strong, with my knife in its stomach, its teeth were still getting closer to my throat. Then suddenly, the wolf went limp. Katie had arrived with more Rangers. She had crushed the wolf's skull with the butt of her rifle.

"Can't I leave you alone for even a minute?" She laughed.

All the rest of the wolves were now in full flight.

"Make sure the guard is doubled." Katie ordered Mark. She then left the stable, without a single word regarding my question.

I saw very little of her for the rest of the evening.

Then the following morning, she was standing next to my bed when I woke up.

"Meet me after breakfast, I have compiled the lists." And off she went.

I ate my breakfast slowly; I didn't feel like rushing. That was a mistake. There was Katie again.

"Are you ready now?" I swallowed the last of my coffee, then followed her.

When we arrived at her office, the others were already there. She quickly introduced the plan for Christmas, which was welcomed by everyone in the room. What was strange is that she explained it as though it was her idea.

She then gave us a list of jobs to do. I never saw her lists before now. The second subject, the dividing of the male and females, with rules wasn't even discussed. I don't know if she was trying to annoy me intentionally. If she was, she was succeeding.

"If that is all, I will take John and Mark, and have a look at the jobs which you have attributed to us." I rose and left the room.

"Katie, I think you are pushing him too far. He looks like he is about to explode." Acknowledged Lana.

"I know, but he is so cute when he is angry." Replied Katie.

Our list:

1. Provide all the food
2. Get a Christmas tree
3. Provide lots of logs
4. Ensure the horses are safe during the celebrations

Basically, we had to get everything that meant going out in the snow, while Katie's team prepared the rest. Well, at least we had plenty of time to sort all of this before Christmas day, then the 25th would be a time to relax and enjoy.

There was one important thing missing from our list. On the 25th we would celebrate the birth of Christ. I would arrange a short talk just before breakfast.

"What's the date today?" I asked. It was so difficult to keep up with the days.

"Sunday the 18th" Replied Mark.

"So, one week to the big day. By the way, if you have a young lady that you have feelings for, don't forget to get them a present!" I reminded Mark.

"Dafydd, there is a woman who I have feelings for. But I don't know what to get her."

I asked him who this lucky lady was. He became a bit shy.

"I have been doing a lot of things with White Eagle, I have become close to her and her children. What can I get her, Dafydd?" I began to smile. An idea had come to me.

"How about this... I will get your present for White Eagle, and you get my present for Katie." He looked surprised.

"Katie? I never knew that she liked you." "Grinned Mark.

"To be honest, I am not sure either. But I do have feelings for her." I went silent for a couple of minutes as these words had some effect on me. "Anyway, are you up for my suggestion?" Mark agreed. "Ok, bring thirty men to the main gate tomorrow at 9AM with two carts and we will go and collect a nice Christmas tree." I ordered, then walked off to find Katie.

"Katie, I have an idea. I suggest that regarding Christmas presents, we should make it a bit different." Katie looked at me with suspicion.

"What are you planning?" She enquired.

"Well, I thought it would be a little more exciting if we added a bit of mystery." She felt that I had a reason for this and wanted to know more before she agreed.

"My idea is, for example, if I want to get Jean a present, it would be Mark who bought her present on my behalf. And I would do the same for the person he wants to buy a present for." I explained.

"So let me get this right... someone who the giver may have feelings for, will receive a gift from someone they may not know very well. Dafydd, can you not see a flaw in your idea?" Expressed Katie. By now I must have been red in the face.

"Ok you made your point; we all get our own presents." I then left the room in search of my present.

The following morning, when I arrived, there were actually six wagons. The extra four would be used to collect logs. I gave orders to ride towards the Mohawk lands.

Eventually we stopped a couple of miles short. I left the team to collect a Christmas tree and logs. While I rode off to try and collect the present for White Eagle.

The night before, it had rained. Therefore, the snow wasn't as deep as it had been. I was aware that Red Shirt was no friend of ours. My tactic was to ride towards the Mohawk village and hope I was taken prisoner, rather than be killed. As I rode through the trees, I was aware that Mohawk warriors were watching me. This was, of course, good news. If they wanted it, I would have been dead by now. I had been to their village before and I believed that I was on the correct route. As I got closer, warriors came out and walked in front of me. Well, I guess I wouldn't have any problem getting to the village, the only question was, would I be able to leave?

They guided me to the middle of the village. Many of the warriors were waving spears at me. They did not seem as friendly as the last time Katie and I visited. Two rather tall warriors pulled me off my horse.

Now I just had to wait for Red Shirt's appearance. I just hoped he was away and it would be his son to appear. I was stood staring at the tent, waiting to meet whoever came out, when I felt a tap on my shoulder.

"Thunder Cloud! I was hoping to meet you here. Where is your father?" Thunder Cloud's face dropped and he shook his head. "My father was killed last month. I am now chief of the Mohawks" I gave him my condolences. "So, Dafydd, what can I do for you?" I now began to grin. "Well, it is in part for me, but it's mainly for you, my friend." I proclaimed.

"Come into my warm longhouse," he offered. I followed him. "Don't worry, your horse will be safe." He smiled. "Now tell me, why are you here?"

"I presume you are aware that we celebrate Christmas? Part of that is that people give presents to each other." I explained.

"If you remember, my Welsh friend, I learnt my English from a man of God. Of course, I know about Christmas. But what has it to do with me?" he enquired.

"I want you as a Christmas present." I grinned. He seemed slightly taken aback.

"I thought you had turkey at Christmas, are you wanting a poor Indian for a change?" he laughed.

"My friend, you have a sister, yes?" I asked.

He was no longer smiling. Memories seemed to be flooding back into his mind of his dear sister.

"She was kidnapped by the Cherokee, many years ago. Why do you ask?"

"She ran away from them, and we have provided her and her children with safe keeping. I have come here to ask you to go with me, and be your sister's Christmas present."

It was quite unusual for Thunder Cloud, but for the time being, he was lost in emotion.

"Yes, my friend, of course I will be her Christmas present! I will leave with you tomorrow." He was so happy; I probably could have asked him for anything.

"I am trying to find a present for Katie. Can you give me any advice?" I begged. I knew the days towards Christmas were running down. He suddenly jumped up.

"I have just the thing!" He searched among the pile of trinkets at the back of his longhouse. "Here it is." He called.

He held a box, he opened the box to display a necklace, plus earrings and a bracelet, made of rubies.

Thunder Cloud was full of excitement from the thought of seeing his sister again. He had thought that he would never see her again.

He quickly went about organising the Mohawks for his departure. The next morning, he was ready to leave.

When we made contact with the rest of the Rangers, I could see they had done a great job. There was a nice Christmas tree on one of the wagons and the rest were filled with logs.

"Well done lads," I shouted. We had taken a total of two days to get the tree and all the logs.

I reported back to Katie, informing her that the tree was here, and that we had plenty of logs. I then walked behind her and put my hands over her eyes.

"Guess who I have brought with me?" I instructed her.

"Don't be silly, that's impossible to guess!"

I told her that it was White Eagle's brother. Now that piqued her interest. She offered a long list of Indian names, but not the correct one.

"Katie, this is the Christmas present for White Eagle. Here is her brother, Thunder Cloud. Katie opened her eyes; she was in shock.

"You are White Eagles brother?" He nodded. "I presume that you have not met your nephew and niece?" She asked. He shook his head.

Somehow, we kept him hidden from White Eagle until Christmas day.

The day began with me delivering a short talk about the meaning of the birth of Christ, followed by breakfast. White Eagle was in charge of the catering. She had a busy day planned.

I sent a message for White Eagle and her children to report to us in the main hall immediately. She clearly thought that she was in trouble, or that she may be asked to leave.

"White Eagle, it is a custom for us to give presents at Christmas. As you will be busy today, Mark had asked if he could give you his present now." Her eyes lit up with excitement. Mark walked into the room.

"White Eagle, I wanted to give you a special Christmas present. Please close your eyes." This she did. Then Thunder cloud entered the room.

"Ok, open your eyes." Grinned Mark. She opened her eyes to see her brother, who she had thought that she would never see again. She broke down in tears and rushed over to give him a hug. We all left them together; they had a few years to talk about.

What an amazing day, everyone's spirits were lifted.

I went to find Katie, she was alone in a room.

"Katie, I hope you are having a brilliant day. I got you a small token of my love." I passed the box to her.

She opened the box and stood for a while just staring in shock at the jewels.

"Dafydd, where did you get these?" This sounded like I was in trouble.

"I got them from Thunder Cloud, he had them stored with hundreds of other precious gifts." She grabbed my arm and pulled me close to her.

"My Dragon, you have probably got me the best gift I could ever have. These belonged to my Grandparents. They were killed in an Indian raid many years ago. I am so happy to have these restored to me." Tears were now running down her cheeks. I wasn't quite sure what to do with myself. I decided that I was needed elsewhere, so I went towards the door.

"Where are you going? I have your Christmas present. Don't you want it?"

I walked over to her; she tapped the seat next to her. I sat down and waited for my gift. She turned to look at m

"Dafydd, I have had feelings for you for ages. I have tried to control my feelings, as I thought it may affect discipline. But I was wrong. Love is something which should be allowed to grow, to be nurtured, not locked away in a box. I love you Dafydd." She then pulled a small box out of her pocket. It contained two rings made of string.

"Will you exchange rings with me?"

I pulled her into my arms. I hugged her tight and kissed her longingly." I had been dreaming of this moment for a long time. It lived up to and exceeded every expectation I had.

"It would be a pleasure my love." I said with the biggest smile on my face.

It was the best Christmas ever. She never discussed the situation regarding the male and female bedrooms, and the ones for married people. I expected we would get back to that at some point.

Spring came and went. We all spent time training, we were aware of big battles to come. June and July passed us by, then on the first of August, we received orders to support General John Stark. This was to be our first real battle. We would now be fighting against British and German professional soldiers. We would also feel the effects of fighting with cannons.

We arrived on the morning of the 14th August.

When I was serving in the British army. I was told that during a big battle, we would never really know what was happening. We would just follow orders and do our best. At the end of the battle, we would either be alive and celebrating, or lying dead in some field, far away from home.

Our orders were very limited. We would be fighting against mainly German soldiers, backed up by British marksmen and Indians. The Germans would have artillery and dragoons, mounted infantry that used their horses for mobility, but would dismount to fight on foot. We have never fought against either of these. We would have to learn quickly, or we would be leaving.

On the 15ᵗʰ, the general ordered Katie and myself to disperse The Rangers into the surrounding forests to act as Skirmishers. We were to probe the German lines. Now this is what we had been trained for.

It had been raining hard since we arrived, which would give us problems keeping our powder dry.

The Rangers were skilled Indian fighters, they would move through the trees in total silence. But the rain soon became a problem, as we were soon up to our ankles in mud. Although, it did make it easier to follow the enemy footprints in the mud.

On our return to the main force. We were informed that we had received reinforcements during the day.

August 16ᵗʰ finally arrived. The day of the battle.

By midday, the rain had finally stopped. Blue sky was breaking through the clouds. The rain may have stopped, but when Cannons are being dragged across a field, massive furrows are made, which doesn't help the soldier or his horse.

General Stark ordered everyone to be ready to attack. He then made a rallying speech - or so we were told, as we were out reach of his voice.

The German soldiers, who spoke no English, had been told that the Loyalist soldiers had bits of white paper adorning their hats, and they must not be fired on.

Most of General Starks' men soon heard about this, and many began to add white paper to their hats.

The fighting broke out around 3pm.

The German position was immediately surrounded by Gunfire. General Stark described this as 'The Hottest engagement he had ever witnessed'.

Katie and I kept our Rangers together. We did feel responsible for them. These Rangers were making themselves a name.

While crawling through the mud, they were still able to pick off German soldiers and British Marksmen with ease. All those months of training had produced Rangers who never missed their target and could reload faster than most.

After the Battle, Stark's militia men began to disarm the prisoners and were looting their supplies. The Rangers did not get involved in this.

Suddenly, a German officer named Breymann arrived with German reinforcements. Stark's men were in disarray, so he launched a surprise attack. Katie quickly saw what was happening and ordered The Rangers to engage with the attack.

We were able to shoot quite a few German soldiers, which gave Starks men time to hastily regroup. We all gathered together to try and hold the high ground, but were soon pushed back. Soon, others arrived to reinforce our troops. A pitched battle continued until dark. It was a nightmare. Katie and I were fighting back-to-back. Cannons were still sending iron balls of death into our midst. There was thick smoke causing us to choke as we both slashed left and right.

Eventually the Germans retreated. They had apparently lost a quarter of their troops, and all their artillery pieces.

Looking at the dead soldiers around Katie and I, it looked like most must have died here.

It doesn't matter how much training you have done; nothing can really prepare you for the real thing. Our arms were aching and we were both exhausted, but we were alive. Unlike those who would be buried in this foreign field, never to see their loved ones again.

We put out a call for The Rangers to gather. Katie held my arm tight.

"I do hope that they all survived." She was almost pleading.

Eventually it looked like everyone had gathered. I could see Jean, Lana, Mark…

"Where is John?" I asked.

After a final count. We had lost twenty. Four women and sixteen of our men. This included John Deacon, who had not returned. Both him and his brother had now given their lives to free our country from the British.

I gathered everyone and said a prayer for our fallen comrades. That night we all slept on the battlefield. We were too exhausted to do anything else.

The following morning, we marched to a small lake not far away. We stripped down to our underwear and jumped into the water. We washed all the blood off our skins and tried our best to scrub the blood out of our clothes.

By noon the August sun had dried most of our uniforms. We also found some food distributed among the German dead. We ate a good breakfast then went to collect our horses. I was glad that we had walked and not taken our horses into that bloodbath.

As we were all walking back to collect our horses a messenger arrived. Katie and I had been ordered to attend a meeting with the other officers, including General John Stark.

We arrived at the tent where the meeting was to be held and both stood outside like naughty school children waiting to be called in to see the teacher.

A voice came from behind us.

"As the stars of the show, I think you two should enter first." It was the general. We both saluted, just before he pushed us both into the tent.

Apparently, this was a very important battle, winning here would help Washington's army in later days.

The Rangers were praised for their bravery and shooting skills.

Then we were called forward. General Stark began to speak.

"As I oversaw the Battle, my eyes were drawn to two young officers who were fighting back-to-back. I could have sworn the Germans were throwing their whole army at you. The more that came, the more you both cut down. I have heard a rumour that you are called The Dragon and The Eagle. I cannot think of any more appropriate name for the two of you.

In future those are the names I will use when we meet. You have both earned them well. As well as these medals." He called us forward and pinned a medal on each of us.

Everyone was praising us. Eventually we managed to escape, but it was well past dark by then. On our way back to our camp, we passed the lake.

"Shall we?"I asked Katie, gesturing to the lake.

She nodded. We both threw our medals into the lake. Then we both laughed and had a little dance. Medals are given to individuals. We were part of a team of brave and very skilled fighters called Katie's Rangers. As we couldn't share the medals, we didn't want them.

We finally arrived back in camp. There was a massive fire burning. The Rangers had also done a bit of hunting, and we had meat. We were celebrating our victory, but we would never forget our dead.

"Katie, what did the General say to you? Something about heights."

"Let's celebrate tonight my love. We will leave heights or whatever until the morning."

CHAPTER 9

THE BATTLE OF
BEMIS HEIGHTS

When we returned to The Rangers, we gathered the sergeants. We had discussed their reward last night.

"Everyone did an amazing job at The Battle of Bennington. We are promoting you all to second lieutenant." I announced. "We would like you each to select one man or woman that you think has shown great leadership skills, to promote to sergeant."

We returned to our headquarters for a rest after the battle. As we approached the school, hoping that we could spend a month there in the summer sun.

About half a mile from the school, we became alarmed by the noise. Yes, the British had returned.

"That's bad news Katie. Now where will we find somewhere to recuperate for a month or two?"

Katie thought for a while before replying.

"I think the British have taken over most of New York and the surrounding area. We may have to search for somewhere a bit further out."

We had ninety Rangers with us, some still carrying wounds.

"Mark, take your sister and go in search of a suitable place for us to hide away for a couple of months." He nodded and was soon on his way.

He had a lot on his mind. After Christmas, White Eagle, who he had feelings for, returned with her brother Thunder Cloud, to her people.

She told him that she had to visit her family who she hadn't seen for years, but she had promised to return. They had both declared their feelings for one another before she left.

It was now late August; summer was drawing to a close. We had been given a couple of months off to rest and recover, ready for our next encounter. This was not far from New York. A place called Freeman's Farm. ten miles south of Saratoga.

It was getting dark; luckily, it was a warm summer's evening. Katie ordered us to set up camp in a nearby woods. About 9pm, Mark and Jean returned. They had found a deserted farm. It looked like the previous occupants were Americans who had feared that the British would pay them a visit.

Katie and I decided to go for a walk. There was a large summer moon overhead.

"Katie, when we get settled into the Farm. We need to discuss what we were talking about last Christmas. The Rangers are fit fighters. They could all be dead in our next battle. I expect that many live for the day. Some may have feelings for each other. As their leaders, we need to say something." I paused for a moment and added. "Apart from them, what about us?" She walked a few steps, before turning to me.

"What about us?"

I pointed my finger with the ring made of string. She smiled.

"Ok I understand, yes we will talk with them."

"We are all red-blooded men and women, filled with hormones. They, as well as us, are looking for guidance."

At 7am the following morning, Thunder Cloud rode into our camp with his sister and her children. As soon as she saw Mark, she jumped down from her horse and ran to him. They wrapped their arms around each other.

"I am sorry that I have taken so long to return. My family wanted me to stay with them. I'm glad we were able to find you, we saw that the British had taken over the school, but we thought you wouldn't be too far away."

Mark just stared into her eyes.

"I am so glad you returned; he has been wandering around like a lost sheep since you left" Jean laughed.

Katie appeared from her tent.

"I want everyone ready to move at noon. We need to reach our new home before it gets dark." Then she dived back into her tent. I walked over and stuck my head inside.

"I am going over to see this farm before everyone arrives. I will meet you all there." She came out to me with her hair covered with a towel.

"Ok, we will be there before dark." I asked Jean to come with me and show me the way.

The farm was only an hour's ride. On the outside it looked like what it was - a run down, deserted farm. I was a bit concerned. If any British or German soldiers passed here. It would be impossible to conceal The Rangers, and they would likely be heard miles away. It wasn't really suitable for our needs.

"Jean, did you see any other suitable buildings?" She nodded.

"About a half hour away, I think there is an abandoned church. There used to be a small village near the church, but I believe the people moved because of Indian attacks. We didn't scout it though as we found the farm first."

"Now that is interesting." I smiled.

We rode on until we found this abandoned church. There were also a few of the cottages which were still habitable, but the church was my main interest. Below the church were many rooms. Apparently, when the village was under attack by Indians, the villagers had sheltered in the church.

"This is the place Jean, the top floor can be left as it is, visitors won't suspect that we are living below." I beckoned to her. "We had better get back to the farm before everyone begins to wonder where we are."

Katie and The Rangers had arrived just before we returned. They were beginning to unpack their luggage.

"Stop! We are not staying here." I called over to Katie. She walked over to me and asked why not. "This place is too exposed. We have found a safer place a bit further away."

I suddenly held Katie and put my hand over her mouth. Then with my free hand, I waved The Rangers to take cover.

There must have been four hundred German dragoons, riding towards the farm, they must have had the same idea as us. The German troops were concentrating too much on what they were doing to hear us. We slowly crept away, and on our way to the church.

"That was lucky. If we had returned another half hour later, you would have been unpacked. And facing a charge by the dragoons."

"Well, this looks interesting," admitted Lana.

"True, there is a lot of room under this church. And no one will know that there are nearly a hundred Rangers living here." Agreed Jean.

Katie was standing with her arms folded and smiling.

"I hope someone has lots of candles, it will be very dark when the sun sets."

I had to admit, the lack of candles would be a problem. 'It's not like we can just pop to a nearby market and buy some.' I thought.

"Katie, I think before it gets dark. You need to talk to our Rangers about the plan we came up with last Christmas. It has become necessary now." I declared.

"You are right, ok I will explain the rules."

"Rangers," she hesitated, trying to form her words. "We are of both sex's. We are also adults with hormones and attractions to other Rangers." She was waffling. I had better help her out.

"What Katie is trying to say is, we need to define sleeping quarters. There will be sleeping quarters for single males. The two cottages across the road, will house you, for tonight at least. Single ladies will sleep below the church. And married couples will sleep up here in the church. But… As this is a church and a place of God. I will, as an officer, be conducting weddings. If any couple wishes to marry, let me know by tomorrow evening. It's almost dark, owing to the lack of candles. I suggest you unpack quickly and depart for bed." I moved aside and indicated for Katie to finish up.

After everyone had dispersed. Katie turned to me.

"Are we going to marry?"

I already knew what my answer would be.

"As a Christian, I could never sleep with you unless we were married. So..." I then knelt on the cold stone floor.

"Katie Brooks. Will you marry me?" I then pulled a ring from my pocket. It was my parents ring, the one which my father had used to propose to my mother. Katie looked at the ring, tears began to run down her cheeks.

"My dear Welsh Dragon. How can I possibly refuse your offer? Yes, of course I will marry you." She then took the ring and put it on her finger.

Two days later, all couples who wanted to marry came to the church and I married them in front of the rest of the Rangers. Mark, as another officer, married Katie and I.

Things were going well; it was an early afternoon in the middle of September. I was lying in the grass near some trees with Katie, when suddenly about fifty German dragoons rode up to the church. Two officers at the front, dismounted and began to look around. Leaving their men on the outskirts of the village.

I signalled Katie to go to the cottages and alert the men. I slipped into the back of the church. Lana was in the church when I entered. I signalled for her to alert the others down below. Lana alerted the others then returned to stand by my side. The German captain saw us first, but before he was able to speak. Lana's knife stuck in his throat. She was a great knife thrower, with amazing reflexes.

The general saw his man go down and pulled his sword from its scabbard.

In broken English he insulted The Rangers, and called me a 'scruffy lout'.

"Well General, I have to admit, I am a bit scruffy, and maybe I am a lout, but I am also a better swordsman than you are."

I then drew my sword. I have to admit, he was good. He kept talking about how good German swordsmanship was so much better than the English. Well, he was about to see how good Welsh swordsmanship was. I sped up my attack and it wasn't long before his sword had gone and my sword was pointing at his throat.

His hands were tied behind his back, then he was marched up the front of the church. His men were shocked when they saw him. I made him order all his men to drop their weapons, which were gathered up. I was sure that we could make use of them.

His men were all tied up and placed below the church. The General was still shouting various insults at me.

We were due to meet at Freeman's Farm during the first week of October. Katie and I decided to leave a little earlier. We took fifty men with horses, swords and pistols. It would be too difficult to hide, especially if the British came into view.

We eventually arrived about half a mile from this farm.I sent two Rangers out to check the area for British or German soldiers. They both returned an hour later, both their faces white as a sheet.

When they were finally fit to give a report. It turned out that the farm was commanded by the British. What turned their faces red was the amount of blood still lying on the ground. There must have been a really bloody battle earlier. The British were fortifying their positions.

It seemed that the British, having won the battle, were waiting for support - they had obviously lost a lot of men in the battle. I presumed that as well as more men, they would also be waiting for more supplies. The problem with a lack of supplies is that the British would be forced to decide on whether to attack us or retreat, and I doubted that they would want to retreat from their bloodily won position at the farm. They may be planning an all-out assault on the American army, which of course would include our Rangers.

We needed to leave this place quickly and find out where the other American forces were based. We quickly retreated back to where we left the rest of the Rangers then departed towards Bemis Heights, the next place that had been mentioned in our orders.

We arrived just in time to be warned about an imminent attack by the British. I ordered White Eagle and her children to follow me. We drove the Ranger's horses with us, as well as the German horses we had acquired.

My target was the area where the men in charge of the battle were. They sat in comfortable chairs drinking wine and eating niceties, while we were fighting up to our necks in blood. We rode directly towards Major General Arnold. We presented ourselves. Then I gave him the gift of fifty horses, plus swords and pistols. He was totally amazed.

"Thank you, Colonel, and what can I do for you?"

I smiled. "Sir, I would like to leave The Rangers horses up here in a safe place, as we will need them after this skirmish.

I will leave White Eagle behind with them to take care of them." He shook my hand, and promised that I could leave them here in safety.

The British were deployed into a battle line at Barbers Wheatfield by General Fraser. On the left he had the British grenadiers - in my short time with the British army, I came across the grenadiers, they were one of the top regiments, brilliant fighters. In the centre were German troops. Then on the right, he had light infantry.

Major General Gates, who was in command of our army, dispatched General Morgan's men to attack the advancing British forces. The Battle began at a little after 2pm.

Morgan was joined by light infantrymen, armed with muskets and bayonets. They worked in tandem with Morgan's riflemen. While the rifles were more accurate, they were slower to reload, so after firing, they fell back behind Dearborn's bayonets, to prevent the British breaking through.

This is where Katie's Rangers joined the battle.

I heard that where we left the horses, while the officers were taking lunch, they could hear the growing sounds of battle. Arnold wanted to be allowed to take the fight to the enemy.

On getting permission, he rode down towards the American lines. A cheer went up as he rode into the fight. The American troops fought their way forward. Somehow, I had drifted away from Katie, normally we fought shoulder to shoulder. Then it happened. The only thing that I could remember was a thud to the back of my head, then lying in the blood-soaked mud, thinking to myself, that this was the end.

Katie had begun to wonder where I was.

"Has anyone seen Dafydd?"

Two of the Rangers who had been fighting alongside me spoke.

"We have been looking for you Katie. The last we saw of him was over to the left." They pointed. "He was surrounded by maybe ten British soldiers. Then he disappeared. We tried to get to him, but the fighting was too fierce and we were forced back. People who were with her said that she suddenly went silent. Then her cheeks turned red.

"Everyone has seen my Welsh Dragon on fire. But people haven't yet seen The Eagle in her true form. It is time that I spread my wings and show my talons."

She tucked two pistols into her belt. With a sword in one hand and a knife in the other. She ordered twenty Rangers to follow her.

This Eagle was fighting for the love of her life. Only a fool would confront her. She was soon slashing left and right with her sword in a flurry of blows, and wielding her knife in the other hand. On one occasion, she stuck her knife in her belt and drew out a pistol. Eventually the blood-covered Eagle reached her loved one. She gave orders for her dragon to be picked up and taken to safety.

I was finally regaining consciousness, trying to figure out where I was. I had a raging headache. Blood was still running down my head. I looked up at my saviour, who was starting to come into focus. She looked terrible - blood was leaking from so many cuts all over her body. Finally, she collapsed on top of me. I put both arms around her, and hugged her.

"Not too hard my love, I have a few sore places." Then she lost consciousness.

What a woman! I didn't want to see too much of this Eagle though - she was badly injured. We were both carried from the battlefield.

Soon after we left, the Rangers supported the rest of the Americans as they broke both flanks, and the British began to withdraw in disorder.

Later we found out that The British, under Fraser, attempted to reform their lines between the Wheatfield and the British

Fortifications. At this moment, Fraser was hit by a stray bullet in his stomach. He fell from his horse, mortally wounded.

The British then lost all order - they broke and ran for their lives at Freeman's Farm, with American soldiers following.

Arnold wanted to break up the British formations. With both flanks crumbling, General John Burgoyne, the British commander, rode back to the British entrainments to prepare for a defence.

The British put up a determined stand against the surging American forces. The Germans were pushed back, and the Americans now held a position on the British flank.

As the sun set and darkness covered the ground, those who were uninjured rested. The injured were treated, a minor bullet wound would not be too much of a problem, but many lost limbs that evening - they may spend the rest of their lives as cripples, begging for support. But at least they were alive. Many American and British young men lay in their own blood, never to see their loved ones again. The battle had been a disaster for the British. 600 men were killed, wounded or captured.

Burgoyne and his 5,000-man army fell back towards Saratoga.

On October 13th, Burgoyne had no other option left. He offered to negotiate surrender. He agreed to surrender with a condition that his captured men would be sent back to England.

Congress agreed but later went back on the agreement, and the British soldiers spent the rest of the war in a prison of war camp. This was the first British army to surrender in world history.

Katie and I were put in beds next to each other. Well, it made visiting easier.

As soon as Mark arrived, I ordered him to go immediately to where White Eagle was looking after our horses and retrieve them.

"And, don't forget to bring White Eagle back." I joked. He nodded.

"Now, my Eagle, I understand that you opened your wings and became a one-woman army. Have you anything to say?" She shook her head

"I was a just worried that the British may torture you, and I know you would give away all our secrets."

Now that was funny, as I didn't know any secrets. Well, apart from where Katie was ticklish.

The following day I was back to normal again. Lana, paid her first visit to us.

"Lana, I married a lot of couples the other day. Don't you have a boyfriend yet?" Katie threw something at me. Then shook her head. What had I done?

"It's ok, he doesn't know. You see, I was in love with a young man. We had planned for you to marry us, but we were too late, so we decided to marry when we returned from this battle."

There was silence, and tears began to run down her cheeks. I sat up in bed and grabbed hold of her. I pulled her towards me, and held her close. I began to think, how I would feel if Katie was killed.

"I'm so sorry, shed your tears on me." I said softly.

"Lana, we have good news for you. And a special commission. You will have to be strong. We will give you two days to grieve the loss of your loved one. Then we will want you to return to us and enquire about this commission. Or if you'd prefer to walk away, you have every right."

Katie was now staring at me, with a confused look on her face. She was wondering what this commission was. The thing is, I was also wondering what it was. But I had two days to come up with an idea.

Lana left the room, no longer crying, I think mentally she was also grabbing at the thought of something to throw her time into.

Katie had cuts all over her body and had lost a lot of blood. She must have been magnificent, fighting her way to save me. It seemed like The Dragon and The Eagle were becoming true heroes of this revolution. She had one deep cut across her back, which was causing most of the concern.

I was technically ok to leave the hospital. Of course, there was no way that I was going to leave Katie until she was fully healed. Like all battle grounds, when the Battle is defined as over, injured soldiers are rushed to the field hospitals. Often limbs are removed and a pain-killer, normally morphine, would be used to ease the patient's agony. The bigger the battle, the more injuries, resulting in the morphine being used up quickly. Katie was in the situation, where especially during the night, the cut across her back brought her a lot of pain. The morphine was no more. All I could give to help relieve her pain was my love for her.

I shared her bed, when the pain came, I held her tight, and kissed her. Sweat often poured from both of us. Somehow my kisses helped to take her mind away from the pain.

Two days later, her wound began to heal and the pain subsided. I was so happy. I was finally able to take her for short walks. Truly, my Eagle was on her way back to health.

"Hi Lana," Katie, called out. I turned and yes, Lana had returned, two days exactly from her last visit.

"How are you feeling Katie, you look a lot better than when I last saw you." She acknowledged.

Katie was now sitting on the edge of her bed.

"I feel like I have been to hell and back. But the love of this man has helped pull me through." Katie made a somewhat weak smile. It was still early days.

"What have you been doing?" I asked.

"For the first day, I could not stop crying. Yesterday, I visited our wounded Rangers. In case you didn't know yet, we lost five Rangers and fifteen were injured. Two lost limbs - they won't see any more fighting. I was talking with their wives, they both have children and are now concerned about what life lies before them, with their men unable to work. I was at a loss as to what to say to them." Lana disclosed.

All at once it hit me. I had spent the last two days worrying about Katie. I had completely forgotten about our wounded Rangers and the families or our dead. I felt so ashamed.

I finally managed to pull myself together. During the last two days I had in fact come up with a commission for Lana. With the news that she had just brought us, the commission which I was about to offer her became more relevant than ever. It was as if this was the will of God. I had not been able to talk about Katie, about the commission as she had other things on her mind, like getting better.

"Katie, my love, I have not been able to speak with you about the commission which I am about to offer Lana. Will you trust me with it?" She smiled and nodded. I turned to Lana.

"Firstly, I am promoting you to Lieutenant." I looked at Katie for approval. Again, she nodded.

Lana, was so happy about getting the promotion, although couldn't hide that she was a bit concerned as to why.

"Now, the commission. First, I want you to form a team to help you manage this scheme. Anyone who you appoint on your team, will receive the rank of sergeant. Your first responsibility will be recruitment. Since the summer we have lost 35 Rangers, as well as the two who will never fight again." I informed her. "The second is to form a team of people who are medically trained, to take care of our wounded. Katie and I will work on our own commission, which will be to somehow, find a way to look after the families of our dead and those who are unable to work anymore." As I spoke those words, a lump filled my throat. "Will you accept this commission, Lieutenant Lana?"

She smiled as she saluted, then grabbed hold of my hand.

"Yes Sir, it will be an honour." She nodded to Katie, then turned and rushed off. I looked at Katie and we both broke out into a big grin.

"Come on, let's go for our walk." She took my arm and off we went.

On our return, there was a messenger from George Washington. 'Now what have we done wrong?' I giggled to myself. I opened the message.

"Sit here my love, and read it to me." Katie instructed me. So, as ordered, I sat beside her.

"Our commander in chief has offered our Rangers an opportunity to join The Continental Army at its winter retreat, near Philadelphia."

"That's good. It will give us a chance to heal our wounded and for our new Lieutenant to begin her commission." She nodded. She was clearly feeling a lot better now.

CHAPTER 10

VALLEY FORGE

I was now fully recovered; Katie would be ready to travel in a couple of weeks' time. Alas we had about ten Rangers still unable to travel. We wouldn't leave without them.

Two weeks ago, The Continental Army collected the fit soldiers who had survived the battle, then they continued on their way to Valley Forge - their winter retreat.

Lana was a bit concerned as to the conditions at Valley Forge. After all, there would be at least 12,000 soldiers staying there. So, using her initiative, Lana gave orders to four of the fit Rangers going to Valley Forge, to stay for a week, before reporting back to us about the conditions.

"Sir, I would like to recommend Jean, for promotion, she will be in my team."

I must find out and remember everyone's surnames - it would not do to be referring to officers by their first names around others.

"Ok, done. Please ask her to come in and see me for her promotion."

She called Jean, who had been standing outside.

"Well done, Jean, you are now a Lieutenant."

"Thank you, Sir.

I was pleased that Lana had made a start on the commission that we had given her.

The idea of taking our Rangers to a winter retreat seemed, on the surface, a great plan. Provisions and food would be supplied. We, the officers, could get some rest, while our troops would be trained to new levels of fitness. This would give us the time to plan for the families of our sick and wounded, and of course the deceased.

Two weeks later, our Rangers returned from Valley Forge. It was all bad news.

They had observed what was happening at present, plus there was always someone willing to tell them about what had happened before they arrived. In the summer, The Continental Army's quarter-master, General Thomas Mifflin, decided to station a large portion of the army's supplies in outbuildings around the forges.

Some officers voiced disapproval, as such a large concentration of military supplies would become a target for British raids.

On September 18th, after the Battle of Clouds on the 10th, several hundred German soldiers, under General Wilhelm Von Knyphausen, raided the supplies at Valley Forge.

After this, two officers decided to evacuate the supplies from Valley Forge. Crown soldiers captured the supplies, destroying them and burning down the Forges - reducing Valley Forge, to a place not fit for purpose.

Thomas Paine wrote a description of his army's march into Valley Forge:

"To see men without clothes to cover their nakedness, without blankets to lay on, without shoes, leaving bloody footprints. Without provisions, marching through frost and snow. To see them sit down famished and maimed by the inclemency of the season, without a house or a hut to cover them from the rigours of the weather, and at the same time, withering under an idea that their countrymen in ease and plenty were indifferent to their sufferings."

On arrival at Valley Forge, the soldier's first job was to build a number of log-cabins.

The Rangers observed that as well as the 12,000 soldiers of The Continental Army, there were many women, children and slaves. The allocation was 12 enlisted men to live in each cabin.

The soldiers often had their wives and children with them, which could lead to over 20 people to some cabins. Many soldiers were dying of starvation and disease.

Washington had been unable to keep the British out of Philadelphia. While his army suffered at Valley Forge, The Redcoats were warming themselves in the homes of the colonists.

Washington had become annoyed when he heard that local farmers were hoarding food, waiting to earn higher profits in the spring. Some farmers even took grain into Philadelphia to sell to the British, as they would pay in gold or silver. Buying from markets was difficult, as Washington had no hard currency. Also, there was massive inflation.

Apparently, during the first few days of construction of the cabins. The troops ate mainly fire cakes. A mixture of flour and water, cooked on hot stones.

The weather wasn't that harsh, but many soldiers were still not fit for duty, owing to illness and disease, as well as lack of proper clothing. Many had neither coats, hats, shirts or shoes, their feet and legs would freeze until nearly black. They had not even been at Valley Forge that long.

Disease was already rife - as with any large number of people gathered together in unhygienic conditions. The scouts had witnessed dead horses laying in the mud; Scabies; Typhoid; Dysentery; Pneumonia; and even rumours of Smallpox had been talked about around the camp.

So, summing everything up. There was a lack of food and supplies. The cabins were overcrowded even before we arrived. Disease was spreading. If the Typhoid and Smallpox weren't isolated soon, they alone would kill everyone there." I turned to Katie.

"There is no way that our Rangers should enter Valley Forge. Perhaps we should camp a little way away and try to support the army in our own way." I suggested, looking at Katie for her response.

Before she could speak, one of the Rangers who had not spoken much in the reporting of Valley Forge, spoke up.

"They do have a new man in charge of training at the Forges. His name is Baron Friedrich von Steuben, a former Prussian drill master. Those who are able to turn out for training are showing massive improvements."

"This is my idea, Katie. We should go to Valley Forge, but not into the camp. We should make our own village in the forest nearby. Like our friends, The Mohawks, we can make some longhouses. They are made from trees. I know that the leaves have fallen, but we don't need the leaves, only the branches and twigs. White Eagle can be in charge of the building, as she is the expert."

We can try to obtain food and supplies to help the troops. Coats and blankets would be helpful. The way I see it, the people who want a free country must be willing to give us what the army needs. Our soldiers are willing to give up their lives to gain freedom from the British. So, I'm sure they can give a few cows or bundles of grain. Also, the British may need some help to carry all their gold and silver. We should offer our help to carry it." I grinned.

Then I turned to Lana. "During this winter, I am expecting Lieutenant Lana to recruit new Rangers and to find medical personnel who would like to be part of our new mobile hospital. Does anyone else have any thoughts on any of this?." I finished and stepped back.

For maybe two minutes there was total silence, but eventually, comments began to flow. Overall, I think they all agreed with me.

"Dyfydd, can I take ten Rangers with me?" Lana was of course the first to speak up. I nodded. "Also, we can't go in our uniforms - we may have to visit people who live near the British. Have we got anything else we can wear?"

Katie nodded and told her that she would sort something for them.

I was beginning to run things through my mind. Katie's Rangers would live outside of Valley Forge. Lana was going to find medical people to help us and look for new recruits. What else could we do to provide help for the army? There was a priority in the need for food. One of the reasons that Washington couldn't buy food and supplies was because we did not have any gold or silver. This was the only currency which farmers would accept.

"Katie, I think that we should pay a visit to Philadelphia before we head to Valley Forge."

"Are you planning to steal some of the food, which the British seem to have so much of?" I smiled, then shook my head. "Food and supplies are too bulky; it will be difficult to escape from the city with hundreds of dragoons in chase. We are going after gold and silver." I grinned. "By the way, I have a surprise for you." I added.

She was now becoming very curious. I went to the sack where I kept my cartridges. I pulled out what now may be recognised as something akin to a wad of dollars. She began to read what was written on the notes.

"I promise to pay the bearer on demand." There then was a gap for the sum of money to be added. "On behalf of the American Government. Signed George Washington." She frowned, then asked what they were.

"They are an 'I owe you'. When George Washington needs food and supplies. At present, farmers are refusing to sell their goods as our currency is unreliable due to inflation. Therefore, the soldiers are lawfully able to take whatever goods they require and give the farmer one of these. All the officer is required to do is fill in the amount he owes the farmer. When the war is over, the farmer then has to present his I owe you, and he will receive his money. The only problem with this is that if the British win, it may be difficult to claim their money."

She was now laughing.

"So, all those greedy farmers or stallholders at the market will have to give their stock to the soldiers in exchange for one of these pieces of paper." Katie now broke into a fit of laughter. "You are a clever Dragon," she grinned. "Ok everyone, have an early night, I will take thirty Rangers with me tomorrow to visit Philadelphia."

I was happy to have an early night with my wife, but what was all this about her taking thirty Rangers? I thought that I would be going - after all, it was my idea.

"Come on darling, let's get to bed. I will explain things to you there."

With that, we retired to bed.

"Philadelphia, is a large city. There are some poor people, but there are also many ladies and gentlemen, 'well-off' people. I doubt if you will find any good looking Welshmen who speak with a strong, albeit sexy, Welsh accent."

I thought for a while then had to agree.

"I will once again become a lady, with my servants and body guards. This will enable us to move around the city undetected. I can't have you there blowing my cover."

What could I say, when Katie makes a decision, it becomes law. Katie's problem was that, although I was brought up in the Valleys and I had a strong Welsh accent, she didn't know that I had a great ear for accents and was perfectly able to put on a posh accent.

As soon as Katie left, I jumped upon my horse and began to follow her. I had packed some old clothes to wear when I entered the city. I intended to find a set of posh clothes when I arrived. I had given Mark orders to take command until we returned.

Katie decided to take a break at a pub near the city. They all had a hearty breakfast and a few tankards of beer. While they were all relaxing, six British soldiers entered the pub. They sat at a table in the far corner of the pub. I had entered the pub earlier, without being seen by the Rangers, and I was sipping my beer when the soldiers sat at the table next to mine.

"Why is that beautiful woman sitting with that collection of rogues?" I heard one of them say.

Katie had chosen her best fighters to take with her. The problem was that most of them were ex-mountain men, incredible fighters but little did Katie realise, they may find it difficult to pass as a lady's servants. The soldiers were aware that they were outnumbered, and so one of them went to get backup. Katie's attempt to collect some gold may just end before it had properly begun. Lucky for her, I made an exchange of clothes with a passing gentleman in the toilets. Ok, he may have been unconscious at the time.

I approached the soldiers.

"I say, old chaps, I have been listening to your conversation and I totally agree with you. How can such a beautiful lady be with them?

I think that she must have been kidnapped by those rough men." I was speaking with a posh accent. The officer took the bait.

"Men, let us rescue the lady!"

They all drew their weapons, and advanced towards Katie's table (or tables, as they were taking up four tables to be exact). All the soldiers had positioned themselves in order to have a good view of all the rough looking men.

He began to speak again.

"All you kidnappers are under arrest. You are free now, your Ladyship."

Katie exploded, jumping to the defence of her team.

"These are my servants and some are my bodyguards."

It was a nice try by Katie, but as she finished talking, the door flew open and fifty British soldiers entered the pub, led by a Captain. It looked all over for Katie.

"Captain, my brother is the Duke of Wessex. He is commander of The Grenadier Guards. I presume that you are aware of this?" He began to bow and apologise for not recognising me. "Well, I am a close friend of Lady Brooks. We will be getting married sometime next year. The king has promised to attend." I wondered if I was getting a bit carried away. "Lady Brooks always chooses her personal body guards from the mountain men, because, as I presume you are aware, they are the best fighters. I have talked with her in the past about their attire. I asked her to have them shaven, and smartly dressed. I hope that she will realise that I was correct, and that she will have them more well kept in future."

The captain apologised to Katie again, and exited the pub with all the soldiers. Well not quite all - one of the sergeants was asleep under the table I was sitting beside. I walked over to Katie.

"Good afternoon, Lady Brooks."

She laughed at my accent.

"Well done my handsome husband, it seems that I underestimated you." She grinned. I think we should collect this young man and get away from here quickly, in case they return." She gestured to the drunk sergeant.

At some point in the afternoon, he volunteered the information as to where the gold was stored. Katie sent four of her men to bring the carts. It didn't take long for us to take out the guards and soon the carts were filled with gold. Everyone was on their way out of the city, driving the four heavily loaded wagons.

We were about an hour outside the city when we heard horses pursuing us. I ordered the carts to stop. Twenty-five Rangers, including myself, dismounted. We were all lying in a prone position on the ground, waiting for the owners of the horses to appear. The carts loaded with gold continued. We waited.

Then it happened, fifty horses came around the corner. The Rangers all lay in silence, waiting for the order to fire. Twenty-five British soldiers died in the first attack. But they kept coming. Another eight died. They were soon in retreat. We now had a lot of horses to round up, that was a bonus, then set off in pursuit of the gold.

On reaching Valley Forge, Katie and I went in search of White Eagle - we needed to know how long it would take her to build five longhouses.

We followed her into the forest. Then in total shock, we saw eight longhouses.

"How did you manage to build them so quickly? No one is that fast!" Katie was so excited.

Mark was laughing.

"White Eagle is just that good! Five are for us, the other three are spare to use when needed."

All the Rangers were at our camp near Valley Forge now. Lana had brought six doctors, six nurses and twenty raw recruits.

We began talking to the doctors and the nurses about the various illnesses going around Valley Forge. These could kill every soldier in the camp at any time. I began to tell them a story.

"When I was young, I used to do many jobs, in order to put some food on the table. One of my jobs nearly cost me my life. I had an early morning job, looking after the milk maids. Sometimes, when they were sick, I used to milk the cows. One day I caught the dreaded Cowpox. I had a fever, swollen glands and large painful blisters. I thought I was going to die. After a week, I began to recover. I heard later at the farm that the milk maids often caught the Cowpox. There was also a strange rumour. It was said that these maids, as well as some other people who had caught Cowpox in the past, had all recovered from Smallpox when they came into contact with it."

"Hmm… that's very interesting!" Said one of the doctors.

"Yes, I have heard of similar rumours elsewhere." Confirmed one of the nurses.

"There are no cows, with or without Cowpox, within ten miles of Valley Forge. If they were out in the Snow-covered fields, the wolves would have killed them. But I may be able to help look after the smallpox patients." I suggested.

"Perhaps a local farmer has some infected cows in his sheds. A cow with large blisters on them would not be bought for eating." Added Katie.

I ordered ten Rangers to ride wide and check if any farms had cows with pox blisters. My thought was that if we could collect some Cowpox pus, we could infect some Rangers, who would recover and then be able to help me with the Smallpox patients.

On January 7th, we saw ten teams of oxen being driven past, heading towards Valley Forge. They were being driven by Philadelphian women. They also brought with them 2,000 shirts, smuggled from the City.

Over the course of the winter, the weather improved somewhat. Food and supplies trickled in from the surrounding countryside and the gold was used to purchase enough for The Continental Army to begin to recover. Morale and discipline improved with the better supply of better food, supplies, and weapons.

We were informed that France and America signed a treaty on February 6th 1778. Strangely enough, Britain declared War on France 5 weeks later, on March 17th. Living in the forest, we were the last to be told anything.

Eventually, Washington held a meeting of officers, and Katie and I were invited to attend. Washington informed us that he would break Camp on June 19th. He then made a short speech:

"We entered our winter retreat, a beaten, tired, dejected army. During our time here, a thousand soldiers, plus 1,500 horses, have died. But we have come out fitter, better organised and with high morale. We have less troops, but those who have survived, have become a superior fighting force. We will be able to confirm how much The Continental Army has improved in 9 days' time, on the 28th June."

As The British marched through South and Central New Jersey, on their way to New York City. They destroyed property, and stole supplies and food.

This inspired growing hostility among the area's civilians. Meanwhile, small-scale operations between the Continental and New Jersey militia harassed the British. The Battle of Monmouth had begun.

The two armies met on the morning of June 28th and fought for approximately 5 hours in ferocious heat. That night, the British moved their army to resume their attack on Manhattan.

What we, Katie's Rangers, had achieved during our stay at Valley Forge, was our first hospital. In order to protect the hospital from our enemies. We made it known that no one would be turned away.

The doctors and nurses were treating both American and British injured. The bonus was that both armies were sending medicines to the hospital. The last that we heard. They were using thirty longhouses. What gave me personal pleasure was that a group of doctors and nurses had been infected with cowpox. They all recovered well and they now ran a special longhouse, which specialised in Smallpox treatment.

I remember thinking that I would die from the Cowpox. But all that pain was worth it, as we are now hearing our medical people are winning the war against Smallpox.

CHAPTER 11

THE SIEGE OF BOONESBOROUGH

Katie walked into the room with a massive smile on her face. I have just received new orders. She walked around the table in silence. Thinking back, she was like an angler, waiting for the fish to take her bait.

"Ok Katie, where are we going to fight next?" She continued to smile.

"I understand that some of you may have heard about a certain person. Can anyone guess who I mean?" We were all hanging onto every word.

"Come on Katie, either tell us now, or we are leaving." She realised that her bait had been taken.

"Have you heard of Boonesborough?"

She had just spoked the magic word. Everyone knew Daniel Boone. Even I used to read about him in comics back in Risca. I decided to play things cool.

"Well, I may have heard of that name. How is it relevant?"

She was enjoying this.

"It's ok, if you have never heard of him I will just tell General Martin that we are unable to help."

That did it. Everyone, apart from me, was surrounding her, begging to know what the orders were.

"We are the best Indian fighters, and have been given a special commission." She began to read. "As you Daniel Boone followers know, in 1774, the colony of Virginia defeated a large war party comprising of many Native Americans, but mainly Shawnee. In the Dunmore's war. A treaty was made that established the Ohio River as the boundary between the Shawnee lands north of the river and Western Virginia, which includes most of Kentucky, to the south. In 1775, Richard Henderson of North Carolina bought a large amount of Kentucky land from the Cherokees. Henderson then employed Daniel Boone to blaze a trail through the wilderness and to build Fort Boone, which has since been renamed Boonesborough. The Shawnee were not happy about the American expansion and began to sporadically attack Boonesborough. Meanwhile, the American War of Independence had begun in the East. In 1777, British officers opened up a new front in the war with the American colonists by recruiting and arming Native Americans. War parties raided the Kentucky settlements.

"Wake up! I have a lot more to tell you," Katie exclaimed. We were all falling asleep, that's true.

"Let's just get to the important bit," I said.

She looked into my eyes.

"Ok, ok, I got your message. Daniel Boone has been captured by the Shawnee and escaped. There were some negotiations, which ended up in a fight. Boonesborough is under siege. They have about 40 people defending the town. The Shawnee who are attacking are reported to have about 440 warriors. What shall we do about this?"

As expected, everyone went to find their rifles and started to pack. They were well aware that riding through the night is dangerous. Therefore, most of the Rangers went to sleep early. They might not get any more sleep for a few days.

"Lana, are you ok? You are working very hard of late, and I think that you are looking pale because of it." Explained Katie, with a very concerned look on her face.

"Katie, my heart is broken. The only thing that I have to live for is my work." She then began to cry. Katie took her into her arms, and held her close.

"That's ok, just cry it out." Lana's tears were running down her cheeks and soaking into both their clothes. Eventually, she pulled away from Katie and wiped her face.

"I loved that man so much. We never had enough time together for me to be able to introduce him to you. Every moment we had is precious to me." Wept Lana. She composed herself a little. "Let me tell you how Jean and I are progressing with the commission. I know that you and Dafydd have now created a hospital for the long term injured. We are continuing to recruit more doctors and nurses to expand that."

Katie smiled.

"This we know and are waiting for a suitable time to thank you both." Lana bowed.

"We have also recruited thirty newbies. They are not quite ready for The Rangers yet, but we do have enough to bring The Rangers tally up to a hundred again. One of our new recruits, a black-haired giant of a man, is not only good with his rifle, but has good fighting skills as well. Plus, he shows leadership potential. I want to recommend him for promotion to Corporal." She was smiling now.

Katie took notice of Lana's change from being depressed and crying, to proud and smiling, when she began to speak about this new recruit.

Jean then appeared.

"Who are we talking about?"

"You know Pete, he is doing so well!"

Jean also began to smile.

"Yes, I bet he will be one of the best fighters in the Rangers!"

Katie has good intuition, and she was feeling that something was wrong here.

"Ok, promote him to Corporal, I will check him out later." Both Lana and Jean began to giggle like two little girls.

"You won't regret it." replied Jean. "He is so handsome." She added. Lana suddenly stopped smiling. Tension began to fill the room.

"Ok, let's get some sleep, we will be starting early tomorrow." Ordered Katie.

"Dafydd my love, I think we may have a problem." I turned over and gazed into her beautiful eyes, how could I not fall in love with her?

"I just want to talk with you. Nothing else." she said sternly. I chuckled.

"Go ahead, I am listening."

She checked that she had my full attention before starting.

"Lana and Jean have recruited a new man. They just asked me to promote him - he only arrived two weeks ago. They are gushing with praise about him. That 'he is the best fighter; he is so hand-some.' I gave a short yawn.

"Are you getting jealous?" I grinned.

"Well, he does seem very attractive, maybe I should take him under my wings." I was now regretting what I had said. I put my arm around her, pulled her close and kissed her passionately.

"Ok, I will keep you a little bit longer." Then we both began to laugh. "But I am worried, both Lana and Jean appear to be infatuated with him. Also, if he is such a good fighter, he could be a British spy."

I nodded, taking it a bit more seriously now.

"Ok my love, I will give him my personal attention from tomor-row. But for now, can we get some sleep?"

I woke up to the smell of venison steak. Not an ideal breakfast, but good protein to prepare us all for the defence of Boonesborough.

"Katie, how are we going to get 100 Rangers into a fort that's under siege?"

She looked towards the roof, then replied.

"A straight charge during the night, under cover of darkness."

I gave this some thought while eating my breakfast.

"If it's dark, the Indians won't have a good view of us." She nodded. "Then the Boonesborough defenders won't be able to see us either." Again, she nodded. "Won't they think we are Indians and shoot us?" Again, she nodded.

"How about this… We set fire to some of the trees to draw them away from the fort, which will give us a chance to make a run for the fort in daylight. Those who light the fire will have to ride away as quickly as they can, before the Shawnee arrive."

"That, my husband, sounds like a better option. So, let's get on the road." She said, seeming a bit more confident now.

The horses and Rangers were all well rested. We now just had to arrive at Boonesborough while the defenders were still alive.

"One minute. Bring this Pete over to me." I ordered Lana. Before she could move, Jean came into view with a tall Corporal.

"Did someone want me?" he asked, then he put his arms around both Jean and Lana. "These are my best girls." He said in a slightly slurred, half drunken voice. He had obviously been celebrating his promotion. I had come across many of these drunken womanisers, they often went off with my girlfriends, but not this time.

I slid my leg across my horse, and jumped to the ground. Katie was watching me, but she knew that what happened now, would set the course of things to come. Both Lana and Jean were aware that Pete had crossed the mark. They realised that I was not coming over to welcome him to the Rangers. I stood two feet in front of him. Many of the Rangers had now gathered around to see what was going on.

"Yes Corporal, someone does want you." First you have failed to address me as Colonel Rhees. You put your arms around two of my Lieutenants, and call them 'your girls'. Do you have anything to say for yourself?" Pete staggered a little. "Oh and I nearly forgot; you are drunk on duty." I ordered Mark to arrest him, tie his wrists, then throw him over a spare horse, to make sure he did not fall off.

"Oh and if it wasn't clear, you are no longer a Corporal."

I then turned to Lana and Jean.

"Lieutenants. What the hell are you two playing at? Back where I was brought up, there were hundreds of womanisers like him. Women would fall for their good looks, then later be replaced by another, and after being used, they would be left in tears." Before I could say any more, Katie interrupted.

"We are about to leave, on a mission to save lives. Let's deal with this later." When this dragon was shooting fire, The Eagle was the only one that could douse the flames.

"Ok, mount up Lana and Jean, we have people to save."

126

It was early morning when we arrived. I was hoping that any Shawnee sentries would be asleep. Our horses were nearly finished. I gave the freshest horses to Lana and Jean and told them to take eight Rangers and set fire to the trees which I was pointing to. They both nodded obediently, gathering up the Rangers they needed, they rode off to the trees.

Fifteen minutes later, there was a huge explosion. The trees seemed to all burst into fire.

I gave the Shawnee about 5 minutes to react to the distraction, before I gave the order to charge. Bent over our horses, we came in from the east. Jean, Lana and their team came galloping in from the west. Lookouts on the terraces could see us coming, and they rushed to open the gates.

I was amazed that all hundred Rangers made it to the fort safely. I quickly ordered The Rangers to look after their horses: feed them and rub them down, they had just completed a journey that pushed them to their limits.

Lana and Jean reported. The fire was a great success. Now it was time for discipline. I left Katie to take care of it. I felt she would be more rational about it.

"Lana and Jean, you are both our friends. You are also both adults. We put you in a position of authority, but you both have allowed the good looks of one man to distract you from your duties. Although nothing too bad came of it this time, you must now understand the potential risk you brought upon the entirety of the Rangers."

Both of them had been hanging their heads in shame. They nodded.

"Dafydd and I have agreed that you both made a mistake, and you must learn from it." Katie held out her hand. " This time, we will forget all about it and move on. Just don't let it happen again. Let's begin our fight for freedom."

Katie left them standing there in shock to take in what had just happened and consider their mistake.

Katie had gone to talk with Daniel Boone, my hero. How did she get to him before me? I hurried over, trying not to appear too over the top.

"This is my husband, Dafydd. He is a fan of yours." Thanks Katie, I thought I could already feel my face turning red.

"Glad to meet you, what was your name again?" He quipped. Great, he couldn't even remember or understand my name when it was said just moments before.

"My name is Fred. Pleased to meet you." I joked. Katie was now in tears of laughter. "Are you in command?" I enquired.

"No, I am only second in command. I am pleased to see Katie's Rangers arrive. Did your Rangers bring rations with them?"

I asked why. It turned out that they were short of food. An extra 100 Rangers to feed may be a problem.

"Well, we all had a large breakfast before we left, and I expect that we will be too busy shooting Indians, to think about food." A big grin filled my face. "Mark, get Lana and Jean over here please."

They both came running.

"Let's forget the past, well not all of it, you are both top Rangers. I believe that you were both fooled by Pete, you were not the first to fall for someone like him. A lot of my former girlfriends did as well." There was an awkward laugh. "What did you do with him?"

There was silence or a moment. I think they were both expecting the other one to answer.

"Oh no! I left him tied over his horse." Blurted Jean.

"Don't worry, I locked him up in one of our cells." exclaimed Daniel.

"Which one? I need to have a chat with him." Daniel pointed to his cell. "By the way do we sleep in shifts?" He shook his head "My dear Mr Dragon, we stay at our posts, until the Shawnee leave, or we die." I nodded and walked over to the cell where Pete was being held. The cell door creaked as I pushed it open.

"Get up." I ordered. "Maybe I was a bit hard on you, but I care about Lana and Jean, and I won't have them being mistreated. You got that?" He nodded. Anyway, we are trapped in the fort surrounded by Shawnee. We could use your shooting skills on the walls. Here, take this rifle. Report to Daniel Boone."

He grabbed the rifle and a handful of cartilages. He could not believe his luck. He had been freed and given a rifle. I placed myself not far from Pete. I wanted to keep an eye on him.

I took my place on the wall. My orders were simple. Just shoot as many Shawnees as possible.

Dusk came early now it was September, in fact it was dark by 8pm. It was strange not going to bed. He was of course right though, stay awake or die. It was like a funfair shooting gallery. Every time a head popped up; I shot it."

"Davy, it's getting Dark, they will be coming over the walls soon. Pass it on to your Rangers." Instructed Daniel.

"Davy. Who is Davy? Do I look like Davy Crocket or something?"

Katie and I decided on a plan between us. Lana and Jean were moved to where I had been. They could keep an eye on their friend Pete. Katie and I were going to work our way around the fort, supporting anyone who was in trouble.

"Davy, sorry, David, I just saw Pete bring two coloured handkerchiefs out of his pocket, he is waving one over the side of the wall. I think they are white and red."

I looked towards him. And then to the other side of the fort.

"Keep an eye on him, Katie."

Lana was near us. I grabbed her arm and indicated for her to follow me. We moved to the other side of the wall. We could see clearly what he was doing. He was waving either the white handkerchief or the red one, back and forth. I don't know what the signal meant, but we both could see someone who looked like Chief Blackfish, the leader of the Shawnee, replying by also waving white or red pieces of cloth. He was clearly directing the Shawnee attacks indicating the weak points.

"Well, Captain Zakharon. What action shall we take?" She was cool, taking my rifle off me, she loaded Kate (yes, I named my rifle after Katie) and aimed. As Pete turned towards her, she shot him straight between the eyes.

She then returned my rifle.

"That's the end of that. Now, let's give these Shawnees a beating."

During that night, there were many attempts to climb the walls. A few times, some of the Shawnee would manage to get over and attack the defenders, but they were always beaten back, without any casualties. Our main problem was that many of the defenders, after fighting all day and into the night, were beginning to fall asleep at their posts. Katie and I saved a few sleepy lives during the night.

Katie had noticed two of the new Rangers working together.

"Dafydd, have you noticed the two new Rangers. They are working together; one is covering the other so one of them can have a quick nap." I had not noticed, but I paid attention now.

"It looks like their system is working well. Let's pair The Rangers up. But make sure that everyone knows they need to all be awake if the Shawnee make a full-on attack. Napping then will not be tolerated." I stressed.

Well done to Lana and Jean, they had recruited well. I positioned myself next to the genius pair of newbies, picked up my rifle and began shooting at the attackers. I was glad that dawn was finally arriving, trying to hit your target during the night is difficult to say the least.

Suddenly there was a withdrawal.

"Maybe they are off for their breakfast," said one of the men. That made me laugh.

"I haven't seen you before, I presume you are both new recruits."

One of the men had black hair, while the other's hair was blonde. The one with the black hair began to tell me about himself.

"My name is John; this is my brother Nick. We are Canadian, but the British are more or less in control of our country now, so we decided to move south and join The Continental Army. As it was, we were having a nice meal and having a beer, when Captain Bennett, and Captain Zakharon, were making an appeal for good fighters to join Katies Ranger's and fight the British. Their offer appealed to us so much that we even left a steak and a cool beer behind in order to enlist."

"We are basically creating a new life for ourselves." His brother Nick explained. "Back in the village where our family lived, we were happy. Our Mum and Dad worked the farm and our twin sisters helped them. We also helped of course - we often had to take stock to market, or buy things for the farm. To us, to fight the British is fair, we both fight under the same rules of war."

At that point, Nick began to choke up, and had problems continuing. John put his arm around his brother.

"When the British involved the Indians, the rules of war changed, basically there were no longer any rules. One day we went to the market to sell two bulls and buy some grain. As we were maybe half a mile from the farm, we could see smoke curling up into the sky." Now both Brothers had tears running down their cheeks. "We hurried back to the farm, to be greeted by dads body. He must have been killed before the family were aware of any danger. We could not find our mum or our sisters. It was only when the fire was nearly out that we were able to enter what was left of the cabin." They were both silent again, as the nightmare of their memory's returned. "We found the bones of all three of them. It didn't take us long to picture what had happened." He paused.

John began again.

"We followed that war party for three days and nights, until we finally caught up with them. Twelve Ottawa Warriors. We waited until dark. They had found some of my dad's home-made beer, and brought it with them. They never thought that anyone would have followed them. About midnight they were all asleep, they didn't even leave any lookouts." Explained Nick.

"We killed them all as they lay sleeping, and scalped them." Grinned John,

"Why did you scalp them?" I asked.

"They believe that without your scalp, when they die, they will wander around and never get to the happy hunting grounds." Replied Nick. "We are now where we belong, fighting Indians."

Talk about bad timing, at that moment, White Eagle arrived. She was bringing water round to all the defenders. She offered a tin cup of water to Nick, he knocked the cup out of her hand.

"I don't want anything from an Indian." He spat.

His brother pushed White Eagle. I punched him on his jaw. Lets just say he had the best sleep he had had for a long time. Nick attempted to grab hold of me, only to be greeted with about six rifles pointing at him.

"Nick, I am sorry for your loss. I too lost my father to hatred. You will learn that there are good Indians like White Eagle and her brother Thunder Cloud, as well as the bad ones like Chief Blackfish of the Shawnee. Don't let hatred fill your life. We want you to be a Ranger, and fight bad Indians as well as the British and German soldiers. But that doesn't mean that all British, Germans and Indians are all bad. We would love both you and your brother to stay with us, but you will have to get rid of your hatred of all Indians." I pleaded.

He stood for a while, contemplating.

"I understand. It may be difficult for us, but my brother and I will learn. It was just such a horror, what happened to our family." He replied.

"Do you think that horror only affects white men? When my brother and I were about twelve. White men came to our village. My father, the chief, was away with the warriors. Only old men, women and children were left. As they galloped into the village, they began to cut down those women and children. The old men tried to protect the village, but for that they were all killed, I even saw babies being thrown against the ground. Everyone ran away in an attempt to escape death. My brother and I were two of the few who survived that day. Most of our relatives, including my mother, died that day."

"Was it the British who did this?" Asked Nick.

"No, the attackers were Americans, the so-called settlers. My brother and I have good reason to hate white people, but hate only twists your mind, and destroys your life. We both refused to hate all Americans, we always judge people as individuals."

Mark had arrived part way through this conversation.

"This woman is my wife; I love her with all my heart. She is not white, or red, or yellow or brown or black. She is not any colour. She is just a human being. Despite the hurt Americans brought into her life, she offered you both water, to ease your thirst, she will also tend your wounds. She does this out of love." Explained Mark.

Both the brothers were awake by now and heard what Mark had to say. They both stood up and apologised to White Eagle. John asked her to treat a cut that had appeared on his jaw.

I turned to Katie, who had come over to join us.

"I think we have two top class Rangers here." She nodded and smiled.

Early the following morning, September the 11th, we could all hear a lot of noise. An order went out to search the fort, we needed to know what was causing the noise. After searching the entire fort, the conclusion was that the sound was coming from outside somewhere. Hundreds of keen eyes were searching the whole area surrounding the fort. Finally, the site of the noise was narrowed down to an area near the river.

A shout went up.

"They are mining!"

Daniel, Katie and myself rushed to the side of the fort with the best view of the river.

"They are digging a Tunnel from the river. They must be planning to dig under the fort and lay explosives. You men, gather a crew and start a counter tunnel." Ordered Daniel. "We will bring their tunnel crashing down."

The Shawnee continued with their attacks, the same time as they were digging the tunnel.

"If they can get barrels of gunpowder under our fence, they will be able to smash a hole in our defence and we will see hundreds of Shawnee pouring into the fort." Warned Nick.

"My Father was a Methodist minister. He used to tell me, 'have faith in God!'. I have seen him perform many miracles. I am going to pray for their tunnel to collapse." I knelt where I had been standing.

Others joined me in prayer. At the end, we all stood.

That night, the heavens seemed to open. Rain poured from the skies. The river rose, and the Shawnee tunnel collapsed. Many voices shouted praises.

On the 17th, The Shawnee gathered all their warriors for a massive attack.

"This is it. They are giving everything in this next attack. If we can continue to hold them back, then hopefully they will lose interest and leave!"

All the Rangers went to their positions. Katie and I were joined by Lana and Jean. Our job was to support any section of the wall that was under pressure.

The fighting was fierce. The crack shots of the Rangers made themselves very effective. So many Shawnee warriors had fought their last battle. A couple of times the attackers managed to climb over the wall. Once, Lana got herself separated. Three Indians were after her. A tall blonde-haired man appeared. He leapt on the backs of two of the warriors, bringing them down. Before they could react, they were both dead. The third one was of course killed by Lana.

On the other side of the fort, John and Mark were fighting together, when John saw two Shawnee attacking White Eagle. He jumped from where he had been fighting, directly on top of both of the attackers. White Eagle turned in surprise. Nick had killed both of them, but received a cut across his chest. White Eagle ran to attend to him.

"Thank you for saving my life." She said, a tear welling up in her eye. Nick laughed.

"That's ok, I think you are about to save mine now." They were both laughing.

As soon as dusk came, The Shawnee withdrew and disappeared into the forests.

"Daniel, it's been nice to meet you, but we have more battles to fight." I grinned as I shook his hand. "We are off to New York now. I am hoping we may get at least a day's rest before the next battle."

He bid us good luck and went to deal with other issues around the fort. The Rangers waved to the town's folk as they rode off in the direction of New York.

"We only lost one Ranger." Stated Katie. "And Lana shot him." That made us laugh.

CHAPTER 12

PHILADELPHIA

We had ridden for about six hours when Katie called a halt. Her Rangers had been fighting without a proper sleep for nearly two weeks. They needed a really good rest. She ordered everyone, except the sentries, to go to bed. Of course, their beds were just blankets, but they were all so tired that they could have slept on a pile of rocks. We, the officers, took turns doing sentry duty. Everyone needed a good rest.

The people from above, had finally realised that the Rangers had been fighting almost nonstop, and needed to recuperate. We also need to recruit more members. Katie had received new orders, but she could only share it with me, as most of the others were asleep.

George Washington had driven the British out of Philadelphia. They were now in full retreat, back to New York City.

As The British had been abusing the citizens of the city for some while. Our commander in chief thought that the city may be full of potential recruits. We both agreed, then slid under our blankets. As she turned over, trying to make herself comfortable, her body touched me.

"Sorry my love, I am too tired tonight."

She chuckled to herself. Then whispered under her breath.

"Even if you were not tired, your luck would not be in tonight."

It took the Rangers three days to finally recover from lack of sleep. They all had a good meal, and a wash in the stream. The men and women took turns of course.

We began our journey to Philadelphia. We did pay the city a short visit last winter, leaving us with some memories.

Katie remembered a Tavern with a large meeting room. She sent three Rangers on ahead to book the whole Tavern for two weeks. It seemed that she also had orders for another operation after our recruitment drive. Her plan was to use the 'Rising Sun Tavern' for meetings. But we would split into two groups and book rooms at two different places to sleep.

We arrived just after dusk. Katie decided that we should eat, then all sleep in the Rising Sun Tavern, rather than try to find our rooms so late in the day. As there weren't many rooms, most of the men had to sleep on the floor of the meeting hall. Including me.

Sleeping on a hard wooden floor, next to a couple of men who stunk of beer, instead of my sweet-smelling wife, doesn't put me in the best of moods.

Katie arrived and wanted to give out her orders even before we had eaten. 'This is going to be a bad day' I thought.

"Dafydd, Lana, Jean, Nick and John. Please join me here." Ordered Katie.

Of late, Katie had been annoying me by seemingly taking sole command of the Rangers. We were equal ranks. Therefore, I should be aware of the contents of orders at the same time as she does. She had been treating me as the same rank as Lana and Jean. We would have to have a chat, and very soon.

"Rangers, we have a well-earned break between battles. It has been decided that we should use our break to recruit a few more Rangers. Rather than send a hundred Rangers around the city, I am going to divide us into two groups. Team 1 will be led by Lana, Jean and myself. Team 2 will be led by Mark, Nick and John."

There was total silence. Everyone was wondering why I had been left out. I stood there feeling like a right idiot.

"Both teams will scour the city for people who may be interested in joining the Rangers and set up meetings with them. At 6 o'clock each evening, both teams will return here and discuss the day, before returning to their place to eat and sleep."

I had had enough. I picked up my rifle, jumped off the stage where we were standing and headed out of the door. Katie shouted after me, but by now I wasn't listening. 'Where to first?' I thought. 'I know, I need a change of clothes. If I am seen wearing my green uniform, people may realise that I am a colonel in Katie's Rangers.'

It was still early morning, and some kind ladies had left their washing on the line overnight. I managed to collect enough dry clothes to make me look quite respectable.

As soon as I changed, I tucked my greens inside my rucksack. Then began to walk toward the 'White Duck Tavern.' I only chose that one because the name made me laugh.

I pushed the door to the tavern open and entered. I leant on the bar and asked for a hot meal and a cool beer. I often wondered where mountain men chose to drink, when they visited cities to sell their beaver skins. I'm pretty sure that I had just found the place.

One of them, a hairy man, about 6 ft 4 inches tall, stood next to me. He stunk.

"Bartender, I want a hot meal and a Cool beer." He was imitating what I had said. At the same time my meat came into view. "That will do me." He said as he attempted to take my plate. As he turned towards me, with both his hands holding the plate. I grinned at him.

"Enjoy your meal." Then I punched him hard in his stomach. As he bent forward, I hit him with an uppercut. He crashed backwards, his meal landing on top of him.

"That's his meal. Can I have mine soon please?" I said as I stared at the bartender. I then heard chairs scratching the floor as his friends began to move. I turned and stared at maybe twelve men, all hairy and smelly.

"It is a bad day to wake this Dragon." I warned them. Knives and batons appeared. I grabbed a stool and smashed it across a table, leaving me with a wooden leg in each hand. The first one ran at me; I side stepped and brought a leg down on his head.

"Good night." I whispered.

Then they began to come in pairs. I ran and jumped up on the table, then jumped down behind them. A couple of quick blows and that was four down. A club caught me on the back of my shoulder, I spun round and punched the holder so hard that I think that I broke his jaw. The rest just charged at me; it was like fighting the pirates back on the ship coming to America. I was hit many times by clubs, and I felt a few stab wounds. In the end, I was once again the last man standing.

I staggered over to the bar.

"A large tankard of beer please." Then I collapsed onto a stool, which luckily was next to me. As I drank my beer, one by one, the hairy ones began to struggle to their feet.

"Give them all a beer when they wake up." I paid the barman in gold.

"What's the matter with him?" Inquired Katie.

"Are you for real?" said Lana, "You just insulted him in front of all the Rangers. He is the same rank as you, but did you discuss your plan with him?" She asked, then cut Katie off before she could answer. "No, of course you didn't. Then you gave the leadership of team 2 to Mark, leaving Dafydd without any responsibility. Did you not notice how angry your husband was?"

Katie began to make excuses.

"I had a very important job for him. I wanted him to go round the Taverns, checking if there was anyone who we should enlist."

"Mark could have done that job," added Jean, "in fact any of the Rangers could."

Mark had said nothing up till then, but felt that he had to say something.

"Katie, you are a great fighter, and I thought you were a good leader, but I can't believe that you treated your husband like that." He turned and walked away.

Katie went silent. She pondered over her actions; it began to sink in how badly she had acted. She jumped off the stage and ran out of the door I had used to vacate the building. Two of the Rangers saw her leave and followed her.

She ran from Tavern to Tavern, looking for me. But I had left. I was moving into the centre of the city. She entered one Tavern.

"Has anyone seen a Welshman?" She shouted.

"No, but we can look after you until he arrives." Was one of the replies she received. The Rangers raised their rifles. The message was sent. They then told her that I had left ages ago. So, they all returned to the hall.

The teams had to find somewhere to stay before dusk. She ordered team two to work the left side of the city, while her team would work the right side of the city. But their first job would be to book rooms to spend the nights.

I had managed to book a room for two weeks in a nice hotel overlooking the city's main square called The White Hotel. I was taken to my room. After sleeping on the ground the last few weeks, this was paradise. I even had a nice bath. I laid on my bed and fell asleep.

"Mark, what are your plans? I thought that we should promote a couple of big meetings." Suggested Nick.

"Yes, that sounds like a good idea." Mark agreed. "I am a little worried about Dafydd." He admitted. "But I also know that he can look after himself."

They discussed where the best squares in the city may be and where they could get posters printed. None of them knew, so they decided to ask people.

It was getting dark. I decided to visit another Tavern to get my dinner and another beer. 'The setting Sun' was not far from me. That would be good, especially if I had to stagger back to my hotel. I walked in and went up to the bar, just the same as before, in my previous attempt to get a beer. While I was waiting, my mind wandered. I can't remember exactly what I was thinking about but it made me laugh aloud. The Tavern was the same as the previous one, full of tall hairy men. I must've been in the 'mountain man' district of the city.

"What are you laughing at, stranger?" One of them asked. 'Not again', I thought.

"I am sorry if I annoyed you, please forgive me." I pleaded.

"That won't do." Replied the man.

A man sitting near him reached across and put his arm around him.

"Unless you want this to be your last evening on earth, I think you should calm down and apologise to the Welshman." This man then stood up and spoke a little louder, so people around could hear.

"Are you ok, Welshman? My boys are all sorry we misbehaved earlier today." He smiled and put out his hand. I grinned and shook it. This was the hairy man, who took my breakfast.

"What's your name? I'm Andy. We are all mountain men. At this time of the year, we all venture into the city to sell our furs." I stood back.

"So, you are mountain men? I thought you were all bears. You must admit, you do smell like one." I jested. We broke into laughter.

"You are right, but it's difficult for all of us to get a bath in this city. Most of the hotels with baths won't let us use them." He moaned.

"You asked why am I here. Well, I am recruiting for Katie's Rangers. We are looking for strong people, who hate The British. Andy, do you know anyone who hates the British?" I grinned.

"We all hate the British here. For a start, they stopped us selling our furs to our normal customers. They wanted to buy our furs for next to nothing." He complained. "Welshman, I am with you." He then turned to the others.

"Will anyone else join me?" He asked the others. To a man they all stood up and cheered. "I think you have found a few recruits here."

I walked among them, shaking their hands.

"What I can offer you is lots of fighting, a good rifle, and a bath. After you have shaved and had a bath, then I'm sure you will all become girl magnets, just like me." I winked.

That did it. They grabbed me and continually tossed me up in the air.

"Well, Dafydd, how about this bath? enquired Andy.

"Follow me lads." I walked out of the Tavern with about twenty ex-mountain men behind me. We were soon all standing in front of my hotel.

"They won't let us in here, Dafydd." Stated Andy.

"Well, let's have a bet."

Andy was a betting man, and I clearly had his attention.

"For the next two weeks, this hotel will provide any mountain man who signs up with Katie's Rangers, a good meal, a hot bath, where they can shave as well as soak in scented water, plus I will arrange a market here in the main square. where you can auction your furs."

"That sounds great Dafydd. If you succeed in doing all this. What do we have to do?" There was a little concern in his voice. "All you or they have to do is spread the word about my offer. Are you up for it?"

Andy shook my hand and began to run into the hotel. Luckily, I was faster than him.

"Wait. I have to have a chat with the owner of the hotel first." I laughed.

I walked up to the front desk.

"Which room does the owner use please?" The young lad, facing all these rough hairy men, began to stammer. "His room is number 10." He stammered. "B…But he won't see you." He added.

I ignored him and walked up the stairs, then knocked on the door of number 10. A young blonde woman opened the door.

"I am sorry, I think you have the wrong door." I smiled and pushed the door open wide, then entered the room. There was a man lying on the bed.

"You can't come in here!" He screamed.

"Why do people tell me what I can't do, after I have already done it? I can never understand it. How much will it cost me to book this entire hotel for two weeks?" I asked.

"It's not possible, we are fully booked. Now get out of my room!"

I opened my rucksack and took a handful of gold out. This made his eyes almost pop out of his head.

"Well, I suppose it is possible, but it would cost you a lot of gold." He said as he sat trembling.

"The whole hotel for two weeks, with large cooked meals for everyone staying and full access to the bathing facilities."

"That will cost you two handfuls of gold nuggets."

He was no longer shaking. But his eyes were still wide with glee. I took out two handfuls and placed them on his bed. His eyes seemed to light up at the sight of the gold. Then I added another handful. At the sight of the third handful of gold, he sprung out of bed and opened a draw to his dressing table. He pulled out a contract, which I signed as having total use of the hotel for two weeks. He then woke his staff up and sent them room by room, throwing the occupants out.

I went outside to give the good news to Andy.

"What did you do to get him to agree?" He asked, shocked that I was successful.

"The key to any business owner's heart is always in the gold." I replied.

"Where did you get enough gold to buy a whole hotel?" Asked Andy. A few angry guests had begun to leave. "And to get them to kick out other paying customers!"

"Well, we paid a visit here last winter and realised that our notes were not acceptable currency. So, the British *insisted* on giving us all their gold. Funny that." I laughed.

Then I grabbed Andy;s arm and led him to my room, then into the bathroom.

"There you go. When I see you again, I want to see a new man." I smiled and left.

"We have been delivering posters all day, I hope that we get a big turn out tomorrow" said John, almost pleading.

"Me too. My boots are almost worn out!" Nick grinned. "Let's get to the 6 o'clock meeting quickly. Then, back to our hotel for a meal and some sleep."

Mark had disappeared with some Rangers; they were not sure where he went. They assumed that he would turn up at the meeting.

Katie, Lana and Jean, had also spent the day delivering posters.

"Katie, why did we not bring our horses into the city? It would have been much less tiring if we had been riding." Moaned Jean. Katie nodded in agreement.

"True, but they would have become a problem in the city." Clarified Lana. "Anyway, we have booked a place to hold a meeting the day after tomorrow, and we have delivered, I think it was two hundred posters." She noted.

The meeting did not take long. Team 2 had booked a public meeting for tomorrow and team 1 booked a public meeting for the day after in the main square. Both teams had spent the day handing out posters, and both teams would be pleased to get to their hotels. She closed the meeting early so everyone could all set off to get some well deserved rest.

Katie was the first to reach team 1's hotel. She had booked rooms in The White Hotel, as it was one of the more frequented hotels in the centre of the city.

I was sitting across the square, when she and the rest of team 1 arrived. She was greeted by a queue of tall, smelly, hairy men, and funny enough, there were actually a few women among them.

"If you want a meal and a bath, love, you will have to wait in the queue. Or you can share my bath." A man towards the back of the queue laughed.

A few others enjoyed his joke and joined in with his laughter. Katie rose above his joke.

"I have booked most of these rooms for my Rangers." She addressed the man.

"Haven't you heard? All the rooms here are now only for the use of us mountain folk." Another man claimed.

I was holding my breath, hoping that she would not provoke a full-scale fight between the mountain men and her Rangers.

Katie sighed. "Let's leave. We are here to get these men to become Rangers, not to fight them. We will have to find another place to stay."

Lana stared at the long queue.

"Isn't it strange that so many mountain men are all coming here for a meal and a bath?" They both agreed. And left the hotel.

"Send runners to all the hotels in the area. Get them to book whatever rooms they find." Ordered Katie. There was a slight sound of panic in her voice.

I looked at the sky, it was white, maybe we will have an early snowstorm this year.

After a couple of hours, the runners returned. I was still sitting, waiting to find out if she had found enough rooms. Well, it seemed that they had found rooms for everyone apart from six of them. I was now laughing under my breath.

"tell the Rangers to sort out those rooms between themselves. We, the officers, will have to spend the night here in the square."

She may have annoyed me this morning, but I still loved her, I could not leave her sleeping out in the cold. I slipped past them and into the hotel. I asked the owner to go and invite the six of them to use two of the rooms (luckily there were still a couple left - I would've hated to have to kick out some of the new recruits), and give them a hot meal each.

I then went to my room and spent half an hour in the bath before putting a new set of clothes on. I went down to dinner, and sat in the far corner of the room. I could see Katie and the other five towards the middle of the room.

The rest of the seats were taken up with dirty mountain men. I was not happy; they were supposed to bathe and shave before coming for their meal.

"Why are all these dirty men eating here?" Asked Jean. "It's meant to be a nice hotel!"

"They stink. It's enough to put anyone off their food." Remarked Lana, picking at the meat on her plate.

"Are you talking about us, lady?" Shouted a man from the next table.

"Leave it, we don't want any fights." Ordered Katie. She turned to the man. "Please, we don't want any trouble."

Now the man was standing. He was clearly drunk. He walked round to where Katie was sitting. He stood behind her and began to massage her shoulders.

I was now getting annoyed; how dare he put his hands on the woman who I loved.

"Take your smelly hands off me." She ordered.

"Give me a kiss first." He demanded. He was as stupid as he looked, I thought. Katie picked up her knife and stuck it in the middle of his hand, pinning it to the table. He screamed.

"I'll kill you woman!" He shouted. With his right hand he knocked Katie onto the floor. Then he pulled the knife out of his left hand, and made to stab her. I had had enough. I threw my knife across the room. It sunk into his chest. As he crashed to the floor, maybe ten of his mates stood up and turned towards me. I leapt onto a table and pulled my pistol out of my belt.

"Katie, that's Dafydd." Whispered Lana.

"I know, I saw him some time ago. He looks quite smart tonight." She grinned. The man's mates were now approaching me.

"If you want to live, I suggest you all sit down. The man you are looking at is your benefactor. Dafydd, the fighting Welshman, known as The Dragon." It was Andy.

"Good timing Andy." I said, walking over to him. "Look after those ladies, and make sure no drunks try to enter their room." I ordered. Then I jumped off the table and left the building.

"What a man! If you don't want him, Katie, can I have him?" Grinned Lana.

"That man is all mine ladies." Insisted Katie.

All six of them went to their rooms after their meal. Jean and Lana were soon asleep. But Katie could not fall asleep. Her darling husband was on her mind.

The following morning, the first open recruitment meeting took place. Mark intended to do the talking. I was not aware that he was good at speaking in public. John and Nick were backing him up. They had delivered over 200 posters around the area. They now needed people to attend who hated the British and wanted to do something to drive them out of the country.

The meeting began on time. They had chosen 1pm to begin. This would be the time when most people were out and about.

"This looks good Mark, quite a few are gathering to hear about Katie's Rangers." Declared Nick.

"You are right, I am feeling a bit nervous. Although I guess maybe it's more excitement." Mark proclaimed.

I thought that Katie would have attended, to give him support. I had to admit, I think his talk went well.

At the end, he put out a call for volunteers to fight against the British. A few people began to walk forward to sign up. Then to our horror, hundreds of soldiers appeared. They wore blue jackets with red trimmings, white trousers, and a hat with a white feather. They were from the Pennsylvania Regiment. The 5th Light Company. Why were they here?

Then it became clear. They had used us to publicise the recruitment event. Now they were taking over, and getting the volunteers to sign for The Continental Army.

Mark had fifty Rangers. They had brought 200-300 soldiers to block the Rangers off from the volunteers. They were outnumbered by about 6-1. If they had tried to fight them off, the result could have reduced the number of Rangers drastically. There was nothing they could do but pack up and report back to Katie at the hall.

"Mark, I hope it all went well. How many new recruits do we have?" Katie was so excited.

"Sorry Katie, we failed." He said, very deflated. He knew he had been put in charge instead of me and had come back empty handed.

"You never failed," I explained. "You were stitched up." I slapped his back to encourage him.

"Darling, you're back!" She cried out.

"I have never been away; I have been watching all the time." I winked an eye. "Katie, you have a similar event arranged for tomorrow in the main square." She looked at me with a frown.

"How did you know that?"

I smiled.

"I know everything that has taken place. Dragons have eyes everywhere." I was now chuckling. "Are you sleeping with Lana and

Jean tonight? I know of a nice double bed, and a sweet-smelling bedroom." Katie hesitated; she did not want to give in so easily.

"Well, I did like sleeping with the girls, but if you are feeling very lonely, I will think about it." I wasn't falling for that.

"It's ok, I am sleeping well without your snoring," I said, then left to go up to my room.

"You fool." Moaned Lana. "You could be sharing his bed again. But now we will have to put up with you twisting and turning all night."

All three of them had their bath in turns, then they got into their double bed. Lana and Jean were soon asleep. As the last couple of nights, Katie lay awake twisting and turning. Then she finally snapped. She slid out of bed. Opened the door and ran down the corridor, to her husband's room.

She banged on the door a few times.

"Dafydd, I am sorry, please let me in." She begged. I opened the door and she rushed into my arms. "I am so sorry; I have mistreated you. Will you forgive me?" She pleaded.

"Well, that will depend on how you treat me tonight." I grinned, closing the door behind her.

The following morning, we seemed to have two plans. Katie, Lana and Jean had made their plans for the event. My plan was to prepare in case we had another visit from The Continental Army.

I was having breakfast with Andy, who I was now relying on, plus a few other mountain men, and women. If the soldiers decided to interrupt again. We would be ready.

Katie began her talk at 11 am. She was good. Everyone there was glued to every word that she said. Then she made her call for all the volunteers to come forward. Lots of men and women walked towards Katie's people, whose job it was to sign them up.

There was suddenly a blow on a trumpet, and again about 200 hundred soldiers appeared. Katie had her hundred Rangers waiting to separate the soldiers from the volunteers, but that would not be enough. I took an old buffalo horn from my belt. And blew it hard. Katie was wondering what I was doing.

From within the Crowd came 200 ex-mountain men. They were clean shaven, dressed in Katie's green. And they smelt nice. They joined with her current Rangers and forced the soldiers back. Katie and her team quickly began registering the new recruits. That was a day in the history of Katie's Rangers that we would never forget.

"Where did you get these handsome men and women from?" Asked Katie.

"Do you remember all those smelly, hairy men, who were sitting near you at dinner last night?" I was grinning now.

"This is them? How did you do it?" She enquired. "Well, all I had to do was fight 13 men alone and win." I winked at her. "Don't worry, Dragons never lose."

The total of our new recruits was 200 ex-mountain men and women. Plus 80 people who volunteered on the day.

"Katie, this is Andy. I could not have recruited all these people without his help. I have brought him in as an officer. Is that ok?"

"Whatever you say, is ok with me."

I smiled, nothing much to say after that.

We had just about ten days to get the new recruits ready for battle. Katie and Lana were in charge of recruiting, therefore, the newbies were divided into two teams. Team 1, the ex-mountain men and women, were being trained by Lana and Andy. The other volunteers were being trained by Jean and Mark; they would require a lot more training than the mountain men.

October 15th. The newbies would be left here to continue their training. When ready they would join the rest of us in New York. The original Rangers and the 200 ex-mountain men and women are all ready for battle. At 10am, all three hundred of us mounted our horses and began our journey.

CHAPTER 13

THE RAID ON UNADILLA AND OUAQUAGA

We received orders to meet up somewhere north of New York. Before we left, Katie filled us in on the situation. Apparently, the Iroquois were killing settlers.

In early October, Lieutenant Colonel William Butler, of the 4th Pennsylvania Regiment, descended on the Iroquois towns of Unadilla and Ouaquaga. He destroyed the towns, and burnt down the buildings, burning all possessions. This included their winter supplies. The raid was conducted because of a series of raids on frontier communities.

While the raid was taking place, The Mohawk war chief, Joseph Brant, and his force were raiding frontier settlements in the Upper Delaware River Valley. They had been joined by Seneca warriors. We all knew that Thunder Cloud was the Mohawk Chief, but it seemed that was the case only in times of peace.

In late October 1777, this turned into a frontier war.

On the 11th November, a joint British, Seneca and Mohawk force attacked Cherry Valley.

Walter Butler, of Butler's Rangers, was in charge of what turned out to be a massacre. His leadership was nothing less than criminal. The Indians ran through the valley slaughtering anyone they met. Men, women and children, completely unchecked.

Joseph Brant himself was upset with the horror of that day. Wells, Campbell, Clyde and the Reverend Dunlop were people who he described as his friends. It seemed that 70 women and children were taken captive. Most were exchanged later.

"We have 300 top Indian fighters with us now, but we will still be outnumbered if the tribes of the Iroquois combine their warriors. Apparently, there are six tribes in the confederation. The Tuscarora and the Oneida are on our side. While the Mohawk, Seneca, Cayuga and Onondaga are fighting with the British."

I nodded at Katie; she had delivered all the information we would need.

"I suggest that we start by visiting our friend Crazy Buffalo. After that we will need to send envoys to Thunder Cloud." I implored.

White Eagle came forward.

"The only people capable of meeting up with my brother are myself, you and Katie. I will go with you two as security, to prevent any loose arrows on the way." She smiled.

"Ok Rangers, we will be leaving at midday. Prepare yourselves as there may be fighting."

We arrived not far from the land of the Tuscarora. Katie decided to rest overnight, it would not make sense to approach anyway, during the night.

"Lana. Can I call you Lana?" asked Andy.

"Of course, after all we are both officers on the same side." She replied.

"I heard a rumour, that you have had an encounter with a General Whitelaw…"

Lana, went white in the face. We had found out a little while ago that General Whitelaw had apparently escaped after we had taken him prisoner.

"Yes, I have." She stated.

Andy was looking into her eyes. She held back the tears well.

"I thought that as well. Would you like to know how I came into contact with him?" Lana was now staring in Andy's direction. She seemed to feel the hurt he was suffering.

"He killed my mother after she befriended him. He appears in my nightmares every night. I do hope that he has done nothing as bad to you." Andy could feel the sincerity in her statement.

"Lana, I used to own a farm in the Mohawk Valley. I had a beautiful young wife; we had been married for four years. We had a boy, 3 years old, and a daughter of one. My daughter was so cute. And my son was going to be just like his old man." He stopped for a while; it was as if his throat was blocked, preventing his words. "One day we had a visit from General Whitelaw. He told us that he was a deserter from the British army. That he and his friends wanted somewhere to spend the night.

I was a bit concerned as his two friends were Senecas. I was well aware that the Senecas were fighting on the side of the British. There was little else we could do but play at being nice to them. My wife made them a meal. If I only had put poison in their meal - things would not have happened as they did. After their meal, Whitelaw produced his pistol. His Seneca partners took our children into the kitchen, and killed them. I heard their screams, and turned the table over in an attempt to get to them. But a blow on the back of my head, sent me crashing to the floor.

I woke to find myself tied to a chair, wondering where my wife was.

Then the Senecas dragged her back into our front room. You can guess what they had done to her. Whitelaw, stood in front of me with his knife touching my wife's throat. He demanded to know about the movements of Washington. How was I supposed to know? I spoke. A flick of his wrist and my wife fell to the floor in a pool of her blood. The ones I loved were all dead. My life was turned upside down in an instance." Tears were running down his face freely now.

"I was pleading for him to kill me. But all he did was laugh. Eventually they tied me to a pole, and smeared me with honey, jam and whatever other sweet tasting foods they could find. They then left me, with my memories filled with the deaths of my dear family. He was obviously hoping that I would receive a visit from one of the black bears that lived near to me.

They set fire to my farm and the hay. This was obligatory. Two hours later a black bear did appear, but as he was deciding where to begin his meal, a shot rang out and the bear fell dead. Personally, I wished that the shot had hit me, then I could have joined my family in Heaven."

This tough mountain man had dissolved in his nightmare. Lana could only put her arm around him and pat his back. Tears were also running down Lana's cheeks. She felt his agony.

Eventually he pulled himself together. He then apologised to her.

"You have nothing to apologise for," she replied." I truly felt your pain."

Andy scratched his forehead.

"That was when I became a mountain man. I would get lost in the woods for days. Just me and the animals. The Indians knew well to keep away from me." He agonised. "Anyway, that's where you will find your General Whitelaw. With the Seneca tribe." He lamented.

"We will catch this General Whitelaw; He escaped after we caught him once. He will not escape a second time." I confirmed.

"We will all enter the camp of the Tuscarora in the morning, so get some sleep tonight." Ordered Katie.

"If you want, I can sleep outside your tent, in case you have any nightmares." Offered Andy.

"To be honest, I think that tonight, I will be dreaming your nightmares." She laughed awkwardly. "I'll be alright, thank you. But I hope that we can be friends." Requested Lana.

"That would be great. Sleep well." Andy departed.

"Sleep outside? How romantic." Grinned Jean.

"You were listening?" Shouted Lana, as she threw her pillow at Jean.

"You have to admit, what happened to him and his family was nothing less than horrific." Acknowledged Jean.

"I am going to try and get to sleep now, But I doubt if I will get much. My head is buzzing with so many things going on. Night." Said Lana.

There were up to twenty men in the male Ranger tents.

"Are you ok Andy?" asked one of them.

"Yes thanks, after so many years of pain, tonight I feel a bit more at peace after sharing my pain with Lana." Night everyone, He shouted.

White Eagle, and the children, shared Mark's tent. They did not share the same bed, at present, White Eagle was unsure about marriage. She was excited, thinking about visiting her brother again.

"Good night, my love." Whispered Mark. She looked down to where he lay every night on the floor.

"And all my love to you, sweetheart." She also whispered, not wishing to wake the children.

The following morning, Katie and I went ahead of the Rangers. We did not want Crazy Buffalo to get the wrong impression. He, of course, was pleased to see us both. When the rest of the Rangers showed up, he was amazed.

"What are you doing here?" he asked. He knew what Katie was about to say before she spoke. "Are you planning an attack on the Seneca and the Mohawks?" he enquired.

"First, we need to bring all the settlers from their farms into the fort. Then, yes. We will go up against the Seneca. The Mohawks are a different problem. Their chief, Thunder Cloud, is our friend." We admitted. "We, the Tuscarora, will support you against the Seneca. Together we will crush them." He was smiling.

"This is White Eagle, the sister of Thunder Cloud." Katie introduced.

He put his arms around her.

"I thought that you were dead! I am so happy that you are alive." He continued to smile.

"Can we leave our Rangers here? We need to visit Thunder Cloud on our own."

He agreed as expected. The following morning, six of us began our ride to the Mohawk Camp. Crazy Buffalo, had provided us with an escort to protect us on our way to the Mohawk lands. We were about an hour's walk to the village when they left us.

Although the Mohawk had an alliance with the British. Many of them are friends with us, and of course, many were relatives of

White Eagle. Eventually we burst out of the forest and into the village. Immediately we were surrounded by armed warriors. They guided us towards the chief. It was the war chief, the one and only Joseph Brant. He pointed at us and told us to sit on the ground.

"I am sorry that your brother is not here today. He had to go on a trip. So, how can I help you?" His English was very good. I believed he went to school in one of our towns to learn our language.

"We came to visit our friend Thunder Cloud." Katie informed him.

"White Eagle is a child of the Mohawks. She can speak with her relatives until her brother returns." Stated Brant. "But we are supporting the British, and the five of you are our enemies. So, what shall I do with you all?" He grinned. "How about we have a little fun?"

I understand that you are all great Indian fighters. Here it is. The five of you will fight 20 of my warriors. Its ok, we will all have clubs." Laughed Brant.

That's 4-1 against, I thought.

"Ok, we accept your challenge. We will fight against 20 of their men. "Have heart, we will all be okay. We will win together." I assured the others.

Brant was now laughing. Twenty of his best fighters were now standing before us. Each holding a wooden club. At a wave of his arm, hundreds of his people moved and created a ring, which is where our fight will take place.

"Your warriors have clubs, where are ours?" I asked. He gave a puzzled look.

"Yours? You misunderstood. I said 'We' will have clubs. I never mentioned your people." He chuckled.

I was now wondering what tactics we should use, when I saw a group of people waving in our direction.

"Quick, move over to where those people are waving at us. They must be our friends; we will fight with our back towards them. They will cover our backs and we will then only have to worry about people in front of us."

"Lana, get behind me, I will cover you." Ordered Andy.

"You are new to the Rangers; we don't have men and weak women. We are all Rangers and we all fight as equals." Explained Lana.

We formed a semi-circle, with our friends protecting at the back. I saw White Eagle among them. These club wielding warriors were not playing games, they were here to kill us. We need weapons to defend ourselves. It was time for The Dragon to rise. Someone then bumped into me.

"Would you like an Eagle to give you a hand?" Katie smiled; it was as if she had read my thoughts. I began thinking of how well she must have fought to save me, not so long ago.

"Ok, let The Dragon and The Eagle teach these Mohawks a lesson."

I blocked the attempted blow from the nearest warrior, then punched him in his stomach. Followed by a blow to the back of his head.

"Here my love, have a club." I laughed, throwing Katie his club. The next of my attackers fared the same.

"Here Lana, have a present." I shouted.

"It's ok I have one." She said, taking one from the person she had just defeated."

I finally got to see why Katie was known as the Eagle. What a fighter.

Mark went down under a blow from a club. The warrior moved in for the kill. Surprise, surprise, White Eagle pushed her way through the crowd and stood over her loved one. She had brought a knife with her, and plunged it into the gut of the one who was looming over Mark before he could harm him any further. I had seen Andy go down, from a blow to his head. Lana stood over him and was now using her club to protect him.

"Shall we?" I turned to Katie.

She turned and nodded. Apparently, I was not the only one with the ability to change from being an ordinary fighter. I could almost see the surge of adrenaline pumping through Katie's veins. I felt it myself as we both were taken up a few gears to fight as the characters we are named after. I'm not sure what twist of fate had brought us together, but it was meant to be.

We began to fight ten times faster, with far more power being unleashed. Soon, the last three warriors were running for their lives. I turned to Katie, and grinned. I could see White Eagle standing over Mark, and Lana standing over Andy. That was funny, as I had heard them promise to protect the girls.

Joseph Brant was not a happy man; we had not played his game the way he wanted. He stood up and grabbed his tomahawk, then waved many warriors to join him. We gathered together. Things were not looking good. Some of White Eagle's family and friends had joined to protect us, but we were still well outnumbered. If we fought, we would likely all die.

Closer and closer came Brant and his warriors. Then an arrow stuck in the ground between both of the groups.

"Stop!"

It was Thunder Cloud.

"What are you doing with my friends?" He shouted. "How dare you mistreat them."

Chief Brant was furious. Brant believed that he was all power-ful, and that Thunder Cloud was a man of the past.

"I am the Mohawk Chief. You no longer have any power here. You are challenging me, and committing treachery against your own people." He then gave orders for Thunder Cloud to be tied up and thrown in a Longhouse. "Tomorrow you will be banished." Thunder Cloud was taken and his hands were bound. Brant also ordered us tied up along with Thunder Cloud.

Lying in the dark, I felt a movement. It was White Eagle; she had escaped her loosely tied bonds (her people had obviously been gentler with her) and had come to cut us free.

"We must all escape under the cover of darkness. Or you will all die in the morning." Whispered Thunder Cloud.

It seemed like a long night, but when the sun began to rise, we were all far away from the Mohawk village.

It took the rest of the day to reach the rest of the Rangers. We were beginning to get a lot of camp followers. This made me feel warm, it was beginning to feel like a family.

The following morning, we split our force into three teams of a hundred a piece. While two teams were out checking on the farms, the third team was in reserve, ready to back up any team that needed support.

Team A, was led by Andy and Lana. Team B, by Mark, Jean and Thunder Cloud, and Team C kept Katie and I busy. We sent our teams along Mohawk Valley.

One team would work north to south. The other, south to north. We arrived at one farm just as the Seneca had left. It was heart-breaking, why did they have to be so cruel? Another farm, we had arrived, just as they were about to attack the main house. Katie and I, plus some Rangers had managed to get into the house via the back door.

The Seneca set fire to the outbuildings first. Then made their attack on the Farmhouse. We were waiting for them, having first taken the farmer and his family out of reach of the attackers. Now it was time to take revenge for the poor souls who had been slaughtered, at the previous farm. A tall warrior covered in warpaint smashed his way into the house, believing he would find helpless settlers. The look of shock on his face as I brought my tomahawk down on his head will live in my mind for some time.

It took a month to get what was left of the settlers to the fort. That was part one of our orders.

"Katie, do you have any plans to destroy the Seneca?" I enquired.

"Let's spend a few days in the fort, we may be able to come up with some ideas there." She confirmed. I agreed, well a rest would be good at least.

The commander of the fort was pleased to be able to give us something in return for bringing many farmers to safety inside the fort.

He did not have any rooms for us, but he provided army tents.

"Jean," began Thunder Cloud, "would you like to go for a walk with me? You will be safe with me." He tried to encourage her.

Jean looked up at the cloudless sky.

"I would love to. There has been too much killing over the last month. It will be nice to get away from it all for a little while." She confessed.

They slipped out of the gates, then they strolled by a stream which was not too far away. Then they sat and looked at the fish swimming in the river.

"It is so peaceful; I wish it could be like this forever." She sighed.

"One day our world will be at peace with one another. I just wonder how long that will take." Thunder Cloud said, shrugging his shoulders.

"We can all grab a small part of love in our own lives, find someone that our heart calls out to, then hold them close throughout all the horrors of this life." A small tear ran down her face.

Thunder Cloud put his arm around her shoulders. Then he blacked out.

"Lana, have you seen Jean? I have not seen her of late. "I asked.

"The last time that I saw her, she and Thunder Cloud were leaving the fort." Lana had a worried look on her face.

"Outside this fort, is teaming with Seneca and Mohawk warriors. Has he gone mad?" I fumed. I looked around. Aha. I had been looking for a Ranger with a bugle.   "Ranger, call all Rangers here now!" Then Katie came running over.

"What's wrong, my love?" she asked, with a concerned tone in her voice. "Thunder Cloud has taken Jean out of the fort." Katie could not believe what I had just said.

"Surely, he can't be that stupid. Outside this fort…." I stopped her as I had just made this sentence.

"I have summoned all the Rangers to go and find them." Sending a few out would leave them open to attack. The Rangers are well trained and within twenty minutes, we were leaving the fort together. White Eagle rode up to me.

"Did you say that my brother and Jean have gone out of the fort, by themselves?" She sounded worried. I just nodded. "The Seneca will have no interest in my brother, but they will be after Jean." She warned.

We eventually came across Thunder Cloud. There was no sign of Jean.

I jumped down from my horse and knelt down beside him, pouring some cold water over his face. I was soon joined by White Eagle. As he began to regain conscience, his sister slapped his face.

"Why did you take Jean outside of the fort?" she was almost screaming at him. He opened his eyes, then it came to him.

"Where is Jean?" He asked, panicked. He had a bad cut on his head, blood was running through his hand and down his face. There was no point in questioning him more, it was clear as to what had happened.

We took him back to the fort in order for him to be treated. Then, the Rangers prepared themselves for battle.

We were not aware how many warriors the Seneca had in their village. But they would be facing the best Indian fighters in the country. We were all about to leave when horses were seen trotting towards the fort.

The eighty newbies, left behind for training, had arrived just in time for their first battle. All three hundred Rangers were clapping and whistling.

Katie ordered a break, to give the newbies time for a drink and a bite to eat. Who wants to fight on an empty stomach?

Katie and I were waiting with Andy and Lana, when two Rangers rushed in and came at us, shouting. We didn't get much of what they were saying, apart from the name 'General Whitelaw'.

"Calm down, we can't understand all this noise." Shouted Katie.

"Jean has been kidnapped by a group of Seneca's. we presume that she has been taken back to their village. And yes, we also believe that General Whitelaw is also in that village."

Andy and Lana, both rushed towards the exit, but they both stopped when they heard both of our pistols cock.

"They won't fire. Let's go." Shouted Andy. Lana on the other hand, knew better. She put her hands in the air as she turned towards us. "Andy, you don't know them, if they believe our actions will cause a problem with their plans. They will not hesitate to shoot us. Maybe not to kill us, but they will shoot." She accepted.

Andy got the message; he held his hands in the air as a sign of obedience.

"Both of you listen, if you go rushing into that village trying to kill him, you will both be killed and Jean will also die. And remember, they prefer their enemies to die slowly. If you promise to obey everything that we tell you to do, we will let you both go with us. We will be entering the Senecan village as soon as it gets dark. We have to rescue Jean before the main body of Rangers charge into the village. If, and I say *if*, we come across your general, you can do what you like with him. Just do it quietly." I emphasised.

The newbies had rested and the sun was setting. It was time to leave

We stopped about a quarter of a mile away from the village. Katie, Lana, Andy and myself left our horses with the rest of the Rangers and began to jog towards the village. On arriving, the sun had gone and there was only a crescent moon to greet us. There were a few lookouts who were there to warn the village if anything happened. We left Andy to take as many of them out as possible. We knew that the ex-mountain man would not have a problem with that. He sent six to dreamland and brought the seventh back to us. Luckily, Andy spoke enough of the Seneca language to enable us to find out which tent Jean was being kept in.

All of us managed to get to the back of the longhouse where she was being held. The problem was, how many other people were also in the longhouse? Lana crept to the front of the building. There was no talking at all. Of course, the inhabitants could be asleep, but it was only 8pm.

We had to throw caution to the wind. All four of us entered the building with our rifles raised. The longhouse was empty. Then we heard someone rolling around in the corner. Katie quickly checked. It was Jean. Katie cut her free.

"Let's get out of here quickly, and head back to the other Rangers." Whispered Lana.

I poked my head out the door.

"Welcome. I have been waiting for you all to return." Grinned Brant.

"You!" screamed Lana.

Beside Brant, was General Whitelaw. I spread my arms wide to prevent both Lana and Andy, attacking him. If I had failed to stop them. They would both be dead by now.

"Did your mother have a nice funeral, Lana?" He asked. "You will be joining her soon." He began to laugh at what he thought was a joke. Then he saw Andy. "Ah, you as well… Your children were awfully noisy at the end." There was no reaction from Andy. He was fully charged inside of his mind. Today would be the day his nightmares ended.

There were hundreds of warriors waiting for the order to attack us. Katie looked at me. It was that time again. We were both somehow able to release an excessive amount of adrenaline into our bodies when we concentrated fully. This enabled us to move at an almost unbelievable speed. We become stronger and we think quicker and clearer. While our opponents became tired, we were able to continue fighting as if we had only just begun.

I told the three others that we would handle this fight. They were to set fire to the longhouse to inform the Rangers that it was time for them to do their bit.

The two of us armed ourselves and prepared to move towards the warriors. It was now the time for The Dragon and The Eagle to perform. We both knew that although moving as fast as we could, it wouldn't prevent us from taking blows and cuts.

So, the stage was set. The longhouse behind us burst into flames, then the three of them picked up their rifles. Katie and I launched ourselves forwards into the midst of the warriors. We were fighting back-to-back. Bodies were beginning to pile up around us. We both had many cuts and although our stamina lasted a long time, it was beginning to wane; we were hoping the Rangers would arrive soon. The other three were fighting together also with their backs to each other.

Then a beautiful sight befalled us. Katie's Rangers came crashing out of the trees and smashed into the first Indians they came across. Katie dropped to her knees. I stood over her, but I also was nearly finished.

I can't explain the happiness, when the Rangers horses passed us and cut into our attackers. My legs then gave way and I dropped to the ground next to Katie. The Seneca were now in retreat. Nearly 400 Rangers had them on the run.

Andy and Lana saw their opportunity to find General Whitelaw and take their revenge. Two Rangers stopped near them and presented all three of them with horses. They did need a bit of help mounting their horses, but they were soon off, hunting the general.

What they eventually saw shocked even them. Some of the lower chiefs blamed their failure on the only white man they could find. Yes, General Whitelaw.

He felt the full revenge for the Seneca defeat. Lana and Andy had wanted to kill him in revenge for the death of their loved ones. But the way he had died in the end was too horrific for even them to have wished.

The Seneca had been taught a lesson. Mission complete.

When we reported back to Headquarters, we were informed that an expedition consisting of 4,000 soldiers was planned to take on the Iroquois. The name of the expedition was: Sullivan Expedition. They planned to set out at some point in 1779. We wished them all the best. I do think that Katie's Rangers may have softened them up a bit.

"Well, another challenge has been conquered. I think we can say it was all quite successful." I was grinning as I thought about all the new recruits.

"You are right, my love. And I think we may have a few new romances on our hands." She was smiling now.

"What, do you mean Mark and White Eagle?" I said while scratching my chin." Are you blind my husband? Have you not noticed Jean and Thunder Cloud. Also Lana and Andy, are spending a lot of time together." She walked away shaking her head.

162

CHAPTER 14

THE BATTLE OF BEAUFORT OR THE BATTLE OF PORT ROYAL ISLAND.

Katies Rangers had returned to what they now called their home. When we had the hospital built near Valley Forge, Katie and I also arranged for another building to be built. This has become our official base.

We had been there for a few months now. We started with a good rest, then it became a training camp. It was January 1779. Everyone was becoming bored of the same monotonous routine. Katie's Rangers were trained to fight.

"Katie, have you any news yet about a new commission? We have been stuck here for ages now. It's like we have been forgotten." I moaned.

"I am just as bored of this as everyone else. I will send a rider to the head office. Perhaps they will have something for our nearly 400 Rangers." She advised me.

When we were at our home, without any fighting to do, romance seemed to fill the air. Lana had been hurt by Cupid's arrow a couple of times. Although she was really keen on Andy, she was being careful. Andy, on the other hand, was madly in love with her. I think that Cupid must have emptied his quiver into his heart. Then we had a brother and sister falling for another brother and sister. It was all too complicated for me.

Finally a rider arrived with what we all had been waiting for. A commission. I grabbed the message off the messenger, Katie saw and raced after me, eventually we laid on our bed and read the orders together. Passers-by could hear us shouting abuse as we read our orders. What we wanted was like before, Orders where we had a job for only us to carry out. What we hated was being sent as support for the Continental Army. Instead of fighting Indians, we would be fighting the British and German soldiers.

"Where are we going? "I asked. "We are going to a town called Beaufort, in South Carolina." Grumbled Katie. "They even have given the history behind our encounter. Let me read it…" she announced.

"The British have consolidated control around Savannah, Georgia, which they captured last December. They then sent what they called 'The New York Expedition'. It was under the command of a Lieutenant Colonel Archibald Campbell."

"What a name?" I laughed. Katie continued.

"Apparently, he captured the town on December 29th 1778. A Brigadier General, Augustine Prevost, arrived a couple of weeks ago. He assumed command of the garrison there, and on the 22nd, sent a force to Port Royal Island. Where they had been led to believe that Loyalist sentiment was strong.

"Dafydd, wake up!" She nudged me.

"I am listening." I assured her. She continued.

"It seemed that the only garrison on the island was Fort Lyttleton, which had some Continental troops, under Captain John De'Treville. When he heard that a large British force was on its way, he spiked the fort's cannons and blew the main Baston.

"What's a Baston?" I asked.

"I don't know, now be quiet or I will never finish this! Brigadier General William Moultrie, with 300 soldiers, was sent to Port Royal Island. He is on our side. After De'Treville had finished destroying the fort, he crossed over to the island and occupied Beaufort. Are you still with me Dafydd?" I nodded. "Then Major William Gardner,

THE DRAGON AND THE EAGLE

who is British, landed on Port Royal Island with his 200 infantry. This is where we come in." claimed Katie.

"Let me get this straight. There are various units of American and British soldiers already on this Port Royal Island. Our leaders want us to gallop all the way to South Carolina." I was now shaking my head. "If the battle hasn't yet finished, we are to support our soldiers. Remember I will never march in lines towards an enemy's guns, or order others to do so either. That tactic is almost certain death for many soldiers. Katie, can you imagine lines of soldiers marching towards our Rangers? Our Rangers never miss. It would just be a massacre. So, in the end, if we arrive on this island before the battle is over, we will really be used as sharpshooters. Am I correct, Katie?"

She could only agree with me.

"But, dear husband, orders are orders. Can you inform everyone that we leave first thing tomorrow morning. Nine o'clock to be precise."

As ordered, we were all ready to leave on time. We rode as fast as we could, taking into consideration the needs of the horses. The journey was nearly 700 miles. With rest breaks, we could be there in about 10 days.

It had been a hard trip, but we managed to complete the ride in 11 days. It was February the 3rd 1779.

As we arrived on Port Royal Island, we could see a detachment of British soldiers heading to secure the island side of the ferry. Suddenly, they were retreating. They were being pursued by Patriots. Then the British commander, Gardner, moved his whole force towards Beaufort, to face The Continental Army.

Our commander, General Moultrie had moved his forces out of the town. It was clear that the two forces were about to fight this battle near the highest ground on Port Royal Island. It was a rise called Gray's Hill, which was about three miles high.

I looked at Katie. "This is where we join this fight." She confirmed. "We will climb as high as we can, hopefully we will have a good view of the British. Then we can see how good we are at shooting." I nodded to her.

The British officer lined his men up at the edge of some woods, near the top of the hill, well in range of the Rangers. Here he had an advantage with his bayonets fixed.

The Americans lined up on an open field outside musket range. General Moultrie positioned two six pounder field cannons in the centre of his line.

After about 45 minutes, the Americans were running low on ammunition. General Moultrie had begun a withdrawal. The British were also observed to be retreating.

South Carolina was most important in the pre-revolutionary British colony. It contained plantations which used slave labour to grow the valuable cash crops of indigo and rice. Indigo was used to make blue dye. It was very valuable.

"So that was it! We spent 11 days rushing down here, nearly killing our horses. And what for? We climbed a mountain and shot a few British soldiers. Katie, this cannot continue. We have 380 trained fighters. We want more than half an hour in a shooting gallery." I moaned.

"Don't blame me!" argued Katie. "I just have to pass on what the top brass order us to do." She seethed.

"I disagree. we have 380 Rangers, we have earned the right to challenge pointless commands." I could see she was becoming a bit upset, I had to tone my complaints down a bit. "I understand why you brought us here though."

"You know why I brought us here? Ok, tell me, I will see if you are correct." She grinned.

She thought that she had caught me out.

"You remembered our greater goal." She was looking puzzled now. "You know, my love, the hospital. You have come down here to try and find more doctors and nurses. And maybe some healing herbs, which don't grow near our headquarters. She moved forward and put her arms around me.

"I am sorry Dafydd, I did not realise that you knew me so well." I was lucky there. But now that I had thought about it, it was a good idea. I turned to look at the battlefield. All over the place I could see dead and wounded soldiers. Moving between them was an army of doctors and nurses as well as others with medical training, deciding who they could save. At one side of the battlefield was a massive tent, this is where the injured were carried.

"Follow me Katie." I ordered. On our way to the hospital tent, we passed Lana, Mark and Jean. White Eagle was with Mark, so I brought her with us.

I grabbed one of the newly promoted corporals.

"Grab as many Rangers as you can find. Tell them to check all the dead for donations for our hospital." I ordered. "Are we talking about our dead or The British, Sir?"

"I can see you are a newbie. The hospital is for the use of anyone, as long as they need medical attention, so take your collection from anyone."

I caught up with the others just before they were about to enter the tent. What a shock, we were all taken back. The first thing we noticed was the intense smell of blood. Beds, tables, surgical implements, soaking into the ground. Blood was everywhere. Even the mountain men could not prevent tears running down their faces. The morphine had apparently been used up some time ago. Now all surgery was carried out without painkillers.

A young woman was laid on a blood covered table. She had a bad cut on her thigh, it looked like it was becoming infected. One orderly jammed a stick into her mouth.

"Bite on this love," he told her.

The surgeon appeared with a large knife in one hand and a saw in the other. He was clearly about to cut this poor woman's leg off.

"Stop!" I ordered.

The man with the saw turned.

"And who are you to order me around laddie?" He asked. I showed my pips.

"I am Colonel Rhees." He went quiet.

"Sorry Sir, I did not recognise you. What shall we do with the girl then?"

I gave orders for her to be carried to one of the tents the Rangers were putting up, after all we had no intention of leaving for at least a day or two.

A large blanket was laid on the floor of the tent. I asked White Eagle to follow me.

"Do you know anything about herbs?" I asked her.

To my relief, she nodded. She knelt down beside the young woman. She asked for hot water and clean cloth, so I quickly ordered that.

"The cut is deep, and a slight infection is becoming worse. But I think I can save her." Smiled White Eagle. She first cleaned the area of the cut, then she made a tourniquet to stop the bleeding. "Keep an eye on her, I am off to try and find some herbs."

"Mark, take two men and go with her." I ordered. Katie and Lana were just standing and watching what was going on. I turned towards them. "You two can make yourselves useful and make some soup. She needs fluids and something warm inside of her." They never said a word, they just turned and carried out my orders. That doesn't happen much with Katie.

Soon, White Eagle was back. She had found what she had been looking for. It wasn't long before she had worked her miracle. The cut had been cleaned and bandaged, herbs had been placed over the infection. The young woman was still unconscious. But she looked a lot better. At least she wouldn't lose her leg.

"She has a fever. If she survives the night, she should live." She acknowledged.

Then a thought came to me.

"Katie and Lana, do you have any clean sheets?" I asked.

"Why do you want sheets?" asked Katie.

"Well, this young woman has a fever. I've heard that the best way to break a fever is to spend the night under the sheets with her. If we sweat together, it should break the fever. I will need to undress, and of course the young woman will also have to be undressed."

Trying to listen to two women speaking loudly at the same time is really difficult. Apparently, Katie and Lana were volunteering for the Job. White Eagle was standing not far away. She stood there laughing.

"I never knew that Dragons were so crafty. I had better watch out for you." She giggled.

With three young women sleeping naked in this tent, I had better place a warning notice for everyone to keep out. Or else. I was going to place a guard outside the tent, but I was not sure that I could trust them. So, Mark and myself took turns guarding the entrance to the tent. Thinking about it, sleeping under the sheets would have been the better option.

The following morning, I put one hand over my eyes, then used the other hand to find my way. I walked into the tent.

Suddenly, my hand made contact with something wet and warm. I jumped back, it was human flesh.

"I am sorry, as you can see my eyes are covered."

"Lucky for you, it's me that you touched." It was Katie. Phew, that was lucky. If I had touched one of the others, I would have been dead by now.

"Has her fever gone?" I asked. "Yes, we are just getting dressed, keep your eyes covered." As soon as they were all dressed, I sat next to the young woman.

"Are you ok? What is your name?" I asked her.

"My name is Valery, Val for short. Val Green, born 1755, in Virginia." She concluded.

"White Eagle said your wound should heal in a couple of weeks. How are you feeling?" I asked.

"A little worse for wear, but thankful I'm alive. Thank you." Val replied.

Later, Katie, Val and myself went back to the hospital tent. As I entered the tent, almost everyone saluted. Apart from the butcher.

"Please listen." I spoke up. "At one time I was in the British Army. The joke was that we would have more of a chance of dying in a field hospital, than in a battle." I decided to make a speech appealing for recruits. "We have built a large hospital near Valley Forge. It is for use by patients from both sides who are very ill. We also train medical staff and send them out to our field hospitals to provide good treatment. We are always on the lookout for doctors and nurses. Please, will any of you join us? We provide good working conditions, good food, and the satisfaction that wounded soldiers are being saved. I will ask you all in the morning who would like to join us."

I returned to our tent. Val came to find me not long after. It turned out that she had some office managerial experience. She offered to help with our hospital admin.

"It just so turns out that we don't have any admin staff yet! I will put you in charge. You are welcome to recruit your own staff. However, please don't feel like you must join us because we saved you. You owe us no debt. Please think it over and give us your decision in the morning." I told her. "Now Katie, my love, I just have to find the boys."

We both searched for them, and eventually they were found. John and Nick were asleep. After waking them up. We made them a proposition.

"Nick, John, the hospital isn't secure. We plan to leave 80 Rangers at the hospital when the rest of us leave for battle. Will the two of you take command of security at the hospital? It will come with a promotion." They were about to answer but I cut them off. "Think it over and let us know in the morning."

All the fit soldiers had left by now. The last of the injured will have been treated by this evening. I gave orders for us to be ready to leave by noon tomorrow.

We both could not wait for the following morning to come. By noon we were almost screaming with excitement. We have added 30 doctors and 38 Nurses. Nick and John were chuffed to be offered the leadership of the hospital's security. The last one, we were not that confident about, after all, we only met a couple of days ago. I was sure that she only offered her services in the first place because she felt like she owed us.

"Hi Val," said Katie. "I understand this is a big decision for you, especially as you haven't even seen the hospital. So, we understand if you choose not to join us."

Val was smiling.

"Yes please, I would love to do it."

We both began to walk away.

"It's ok. We understand." Moaned Katie.

"I will take the job!" Val shouted.

Katie and I looked into each other's eyes.

"She wants the job!" Katie turned around and gave Val a big hug.

Well, I did not think much of the battle, but we had recruited so many talented people. It was amazing.

At exactly noon, we all began our long journey back to Valley Forge.

CHAPTER 15

OH, BROTHER

It was a long hard journey back to the hospital. First, I had to find accommodation for the new doctors and nurses. Katie suggested that Val shared our room just for the night. I didn't see a problem, so I agreed with her.

Our hospital complex was becoming a massive project. We had so many staff now. When we arrived, a team of people came to us, they took our luggage, and also looked after our horses. Leaving us to try and stay awake and find our rooms. I was glad that Val had accepted the job, but with so many people to manage, I was sure she would find it challenging.

I had the latest collection sent to our rooms. We need a massive amount of money moving through our accounts to provide for all that was happening here.

It was now 8pm. I decided to go straight to sleep, I was knackered. The girls wanted to check our collection first. By the time they had finished, I was fast asleep.

"We have a problem here," said Katie. "I was planning for us to share our bed and to give him the chair or the floor, while he finds somewhere else to sleep, but he is already asleep in our bed."

"The bed is big enough that we could both squeeze in next to him." Suggested Val. Katie nodded. They both decided to have their bath in the morning, so they slept in their underwear. Soon the room went silent, interrupted only by occasional snoring.

I was the first to wake up. I turned towards Katie, she smelt so good. I put my arm around her and pulled her closer.

"You had better have a cold bath, we have a visitor." With that I withdrew my arm." A visitor? Who? Where?" I queried. From the far side of our bed, an arm was raised. I was now beginning to think that I was dreaming.

"Hello arm, who do you belong to?" I mumbled. Then I lifted the sheets and got out of bed.

"Katie, I didn't realise your husband had such a good body." I nearly died; the arm belonged to Val.

"You are right there, he is quite fit." At that both of them began to giggle. I grabbed a towel, and ran into the bathroom. There was more laughter.

"Ok, I thought, we can all play this game. I wrapped the towel around my hips, then walked out of the bathroom. Katie went in to use the toilet. Val was now sitting up in the middle of our bed.

"Now this is nice, first thing in the morning." I was so embarrassed.

I thought that Katie would be there. Well, I had better follow my game through. I walked over and laid on the bed.

"Am I interrupting anything?" Katie was back, I was so pleased. I got up to get dressed.

"Katie, where are my clothes?"

She put her hand to her mouth.

"OH, I'm sorry love, I sent them over to the doctors, they had left all their clothes behind in the rush." She explained.

"So, are you suggesting that I walk around all day wearing just this towel?" I heard a giggle from Val's direction.

"Now that is a good idea," she laughed. Katie got undressed down to her undies then picked up her towel and went into the bathroom.

"I presume that she has all her clothes?" I asked. Val laughed again.

"Of course."

Katie did not take long to have her bath, she returned and got dressed. Val got out of bed, she stood at the bottom of the bed then pretended to be about to undress. I panicked and dived under the sheets. They both burst out laughing.

Eventually, some clothes were sent up for me. We all went down to breakfast together. There were different dining rooms. We ate in the officers dining room.

"Well Katie, my love. Was our collection worth collecting?" She just nodded. "In fact, it was quite impressive." I then turned to Val.

After breakfast, we all need to have a discussion about the details of your job. I know you will require help. Then Katie will show you your room." I looked at Katie. "Have we received any new orders yet?" I asked.

She nodded and said that we can talk about it later.

"Just one thing, Katie, where have we got to go? For this next quest." She smiled.

"It's near New York, not too far. And not till July." Now I was nodding and smiling.

That night I was glad to get to bed again, it had been a very busy day.

The following morning, as we were eating breakfast. One of the Rangers informed us that Katie had a visitor.

"A visitor? I wonder who is visiting you, my love." I wondered aloud.

If we both sat at the table all week saying names, we still would not have guessed who it was.

"Richard Brooks! Long time no see. Shall I leave you with your sister?" He shook his head.

"Actually, no. I have really come to see you Dafydd." Katie looked a bit puzzled, she wondered why her brother had not come to see her. "Let me tell you both a story. You may think that it's unbelievable, but it's true."

He pulled up a chair and sat down at our table.

"I was In New York on business. One night, I was bored so I decided to visit a gambling club which I frequent now and then. There were eight of us playing. Now the player next to me was drunk. We all know that to play cards; you need a clear head. Consequently, he was losing badly. He then began to tell me how he arrived at the table" He began to recite the story he had heard.

"I was born in a small village in Wales. It was called Risca. My mother died when I was young. My father could not look after both my younger brother and me, so I was sent to live with my aunt and uncle. One day my uncle told me that my father had been killed. Someone had set fire to his church, while he was in it preparing a sermon. A couple of days later I went to see where my younger brother had got to. I was told that he had joined the British army, and had gone to America to fight The Continental Army. I didn't have any reason to stay in Wales, so I bought a ticket to America, in an attempt to find my brother."

Richard was now staring at me, with a big smile on his face.

"This Welshman told me that his name was Gareth Rhees. I have never before seen tears when someone was laughing. Would you like to guess his brother's name?"

How did my brother find me here? I thought.

"Ok, ok, I can tell you are enjoying this. Where is he?" I moaned.

Richard gave a call, and one of his men brought my brother out of where he had been standing.

So, this was my brother now. I hadn't seen him for twelve years. He was two years older than me. When I was young, he used to bully me.

"Long time no see Gareth. Do you still bully those who are weaker than you?" I asked sourly.

Gareth held out his hand.

"It's been a long time brother. I arrived in New York, then I made enquiries as to what regiment you were serving in. Funny enough, you had left the Army. Or should I say The British Army."

Was he trying to blackmail me? Was this a threat to inform the British as to where I was? I stood up and walked round the table to face my long-lost brother. I would say that I was about two inches taller than him. He was only 27 but he looked older.

"What do you do for a living, brother?" Gareth took his time considering his answer. "Well, you could say that I am a trader."

He opened his left hand.

"I take something," he then opened his right hand. "And what-ever it is, I sell it at a profit." He had a big grin on his face.

I was now staring into his eyes; Information could be one of these products. I thought that I had better change the subject.

"So, my brother, why are you here?" Richard butted in.

"He, or rather you, owe me $10,000. He had lost it that night, if I had not paid off the debt. They would have killed him." I looked at Katie.

"Where am I going to get $10.000, from?" Katie pulled an unhappy face.

"Don't worry, I will find it for you, but he will have to repay the money." I said reluctantly.

Gareth nodded.

"Why are you here? I haven't seen you for years."

"Dafydd, can we speak in private?" He asked. I looked at Katie, she nodded.

"Ok but this had better be good."

He told a story which sounded a lot like mine was, and why I joined the army. When he arrived in New York, he got a job as a control manager.

"I did very well, the manager praised me. But my drinking habit got me the sack. After the game the other night, I had no other choice but to move. Are there any vacancies in the Rangers?" He asked.

"No!" Katie said sternly, walking through the door. "I don't trust you. I am truly wondering if I should have you killed. We can't take a chance on you telling the British where we are.

"Katie, he is my brother. You can't just kill him! What would you do if I threatened Richard?"

She turned and looked at me.

"Richard is different, he is a leader of Vigilantes."

If I continued this line, I would upset my marriage. Thankfully Richard intervened.

"I haven't known this man for long, but I do think that maybe we can trust him. How about I use him with The Vigilantes for a while?"

Katie was thinking.

"Katie, can you guarantee that none of the doctors and nurses we brought back with us are spies from the British?" She knew I was right on this.

"Ok, fine. Let your brother work with Richard for a while, let's see how he turns out."

It was agreed. Richard left with Gareth, and my $10,000.

"Let's forget your brother, we need to talk about our next command."

"Ok my love. Let's go up to our room and discuss it."

This is better, I thought, discussing my brother was getting a bit heated.

"Ok, following the surrender of General Burgoyne in October 1777, and the entry of France…"

"No, Stop! I don't need to know the whole back story. Let's just discuss where Katie's Rangers will be required."

She began again.

"The Continental Army is planning a night attack against British troops at their outpost in Stony Point, New York. It's about 30 miles north of New York City. The British realised that Stony Points represents a vital area that controls that part of the Hudson River, and the entrance to Hudson Highlands, as well as Kings Ferry crossing. This is a fortified position." She informed me. "General Anthony Mad Wayne, has been put in command and various regiments have donated soldiers. We have been asked to support this attack, as our Rangers are the best shots in the army.

The plan is for a night time attack carried out by 1,350 men. That's excluding our 300. Part of the plan is to send in the Forlorn Hope. They will consist of twenty men from each regiment." I frowned. "I expect they will be all the troublemakers. No worries if they are killed." Katie continued.

"The general announced that he would give prize bounties to the first man to enter the works. Also, to any man who distinguished themselves in the action." Katie smiled. "I hope he will give it to women as well."

What the other regiments were planning had no interest to me. Our plans had already been made. We would support the Forlorn

Hope and try to keep as many of them alive as possible. I have never been able to understand the use of the Forlorn Hope. A small group of soldiers stand in lines and slowly walk towards the enemy, who will be shooting at them. It always reminds me of the funfair, when I'm shooting ducks. The ducks have more of a chance than the Forlorn Hope, because the rifles at the funfair are fixed.

My plan was to be the first to enter the Earthworks, followed by our Rangers, who would give their all to win an award. The awards would be money for the hospital, and the Rangers would also take a collection from the dead to help run the hospital.

July 16th 1779. The weather helped us. It had been cloudy, and the clouds had covered the moon. Everyone had been ordered to fix pieces of paper to their hats to highlight our soldiers in the dark.

Katie and I had sent our Rangers to camouflage themselves along the route that the forlorn hope would take. We could see the British soldiers dotted across the Earthworks. As it was a surprise attack, the use of musical instruments was forbidden, which helped the Forlorn Hope to progress somewhat before the shooting began.

I was always amazed at them. Their friends were being killed all around them, but they continued to march slowly as if they had a belief that they would not be hit. The lack of moonlight helped them to stay alive longer than usual. The Rangers were performing what was nothing short of a miracle by hitting so many soldiers in the dark.

I had crawled on my stomach to a point as near as I could get to the gate, thinking, 'It won't be long until the Forlorn Hope make their charge. This is normally where most of them would be killed.'

Suddenly, I was alarmed as something grabbed my right foot. I turned on my side and looked behind me. It was The Eagle. I was concerned that she may get injured or even killed. Our gift made us fight harder and faster, but we could still be killed. She crawled alongside me.

"We will enter the Earthworks together. The Dragon and the Eagle." She whispered. "Maybe we will get a prize each!"

As we were now very close to the Earthworks, we could evaluate the best place to enter better.

The main gate was a stupid place to make our entrance. Their forces were gathered there, expecting the main attack to be attacking the gate.

We had brought a small amount of explosives with us. Our plan was to make an entrance 400 yards further along, out of range of the soldiers protecting the main entrance.

We both crawled through the mud, it had been raining which also helped us. Looking back, the Forlorn Hope were not far away. We placed the explosives, and attached a length of twine, which we lit then dived behind a large stone. There was a far bigger explosion that we had expected.

We could now see the Forlorn Hope running towards the entrance we had made. I turned to Katie.

"They may be running, but they won't beat us into the works." We drew our swords, and ran towards the massive entrance we had made.

By now we were both covered in mud from head to toe. Our swords were doing their work against the couple of guards that had been unlucky enough to be close to the new entrance. It must be strange fighting a mud man in the dark, I thought.

It didn't take long for about twenty or thirty soldiers to come running towards where the explosion had taken out some of their wall. The Forlorn Hope hadn't entered the works yet. The main force was far away. Katie smiled.

"Ok, it's time for The Dragon and The Eagle to spread their wings." She grinned.

We stood back-to-back. We gripped our swords tightly and concentrated. As expected, our adrenaline began to flow. We could feel it filling our bodies. Now if the British had stopped and reached for their rifles, we would have been in trouble. But instead, they were waving their swords. Well twenty odd soldiers against two, they must have thought that this would not take long.

We started back-to-back, but circumstances prevented us from staying together. We were both on fire, so to say. Dead and wounded British soldiers lay everywhere. First the other Rangers joined us, followed by what was left of the Forlorn Hope.

By the time that the main force arrived, it was nearly all over. Katie and I had taken a fair amount of cuts and minor wounds, but we were ok. That was about normal for us for a fight like this.

My thoughts went to our hospital tents that we had set up earlier. Val had come with them, so that she could assess the proceedings after a battle.

Our soldiers took every live person captive, but a lot of British soldiers were either dead or injured.

The British prisoners were soon put to work. They were used to bury their dead comrades (after the Rangers had accepted their donations of course). Then they buried our dead.

To their surprise, Val was directing both injured American and British soldiers to our hospital tents.

One of the British officers was amazed at the cleanliness of our tents, and the treatment his soldiers were receiving. She told him all about the hospital at Valley Forge. She explained that the injured from both sides were treated there, and that extended to our field hospitals too. If any soldier had long term injuries, they would be taken to our main hospital. When British soldiers were healed, they would become prisoners until the end of the war. Some even offered, and were accepted, to work at the hospital, rather than stay in prison.

Eventually, we had a visit at the hospital. It was General Anthony Mad Wayne. Val gave him a tour of our hospital tents, and also explained about the Valley Forge hospital. He was impressed.

"I have come here to present my awards. It has been difficult because I had wanted to give one prize. But in this case the winners came as a pair. Together they entered the works. And together they held off twenty-five soldiers until help arrived. They have names but I believe they prefer to use their nicknames. Will The Dragon and the Eagle come forward to receive their awards."

We walked forward and received a bag of gold each. This was of course given to the hospital fund. After Katie had deducted 10,000 dollars first.

The general himself had an injury which needed treatment. Therefore, he took advantage of our hospital tent. To our surprise, there was a sudden disturbance outside the entrance. It turned out to be two British officers; they had been wondering where all their injured soldiers had been taken. The general gave orders for the officers to be allowed into the tent.

They were both totally amazed, first by the cleanliness and the surgeons' skills. But they also were wondering why their men, the enemy, were being treated alongside the American injured. Val took some time explaining everything, including about our special hospital. They were truly impressed.

"I guess after all we are all humans, obeying orders."

Val did a brilliant PR operation. Top brass from both the British and American forces had experienced and approved of our efforts.

As soon as the fit soldiers had returned to their regiments, and they had removed all the prisoners, we began to find places for those whose wounds were healing. Then the last ones, those with long term injuries, would require treatment at our hospital.

We had finally got ready to leave on the 20th of July. I was pleased with our collection. A lot of British soldiers had died during our attack. They left a lot of valuables for the collection.

I had also been wondering where my brother was. I hoped that Richard had taken him back to New York, where he could keep an eye on him. After all, he did bring him here.

When we arrived back at the hospital, we all got off our horses. A group of people ran out and took the horses. They would be brushed, fed and whatever else was needed. We wouldn't see our horses again until we were ready to leave.

The collection was collected by Nick and John, with some of their men, then carried away to a safe place. All our weapons and luggage were taken. Our weapons would be cleaned and our luggage taken to our rooms.

Katie and I stood back.

"This place is quite amazing." I could not think of anything else that I could say.

Somehow, we managed to get to our room. We both undressed and rushed into the bathroom. We would often share the bath. Then we suddenly heard the door open. Then a voice.

"Katie, Dafydd, are you here? You never gave me a room of my own, so I presume, I am still sharing this room with you?" It was Val. We held each other's hands.

"What shall we do?" I whispered. Then the door to the bathroom began to open. I panicked. I pinched my nose and slid under the water. My legs had to somehow get between Katie and the side of the bath.

"Katie, you are in the bath? That's exactly what I need right now! How about I share the bath with you, that will save some water."

Bubbles began to rise to the surface. Val grinned.

"You had better let him up, before he suffocates." At that point I sat up. I could not hold my breath any more.

This Val was quite cheeky. She even offered to share with both of us, but then decided that there would not be enough room. She even pointed at my chest and said "I remember that from last night." Then winked and left the room.

"Katie, please find her a room of her own. That woman scares me."

After a good night's sleep, I woke refreshed and relaxed. I found some clothes to wear, then told Katie that I would see her at breakfast, I had to check something out first. The first person I bumped into was the last woman I wanted to see.

"Good morning Dafydd, did you sleep well?"

While I was thinking about what to say, she asked me to come closer, as she wanted to talk with me about something. I began to protest, when she put her finger in front of her lips, indicating silence.

"I am not playing now, this is serious." Her face showed a different Val than the one who had been teasing me. I beckoned her back to my room. Katie had just got dressed.

"What are you two doing now?" she asked. Val began to speak. "First thank you for arranging my rooms before we left for Stony Point. Sorry that I had not realised and came here last night. Before I went to bed last night, I went to my office, just to check how things had been going. I opened the door and had the shock of my life. Sitting in my chair, was your brother."

Katie began to blow a fuse.

"I will kill him now." She clearly did not like him.

"Calm down Katie." Whispered Val. "I asked him what he was doing in my office at this late hour. He then informed me that your brother, Katie, had come up with an idea. Richard had a small grocery store in New York. He had made Gareth the manager. Although the store would sell to locals, their main purpose would be to supply the hospital." She said with a worried look on her face.

"So, why was he in your office late at night?" I enquired.

"He told me that in my absence, he was checking what goods he would have to smuggle up to us." Val still had this frown.

"If Richard did set this up… well we do often have problems getting supplies. If my brother can smuggle supplies to us, it would be amazing." I grinned. That was a mistake, Katie was now glaring at me. "Let us all go to breakfast, then if Richard is still here, he can tell us more." Katie, conveniently agreed.

All three of us sat at the table, we even had ladies bringing the breakfast and removing the used plates. Looking around, I began to realise the amount of supplies we must require every day.

"Hi Dafydd, how was your trip? I was explaining to Val last night about the scheme Richard has come up with." Katie, jumped up.

"Where is my brother now?" If I was Richard, I would not want to meet his sister at present.

"He went back to New York, just before you all returned."

That was convenient.

"Katie, can you check how our wounded Rangers are doing? Val and I can sort out this situation." I was now giving her instructions with my head.

"Ok, my love, you and Val sort things out. We can catch up later." She then left the room. My brother got up from his seat and came round to where I was now standing.

"She is a fiery one, your missus."

I turned and punched him as hard as I could.

"Forget my missus, I am The Dragon. Don't you dare play games with me." I warned him.

"Val, can you please check what is really happening? If there is a plan drawn up with Richard, and my brother really is the manager of some store in New York, please confirm it. Then clarify how often he will provide supplies and send him home with a shopping list. As soon as he has left, Katie will calm down."

Val nodded.

"I will try to get him away from here by midday."

I smiled.

"Thanks"

She left, with Gareth following, holding his face with one hand. Peace at last I thought.

Then just as I sat down. Four Rangers burst in dragging a young woman.

"Sir, we found this young lady outside the main gate. She says that she wants to be a Ranger. She said that she had ridden far, then when her horse died, she had to walk."

She looked as if this story was true, she was dirty, her clothes were torn, and she looked totally exhausted. I had her brought to a spare room, and ordered the Rangers to bring her food and coffee.

"Thank you." She whispered. "My family had a farm in South Carolina. One day, I was down by the brook fetching water. I heard my father's gun being fired. I dropped the water and ran back home. On arriving at the farm…" She held back a sob. "I am sure that you can imagine what happened to my father and mother, and my two sisters. After I buried them I found our horse; they somehow missed him. I had seen you and your Rangers in action near Beaufort, so I got on my horse and galloped off with a hope that I could join you. The journey was too much for the old boy. When he collapsed and died, I had to walk. But I have made it. My name is Jen."

Then she collapsed with exhaustion. I called two Rangers over.

"Carry her to my room. I will follow. Also, find Katie quickly and send her there as well."

CHAPTER 16

THE BATTLE OF NEWTOWN

The Rangers and I got Jen to our bedroom, and laid her on our bed. I ordered both Rangers to stay with me until Katie arrived. I didn't want any rumours.

Katie wasn't long. I explained the situation, and told her that she said her name was Jen.

"And where is your brother?" Katie asked. I had forgotten him.

"Val is sorting him out now." At that point in walked Val.

"What is going on here?" She grinned. "Dafydd, don't forget you can't get three in the bath."

Katie intervened to save me. "Leave him alone, you can give me a hand. She looks exhausted. Take her clothes off and we will give her a bath, then after she has had a good sleep, I will find some clothes for her."

Katie began to undo her shirt; Val looked at me.

"Are you going to watch?"

I then began to panic and ran out of the room, with laughter ringing in my ears.

Back in the dining room, I came across Gareth.

"Why are you still here?" I asked. "It's ok, I am off back to my store in about 15 minutes, I was just picking up some food. I had a talk with Val, and she had given me a list of things to bring. They will of course arrive at night, as I have to avoid the British."

"Ok brother, we will give you a chance to prove your worth. Leave me directions to your store, Katie and I may drop in at some point. By the way, how will we pay for our stores?" I asked.

"Well brother, I have thought about that, and for a small commission. I will get your collections exchanged for gold, the favourite currency."

"How much commission?"

Gareth stroked his chin.

"I will only charge you 15%, and that is a bargain, as it will be such a dangerous thing to carry out."

I shook my head.

"I will write a number on this piece of paper. This is how much I will pay, and if you refuse it, I will just have to think of another way to make the exchange."

He thought for a while, then opened the piece of paper.

"5%! You have to be joking." I began to walk away.

"7% and it's a deal." I held my hand. Deal!

He then picked up his food and left the hospital. Now I could see Katie without any more arguments about him.

I hurried back to our room. I wanted to know more about this Jen.

I pushed the door open. Jen was quick and just managed to cover her modesty before I had entered.

"Sorry." I said "Thought that you would be presentable by now." I beseeched her.

Val was going to make one of her, what she feels are, funny remarks.

"Dafydd, where is your brother? I want to have words with him." Katie asked rather aggressively.

"He just left my love. Get Jen dressed, and I will return, I want to discuss something with her." Then I left the room. Katie ran after me.

"She will be presentable in a few minutes; wait here and I will call you in."

Fifteen minutes later, I was called in.

"By the way, my full name is Atkins, Jenifer Atkins." I wasn't sure how to respond.

"My brother has returned to New York to his store. Do I trust him? I don't know, I was eight when we were separated."

"What has this got to do with Jen?" Katie interrupted.

"What this has highlighted is a need for something which we don't have at present..."

All three of them were now staring at me.

"Go on then, what is it?"

"We need a spy network. Maybe five or six people trained to infiltrate the enemy. What brought this to my mind, is my brother. Jen has arrived and asked to be a Ranger. I was thinking that she could get a job at my brother's store. Then she could keep an eye on what's going on. I would need to send you away for training. And the job could be dangerous. But can you think of a better way of avenging your family?" I concluded.

"Can I think about this offer?" she asked. "Of course, But if you do want the job, even before the training, I will be sending you to my brother's store." I smiled and gave her a wink.

The following morning, she gave me the thumbs up. I gave her a letter to give to Richard. The letter informed him that I had sent Jen to be responsible for our goods.

"Katie, what's our next mission?" She looked for our orders.

"Oh no! We have missed our first command. We were to be at a town just outside Elmira, on the 11th August. Husband, what is today's date?"

"Today is August 13th."

"I think we had better get moving, or we will miss the rest of the war!" She shouted. "I tell you what, my love. We can drop Jen off on our way. Where we are going is near New York." She was glaring at me, she hated being late, especially as we may have even missed a battle.

We packed at incredible speed, and only missed the battle by a few days. But we weren't too late to hear all about it.

We had missed the Battle of Chemung.

This battle was probably the most significant engagement of the Sullivan Campaign, and played a crucial role in the war.

After our attack on the Seneca and Mohawks, late last year, General John Sullivan was ordered by the Continental Congress to end the threat of the Iroquois.

They were fighting a series of battles, and burning towns and crops, in order to destroy the Iroquois.

John Butler and Joseph Brant, our old friend. Did not want to make a stand at Newtown. But they were overruled by the other chiefs.

Katie's Rangers arrived on August the 16th. Katie apologised for us being late.

On August the 26th, we joined up with Sullivan as he left Fort Sullivan with 5,000 well-armed troops. We marched slowly up the Cayuga branch of the Susque Hanna to destroy their towns and crops.

On Sunday, August 29th, ten miles upriver from Fort Sullivan. The advanced guard, under Colonel Daniel Morgan, suspected an ambush.

He halted and scouted the area; we were included in the scouting. We discovered hidden Breastworks and informed Brigadier General Edward Hand.

He dispatched soldiers with orders to fire into the breastworks, which would make the defenders attempt to lure the Continental Army into an ambush, but they would be unsuccessful.

He called Katie and I, with his other officers, and made a plan.

Two detachments were sent to attack in two different directions. Ten cannons were used to soften them up. The plan was complex and had been arranged at short notice.

The Battle of Newtown began on the 29th August 1779. The Battle was short and bloody. Luckily, none of our Rangers were injured. After the battle, three more Iroquois Towns were burnt to the ground.

General Sullivan, after a short chat with Katie, where they talked about what we did last autumn, marched north. During the next three weeks, against demoralised opposition, they completed their campaign.

Thunder Cloud was very interested in this. After all, he was a chief of the Mohawks.

"Dafydd, can I have some leave? I need to visit my people. Now Brant has been defeated, my people will need me." He pleaded.

"My friend, you are more a brother to me than my real brother. You can do whatever your heart tells you." We hugged for a minute.

"Can Jean come with me? That's if she would want to." He asked.

"You have feelings for her, am I correct?" I speculated.

"You are right, we are like brothers. Yes, I believe that I have loved her for some time." I could see the pain in his eyes.

"If she feels the same, will you marry her?" I asked.

"Dafydd, do you remember me telling you that my sister and I learnt to speak English at a small chapel?"

I nodded.

"The one that was burnt down, just like my father's church was." He hesitated as memories flooded back into his mind.

"Well, my sister and I gave our lives to Jesus during one of the services, and we are both Christians. So, if she will have me, we will get married in church. We are not believers of the Great Spirit, although he has similarities." He smiled.

"So, brother, what is the reason for the pain that I see in your eyes?" I asked.

He sat down on the grass and patted the ground beside him.

"I have two reasons. The first is, how can I ask Jean to live in a longhouse with other members of my family? My people are not living the life that Jean is familiar with." I understood what he was saying.

"But if you love each other, these things can be overcome." I replied, sounding like my father.

"That is true, Dafydd, but there is also another reason, which may be harder to overcome, or even live with." He sighed.

"What could that possibility be?"

"A small word, which causes so much hurt. Racism!" he said, lifting my hands off his shoulders.

"My people would accept Jean as my wife, but they would look down on her. Many white women were captured and used as slaves in our villages, and many were used by the men. If we left my people and tried to live in the world of the white men, we would both be ridiculed and even hated."

I understood what he was saying. Even I had experienced racism as a Welshman living on a ship filled with English soldiers.

"Well, not for long," I said. "When a certain Dragon has a word with them, their attitudes will change." That made me snigger. "My brother, let me tell you something, which may help you make your final decision. "As you know, Katie created Katie's Rangers. This was not a power kick, or something to alleviate her boredom. She had a dream, which I have bought into now. That woman, who I love so much, created the Rangers to fight for the freedom of the people, who are trying to carve a life out of this new world, against invaders who only see our country as a cash cow.

But her dream did not stop there. All wars begin and end. At present we are fighting over what is a small strip of this country. When peace is declared, she wants to take The Rangers and their families west. They will build a new life for themselves, as they carve a slice of this land for themselves. This world will include people of all races. Racism won't exist there.

Why? Because it will be outlawed? No. The people will love each other, and have no wish to cause hurt. Maybe you and Jean would want to be part of this world?"

There was a noise behind us, and Katie and Jean joined us. Dafydd, I could not have expressed my dream better. And I do love being your wife." We smiled lovingly at each other.

Thunder Cloud looked like a deer caught in the headlights.

"Thunder Cloud, I have loved you for some time. I would also like to be part of this dream."

They looked at each other and hugged.

"Can anyone join in?" asked White Eagle, laughing. White Eagle and Mark came and sat with us.

"Did you hear the gist of the conversation?" Asked Katie. They pretended not, but eventually gave in.

"What I heard; I want this dream to be my dream as well." Exclaimed White Eagle. "I truly love Mark, but I had the same concerns as my brother. You talk about going west. How far is that?" She wondered.

"My dream is as big as we want it to be. We will ford rivers, climb mountains, cross large deserts where water doesn't flow. We will pass through giant forests first, eventually hunting the buffalo on the plains. We will come across the Shawnee, Pawnee, Kiowa, Sioux, Cherokee, Cheyenne, Comanche, and Apache. If your dream is as big as mine, you will hold hands with me overlooking the Pacific." grinned Katie. "But first, there is the tiny matter of this war."

When that woman speaks, I would gladly follow her to the end of the world.

"I will go on my own to visit my people. They will not harm me," nervously grinned Thunder Cloud. "Then I will go with you, my brother." declared White Eagle.

Mark and Jean then spoke at the same time. They both demanded that they should go with them.

"Ok. The four of you are on leave. Report back to headquarters. That's an order." Now it was me who was grinning.

They took some food and their horses, then temperedly disappeared out of our lives.

"May God be with them," I whispered.

"Let's get back to the Rangers my love."

We returned to the hospital camp. As always it was really busy.

"Dafydd, Katie, we have a problem." Said one of the doctors. "We have a top British officer severely injured with us."

I could not see a problem; our hospital is open to everyone.

"What is his name?" They checked then returned.

"His name is Major General Philip Morrison. If he dies, the British will send their best regiments to crush us once and for all." The messenger shuddered. We went to see this Major General. Somehow, he had his adjutant with him.

I approached the adjutant.

"I don't know if the British are aware of our war hospitals. They are kept clean and we have the best doctors working here. More importantly, we treat any wounded, American or British. If we can treat the injured here, then we do. We have built a massive hospital, with all the latest equipment, at Valley Forge. Your Major is too badly injured to be released into your care. If we can get him to the hospital without him dying, there will be a chance that he may live."

The adjutant had noticed the Rangers were searching the bodies and removing any valuables.

"Why do you steal from the dead?" he asked, disgust clear on his face.

"The valuables we collect pays for the upkeep of the hospital and the hospital tents." He looked relieved.

"There is a rumour that your Rangers steal from the dead to line each other's pockets."

He watched the Rangers and saw that everything was put into a large chest, to take back to the hospital.

Finally, all the wounded had been treated, the Americans were sent back to their regiments, while the British were simply released. The adjutant looked on in amazement.

"We have ten seriously injured soldiers, who will require treatment at the Valley Forge hospital. Four are American, and the other six, including your Major General, are British." Explained Lana.

The journey back to the hospital was a slow one. We were concerned that some of the wounds may open up if we went too fast over bumpy ground.

After a nerve racking journey, we eventually arrived at Valley Forge. The adjutant insisted on being with the Major all the time. Eventually we all arrived at the ward. He was undressed and hospital white clothes were put on him. A team of doctors came out to meet us as we arrived. The main doctor turned to speak with the adjutant.

"If you have a God, I would start to pray now. Your major is in a very bad way, I am amazed that he has made it here alive."

He then left. I placed a chair for him to sit on. He looked around the ward. There were British and American soldiers equally spread around the ward. They were talking to each other about their loved ones, as if they were friends.

"The major will be ok if you leave him for a while, would you like a tour of the hospital? We can get some food and drink." He nodded.

A tour of our hospital involved a lot of walking. We were both glad to arrive at the eating room afterwards. A plate of food was presented to all four of us, and some tea. Americans seem to like coffee, but I will always drink tea.

"Listen, we are aware of this hospital. There are rumours as to who it treats. But the important thing is that the organisation which runs it, is well known to be Katie's Rangers."

I looked at Katie. "Wow you are famous!"

He grunted. "That is nothing good. Your Rangers are fighting against us, the British, you are our enemies." That stopped my laughter.

"Don't you agree that a lot of good is performed at the field hospital and here at the main hospital?" He was still not smiling.

"Owing to the fact that you even treat your enemies. This is an amazing place. But we can't get away from the fact that you and your rangers are fighting against us. It would not surprise me if a large army was sent here to destroy Katie's Rangers. Please be warned. You need to separate Katie's Rangers from this hospital. Otherwise, it will all be destroyed."

One of the Rangers took him back to the ward.

"Katie, we are in trouble. What are you going to do?"

At that moment, someone called for me. Our stores had arrived from Gareth's store. Katie was first to meet them, she even for a few minutes forgot that she hated my brother. That did not last long.

"Where is Jen? Dafydd sent her to look after our stores." Jen jumped out of one of the wagons.

She ran up to Katie and saluted.

"Everything you ordered is here."

My brother and I said very little. We unloaded the stores and I paid him. Then he was away as quick as he came, back to New York.

Jen stayed behind. She had something to tell us.

"I took your letter to Richard. He took it to your brother. He ordered you brother to put me in charge of our stores. I have worked there for about a month. Every night he goes out gambling and drinking."

"What about Richard?" I asked her.

She told us that Richard left. He told us that he had more important things to do. That left my brother in sole control of the store.

"One day, I had a customer. Your brother was in another room with someone who he called an 'important customer'. I had to go to the room next to the one that he was using. I heard the two of them talking. I could not catch it all; just the words 'hospital', and 'Katie's Rangers'. I wanted to stay longer, but we were busy and my customer was waiting."

The word 'Spy' ran through my mind.

"Katie, we know that the American leaders are on our side. We need to speak with a high-ranking British officer. If they both would agree to make the hospital and the field hospitals neutral ground then we would have nothing to worry about."

"Well, it is used by both sides." Katie agreed.

"Then all we would have to do is move the Rangers away from the hospitals."

Katie nodded. "This would distance my Rangers from being part of the hospital, thus ensuring their safety."

I nodded in agreement.

"How about I return with Jen to the store. Of course, I won't enter the store, after all my brother is still under suspicion. Then I will try to meet up with some British general. If we can get him on our side. We can then arrange a meeting with an American General."

I could see that Katie wasn't fully sold on the idea.

"I think this plan is filled with danger. If you want to go ahead, then take others with you."

I agreed. I decided to take John, Nick and Andy. The four of us, and Jen, set off towards New York.

We had taken some gold nuggets with us, to use as money, we knew that the American dollar would not be worth much in a British

controlled city. On arriving at the store, we left Jen and began looking for a place to stay near the store. When you have gold nuggets,
everything is available to you. We soon found a nice place overlooking the store. Our next job was to find a British general to have a chat
with. New York, being a British city, was crawling with officers of all
ranks. We decided to have a walk around the city and get a meal, to
help us get the layout of the area and try to formulate a plan.

We finally decided that the best way to arrange a meeting with
a general would be late at night. We had seen all ranks staggering out
of the taverns, drunk. In the meantime we caught up with Jen. She
informed us that my brother often has visitors, but mainly a certain
'Captain Simon Blake'. I asked her to identify him to us, on his next
visit. We would have one of us watching the store from our window.

"Dafydd, how long will we have to stay here? Kidnapping a
British officer will be so easy, I can get you one any day." Moaned
Andy. Cities were not the best place for an ex-mountain man."

"Andy, my friend, this captain knows a lot about my brother.
He is the one I want. Anyway, if we have to spend the winter in this
city, we will avoid all the discomforts of living outside during the
snow." We all laughed.

Two weeks later, the mysterious Captain appeared. Jen made
an excuse to wave a red cloth in our direction. Nick was on lookout
that day.

"Dayfdd, quick, take a look at your captain." He said, pointing
at a man walking into the store.

I memorised everything about him. Then I ran outside, I
planned to follow him when he left.

He eventually left after a rather long chat with Gareth. We followed him for maybe half an hour. Our walk was well worth our
time. Our captain did not live in the barracks, he had a nice place of
his own in the city, not too far from us. I stood there smiling.

"Lads, I think that we will be introduced to our captain tonight."

I gave them all the rest of the day to themselves, with a warning
not to get into any trouble. Then I went back to the store. I wanted
to have a chat with Jen. She was left in the store serving customers
most of the day, I was not sure what my brother did.

The store was always closed for lunch. I passed the store's window and indicated to Jen that I wanted to meet her in our flat during her lunch break. She nodded. I went to a hot food stall and bought enough hot food for Jen and myself - it was her lunch break after all.

CHAPTER 17

WHERE SHALL WE GO?

Jen arrived just after 1pm. She welcomed the hot food. I was not sure that she would welcome what I was about to ask her to do though.

"Jen, tonight, I want you to help us lure the captain. We plan to kidnap him, then have a chat." She looked a bit puzzled.

"What do you want me to do?" she asked.

"Well, I recognise him. He always has a drink at The Railway Tavern, before turning in for the night. When he leaves the tavern slightly drunk, I want you to stand in front of the alleyway, which is to his right, and entice him from the tavern to the alleyway. When he arrives, we will grab him."

Jen stood thinking about this. Eventually a grin appeared on her face.

"Do you think that I could be a temptress?" She was now walking towards me, with a seductive look on her face.

Pack it in, I had enough when you and Val were teasing me the other night."

"Who said I am playing," She continued. "I find you a handsome, strong, sexy man."

At that point Andy entered the room.

"Thank God you are here!"

Jen burst into laughter.

"You are right Dafydd, I think that I would be a great temptress. I was wondering what you would do if Andy had not arrived." Andy was now looking at me.

"And what would you have done?" He asked.

I nervously scratched my chin.

I rushed over to the window and changed the subject. I could hear both of them laughing behind my back.

Jen had to return to work, while the four of us just laid around feeling bored. Jen returned at 6pm when the store closed.

"I see the four of you have been working hard all afternoon."

There was no answer to that statement, we knew what little we had been doing apart from sleeping. Then I had an idea, we could not make our move on the captain until later.

"How about us all going for a drink and a meal?" Jen was the first to respond. I say respond, she was out the door and half way down the stairs.

"This is a big city; let's try the taverns on the other side." Suggested Nick. We were all in favour.

Eventually we came across a nice tavern near a river. They even had some tables and chairs outside. We preferred to stay inside. After all, we were still the enemy. We ordered a steak meal each, with a large tankard of cool beer. I had only brought gold nuggets as money. I had assumed that gold would be taken everywhere. Well, I was correct, he was willing to accept our gold, the problem was the exchange rate. He was wanting to give half the true value of our nuggets. Our steaks were already half eaten, so it would have been difficult to return the meal. I surveyed the other tables. It appeared that the tavern we had chosen was frequented by off duty British soldiers. More to the point, they were making us the centre of attention.

"I am sorry, we are new here and had not realised the value of our nuggets here." I handed him what he asked for. "Thank you for such a wonderful meal." Jen was the first to punch me in my side. "What do you mean by saying that rubbish?" I grabbed her hand and began to squeeze it.

"Dayfdd, you are hurting me." I had gotten her attention.

"Shush, we don't want a fight with the British army, over a few nuggets." I looked at the others. "Eat up, we are leaving." They finally got the message and began to look at the other tables. Most seemed caught up in their own meals and conversation. But the message that we were carrying gold nuggets had been noticed by some of them.

We waited until dark before leaving. I ordered the others to visit the toilet, then leave quietly out the back. I was the last to leave. There were about ten ruffians staring at me.

I was soon out the door. I met up with the others around the back of the tavern. Then I saw them, all ten of them. They were a bit concerned when we had all disappeared. They walked down the street searching for us. Then their dreams, or rather nightmares, came true. Five of us hit them from behind. Sometimes it's best when your wishes don't come true.

It would soon be time for our saucy temptress to go into action. The stage was set. We had spotted him drinking inside the tavern through a window. All four of us were inside the alleyway. Jen was wearing a short cut dress, revealing her long legs.

"If I did not love Katie so much, I could become entrapped by her."

Jen turned and looked down the alley.

"I heard that Dafydd."

We had to wait for Jen to signal when our Captain left the tavern. We had had a warm summer, but it was now late at night, and it got very cold quickly.

Jen began to whistle. That was the signal. We were not far away from Jen, maybe four steps.

"Hi good looking, it's cold tonight, can I warm you up?" We could not see what his reaction was until he finally spoke.

"Pretty lady, I just came out of a warm room, maybe I will warm you up, let me take you home with me." It's funny but I feel personally responsible for all my Rangers. At this moment in time, I wanted to hit this captain. There he was, trying to get his arms around Jen. He had awoken the Dragon. The rest of the lads were startled by the speed at which I passed them. It only took one blow to send him to dreamland. We carried him to our room and tied him to a chair.

It was 1am when he finally came to. I asked Jen to do the initial introduction. Coming from her lips, would seem less threatening.

"Good morning, captain." She began. "We just want to have a chat with you. If I untie you, will you promise to refrain from trying to run away? I promise that you will sleep in your own bed, unharmed, after we have finished our chat." He nodded and she untied him. "Would you like a drink?" She offered.

"Have you anything warm and caffeinated?" he asked.

"We have tea or coffee."

"Tea with two sugars and milk, please." I smiled, that's the same as I have it.

He had a few sips of tea, then wanted to know what we wanted.

"We want you to arrange a meeting between us, and a British general. This could even mean promotion for you." Claimed Jen. "I'm sure you are aware of the hospital that the store supplies."

Again, he nodded, pretending to show little interest.

"Well, we were treating a British officer whose adjutant gave us a warning. He told us that we should arrange a meeting between high-ranking officers from both sides, then get them to agree on both the hospital and the field hospitals, becoming neutral ground. Of course, in order for this to take place, the Rangers will have to leave the hospital grounds."

She then had a few sips of her tea. Our captain was now grinning.

"You want me to arrange a meeting with a top British officer? Is this correct?" he asked.

"Yes, that is our request." I replied. "And we are sorry that we had to use such a rough invite."

"Ok agreed." He got to his feet. "Tell me, I notice that you have a similar accent to the store manager. Are you related by any chance?" He grinned.

Fear had now gone from our visitor. I began to feel like a mouse being played with by a cat, before it made its kill.

"You are welcome to return to your home now. I will return to work at the store. When you have arranged this meeting, let me know and I will inform the boys. Is this ok?" She asked the captain.

I had been studying him for the last half an hour. He clearly was thinking that all his Christmases had arrived.

Jen shook his hand and he scampered down the stairs.

As he left the room, Jen swore.

"What a slimy snake. We had better leave this place now. He could return soon with hundreds of soldiers."

When I lived in my small village in Wales, I was a timid lad, with little knowledge. But I had changed. I had anticipated that this may happen. I had already booked another room a few streets away.

"Come on, let's get out of here." I ordered.

Half an hour later, we were sitting around a new kitchen table, down the street.

"Jen, I am sorry but I must ask you to continue to work in the store, he won't harm you, as he will need you to inform us of the meeting." I turned to the boys. "Tomorrow, I want the three of you to return to Katie. Inform her that a large army may be coming to the hospital in the near future. I will stay here and attend the meeting, which I am sure he will arrange." I took Jens hands in mine. "You, Jen, have been brilliant, but after you give me the information about the meeting, I order you to get your horse and also head to the hospital. I believe that my brother and I will be at the meeting, and I am not sure if we will get what we are after. Either that or I will accompany a large British force on a visit to the hospital." I looked at each of them. "Are you all clear?"

"Yes Sir," they were all nodding.

"I don't want anyone trying to be a hero, just follow orders." We were all very tired. "Let's get some sleep, I think we may all have a busy day tomorrow."

To my surprise, Jen arrived at 11am with the message about the meeting.

"I did not expect the meeting would be this soon." I looked out of the window. "Jen, you have been followed."

He was leaning on the wall at the corner of the road.

"Jen, follow me. When we get outside. Just stand by the door looking at the sun. I will pay your stalker a visit. Then you run away.

Get your horse. I will see you back at the hospital in a couple of days."

I soon put Jen's stalker to sleep, I then returned to finish my breakfast.

The message requested me to meet our captain and a general, at the back of the store after the store closed at 6pm.

I spent more of the day sleeping, I had this feeling that I would not get much sleep that night.

The sun had nearly set, the moon was beginning to shine through the clouds. It was 6pm exactly. I was wondering how I was going to get to the back room, especially as the store was closed. I pushed the front door and it opened. I entered. I could hear some people talking. That must be the back room I thought.

"Come in Mr Rhees." requested a familiar voice.

"Good evening captain, I hope you had a pleasant day." As I came into the light; I could see the captain and my brother.

"Let me introduce General Hoskins. He is my brother. We thought that we should share the promotion on offer."

He then waved his arm and maybe twenty soldiers appeared.

The general began to speak.

"I understand from your brother that one of the most vicious thorns that my soldiers have had to encounter, 'Katie's Rangers', are quartered at that hospital?"

I stared at my brother; he was indeed a spy.

"I am sorry general; I believe that we are here to discuss the hospital being classified as neutral ground."

The general signalled the captain, who came forward and punched me in the stomach. That hurt.

"This will hopefully be a short meeting. We will be taking 2,000 soldiers to the hospital in the morning. There we will crush Katie and her Rangers. Then we will take over the hospital and kill all the American patients. Leave it as a British hospital."

The captain then began to speak. "What we need from you, is to know exactly how many Rangers are there at the hospital."

This was normally the time that I would call on the Dragon. But I needed to know more. Also, I had not met the right general. Four soldiers tied me to a chair.

"Now, Mr Rhees. How many rangers are at the hospital?" The captain asked. Then again punched me in the stomach.

"Stop it!" shouted Gareth. "You promised to ignore the fact that he is a Ranger, in exchange for my help." The captain smiled. "I have, as agreed, but he is also guilty of other crimes. Such as desertion from the British army, and murdering an officer. Am I correct, Mr Rhees?" There wasn't much that I could say, I had forgotten about that, it seemed to have happened so long ago.

"The officer provoked me and murdered my best friend; he got what he deserved." I reckoned.

"Lock him up in one of the store rooms, and place two guards outside his door. He is going on a little trip with us in the morning." Ordered the captain.

They dragged my chair into a store room and locked the door. This was what I had expected, I hoped that all the Rangers had left the hospital grounds by now.

About 15 minutes later, I heard a noise outside the door, then I heard the key being turned. Was it time for the Dragon to rise again? I thought.

The door slowly opened. To my surprise, in stepped my brother.

"Quick Dafydd, the guards are asleep. We need to get away now." He cut my bonds. "Come on Dafydd."

There wasn't much point in moving, I could see two soldiers with pistols pointing at my brother. And of course, the captain was also present.

"So, it turns out that you are a… what do they call it - a double spy? You spy for both sides. Please sit beside your brother. And be ready to leave with him in the morning." Then they all left the room, and locked the door again.

For a while we both sat in silence.

"Tell me why, Gareth."

For a while he maintained his silence. Then he began to speak.

"Just after dad died…"

I had to challenge that statement. "Dad did not die. He was murdered." Gareth nodded then continued.

"After Dad was murdered, uncle chucked me out of his house, telling me that he could no longer afford to feed me. I was out on the streets with nothing to my name."

"Do you think I had things any easier?" I grunted." That's why I joined the army. The army is not a fun job, it was just a means to get to America, and maybe a new life." He again went silent.

"You are right, I am weak. I managed to find enough money to buy a ticket to New York. But it was the cheapest I could afford; I and the others spent a lot of time locked below deck. On arrival in New York, I managed to get a job. It was hard work, but I had to earn money somehow." I looked at him with disdain.

"I would rather die than spy on my friends." I spat at him.

"That wasn't the problem at that time. You see I have another couple of weaknesses. Drinking and gambling. Every night I would go to a tavern, get drunk then lose all my money."

I stared at him for a moment.

"Don't tell me. You got into debt big time."

He nodded.

"You got it Dafydd. And they were willing to take the debt in my blood if necessary."

For a second I felt sorry for him, but there were lots of people in that situation, they didn't all become spies.

"One night, they were really applying pressure for their money. When a man asked if he could sit next to me, he ordered my debtors away, and bought me a beer and a meal."

Oh no, I thought, is my brother really this stupid?

"He seemed to know more about me than a normal stranger. We chatted and became friends, he then offered to pay my debt off. He then laid out his plan for him to be able to pay my debt off. Somehow he knew that I was your brother. He just wanted me to manage the store, and let him know how you were getting on."

A swear word came to my mind but I do try not to swear.

"Did you not realise that he was asking you to spy on me?" Gareth went silent for a minute or two. "Of course I did. But I had no choice, and I wasn't being asked to do anything that might harm you."

So that was it. Deep in debt, he accepted an offer to spy on me, which he accepted as it would not be of any harm to me. This weak foolish brother of mine had not taken into consideration others who may be affected.

The following morning, we had an early visit from our captain. Captain Simon Blake, to be exact.

"Good morning, have you brought our breakfast?" I asked.

He laughed.

"I am glad to see you are in a good mood today. You have a long journey ahead of us, followed by a trial for treason." Then he raised his finger. "Sorry I forgot. followed by the execution of you and your brother." He then raised his finger again. "You will of course be joined by the shop girl Jen, and this Katie, if I can find them."

When he mentioned Katie, he had made it personal. If anyone threatens my Katie, they also threaten me and The Dragon. He would regret this before the day is over.

At 10am, we both had our hands tied behind our backs, then we were pushed out of the door. Our captain was seated on a horse just in front of us.

"Captain, when you were our guest, we gave you tea and a biscuit. We still haven't had any breakfast." He moved his horse closer to me, then he kicked me. I fell backwards and hit my head on the floor. Again, The Dragon inside me began to stir.

We were to ride at the back, so that we would have to face all the dust on the journey. I began to count how many soldiers he was bringing with him.

I eventually lost count, there were over 2000 soldiers. He clearly wasn't going to our hospital for tea.

We arrived at our hospital near Valley Forge late in the day.

Captain Blake had ordered his troops to surround the whole hospital compound. Waiting for him was Katie, Jen, Val and Lana.

"Good evening, Jen, I have missed you." Said the Captain. "Please tell me which of you is the fabled Eagle?" She had no reason to avoid telling him. I was praying that Katie had sent the Rangers away. I did not want any fighting, especially against so many British troops.

"My name is Katie; I am sometimes known as The Eagle. Could you please tell me why my husband is tied up?" He turned to face me.

"I am afraid that your husband has committed treason. After we have had tea. I will be conducting trials. It is likely that your husband will be found guilty and be sentenced to death." Val and Lana held her back. "Don't worry, I think that you will be found guilty of some crime and die with him."

He dismounted, then turned to one of his men and gave orders for Katie and the others to be arrested. They all had their hands tied behind their backs, the same as my brother and I. We were all lined up in a row.

I, for one, believed that this was my last day on earth. I was next to Katie, I had a lot to say to her, but these were difficult times.

Eventually, the firing squad was selected. They also stood in a row. There was a little banter around blindfolds.

"Katie, we can't die like this. Both The Dragon and The Eagle have been waiting for this moment."

She shook her head.

"Not yet, wait for a few more minutes."

"Do you have a chair, Dafydd." It was the adjutant. Perhaps his leader, Major General Phillip Morrison, was well enough to attend this barbeque. I sniggered.

I could not understand why he was asking someone with their hands tied together. Then the reason was made visible. Major General Philip Morrison, accompanied by Mad Anthony, arrived. Chairs had been hastily produced. The Major did not look fully recovered just yet. He whispered to the adjutant.

Captain Blake looked nervous, his face had become pale. The adjutant took charge of the proceedings.

"You, Sergeant." he pointed to Captain Blake. He looked around before realising that the adjutant was speaking to him.

"I am a Captain Sir." Was his response.

"When you return to your Barracks, you will find orders. You have been demoted as of today, and sent to serve in India."

Lying on the ground was very uncomfortable. But I did feel a little better watching this.

"Sergeant! Pick these two men up. Free them from their ropes, then bring them to their seats beside me, and bring them tea and biscuits."

Now I was laughing so hard, I was having difficulties breathing.

"Now!" Shouted the adjutant.

Sitting beside Katie and the gang was something I thought would never happen again. The adjutant continued.

"Today we are in the presence of Major General Phillip Morrison. Who will be representing the Crown at this meeting. Beside him is an American officer who, after having spoken with George Washington, will represent the Continental Army."

He then produced another officer. General Brownlow. He had already been given instruction as to what his orders were. He took control of the two thousand soldiers. Most of them he ordered to return to New York. The rest were given jobs around the hospital.

"Shall we move inside? Suggested the Adjutant. We were directed to the main dining room, which had been cleared of everyone and everything, except for a very large dinner, which had been prepared for us. I think some people call this a business lunch. Major General Morrison took the floor.

"Firstly, I want to thank you and your team for saving my life. I truly thought that I was breathing my last breath. What you and your Rangers have built here is nothing less than amazing. I also thank you for opening your hearts and thinking about the lives of your enemy. Those people who not so long ago were trying to kill you." I tried to put in but was told to be quiet. "As I have informed the organisers of this complex. If this hospital continues with Katie's Rangers based here, one day, like today, the war may be brought to your doorstep. Katie's Rangers must be kept separate from the hospital."

Katie and I were both looking at the floor now.

"The British and the American governments have agreed to manage this complex together. This is what I believe was the real objective when the hospital was planned."

We were both nodding now. This time I insisted on speaking.

"Sir, the Rangers have already left. We will join them in a few days, and find a new place as our headquarters." Katie then joined in. "Sirs, you are correct, we took the hospital as far as we could, we needed governments to take it to the next stage. This day is the answer to our dreams. Thank you all."

Major General Morrison quickly stood up again.

"No, it is us and the thousands of soldiers who have recovered from injuries, who thank you." Now that was a bit of a tear jerker. Time to move on.

"Sirs, I thank you for accepting our dream and promising to continue our work. We now need to find a new place for a lot of homeless Rangers. We would like to bid you all tonight. We hope to disappear from here early tomorrow morning. We wish you all the best. And good night."

Us remaining Rangers disappeared to the sound of applause. We all gathered for the last time in our bedroom.

"Jen, will you come with us and help us form a spy agency?" She nodded. "Val, will you also come with us and take control of the administration for our new home?" Again, we received a yes.

I looked at Nick and his brother John. I did not need to ask a question. They nodded, without a question. Katie then looked at Lana, and winked. Something was going on there.

"Ok, let's get to bed. We have to leave early tomorrow". Lana raised her arm. I was now really tired as I had little sleep the night before tied up in the store.

"Have you forgotten Thunder Cloud and the rest?"

We agreed that we would go to their village as soon as we knew where we were going, to inform them.

They all started filing out of the room. Time for bed. I began to start undressing. Katie pushed me.

"What? Katie I am very tired." I then realised that she was staring at something. I turned around, it was my brother. I had forgotten him. What a nightmare, I wonder if Katie still wanted to kill him.

"Gareth, please leave our room, go and find somewhere to sleep. We will have a chat in the Morning."

Katie wanted to deal with this now. I was having problems standing. I finally opened the door and told him to disappear until the morning.

"Katie, I am very tired, please let us get to bed."

She looked at me and took pity.

"Ok my love, tomorrow is another day."

CHAPTER 18

A PLACE TO CALL HOME

I woke up nice and early, or so I thought. Standing beside the bed fully dressed was my dear wife. I was feeling refreshed and at peace with the world. Going by the look on Katie's face, either she did not sleep much, or had something else on her mind. Then it came to me. My brother. I sat on the side of the bed with my head in my hands. I looked into her eyes pleading for some peace.

"Dafydd, we need to get the future of your brother sorted soon. Ok I have gone off the idea of killing him. but he needs to be dealt with."

I looked at her with my best puppy dog eyes.

"Ok, when we find a place to stay tonight. We will form a court where his future will be discussed." I gave a weak smile, and got out of bed. I had a feeling that this could be another long day.

We were on our way at 9am. I had given instructions for them to follow the road to Philadelphia. The British had been driven out. Now the city was filled with Patriots.

"Dafydd, shall we send in a group to select possible sites for us to build our new headquarters?" She was smiling again. Maybe she had forgotten my brother.

"That's a brilliant idea, but how many shall we send? We are on our way to a big city. Shall we first think about what kind of place we want to build our new home in?"

This got us all thinking. There were the mountains in the north. We could build beside the Delaware river? Or my personal favourite. Why not build our headquarters on one of the islands in the river? We could set up cannons on the island, in case of attack. Also, if we had boats there, and we needed to escape, the river would be a great escape route.

Suggestions were cautiously thrown about, until we finally caught up with the others. To my delight, it seemed that the island was the favourite.

"And what do we do for money? Islands are seldom free." Val added.

"Follow me. I saved a few trinkets from the hospital funds. After all, it is now funded by two governments." To which we all agreed. Katie had brought six trunks of goodies with us, of course.

I am talking about the trinkets and money which we had taken from the dead on the battlefield. This may seem a bit gruesome, but we used this to help others who are injured. The first thing would have to be, finding a broker. The last visit we made to the city, I passed a couple of them and made a note of their addresses.

Katie agreed that we should go ahead and try to make an exchange, as we couldn't purchase anything without money. We asked Val, Jen and Lana to go with us. Then Andy asked to join.

"Andy, you are a mountain man, I am not sure negotiating a deal is quite up your street." I said.

He looked at me and grinned.

"Dafydd, have you ever tried to do a deal with the Indians? You would be on your own, surrounded by many excited women and warriors. Many have their knives and tomahawks near them. To make a good deal and get away with your scalp intact requires skill." I understood what Andy was saying.

"Ok Andy, you are with us."

My brother's name came up, but Katie vetoed it quickly.

The following morning, six of us left with a few samples. We visited the nearest place. I suggested that Andy should be our lead person. I wanted to see how he did. We all stood back as he approached the man.

He had the face of a weasel. There were about ten rough looking men loitering about. They all carried knives and pistols. When the girls produced our samples, their expressions changed.

The dealer stood for a while turning our samples over.

"Well, I hope you are not under the opinion that these trinkets have a lot of value." Said The Weasel. "To be honest, I have enough of these types of things." He then looked up. His eyes shot around the room hoping that we had a dejected look.

Andy knew a bit about their value, as well as haggling.

"As you look like you have come a long way, and I hope to gain your loyalty for future trades, I will offer you a bit more than their value." Andy was now smiling. Not at the offer of a better deal, but it was the patter of the weasel. "You have brought 20 items, some could be gold, others who knows. $40 Dollars is my best offer."

Andy laughed. He produced his knife and stuck it into the table. Those who had been observing, moved for their weapons.

"Let me make the offer." Andy suggested. "For these 20 items, all solid gold, we will accept $30 each." He then began to remove them.

"Don't be so hasty, let me think again about my offer. His hand slipped below the table. Andy grabbed hold of his knife. As The Weasel's pistol came into view, Andy's knife sliced through the air and pinned his hand to the table. The Weasel screamed. Katie and I were ready for the rest of the gang, we gently pushed the others aside. We nodded to each other. Hands clenching tightly, we increased concentration and soon felt the adrenaline rising. They had made the mistake of provoking The Dragon and The Eagle. In minutes they were all asleep. We had a couple of cuts each, but we were still alive.

Now back to our friend, The Weasel. Andy picked up our samples.

"I think we will take or trade elsewhere." Andy said. We left with Katies final words.

"Let us know if you still want to trade with us."

He lifted his eyes towards her, his hand was still pinned to his desk.

"I don't think so," he said through clenched teeth.

"Does anyone know where the woman dealer lives?" Asked Katie.

I sat on the other side of the tavern. We had come for a drink before moving on.

"Come on, someone must have her address." She shouted again.

Then her eyes caught me, sitting with a beer in one hand and a massive grin on my face. My Katie is a very loving woman, but if she thinks that someone might be ignoring her, or playing games, she has a slight temper.

I knew what was coming as soon as she looked at me. She was well aware that I had the woman's address, by the look on my face. That's how close we are. I ducked quickly as a tankard of beer smashed against the wall behind me. I leapt off my chair and rushed to her, hugging her close, and apologising. We kissed to some wolf whistles.

"Ok, I know where she lives. It's about a couple of miles away. Shall I lead the way?" She slapped my back and told me to get moving. She always makes me laugh.

"Let me do the bargaining this time?" Asked Jen. I agreed, maybe it should be a woman-to-woman thing.

As before, there were ten men hanging about, but these were dressed in suits. More business-like, but I expected that they were still good at fighting.

Jen spread our samples across the table. The woman was, I would say, in her late 40s. Her name was Lady Jane. I was not sure if she was indeed a lady, but that was what she wanted to be called, so who was I to argue. She examined all our samples.

"I expect that you have visited my rival, across the city."

How did she know that? I thought. She then answered my question.

"Two of you are carrying cuts on their arms, they can't have gotten those through tripping over." I was beginning to like this woman. "I'll cut to the chase. I know that you are members of Katie's Rangers. I also know where these have come from." Katie could see that she was no ordinary woman. Katie decided to join the exchange.

"You are correct, we are part of Katies Rangers and I am Katie." The two women shook hands.

"Let me tell you a story," Lady Jane began. "My husband owned a gun shop. We ran it with the help of our children. One day the British invaded the city. Some drunken soldiers visited our shop. Seeing all the guns and ammunition, they decided to help themselves. My husband tried to stop them." She took a deep breath. "He was brutally killed. Then the drunken soldiers abused me and my teenage daughters. One of them has never spoken since that day. My younger daughter suffers from depression.

Some people say that we can't blame all the British for the crimes of a few. We went to the commanding officer, a man named Captain Blake. He had those responsible brought to him. We recognised them all including the one who killed my husband. We waited to hear their punishment." She went silent for a moment.

"He asked them 'where were his guns, and was there any money.' Then he approached me, he put his hands on my face, telling his men that I was attractive. I kneed him in the groin and ran out of the room with my daughters as quickly as I could."

We all stood about, not knowing what to say. They must all be broken inside.

"We have met that man; he has been demoted and sent to India." Katie spoke softly.

Emotions were running high; it was not a time for loud noises. Lady Jane again began to speak.

"I want revenge against the British. They allowed people like that to ruin others lives in the name of war. I am going to make Katies Rangers an offer. They can accept it in full, or reject it in full. I will allow my men to make sure that you are all comfortable. I will wait for your answer in the morning. So you have time to mull it over. Is this acceptable?"

We had nowhere to go, so we accepted.

"We know that you are looking for new headquarters. I assume it will need to be a very large place with room for all your horses. One of your present problems is that you don't have any money to purchase any land or buildings. You have six chests of items like these."

She moved them around the table. "But you don't know where you can find a buyer for them. I also know about your hospital. My husband was injured during the Battle of Bennington. His life was saved in one of those hospital tents. I want to make a deal with you." This sounded like a request, but came over more like an order. "The British stole our guns and some money, but our main fortune is buried in a safe in our back garden. We also own property. Before I make you an offer. There are things I want guaranteed. First, give me all your trinkets, I will find a buyer for them and get you a good price. I can do this regularly if you wish. My daughters and I will work with your Rangers - there is one man we want. The former Captain Blake. If you can agree to our terms, then I will tell you what we can offer."

I looked at Katie, we had no problems with this.

"First, I own an Island in the Delaware River. It is large and never floods. This would be an ideal place to build your headquarters. If you are willing to leave this to my daughters and I, we will have it constructed and we will finance the work. We will make sure a hospital will be included during the building, you never know if Rangers may return with injuries, and I understand that you have some doctors and nurses with you." We were both speechless. This would have been more than enough for us, but she continued.

"We also own various pieces of property around the city. Some of these can be used if necessary."

We were just listening in amazement.

"Is this of any interest to you both?"

I stood up. "I am lost for words to describe how amazed I am with your offer. Thank you."

"Please take your time to mull it over tonight and give me your answer in the morning." She got up and left us to discuss.

I was wandering around the house, when I saw a young woman leave the house. I don't know why, but I followed her. Yes, I did believe she was one of the daughters. She was wandering aimlessly. Then she found a seat. I was lying against a nearby tree. Then what I had feared happened. Six drunk men, with two women egging them on, approached the young woman. Two sat on either side of her and began to talk with her. One put his arm around her. She pushed it off and stood up. I could feel The Dragon rising. The other one got up and put his arms around her, trying to give her a kiss, but she was trying to fight him off.

I walked forward.

"Leave the woman alone." I ordered. Both of the men attacked me.

A punch to the stomach of the one on the left, followed by a hook to the other one's chin. I caught the third man's arm as he attempted to put it around my neck. I dropped to one knee and he flew over my shoulder, before receiving a knockout punch. The others got the message and ran away.

"Thank you," said the young woman. "I have been talking with your mother. I am sorry about what happened to you and your family. But I promise that you are all safe now. I hope that you will all find a brighter future, in all this blood and thunder." She gave a glimmer of a smile. "Would you marry me and take me to a better place?" I nearly collapsed.

"If I did, my wife would kill us both." I laughed. She was also laughing.

"I presume that Katie is your wife?" I nodded.

"She is and I love her very much."

"That was a nice answer my husband," Katie walked up to us, "and who is it that wants to fight me for you?"

The girl stepped back.

"Leave her alone. She has had enough horror in her life, she is one of Lady Jane's daughters. Look after her." I could see Jen, Lana and Val following Katie. "And you three can look after her as well."

I then returned to the house with Katie. We went to find Lady Jane.

"We don't need until the morning, we will gratefully accept your offer." Katie said excitedly.

Lady Jane gave a big grin. I needed a drink. I left Katie to sort things out, and went into the other room.

"Is anyone up for a drink? I am buying."

There was a rush towards the door. Lady Jane's two daughters were standing beside a wall. I looked at Jen and Val. Lana had already left.

"I thought I asked you two to look after these young ladies. Come on, bring them over." They went to where the girls were standing.

"What are your names?" asked Val.

"My name is Georgie. This is my younger sister, something bad happened to her, and she has lost her voice for the time being. Her name is Anne."

Val instantly felt sorry for the girl.

"My name is Val, this is Jen. We are all going to the tavern across the road for a drink and something to eat. Would you both like to go with us? Don't worry, you are safe with us." Georgie, spoke to her sister.

"Anne, we are going to the tavern across the road, we will be safe. These ladies will protect us." She then put her arm around her sister. She got a slight nod out of her. "Ok we are coming with you." Said Georgie.

When we arrived at the tavern, it was quite empty. Soon after we arrived, Katie and Lady Jane arrived. We were able to put some tables together, so all our group could sit together. I scanned the room. There was a group playing cards, a couple having a drink, and a tall young man with blond hair sitting on his own. He had three empty tankards on his table, and a full tankard of beer in his hand. It came to my mind that he was trying to drown his sorrows.

We put twelve chairs around the table, then ordered food and beers for all of us. Lady Jane's daughters did not drink beer. They had some fruit juice. Katie was sitting next to me.

"Darling, I almost forgot, I received orders last night. I was busy so I just put them away."

"Ok my love, are we off to the New York area again?" She shook her head." There are two villages on either side of the Mississippi river. They believe that the British will send Indians against them soon. It's a small village named St Louis." I shrugged my shoulders.

"That sounds like a French name?" She pulled a face. It's near Fort Carlos, yes that's Spanish, the powers above want us to go there and support the villagers, the problem is it is about a month's journey. We will have to leave tomorrow." I was speechless. First, because we have business here. Second, why should we have to travel so far to support a Spanish Fort?

"Katie, why don't you take 400 of your Rangers, and give those Indians a beating. As you know I love fighting, but I am willing to stay here with a hundred Rangers and all our supporters. We will try to build as much of our headquarters as possible for your return."

She was now staring at me as if I had a different agenda. Well, I did, winter was only six months away. I know we are in a city, but providing for 600 people would be extremely difficult. We needed our headquarters ready for Katie's return. She suddenly threw her arm around me, and gave me a hug, and a kiss.

"Thanks for being so understanding," she declared.

I must admit, I would miss her, being away from her for over two months would seem like a year. A large crowd of ruffians entered the tavern. They looked like they had already been drinking before they came here. They put the remaining tables together. Then began to enjoy their beers.

There was movement at our table. Lady Jane's daughters had left the table, and were walking towards the bar. I looked at Katie.

"I think that I had better keep an eye on them."

Katie nodded. Lana had also left the table and was following the girls. The bar was now a bit crowded. The blond-haired man seemed to have emptied his fourth tankard and was trying to get another beer. Two men were giving him a hard time. Then a third tried to pick his pocket. He suddenly sobered up. He turned and punched the one who was trying to rob him. One of the others hit him with a bottle. I stepped in and banged both their heads together.

"Here, your beer has arrived." I smiled. He nodded, then collected his drink. I could see a couple of the drunks trying to grab hold of the girls, they wanted to get them to dance. As soon as Anne was grabbed hold of, she screamed.

I pushed a couple of men out of my way as I tried to reach the girls. The blond man got there before me. He hit the one holding Anne. Lana held her as tears ran down her cheeks. The drunk's mates rose to support him. As the blonde punched another one, a man carrying a knife appeared behind him. Anne suddenly shouted.

"Behind you!"

The blonde began to react, but I threw my knife first. He wouldn't be drinking here anymore, in fact that was his last drink. Katie was now beside me. She had ordered everyone to leave the tavern, and to take the blonde lad with them. If he stayed, I didn't think he would be alive in the morning. We left quickly before we were surrounded. Everyone was waiting for us outside, it was still cold in the evenings. I was looking forward to the summer evenings.

"Well, what shall we do next?" I asked. Lady Jane smiled. I think she may have drunk a bit too much as well. "I have a nicer place not too far away. We can all spend the night there. Thank you all for protecting my daughter, and Mr," she was now talking to the blonde man, "I don't know why, but my Anne has finally found her voice, because of you."

We were about an hour's walk from this 'nicer place', but it was worth every step. What a place. This would have done me as our new headquarters. Katie and I were given our own room. I had only been acting drunk. That was always the best way of avoiding people speaking to you.

I was tired and dreaming of a nice bed. This one came all the way from dreamland. I had a quick shower then slid between those cool, fresh sheets. Katie shouted from the bathroom.

"I will be leaving early tomorrow"

I laid back on the bed. I thought I saw the bathroom door open, but no one came out. Then the candle went out. That was strange, as there wasn't any wind.

"Katie, are you coming to bed?"

Then I felt warm skin next to me. I smiled.

"I know it's late, but we will be apart for over two months. I turned towards the owner of the warm skin.

The following morning we were both late waking up.

I insisted that she had breakfast before she left. They had a very long journey, one which I kept saying did not belong to Katie's Rangers. They had to first return to the rest of the Rangers and the supporters, deliver the information, then begin a very long ride - about 900 miles.

As soon as I had some spare time, I would be making all efforts to track down the highest ranking officer in this city. Katie's Rangers would not be fighting battles that took a month to arrive at the battlefield.

The breakfast was very substantial. This was needed as they wouldn't know when they would get a good meal again.

I had made a list of who would go to St Louis, and who would stay and help put together our new home.

"Sir, I would like to join the Rangers. I am a good fighter and a crack shot." Asked the blonde man. I wasn't certain if I should say yes, without speaking with Katie, I was sure she would approve, but she would be down for breakfast soon anyway.

"If you want help deciding, just look at my daughter Anne, she has become a different girl." Chimed in Lady Lana.

Anne, the youngest, was 17, and Georgia, her sister, was 19.

Katie was soon at the table and had no problem with Mr Blonde joining the Rangers.

"What's your name?" I shouted across the table at him. I couldn't be calling him 'Mr Blonde' forever.

"It's Dan Richards."

"Ok Dan, you are now in the Rangers, but need to stay with us until fully trained." He raised his thumb, as a sign of acceptance.

Katie stood up.

"This is a list of those of us, who are off to see The Great River. The Mississippi:

Myself of course, Tom, Nick, Andy, Lana, Jean, Mark, plus Thundercloud. We will collect him on the way and inform the others where you are and where we are building our new headquarters.

Everyone else will stay here with Dafydd, their job is to get our new headquarters as near to ready, for when we return. I hope that the bedrooms will at least be completed, as we will all need to sleep for a week after our journey home."

Under my breath, I whispered. "You shouldn't be going in the first place."

CHAPTER 19

THE BATTLE OF ST LOUIS

Katies Rangers finally arrived after a month of travelling.

"I think I will walk in the future." Claimed Nick.

"My backside will never be the same again." shouted his brother.

"We are about two miles from the village, shall we walk the rest of the way?" Asked Katie. Thunder Cloud made signals for silence.

"There are Indians everywhere." He whispered.

"Stay here and don't make any noise." Ordered Andy. "I will take some of our other mountain men and we will scout about and see what we have run into."

Katie nodded, and off they crept. There were about twenty of them.

"We are so lucky that they joined our Rangers, they can move about so silently."

The remainder of them rested, had a few snacks and the last of their water.

About an hour later they returned with both information and a prisoner. Andy began to inform Katie of the situation.

"Katie, there are Indians everywhere. Chippewa, Menominee, Sac and Fox. The Sioux also have a large war party here, maybe 200 warriors. They are led by a few British officers. It seems they are attacking three targets. The village of St Louis and Fort Don Carlos, which is about 15 miles from the village - these are under the protection of our allies Spain. On the other side of the river, is the former

British Colonial outpost of Cahokia. This is occupied by Patriots from Virginia." Got it, this must be why we have been sent here - to support the Virginians." Shouted Katie, who quickly received a sign to be quiet.

I understand that the Lieutenant Governor of Spanish Louisiana led a local militia to fortify the town, as best as they could.

Fort Don Carlos has a force of only 197 men. It was believed that the combined British and Indian force of about a thousand, would overwhelm the fort.

Back in Philadelphia, progress was good. This island was amazing, and Lady Jane was a brilliant organiser.

I don't know why, but she had chosen my brother to help her. Katie and I had never had a chance to decide his fate.

They employed every builder and carpenter in the city. The island had been marked out. The big question was, did we build a wall around the island, or maybe a fence, or just leave it as it is?

Lady Jane made the final decision, as she often did. I had given her a list of our requirements, then she took them away and produced a plan. When Katie left, we were thinking of building one large building as our headquarters, as we had done in the past, like at the school and the church. I grinned as I thought about this. We were still thinking as if there were still just 80 Rangers, not the 500 we currently had. Lady Jane, or rather Jane which she had now asked us to call her. Drew up a plan where there were many, different buildings spread across our island. A hospital, sleeping quarters for the single men, and the same for the single women. Even an office for the newly created intelligence unit, led by Jen. On her plan there was an eight-foot wall surrounding the island, with cannon to protect us.

She had managed to sell all our trinkets at a good price, but when that money was used up, she began to use her own money.

Katie had been away for over a month and I was missing her and concerned that she was ok. I promised myself that this would never happen again.

The captive warrior refused to provide the Rangers with any information. When he saw Thunder Cloud approaching with a very sharp knife, he suddenly opened up, telling us everything that he knew.

Their plan was to launch an attack simultaneously attacking the village, fort and the outpost across the river.

"What is the date, Katie?"Asked Andy.

She wondered why he needed to know that.

"It's the 25th of May." She replied.

"I just saw a large group of Indians cross the river; I think that they are about to attack our people in Cahokia."

Katie had to think quickly.

"Andy, you and Thunder Cloud, take 200 Rangers across the river now. Find places to enable your men to fire at the attackers, without them being seen. And avoid face to face fighting. I want to avoid any casualties." Andy nodded then went off to find Thunder Cloud.

"That leaves the village and the Fort to protect." Whispered Katie.

At about 1pm, Katie heard a shot ring out from the direction of the village.

"That must be the warning that the village is under attack. Lana, go with Nick and his brother, with half our remaining Rangers. Let's see how many of the attackers you can remove before they reach the village."

Lana saluted, then ran off, shouting "at last some fighting to do."

"I love that woman's attitude," grinned Katie. Katie looked around her. "Just the fort to support now. Jean, Mark, alert the rest of the Rangers, we need to get to the fort as soon as possible. I expect they are under attack already."

Lana and the Rangers had found a good place to conceal themselves. With a good view of what was happening, and an effective place to shoot the attackers. What they saw next, made her throw up.

The Indians had captured a few people who had been working in the fields. They wanted to draw the villagers out from the safety of their homes. They decided to brutally kill their captives in full view of the village. Naturally the villagers wanted to charge out and avenge those poor people. But they refused to leave the village. The Wapasha and the Sioux, persisted in attacking the village for several hours.

In an attempt to draw the Spanish defenders out. Katie's Rangers shot many attackers, in order to reduce the number attacking the village. When the Indians finally withdrew, the village of 700 people had lost between 50-100 residents, who had either been killed, wounded, or captured.

Over at the fort, when Katie arrived, the attack was already under way. She bedded her Rangers in and they began to fire at any attacker which came within range. Unlike the other two fighting zones, when they began shooting, some of the attackers noticed where the shots were coming from. There was a halt in the attack on the fort and at least two hundred warriors made a violent attack on the Rangers. Katie's Rangers shot many warriors before they came to the face-to-face fighting.

Katie could see some of her Rangers falling before the attackers' knives and tomahawks. It was time for the Eagle to fly.

Many of the attackers thought that the only eagles flew in the sky overhead. They soon found out that this Eagle fought with her feet on the ground. Soon the warriors were retreating, and returning to their attack on the fort.

Katie began to cry; this was something that few people had ever seen. Katie was The Eagle, strong and fierce. Few had seen her soft side. Looking at her wounded Rangers dug straight into her heart. Out of the hundred she had with her, thirty were injured, and by far the worst news, two were dead.

The fighting had stopped as quickly as it had started. Katie managed to pull herself together enough to give command to Andy, with the orders to get everyone ready to return home in the morning. He was about to have the dead buried. Katie heard his command and flew into a rage.

"Our dead are coming home with us" She shouted.

Over two months had gone by since Katie had left. I was standing at the edge of the Delaware River, looking at something truly amazing. Our new headquarters was finished. There was also an eight-foot wall surrounding the complex. I was thinking how I wished that Katie was with me to share this.

Suddenly I thought that I could hear a familiar sound. Then it came to me, it was the sound of hundreds of horses. Either we were about to be attacked, or could I say it? Katie was back!

My heart began to pound, as the first horse came into view. It was Katie, I would know her horse anywhere. Then the rest of the Rangers followed her.

What an amazing sight. Then I took a closer look. This was not the Rangers who left here two months ago, all bright eyed and ready to fight for a free America. These Rangers looked as if they had been to hell and back. Beside me were hundreds of people who had been waiting so long for their loved ones. They were all keyed up ready to rush into their arms. I suddenly rushed in front of them.

"Look! Take a good look at your loved ones. Look into their eyes, they have been to a bad place. They will need you to be aware of this, to show your love, with care and gentleness. At present they probably won't be able to see the beauty of their new home. Surround them with your love, until the brightness returns to their eyes." I then stepped back, allowing them to get a closer look at their loved ones.

Katie rode her horse up to about three feet from me. She dismounted and ran into my arms. Then she dissolved into tears. There was nothing I could say, we stood in silence hugging each other for maybe thirty minutes. I could feel her heart beating inside her chest. What horrors had the love of my life been through?

Over her shoulder I could see similar scenes everywhere. Andy was holding Lana so close, he might crush her. I had deserted her, when she left for war. I would never leave her again. At that moment I promised to spend the rest of my life shielding her from whatever horror had taken the light from my darling's eyes.

Then it all became apparent. A long line of injured Rangers. Well, we always get injuries in battles. I thought to myself. But the worst was to follow.

Two coffins came into view.

"No!" I shouted. "I know that death often follows a battle, but not to us, not to our Rangers." So, this is what has taken the sparkle from Katie's eyes. I had to take charge, I had to be strong.

I called for some of the ladies to take Katie. Then I shouted orders for the pontoon bridge to be set up. Currently it was in sections alongside the island.

"We need to get the injured into the hospital. Immediately!" I turned to the ladies looking after Katie." Take her to the hospital as well. She needs a rest and I want her checked over."

By now Jane, Jen and Val had joined me. They were taking charge. What a great team. Then it came to me. What do I do with the dead?

"Andy, what are the names of our dead?" Andy checked a piece of paper he was holding. Bill Pritchel and Fred Archer. They both have young families. They were part of Katies first Rangers." I looked at the crowd behind me. Many families were waiting to hear the names of the dead. Many were frantically trying to find their loved ones, praying it was not them. I called Jane over.

"Katie and I have talked about how to look after the families if any Ranger was killed. But we never finalised an answer."

"Husbands are the provider for their families. On their death, families will struggle financially." Val said. "If we provide some form of a pension for them, plus the knowledge that they can call upon us in times of trouble, they will thank us."

"But how are we going to pay their pensions?"

Jane pointed to a large building within our complex.

"Take the families to my office, and I will sort it out." I was so relieved. But I still had to speak with the families. I felt a tap on my shoulder. Now what? I thought.

"Do you need any help?" It was Katie. I was so relieved. "Are you ok, my love?" She smiled softly.

"Do you know what? When you held me in your arms, I genuinely felt your power flowing into me. The Eagle is back. Would you like me to speak with the families? After all, they were two of my first Rangers."

227

While I was still trying to take all that she had said into my mind, she was gone. I could see Lana sitting on some grass, looking kind of lost. I thought I had better have a chat with her.

"You are looking a bit lost." I confessed. She looked at me.

"Every night, I have the same nightmare. I see these helpless men and women, being brutally killed by the Indians. I wake up screaming."

"When I was born, my mother died giving birth to me. As I grew up, I blamed myself for her death. Some years later, my father, who was a local Vicar, was working late in his church, when some son of Satan set fire to the church. I arrived when the fire was not at its peak. I wanted to run in and carry my father out. The firefighters stopped me. They told me that it would not be safe for me if I went into the church. I stood and watched the church burn. I was a coward; I am still sure that I could have saved him. Most nights I dream of my father looking out of a window calling me to save him. I will never be able to convince myself that I could not have reached him. I think I will live with that for the rest of my life." I tried to distance myself from the pain of it.

"But Lana, there are too many broken hearts in the world. We have to do our best to mend as many as we can. So, remember, it was not your fault that those people died. But you can help others who are still in need."

I took hold of her hands and pulled her up, then I whispered in her ear.

"I think Andy really loves you." I winked at her then went to Jane's office. I crossed the pontoon. Soon I found her smart office. She was sitting at her desk, my brother was sitting in a chair opposite to her.

"Dafydd, can you give my daughters a job?" I nodded. I seem to be nodding a lot of late.

"Have you got a job in mind?"

I am not sure why I asked, I knew that she had a job in mind.

"I think that here we will all need some fun times, especially over the next couple of weeks. I think that my girls should be in charge of the entertainment office." She looked at me with a smile on her face.

"And where will their office be?" I asked, knowing she already had it planned. She pointed to a door leading from her office, which amazingly opened as she pointed. There seated behind a desk was Anne and Georgia.

"I presume they have something organised?" now the girls entered the conversation.

"Four hundred Rangers have just returned from war. Let's have a housewarming party, to help them forget the horrors!"

What else could I say but yes. It was a brilliant Idea. I was beginning to think that I was not needed. A thought came to me. I need to visit our wounded. Yes, the hospital. This would be my first visit. It said 'clean and hygienic', as soon as I entered the door. The wounded could not say enough good things about it. There were 28 men and 3 women. The women were separated from the men by a thick curtain.

One of the men told me that it was almost a good thing to be injured. They could get some rest and good food, he joked.

"Are you feeling better Lana?" Asked Andy.

"Yes, I had a chat with Dafydd, he told me that there are too many broken hearts in the world." Andy laughed.

"That sounds like what he would say."

"Andy, Will you marry me?" Andy was a bit shocked but as he had been trying to find a time to ask her anyway. He said yes. They told Mark and Thunder Cloud and they both proposed to Jean and White Eagle.

"All we have got to do now is catch up with Dafydd." They all said together.

Finally, I caught up with Katie. She was a bit low when she returned, but she soon recovered.

"Katie, I have a big problem, and I intend to sort it out tonight." She could tell by my tone of voice that I was very serious.

"What's wrong, my love?" She asked.

"Katie, we are based in the New York area, we have fought most of our battles in this area. There is no way that we should have to fight a month's ride away."

Before she went to St Louis, she had no problems with the journey. But having done the journey and fought the Indians. She now agreed with me.

"Tonight, I am going looking for the commander. I intend to ensure that it will never happen again."

Katie looked into my eyes.

"You look so sexy, when you act like that."

I couldn't hold back a smile at that point.

"Come on, let's find out where he is."

We searched a few places, then we heard about an officer's ball. Well, we were both officers.

"My lady Brooks, would you kindly attend the ball with me?"

She looked at me, then shook her head and said "no thanks."

Lucky for her she is a fast runner, I eventually caught her, but I had cooled off by then.

"Ok, I'll go with you." She was still grinning.

We found the venue of the ball quite easily. But how could we arrange a chat with him? That's simple, we just walk in.

When maybe twenty guns are pointing at you, you have to think that maybe you have made a small mistake.

"May we introduce ourselves? We are The Dragon and The Eagle. Or Dafydd and Katie of Katie's Rangers. We have come here to have a bit of a chat with the commander of the army here in Philadelphia.

"Good evening, I have heard a lot about you two. My Name is Major General Robert Ferguson."

He raised his hand to signal all his soldiers to continue with the dancing.

"We are a bit busy now, how about we meet tomorrow morning?" That did make sense to us, so we accepted his offer and left them to their dancing. I suddenly realised how tired I was.

"Katie, can we go home to bed now, please?"

Katie had been home since early afternoon, but this was the first look at our rooms. She was impressed.

Of course, there was the bedroom, which contained a massive bed. Then it continued into another three rooms, equally as large

- one of the rooms was our office. I walked as far as our bed, then collapsed across it. It was so soft and even smelt good. Katie had managed a couple hours of sleep earlier. She had just a bit more energy left than I had. She undressed me and somehow managed to get me under the sheets, then she undressed herself and slid under our newly pressed sheets. From then after the only sound was the occasional snore.

"Dafydd, Katie, wake up!" It was Val and Jen. We had forgotten to lock our bedroom door.

"It's 1pm!" Shouted Jen.

I managed to open my eyes, but I was still half asleep.

"Who are you?" I asked.

Jen had a lot less patience than Val.

"I am the woman, who is about to push the two of you out of this bed." She replied.

I only provoked her by throwing doubt on her ability to carry her threat.

"Give me a hand Val," said Jen.

I was nearest the door, and an easy target for two angry women. Being still half asleep, I was unable to put up much of a fight. Well, the good news from my point of view, was that on leaving my bed, I finished lying on my front, protecting most of my modesty.

Lana had heard all the noise and had joined in what she felt was fun and had dragged Katie out of her side of our bed.

I pulled a pillow towards my head and began to fall asleep again. It was only the sound of women's laughter that finally woke me up. I swiftly grabbed the nearest sheets and covered my modesty. With the greatest effort, I managed to get myself back on the bed.

Finally, I wondered where Katie was. This question was answered when a topless woman popped up from the other side of the bed.

"Good morning husband." This figure said.

Finally, the three women managed to bring us into reality. They were still giggling as they left the room.

"Katie, hadn't we arranged to meet the Major General at 3pm today?" As I spoke, I looked into her eyes.

We both leapt up and ran towards the bathroom. It was a draw so we shared the shower.

We had two hours to shower, dress, eat breakfast, or rather lunch. Then get into the city and meet up with the top man. Well, we were both awake now, and we were about to vacate the building at 2.30pm. Lady Jane stopped us on our way out.

"Can I accompany you both? I may be of some use during the meeting."

I just grabbed her hand and the three of us began to run towards where we were due to meet the top man in the city.

Despite our late start this morning, we had made the meeting on time. We were all standing outside of the garrison at 3pm exactly. One of the sentries escorted us to his office.

He offered us a chair, then asked if we would like tea. My father had always told me, if someone offers you something for free, then accept it. Two cups of tea and about four biscuits later, our meeting finally began.

I was the one who had demanded this meeting, therefore I had to be the one to begin the meeting.

I began to introduce Katie and myself, when he interrupted me, by telling me that he knew all about us. I then started to introduce Lady Jane.

"Jane, what are you doing hanging out with these two?" Apparently, they were old acquaintances. "Ok, enough of this chit chat, why do you want to see me, Colonel Rhees?"

With any battle, it is best to make the first attack, in this case he had struck first.

"Sir, you seem to be aware of Katie's Rangers. They have fought many battles in the name of a free America." I could see him nodding. "Most of our Battles have been fought within forty miles of New York, with an occasional trip to South Carolina." Again, he nodded. "Katie has just returned from a conflict, which was a month's journey each way. We had 30 Rangers injured, and two died. I want to inform you that Katie's Rangers will not ever make that journey again to fight a battle. We will fight for the freedom of our country, within a fifty-mile distance of New York. Bearing in mind that at present, New York is in the hands of the British."

He sipped his tea, then finally spoke.

"I agree with everything you have said, so why did you want to meet me?"

I continued the attack. "We have come here to clarify this." I felt that this was what I had come for, so stood up to leave.

"We have not finished yet." Jane was now taking control of the meeting. I sat down again. "Robert, we have known each other for some time. I have come with these young people to offer some exchanges on their behalf."

I stood up again "Allow me to properly introduce Jane. She is in command of basically everything in our complex, apart from things to do with the Rangers."

Robert Ferguson sat smiling.

"So, Jane, what deals do you want to discuss?" Her first exchange was that the Continental Army could send badly wounded soldiers to our hospital. In exchange for ammunition. We just sat and listened to the master at work; we were extremely lucky to have found this lady.

CHAPTER 20

BUT OUR COUNTRY ISN'T FREE YET

We returned back to our island in the early evening, all smiles. The governor had allocated an area for our work. The area between Philadelphia and New York - a stretch of 100 miles total, or a circle with a 50 mile radius.

He would take personal responsibility for Katie's Rangers. All our assignments would, in future, come from him. In exchange, we would take care of any of his soldiers who got injured. He would also supply us with weapons and ammunition. No more long journeys. We were so happy.

"Katie, first we need to organise some weddings. Our Rangers go into battle regularly, and they never know if they will return. Let them marry their loved ones and enjoy their lives. Can you arrange this?" I asked. "I also want to have a chat with Jen and her team. I need to know how much progress she has made with her spy network."

Katie was pleased to be involved in arranging the marriages. We had a small Church within our complex, and our own vicar.

I soon found Jen's office. She was in a meeting with her team.

"Sorry to barge in. I wanted to catch up with you and check how much progress you have made?"

She called her meeting to a close. They all seemed to know what was expected of them. She offered me a seat at the table, and had someone bring me a cup of tea. Knowing that I was British, I had a pot of milk and sugar to taste.

"By the way, Dafydd, I have a partner now to help me with my work." I was wondering who it was.

"Hello Dafydd." It was Val. "Would you like a biscuit?" She asked.

I played it cool, and pretended that nothing unprofessional had happened in the past. I produced a large scroll and rolled it out across the table.

"This is a map of the area designated to Katie's Rangers. Any conflict that happens in this area, we will be expected to respond to. So, when your Spy network is finally set up. This is the area to be covered. Are there any questions?"

Jen began to smile.

"I have a team of thirty agents being trained at this very moment. When their training is completed, they will be sent to various places where they will take up jobs in the community. Only my team and I will know who they are. Of course, any information will be delivered to you and Katie as soon as it is received."

I was amazed at how quick they had set things up.

"Both of you, I am truly amazed at how fast you have put things into action. Well done."

It was early October; the weather was beginning to turn cold.

"Good morning, vicar. How are you today?" The Vicar gave a huge smile. He was somewhat surprised that Katie was visiting him, as she seldom came to his services.

"Good to see you Katie, and why have you visited today. It's not Christmas yet!"

Katie knew why he was greeting her that way, she was well aware that this was her first visit to this new church.

"A lot of my Rangers are wanting to get married. We would like you to arrange a mass wedding. "

"Katie, it would be my pleasure to arrange this. Marriage is an important part of God's work. Please give me a date, and I will do my part." She was somewhat taken back with such a quick response.

"Ok I will get back to you. Thanks."

Then she rushed out of the church, wondering what she should do next.

I could see riders crossing our pontoon bridge. They looked like soldiers. As soon as they saw Katie they rode over to her and delivered a letter.

I smiled; I thought it was a long time since our last mission. After delivering the message they rode off back towards the city. Katie had noticed me watching what had transpired. She waved for me to come over to her.

"So where are we off to now?" I asked.

"Your request has been granted. We are off to New York, my love."

I began to calculate. That's about a hundred-mile journey. The horses travel at four miles an hour, allowing for breaks, that's a three-day journey. Well far better than a month.

"When are we leaving?" I asked, hoping it would be soon - most of the Rangers were beginning to get bored.

"I plan to depart the day after tomorrow, we will need that time to prepare." I put my arm around her.

"So Katie, my love, why are we being called?"

She did not seem to be in a rush to explain.

"An army of regulars; Indians and Loyalists are at present destroying homes and farm buildings in a place called 'Stone Arabia'. It's a village about a mile north of Fort Keyser, in Montgomery, New York. A force of Massachusetts Levies and New York Militia have been sent from Fort Paris. We are to join these and end the destruction."

As we departed from our new home. I felt my heart pulling me back. It was indeed hard to leave our new home, but our country wasn't free yet, we still had a lot of fighting to do to drive the British from our shores.

We arrived in the area on the 18th of October 1780. We had taken both Jen and Val with us. I felt the experience would help them.

Eventually we caught up with Brigadier General Robert Van Rensselaer on the 19th, it took us a day to find him.

Late in the day, we found the invading British supporters, they were on a farm owned by George G Klock.

"At last Katie, some fighting to do!" I shouted with excitement.

I could hear the shouting as the message was passed between the Rangers. At the given command we charged the enemy, the battle eventually ended when our forces outflanked the Loyalist forces on the flats of Dederick Failing's farm and George Klocks farm, near the eastern boundary of the village of Johnsonville. Katie gave orders to fall back. She could see that they were continuing briskly but they were now firing on one another. The general had to order his men to retreat to Fox's Mills.

During the heat of the battle two high ranking British officers and our old Friend, Joseph Brant, escaped on horseback to the south side of the river. Leaving their men to fend for themselves. Thunder Cloud had seen Brant riding away.

"Dafydd, this is our chance. Did you see him deserting his warriors?"

I nodded. Yes, I could see his back as his horse disappeared out of sight.

"Can you get all Katie's Rangers to gather here quickly? We have a great chance now to get him relieved of his role as chief of the Mohawks."

Katie and I agreed with Thunder Cloud. We informed our commander, and he approved of our action. With 500 Rangers on horseback behind us, we followed Thunder Cloud. I understood that he was riding directly to where the remaining Mohawks had been left when Brant deserted them.

We arrived just in time. They had been surrounded by New York Militia. I gave orders for the Militia to stop shooting. Thunder Cloud then rode towards his tribes' warriors. Closely followed by us,

Katie's Rangers. We were wearing our olive-green buckskins; they were well aware of who we were.

About a hundred yards from the warriors, Thunder Cloud dismounted, dropped all his weapons, and sat on the grass. We followed suit. We were now unarmed and waiting to see how his tribesmen would react.

One warrior stood up, he held his tomahawk in his hand and ran towards me. Why me? I thought. I sat and waited to see if I would live or die. This was a test, I was sure.

I stood up, removed my last two knives which I had hid on my person, then I took my shirt off. I was standing almost naked. Then to my total horror, a black bear came running out of the nearby woods towards me.

I had no time to mess about, I quickly raised my adrenaline. I side stepped the bear and even managed to grab its fur, then as it passed, I swung across and onto the animals back. I wished the animal no harm, she was just trying to find some food for her hungry cubs. The attacking warrior stopped in his tracks, seeing me riding a black bear. I had every Mohawk warrior staring in disbelief. It was funny hanging onto her back, but I was wondering how I was going to get off her.

Katie had seen her two cute cubs. They were peeping out of some bushes. Clearly, I had come too close to her cubs, she was offering her life to protect them. Katie quickly became The Eagle and joined her Dragon. She ran towards the cubs shouting, they panicked and ran off into the woods. The mother bear, seeing her cubs in danger, turned to the direction in which her babies had fled.

I had still not figured out how to get off my furry ride. Then a low hanging branch smashed into my chest. I virtually flew off her back, as she sprinted after her babies. As I crash landed, I think every Mohawk warrior was in fits of laughter, at my expense. Then one who had gone to attack me offered his hand, to help me get up.

I took his hand in the name of friendship. Then I realised that not only the Mohawks were watching my bear riding. I had forgotten the New York Militia.

Apparently, I became a legend that day. Of course, Katie too. You can't have a Dragon without an Eagle.

The Militia could see that Katie's Rangers were in control. So, they left. Apparently to report that the Mohawks may be changing sides. But I had a feeling that they would also be reporting something else.

We rode behind the Mohawks as they returned to their town. On arriving, we waited outside the town, as the next move was between Thunder Cloud and his people. Well, that was what I thought. They insisted on me being present.

Somehow, I don't think I will ever be forgotten by his people. Thinking back, you don't see many people riding a black bear.

Finally, after a brilliant speech from Thunder Cloud, the Mohawk nation decided to join us in our fight against the British. They asked me if I could guarantee their freedom and sole owner-ship of their lands. As I always try not to lie, I told them that no one could guarantee that. But I also told them that Europeans, in their millions, were coming to this land. They would consider every inch up for grabs.

"There is nothing that your people can do to prevent this from happening." One warrior declared, then threw a Tomahawk at me. It was only my Dragon's reflexes which prevented a nasty incident.

"I came from those lands, many of us are starving and are perse-cuted. We see this land as a land of opportunity. Maybe you will stop and kill the first few, but they will keep on coming."

"Does this mean that the Mohawk nation will become a people who have to beg from the white men?" Asked one of their chiefs.

I shook my head.

"Go west. You can build your own lands out there, you may have to fight the Sioux, the Blackfeet, Comanche, Pawnee, Shawnee and Apache. But there is great land to be won." I put my arm around Katie. "When this bloody war is finally over, we will be journeying west, as we want to carve a piece of this land out for ourselves."

At that point we stood back and walked away. What happened next was between Thunder Cloud and his people.

Thunder Cloud eventually returned to us. He had a massive smile on his face.

"My people have chosen a new chief. Although they will no longer fight alongside the British, they have rejected the offer to join with the Americans. Peace is their new objective. It seems that your promise of a new land in the west is now their dream as well as yours." He was now laughing.

We gave our goodbyes to the Brigadier General. Then began our journey home. The three days seemed to fly by. Maybe it was our desire to be back home that had filled our minds.

When we arrived at the river, it was already dark. It was late October and the sun set early now. Every night the pontoon bridge was removed to prevent any night attacks.

Those at the front fired a few shots to make the sentries aware of our return. Shots were fired in return, so that we knew that they were aware of our arrival. While the bridge was hastily being put together. I was able to catch up with Jen and Val.

"Well, did you gain anything from our trip?" I asked them. "Well, we did learn how to get off the back of a black bear, which will be helpful if we ever find ourselves in that situation." I had asked for that, and I got it.

"Seriously, we did learn a lot. We have a few agents ready to send to New York, very soon. We have also bought into your dream. We both want to join you in your new adventure. I can see us building a town, or maybe a city. I can see our office. Atkins and Green Detective Agency." Laughed Jen.

"Well, we may be unemployed, could you give us a job?" Katie asked.

Val then chipped in. "Well, we may be able to give you two a try, but you will have to start from the bottom. And if you do a good job sweeping the steps, who knows what will happen next." She grinned.

We told them that we would think about it. Then rode off to where the bridge was being set up.

"This has got me thinking, Katie." She looked at me and yawned.

"What are you thinking of?" I told her that I would tell her later, then began to cross the bridge. Visions of my nice soft bed were floating through my mind.

As soon as we had all crossed, the bridge was removed again. People came out and took our horses away to the stables. The head cook was waiting for us.

"We heard that you were back. There is a hot meal waiting for you all."

The thought of a hot meal made me smile.

"What have you made for us?" I asked.

"We made your favourite!" She said enthusiastically.

"My favourite?"

Was that fresh beef steaks, or a nice pie? I do like fish and chips; they always make me think of home back in the valleys.

"We have cooked bear steaks." She then began to laugh and ran off. I laughed as she scampered away.

"You know what Katie; I can imagine one day being captured by the British. They will begin to interrogate me. 'What is the best way to ride a bear?' That will be their first question. I am beginning to go off my meal." She put her arm around me.

"Don't worry, my love. As days pass, people will forget what happened. But seriously, I doubt if anyone else could ride a bear."

"Let's get dinner," I held her hand and we jogged off following the smell.

"I do think we are having fish and chips," she whispered.

We had a wonderful meal.

"Katie my love, let's get to bed. We need a good night's sleep. We can check out who wants to get married in the morning." I opened the door to our bedroom. Katie jumped onto the bed. I closed the door, then pushed the bolt across.

"I don't want any unexpected visitors waking us up in the morning."

I joined Katie on the bed as we laughed, remembering the last time we slept here.

When Katie woke in the morning, I was at my desk, designing some posters, advertising the opportunity to be officially married.

"They look good, would you like me to get them distributed?" Of course, I accepted her offer. "Darling, I haven't seen your brother for ages, have you any idea where he is?"

At the mention of him, I realised that I too hadn't seen him for ages.

"I thought you hated him?" I reminded her.

"Well, I did, but then I realised that I had been unfair. I have decided to give him another chance."

Those words made me so happy.

"Thanks love." I said, then kissed her. "To be honest, I also may have judged him wrongly."

I waved her goodbye and walked to the place I had seen him last. That was in Jane's office. It was early but her office was open. Sitting in her chair was Gareth.

"Hello brother, long time no see."

He stood up and offered me a chair.

"Would you like a cup of tea, Dafydd?"

He knew I could never refuse a cup of tea.

"Are there biscuits as well?" I laughed.

"For you, anything." He grinned. "And what brings you here, are you missing me?" he enquired.

"Believe it or not, yes I was." I sipped my tea; it was made to perfection. Tea, milk and sugar.

"Where is Jane? Are you working here now?" I asked. I had been observing him. This was not the man, who I had accused of being a traitor all those months ago, and who Katie wanted to kill.

"The first answer is that Jane is still in bed. Second, we are now sharing this office; I hope you approve." I remained silent and let him continue talking. "We have found ourselves compatible. We spend all our time together. Dafydd, I think that I am in love with her." He continued. "I know I am only 28 and she is 40. But when we are together, age doesn't make any difference. I know she has two grown up daughters, but we all get on so well together."

I stood up and put my arm around him. It was a long time ago, when I last did this.

"So, what is your problem? Just tell her that you love her. Maybe she is having the same thoughts as you. A bit older than you, been married before, et cetera. Jane is a wonderful woman. Just ask her! Remember, love conquers everything."

He was now looking at his younger brother.

"You have grown into a man, Dafydd, Mum and Dad would have been so proud of you. The way you have turned out."

I was now beginning to feel a bit embarrassed. And half wondering if he was going to ask about bear riding. Then I heard the door knob turning. In came Jane.

"Good morning Dafydd, I hear your trip went well." I must have looked a bit surprised, but I kept talking.

"Yep, The Mohawks are no longer fighting alongside the British. Anyway, we must chat longer another time."

As I backed off towards the door, I looked at my brother and mimed 'I love you'. Then turned and left.

"Jane, I have something to ask you."

"Of course, what do you want to ask Gareth?"

He was a bit nervous, and scratched his ear. Jane, I know that we haven't known each other that long, and that we are from different backgrounds. Also, there are many reasons why we should not get close, but... Jane, I love you."

Then before she could reply. He dropped onto his knees.

"Jane, will you marry me?"

Unknown to them, her daughters had entered the room. As my brother had made his request. The girls rushed in.

"Go on mum, marry him!" They shouted excitedly.

Jane just stood there, stunned. Gareth, stood up and held out his arms.

"I love you, Jane."

This was a moment of tenderness, which should only be shared between two people, not an audience. It did not matter, the two of them were locked in a world of their own.

"I will Gareth." Came her quiet reply, as she wrapped her arms around her would-be husband.

I had left, but my curiosity made me hang around by the door, waiting to see if he would seize the moment, or let it pass by.

As they embraced, I opened the door and grabbed hold of both the girls' hands.

"Let's get out of here. This is a moment for two hearts, not five. Come to think of it, we are soon to become relatives." I grinned.

They both stood thinking about something. Georgia spoke first.

"You will become our mum's brother-in-law." I nodded.

"Then we will be your nieces." Replied Anne. The girl who could not speak, had little problems with it now. That was a point, what had happened to Dan? I hadn't seen him for some time.

"Well nieces, who would like breakfast?" They both grinned.

"Ok uncle, you lead."

'Uncle,' I thought, 'I am part of a family again. That will make Katie an auntie. I can't wait to tell her.' I grinned.

I almost dragged the girls to where most of us eat together. There was Katie, she was waiting for me to arrive. I knew this as her knife was on the seat next to her. We arrived and slumped down on the seats next to Katie. We all sat staring at her. Then the girls on cue both said.

"Good morning, auntie." The three of us were in fits of laughter. While Katie was sitting straight faced. I thought that I had better explain things before she took things the wrong way.

"Katie, their mother has been proposed to, and she has accepted. You are now about to be an auntie. Auntie Katie!"

She sat somewhat bemused. Slowly working things out. Then it finally hit her.

"Your brother is going to marry Lady Jane?" Normally Katie is very sharp minded. Maybe it was too early for her.

"Come on Katie, let's get those posters up."

I said, standing up. The others continued their conversation.

"I haven't seen Dan in a while, I thought that he was a friend of yours Anne?"

She finished eating before making her reply.

"You are right, we were getting very close, but I hurt him." Now Georgia was very interested.

"A few of us thought that the two of you were in love, how did you hurt him?" She asked.

"I was a fool; I had forgotten men have their pride."

Georgia was all over her sister.

"Come on, tell me what happened?"

Tears were starting to flow down Anne's cheeks.

"We were talking about mum's title. How mum truly is a titled lady from Denmark. I stupidly came out with, 'mum will be looking for another titled man, or someone with money to marry me'. As soon as I spoke, I regretted it.

"You truly are a fool if you think that." It was Jane, she and Gareth had come to join us for breakfast. "In this new land, it's people like him who will win the hearts of women. Rich and titled men will not help you much when attacked by Indians, or gangs of thugs. Gareth, have you seen Dan anywhere?" Asked Jane.

He shook his head. "I know that he left with my brother on their last journey to New York. Maybe Dafydd has seen him?"

At that statement, Anne jumped up." I will be right back, as soon as I catch up with Dafydd. We had breakfast with him, not so long ago."

She finally tracked us down at the Chapel. We had delivered most of the posters and we were looking for the vicar to check on how many weddings he could take per day.

"Dafydd, have you seen Dan?" She asked.

"The last time we saw him was when we returned from New York."

Then a close friend of his caught my eye.

"Hey, how is lockjaw?" I asked. That was his nickname.

He indicated that he was ok, but that Dan was looking to earn money any way he could.

"Have you seen him of late?" I asked. Dafydd,

"He is looking for money anywhere he can. The problem is, he isn't just happy with what he earns. He spent a few days in the mountains, trapping beavers to sell their meat and pelts. He also gambles, there is a place in the city he goes to, but I hear it's dangerous."

"Can you show me where?"

Jane popped her head in.

"Can I come with you Dafydd? This concerns my future son-in-law." At that comment Anne's cheeks went bright red.

Now how could I refuse a request like that?

CHAPTER 21

NO ONE MESSES WITH A RANGER WHEN THERE IS A DRAGON AND AN EAGLE ABOUT

We all decided to dress up a bit, definitely no green buckskins. We gathered at 8pm. Me and Katie, Jane and her girls. And of course, no one could stop my brother following his soon to be wife.

We had decided to split up. Katie and I went as singles; Gareth also pretended to be a loaner; Jane went with her daughters, but only she would play.

Fifty Rangers were hanging about outside at various taverns and establishments nearby. We each had a whistle, which we would blow if we required assistance from our boys and girls.

When I say dress up. I don't mean posh frocks. I am talking about characters.

My brother was dressed as a common gambler. Jane, wow, she may be 40, but she looked very sexy in that red dress. Now Katie, well, you could say she was ready for action. No, she wasn't dressed as an Eagle. She was dressed as a gunfighter, with a pistol and a knife tucked into her belt. She caught sight of me and greeted me with a snigger. There was a teacher at my school who I really respected. He was very intelligent, fair and the kids could not mess around with him, as they often did with other teachers. His name was Mr Morgan. Yes, that was me; Mr Morgan, the teacher.

We were all given half a million dollars' worth of gold nuggets each. Jane only lent us the money, it all had to be returned one way or another, but any profit was ours to keep. We had established a couple of covert signals to use between ourselves.

I had been told by his friend that Dan was bringing a lot of money to the game tonight. His plan was to double it, then return to Anne and proudly tell her that maybe her mother would let him court her now.

I used to have a lot of spare time back in Wales, and I did spend a lot of time in places like this. All the tables were rigged, and when it came to Poker, if you wanted to take your winnings home with you, then you would need a lot of friends to help you. In Dan's case, he had brought none, so even if he was lucky enough to win. He would never get his winnings out of the door.

It was clear who the main man of the house was. He was wearing a white suit, with two of his men beside him. Also on the balcony, stood a man with a gun.

Jane sat near to the boss man; her plan was to put him off. Katie sat directly opposite him. I hadn't seen where my brother had gone.

Clockwise, I chose a chair two places before the man in the white suit. I was not clear as to what the rules were regarding stakes. Some places you can only play for table stakes. This didn't appear to be the case here. I understood, by asking the man next to me, that it was dollars only. Gold would need to be changed into dollars before the game started.

The game had been going for an hour or two already, I was not sure why Dan was trying to double his money by playing cards. He had already lost quite a bit. Then I saw Gareth, he wasn't playing. He had found a table and was drinking. At the same time keeping watch over the game. On seeing me, he signalled that the game was bent. My response was to point to the man with the gun on the balcony.

I was betting low, and dropping out quickly if my hand was bad. Gradually players went broke and they dropped out. Katie was losing and decided to leave the table. She joined my brother at his table. We were now down to five people at the table. Jane, me, the man in the white suit, another man with brown hair and glasses and the dealer.

Suddenly, the man with glasses sprung to his feet, calling the dealer a cheat. Then he made the mistake of making a move for his pistol. Both of the men sitting on either side of the boss man, already had their pistols on the table. It took them little time to grab them and shoot him. In no time at all, four men who had been drinking at the bar, picked up the body and carried it out the back door. A couple minutes later, two soldiers burst in and enquired about the gunfire.

The bartender explained that the boys had been messing about and their pistols had gone off by mistake. The soldiers apologised then left.

Now we were down to the four of us. Finally, I got the hand I had been waiting for. I was dealt two cards, the ace and king of spades. I indicated that Jane should drop out, which she did. I placed a high starting bid. Dan finally dropped out. Just me and the man in the white suit.

The dealer turned over the first card. It was the queen of spades. He turned over the rest of them. A seven of hearts and a two of diamonds. I raised the stakes. The man in the white suit raised the stakes again. Next came the jack of spades. I let a big grin fill my face. All I needed was the 10 and I'd have the best hand in the game. I pushed all my money into the middle.

"All in!" I shouted.

The man in white did not have enough money to cover the bet. Finally, he offered the bar. I accepted his bet and he put in the deeds.

The dealer turned over the final card. It was a ten. But of hearts.

"My money," grinned the man.

"I don't think so." I warned.

I turned to the dealer. My pistol was now in my hand.

"I will have my card please. The one on top. Not off the bottom of the pack."

Katie blew her whistle. Many people were looking around, wondering where the sound of a whistle had come from.

The dealer was under pressure from my pistol pointing at him. He dealt the card that should have appeared: the ten of spades. A shot rang out.

Our friend from the balcony was about to shoot me, but my brother shot first. The boss man and his supporters drew their pistols and shots were being fired from all over the place. Katies Rangers had rushed inside via both the back and front door. It didn't take them long to deal with the owner and his men. I grabbed the money on the table.

"Gareth, could you please see that Jane is repaid what she is owed from this, then give any profit to Dan." I then picked up the deeds to the building and waved them at Jane. "Jane, I believe that we are now the owners of this establishment." She took the deeds off me.

"I think that my girls and I can make us some good money here." Jane claimed with this big grin on her face.

Twenty soldiers from the Continental Army rushed in.

"What's going on? We heard gunshots." Asked the captain.

"Have no fear captain, we have placed all the wrong doers under arrest. I will pass them over to you."

The captain was not familiar with Katie's Rangers uniform.

"And who are you? The captain asked.

"If I were you, I would take the prisoners and leave. You are in the presence of The Dragon and The Eagle." It was Major John Martin.

"And what do we owe this visit?" I enquired.

"Well, I was in the area and thought I would pop in and have a look at your new base."

"Allow me to introduce you to Lady Jane; she is our financial wizard. The whole thing is down to her. She planned and financed everything. When we have finally driven the Brits out, George Washington would be a fool not to have her as the country's chancellor."

We headed back to base and gave him a tour. He was very impressed. He stayed the night and had breakfast with us. As he was about to leave, he turned to Katie and asked her a question.

"I believe that you are familiar with Long Island?"

"Yes, I used to go there as a child." She replied.

The penny dropped, that was where our next mission would be.

"Listen you two. The Continental Army, under Benjamin Tallmadge, is leading a raiding expedition; they plan to finish with an attack on Fort St George, at the end of the month. I want Katie's Rangers to support them.

It was still early November, so we had plenty of time to get there.

The Continental soldiers planned to attack on November 23rd. Their target was a fort on the South coast of Long Island.

We met up with Benjamin Tallmadge on the 21st. He had everything planned; he told Katie that we were not required. His plans were to attack the fort of St George, with a small force. He suggested that we sat and watched. I was fuming. We had ridden for nearly three days to be told that we were not needed.

Katie calmed me down. She explained that there was nothing that we could do, apart from have a rest and watch the show.

The fort was a fortified Loyalist outpost and storage depot, on the south coast of Long Island. It had a twelve-foot stockade lined with branches, which had sharpened points, facing outwards.

Major Benjamin Tallmadge led a force of 80 men. They crossed Long Island Sound in whale boats, landing on Mount Sinai. Bad weather forced his men back a couple of times, but eventually they were ready.

Twenty men were left to guard their horses. The rest were split into three groups. They attacked in the early morning light. They were not spotted until they were forty yards off the stockade.

One unit cut its way through the stockade, while the other two units scaled the wall.

Lots of prisoners were taken as well as a lot of stores. I had to admit, we had observed a masterpiece of skilful planning.

We rested for two days and filled ourselves with local food. We were prepared to return in the morning. Then, out of the setting sun, came a rider. As soon as she arrived in the camp, she dismounted and asked for Colonel Brooks. I was naturally a bit miffed - we were, after all, the same rank. I didn't have to point her out as Katie had already seen the rider approaching. She offered her a drink and some refreshments.

"My name is Madge Goldsmith. Jen sent me to New York two months ago. I recently reported back and Jen sent me to you to pass on the information I gathered. I had been informed by some drunken British soldiers that they were part of a regiment, which had been sent to catch up with Major Benjamin Tallmadge.

Tallmadge was to be brought before their Brigadier in chains. Apparently, their regiment consists of eight hundred men. I thought that was rather a large number of soldiers to capture just eighty continental soldiers. Possibly they were going on to other battles." She stopped to drink from her tankard of beer. "By the way, Jen said that I had to return with you to our new home." Katie was beginning to like this young woman. I, on the other hand, felt that she was far too cocky.

That night I had problems sleeping. Why would the British send a regiment of eight hundred soldiers to capture just eighty men? It didn't make sense. Then it came to me. What if they were in fact hunting us? That did it. I slid out of our makeshift bed, making sure that I did not wake Katie. Then I found Thunder Cloud and Andy. I presented them both with the same problem. They both came to the same conclusion as I had.

We found our horses; which wasn't easy in the dark. Then quietly walked them out of the camp. Tomorrow I would be having stern words with these sentries. It was worrying that none of them stopped us.

Madge had told us that this British regiment was due north of our camp. We rode north for maybe two hours.

"Shush," whispered Thunder Cloud.

His eyesight was far sharper than ours. He had noticed camp fires in the distance. We rode on until we were maybe 400 yards from the camp. Then we dismounted and tied our horses to nearby trees. Undercover of the darkness, we crawled on our stomachs until we were overlooking the British tents. They were in the wrong place to be hunting Major Benjamin. They were clearly moving in our direction. Slowly we crawled back to our horses.

We arrived back at our camp just as the sun was rising. I gave Andy orders to wake up all the ex-mountain men and search the area for British scouts.

Half an hour later they returned to me with twenty Brits. I stormed into Madge's tent, waking her up at the point of my sword. I was tired and angry. I did not have time to ask her to dress, she had to make do with the sheet that she had been sleeping on. Katie came to her aid.

"Dafydd, what are you doing?" She shouted. Then added quietly, "she is one of Jens spies!"

I said nothing. I just grabbed both of their arms and pulled both of them into the tent where the British scouts were being held.

"Well, Madge. Can you tell us why we have twenty British scouts observing us. And why there are eight hundred British soldiers just two hours' ride away from us?"

Now Katie was wide awake. She was finally understanding my suspicions. I had given orders to have everyone packed and ready to leave within an hour. I had no desire to share my lunch with the British.

Katie, we leave in half an hour. This discussion will be continued when we have lost the British regiment, who are not far behind us. I leave her in your hands. I then stormed out of the tent. Clearly The Dragon inside had risen.

I split the Rangers into five groups of a hundred each. They were ordered to leave in five different directions., criss crossing each other's tracks. We met up just as the sun was setting. I then sent some of our now tired Scouts out, to make sure that there was no sign of the British. Their orders were to find the British and keep an eye on them, then find somewhere to sleep. Only reporting back to us if they were an immediate threat. Otherwise, they could return to us at some point during the day.

I led the interrogation of the British scouts. All they could confirm was that my suspicions were correct: This regiment was in fact pursuing us, with orders to destroy Katie's Rangers.

Katie arrived with Madge. Katie had heard that the British were planning to destroy her beloved Rangers, she was far from being a happy bunny. The woman had been tied to a chair. Katie was staring at her.

"Katie, I swear I knew nothing about this. What I told you, was what happened." Katie then pulled out her knife.

"Hold on Katie, she could be telling the truth. The British could have used her. Let's look at all possibilities," I looked at the woman, "before you begin doing a bit of carving." I added. That made me smile. "There are three options, as far as I can see."

Katie thought for a while.

"I can only think of two. One is that Madge is a British spy. The second is that the British knew that she worked for us, and fed her the information, which they needed in order for them to catch us."

I was now stroking my chin.

"There is a possible third option. Why did Major John Martin send five hundred Rangers to support a small assault on a fort, which did not require us? Let's break this down a little.

Number one: how did the British know that we were here with 500 Rangers? Provoking them to send a far larger regiment against us. Surely that can't be all guess work.

Number two: is Madge a spy? What is bugging me is that Jen never told us that she had an agent here. Which is so unlike her.

Number three: why did Major Martin send 500 Rangers here at all."

"The answer to the first option: they would not be able to just guess that we were going to be here. They would have to have some form of information." deduced Katie. "The information could come from a spy named Madge. But how would she know that we were coming? Either the British planted her here, but even then, she did know Jen's name, and all about our new home.

Then back to the third question. Why did Major Martin send us here? When quite clearly, we were not needed. Of course, Major Martin could have given her the name Jen, and mentioned our new home. This would after all confirm her as being a genuine spy for

Jen. If Major Martin were also a spy he would have access to all of that information to pass onto other spies."

I am afraid Katie; you will need to ask her a few questions with your knife." Katie picked up her blade, and began to run her finger up and down the edge."

"Call me when you have some information." And I left.

The truth was that I did not want to watch the woman being interrogated. As I left, I heard the first scream.

It wasn't long before a messenger called me back. I entered the tent; the woman was still tied to the chair. I could only see two small cuts, one on each arm. She was lucky, Katie was very upset at the possibility of her Rangers being slaughtered. Not only had the British sent eight hundred soldiers, but they were possibly their top regiment - The Coldstream Guards.

"Ok Katie, what has she got to say?" I could see by the look on her face that she was still annoyed.

The woman, after just two minor cuts, confessed to being involved in a plan, which may have led to the destruction of Katie's Rangers. Apparently, the British knew about the Rangers a long time ago. But as they, at the time, only had about fifty members, they were seen as nothing to worry about. Then when I joined, their numbers grew, and they became very skillful fighters. The top British officers decided that the Rangers had to be dealt with.

Madge admitted that she agreed to feed false information, for a large sum of money. Her father had been killed by Indians and her mother was seriously ill in hospital in New York. She took the job against her beliefs, as it was the only way she could get enough money for her mother's treatment. She had begged Katie for forgiveness. It was too early for that; Katie would need more time to cool off.

I, on the other hand, was brought up to believe in forgiveness. I also felt sorry for her. With her mother dying in hospital, and unable to get money to pay for her treatment. I believe that she deserved a second chance. And we must not forget her mother would still be needing money for her treatment. At last Katie looked up.

"She is a British spy. I sentence her to be shot." This was not the Katie who I loved with all my heart. I shook my head.

"No, she will not be sentenced until we return to our headquarters. There she will stand trial."

Then to my uttermost shock, Katie pulled her pistol out of her belt and pointed it at the woman. Words would not stop Katie at this point. I stepped in front of Madge.

"Katie, my love, this is not you. Please calm down. While her mind was in turmoil, I grabbed her pistol.

Then took her in my arms, tears ran down her cheeks. I could only comfort her, hug her until her heart warmed up again. It did not take long. I sat her down on another chair.

"Katie my love, we will take her back with us, but her mother is seriously ill. Can we take her back to our hospital? Please." The Katie who I fell in love with resurfaced. She nodded. I gave the orders to find Madge's mother and bring her back to our hospital.

I hugged her gently, and kissed her soft lips. My Katie was back again.

She then sat up.

"The main villain of this saga is a man who I have known for many years, we almost grew up together. In fact, he was the one who recommended you to the Rangers when I wanted to reject you. In fact, when I was young, I even had a crush on him. Now not only has he betrayed me; he has put my Rangers in a situation which could have resulted in their deaths." She then looked into my face. "If it hadn't been for you suspecting that something was not right. We would have all been lying dead in pools of our own blood by now. How could he betray us?"

Madge betrayed us because she had a big problem; it was her only way to find the money to save her mother's life. Gareth betrayed us because his life was threatened; I was sure that John Martin had an excuse.

My mind suddenly drifted back to the time that we were fighting side by side against those pirates. Something very important must have happened for him to betray his friends.

CHAPTER 22

THE BATTLE OF COWPENS

We halted a few miles outside Philadelphia. A few of us intend to ride into the city. We hoped that Major John Martin was still in the city. Katie, of course, with Andy, John, Nick and Mark, joined me with twenty Rangers not wearing their uniform. Mark crossed the river and went to see Jen as soon as possible. Orders were given out to have our complex turned over in a search to find the Major. All boats were guarded to ensure that if he was on the Island, he would not escape.

The rest of us searched the taverns. Using just a hunch, we decided to start with the last one we visited, in fact the tavern we in fact now owned. Katie and I did not want to be recognised as we entered, so we came in as a loving couple, kissing and cuddling. We may have been noticed, but no one saw our faces.

I ordered a beer each.

"Don't look round, but you can't believe the nerve of some people!" Whispered Katie. "Over there, playing poker, is the traitor."

I instantly grabbed hold of Katie, if she got to him before me, he would be dead. I signalled to our men to block the exits. We had him now.

I walked up to the table and sat in the empty chair next to our major. He was too engrossed in his hand to recognise me. I joined the game at the beginning of the next game. I waited for my turn. I increased the bid by triple the previous bid. This made him turn and look at me. He turned a very pale shade of white. And it seemed that he had lost his voice.

"Are you surprised to see me?" I asked.

He tried to hide the fear, but he was physically shaking. He tried to stand up. I grabbed his jacket and made him sit again.

"I bet you are surprised to see me here. Sorry, I mean I bet you are surprised to see me alive."

At this point I pushed him and his chair over. This was when I stepped back. Katie wanted a discussion with him.

This began with a kick to his stomach. Some of his men were also playing. On seeing their officer being attacked, they stood up. Some were searching for their weapons. On recognising me, they realised the futility of fighting and sat down again.

"Katie, stop! We need to ask him why he became a traitor. And what was he about to gain that was more important than the lives of us and the Rangers"

Katie obeyed.

"One thing for sure, conspiring with the enemy in time of war is treason. And punishable by death."

We ordered two of the Rangers to take him back to our stronghold and lock him up. Katie ordered them to lock Madge up as well, when she arrived with her mother.

When Jane planned our complex, she never thought that we would need a prison.

By the time the rest of the Rangers had arrived on the island, there was just enough time for a meal, and then it was time to sleep.

The following morning, Katie had risen a couple of hours before me. She woke Jane up, asking her about what we would use as our courthouse, and if we had any lawyers or judges. Jane asked her to return at a more reasonable time.

I was not happy at the speed at which Katie was trying to arrange things. At this rate, they would both be tried and sentenced by midday. Clearly, I had to step in. I managed to get Jane and Katie together.

"I have decided that I will be the clerk of the court. In other words, I will arrange everything for this trial."

Neither of them objected.

"I will ride into the city to find two of the best lawyers to defend the accused. I would like to offer the position of judge to Katie."

Jane was a bit concerned about this decision.

"Katie has not got any legal knowledge. Would this be fair on the defendants?"

Katie was about to speak, but I interrupted.

"The person who has been aggrieved the most is Katie. If I had not checked on a few things, her beloved Rangers could now be lying in their own blood in a field far away from here." I stated.

"But," said Jane, "wont this make her biassed against the defendants?"

"My wife will only deliver a just verdict." I smiled. "If her verdict was delivered as a result of vengeance; she would not be able to live with herself."

At that moment Katie and my eyes met. I felt love flowing between us. They both agreed and I rode off into the city. I had almost forgotten, I needed four lawyers not two, I had to have prosecutors as well as the defence.

I rode to the City Hall. It must have been a busy time of the year, or maybe I was trying to set the trial a bit too quickly. I had no problems getting two prosecutors, but lawyers to defend the prisoners were impossible to find.

Back in Wales, there was a time when I could not find work, so to alleviate my boredom I did read a few books on law. Ok, that did not make me an expert on the law and if I was defending a client from the death penalty, they deserved a lot more than me. But, I may be better than nothing.

Normally, the accused can decide if they want to accept a particular lawyer, in this case, it would be me or nothing.

As the trial was arranged for tomorrow, I brought the prosecutors back with me. Neither Jane nor Katie was happy with the idea of me being the defending lawyer for both of the accused. But it was the only option, unless we were to delay the trial. To Katie, this was not an option, so I was accepted.

Time was not on my side, so I had to visit both the accused immediately. First, I saw Madge. Her only defence was that her actions were guided by the need to save her mother's life. I could see the prosecutor, standing, and stating 'why should fifty-five rangers have to die, in order to save her mother's life?'

If I put myself in her place; if I had a dying mother, and the only way I could save her, the one who gave me birth, who fed and clothed me, who picked me up and cleaned my knees when I fell... Would I let a group of people die to save her?

Next was Major John Martin. The man who fought alongside me against the pirates, Katie's friend from her youth.

I entered the room; he was sitting at a small table. I sat opposite.

"The only lawyer I could get at such short notice, I am afraid, is me. You can of course refuse, but then you are on your own."

He looked like a man who had lost everything.

"It doesn't matter who defends me, I am guilty of the charges. I did consort with the enemy. And I did betray you and Katie. Just get it over with. I presume it will be execution by firing squad?"

"John, I have never lost a case, I believe that for you to become a traitor, there must have been a very good reason." He looked up and our eyes met. "The British are holding my wife and our four children hostage. They ordered me to set a trap so that they could destroy the Rangers, as you and Katie are causing them a lot of problems.

My family is being held by the Senecas. As you know, they are brutal. As the trap fell through, I expect that my family might be dead already."

I was stunned at what the British, the country of my birth, would do to win. I felt The Dragon begin to rise. I called the guard into the room.

"Go now and bring Andy Blackthorn here as fast as you can." I ordered the guard. Then turned back to John. "I may not be able to save your life, but I will do my best to try and save your family. Where is the Senecan village they are being held in?"

Andy arrived in a flash; I ordered him to take four hundred Rangers to the village and rescue Major Martin's family.

"Teach them a lesson and do not lose any of our Rangers. Please try and be back within two days."

I did not have to tell him twice. He was on a mission to save a family.

"John, I plan to try and postpone the trial for a couple of days. Perhaps I can sweet talk the judge," I suggested. That made me smile.

Jane had put together a temporary court room.

"I plan to ask the Judge to delay the trial for a couple of days, I need more time to put together my case."

Jane laughed. "Are you planning something Dafydd?"

I just grinned and left. My next stop was the hospital, I wanted to see how Madge's mother was getting on. To be honest, I would have preferred to be going to Senecan village, rather than messing about here.

I arrived at the hospital and had a word with her doctor.

"You got her here just in time. We have operated. She is still in a coma, but she is a strong woman. We are praying that she will recover soon."

At least this was some good news that I could take to Madge.

That night, I slipped into bed first. As Katie joined me. I had placed my arm under her shoulders. I pulled her close to me and kissed her.

"Judge, as this is your first trial, I would like to make it easier for you." She pulled her body away from my arm, and sat up.

"I believe the word you are looking for is, 'Your Worship'. Also, I believe this is also your first trial, or have you done any that I don't know about?"

This wasn't going as I had planned.

"Your Worship, I would like to suggest, as both the accused are involved in the same offence, as in planning to slaughter Katie's Rangers. That they can both appear at the same time, and I will then defend them both simultaneously." She was thinking.

"And what shall I call you?" I thought before making my response. "I am the defending lawyer, 'The Defence'." She nodded.

"Ok I agree with your request."

I hesitated, then asked, "in order to prepare for both their cases. Can you postpone the trial for two days?"

She was beginning to enjoy this banter.

"Ok, agreed."

Then I had to play my last card.

"Your Worship, would you agree that you would look more impressive, if it was a jury trial. Of course, it doesn't matter what the jury agrees on, you will always have the final say."

Katie considered this suggestion for a few minutes, then agreed.

With her final word, I drew her close to me, and kissed her again. I began to smile; I had never slept with a judge before.

In the morning, I met up with Jane.

"Are your daughters around? I want them to find people for a jury. Also, the trial has been moved to December 15th." I told her.

Two days passed quickly. The day of the trial soon arrived. Katie made me laugh, she was doing this judge thing flat out, she even had a judge's robe made.

I was well aware of what I had planned, and I was worried about how Katie would deal with the situation. My whole defence was to ask for forgiveness.

Three days previously, Andy and The Rangers had arrived near the Senecan Village. It was dusk, the warriors had been dancing and drinking, but now they were disappearing into their longhouses. Andy had sent his men out earlier to remove the lookouts. Now they were waiting for everyone to fall asleep.

Andy had received good news earlier in the day when he had a scout interrogated. The family was still alive. The Seneca had wanted to kill them, but the British wanted them alive for a bit longer.

About 4am in the morning the raid commenced. The family was rescued first. Then lots of buildings were set on fire. After that the Rangers withdrew and returned home.

The trial commenced on time. Madge was first into the box. The prosecutors made their case. It did not look good for her. Clearly, she had accepted money to help The British, fully knowing that the end result would probably result in the destruction of over 500 men and women. She stood in the box being questioned by the prosecution. Eventually she broke down in tears, repeating over and over that she was sorry. I looked towards the jury. I believe that some of them understood her predicament.

Then entered the main conspirator. When asked how he pleaded, his answer was guilty. He accepted full responsibility for everything. He stood in the box, waiting to be found guilty. When the time came for me to question him. He just stood in the box, a broken man. He fully believed that as we had escaped, the Senecan warriors would by now have killed his family. He now felt that he had nothing to live for. It was a sad sight.

The first prosecutor made his case, and asked for life imprisonment for Madge. The second prosecutor delivered his final speech. He ended by asking for the death penalty for Major Martin.

It was up to me. I glanced at Katie. She looked the part in her robes, but gave nothing away in her face. Just a blank stare.

There were ten members of the Jury, five men and five women. They included Georgie and Anne, plus their mum, Jane. Among the men I could see Dan, John and his brother Nick.

I finally began my speech for the defence.

"Today I am representing two people. They are different, yet similar. Both are clearly guilty of planning on behalf of our enemy, the British, an attempt to destroy and kill over five hundred Rangers. But this never happened. Why? You may ask. Because their plan was so simple, that even I was able to see through it.

Yes, there were over a thousand members of The Coldstream Guards waiting to ambush the Rangers. But Madge gave me clues when we met, that alerted me to the plot. Without her clues, I would not have been standing here.

Madge had a massive problem. Her mother was seriously ill. The operation to save her life would cost a fortune. She had tried many places to earn the money, with no joy. Finally, she was offered the money required to save her mother's life. At first, she refused the offer, she did not want to be involved in the death of all those Rangers. But she stood night after night watching her mother's life eb away. Finally, she could not just stand and watch her mother die, and she accepted the offer that she never wanted to take. It was an impossible decision. I beg you all to think about the person you love the most. What would you have done in Madge's position if it were them?

Next, we have a Major in our army. I know this man well, I have fought shoulder to shoulder with him. Many times, he has risked his life for this country. During this war to gain independence for our country, he has given blood, tears and sweat for our cause. I would like to call a final person to testify on his loyalty for this country."

The prosecutor had no problems even at this late notice.

"I would like to call Katie Brooks to the stand."

Everyone looked around the room, wondering who this Katie Brooks was. Eventually, the judge stood up and removed her hat, then entered the box.

She explained how she grew up with Major Martin, they spent pleasant times together, but at no time did he display anything but total loyalty to this country.

Then she returned to her seat and put the hat back on.

"What made a hero of this country's army suddenly become a traitor? I can tell you the answer. The British took his family hostage, and delivered them to the Seneca. For those of you who are members of the jury, The Seneca are cruel to their core. If the British tell them to kill Major Martin's family, it would be a slow and painful death. With this in his mind, the British ordered him to set a trap for Katie's Rangers, seeing as they have been causing too much trouble for the British.

Members of the Jury. I would like you all to put yourself in the place of our major. Could you let your wife and four children be savagely killed by the Seneca? Or would you betray the Rangers?" I looked at the members of the jury, who were all clearly struggling with the decision. "Again, another impossible choice to make. If he had refused to help the British, he would hear the screams of his family in his head forever more. In his mind, their deaths would be his fault.

It is quite clear that both Major Martin and Madge Goldsmith are guilty of the crimes that they are charged with. But I am asking you, the members of the jury, to find it in your hearts to show these people mercy. Both of them had no wish to commit the crimes they are charged with. They just could not desert their loved ones. In the end, no one was harmed.

I then dropped to my knees. I beg of you to show mercy when you cast your votes. They clearly are guilty, as I have said before, but as Christians, God showed us mercy - I now ask you all to show mercy to these two sinners. A vote of not guilty is not a denial of the acts they have done, but forgiveness because of the reasons behind the act.

The jury was then led away to place their vote. People tapped my shoulders and congratulated me on my attempt to save the accused.

Finally, I stood up and walked to my chair, where I waited for the jury to return. I had done all I could. It was now down to the jury and the judge.

In just ten minutes the jury returned. When asked about their verdict, all ten had voted 'not guilty'.

I knew that Katie was very upset and annoyed at an attempt on the lives of her Rangers, but my Katie was far more than that.

She rose.

"Not guilty." She said simply.

I ran over to the judge.

"Please can you ask people to stay a while?"

Katie was now just following what I said. I gave a signal and the door to the room opened. A bed was pushed into the hall.

"Madge, come and say hello to your mum, she has woken up and wants to speak with you."

A Ranger in full uniform then ran into the hall and whispered to me.

"Ok please take your seats once more."

Once again, the doors were opened wide. In marched ten Rangers. Behind them, five civilians entered the room - a woman and four children. I could see John Martin with tears streaming down.

John could not believe what was before his eyes. His wife and children were alive.

I stood up on a row of chairs.

"This is a message to you all. We have Rangers who can rescue anyone, and brilliant doctors. So, let us not betray our Rangers to the British, but ask them for their help."

The room was filled with clapping. Katie removed her judges' robes and ran over to me, where she threw her arms around me.

"Judge! Are you allowed to do that?" I asked. We both laughed.

It had been a long day, it was time for a well earned rest.

The next morning, a messenger came to our room and handed me a letter.

"Katie, orders have just been delivered. Brigadier Daniel Morgan is marching west of the Catawba River. He plans to forage and replace his troops' supplies. His spies brought back information that the British believed Morgan was planning to attack the strategically important fort of Ninety-Six.

General Charles Cornwallis dispatched dragoons, commanded by Tarleton. Upon learning that Morgan's army was not at Ninety-Six, Tarleton, bolstered by British reinforcements, is now in hot pursuit of Morgan's army, who are retreating north to avoid being trapped between Tarleton and Cornwallis. We have to meet up with Morgan's army at the Broad River."

We grabbed as many provisions as we could, then all of us mounted our horses and were off. It was clear that Morgan was in trouble, with the British so close to him.

When we arrived, we were all knackered, especially our horses. Our leader had selected a position on two low hills in open woodland. We set up camp.

We had heard the Tarleton's Brigade did a lot of rapid marching across difficult terrain. When they reached the battlefield, they were exhausted and malnourished.

It was January 17th 1781. A few minutes before sunrise, Tarleton's Vanguard emerged from the woods, in front of our position.

He ordered his dragoons to attack the first line of skirmishers. We saw them begin to open fire and quickly shot 15 of them. The dragoons promptly retreated. He then ordered an infantry charge.

The British, with 40% of their casualties being officers, became confused?

Tarleton continued sending his soldiers on head on attacks. Morgan's army went on the offensive, wholly overwhelming Tarleton's force. His light brigade was wiped out as a fighting force.

Morgan's casualties were 25 killed and 124 injured. Tarleton was almost completely eliminated, with 30% casualties and 55% of his forces captured or missing. The annoying part was that Tarleton escaped with 200 of his troops.

"With idiots like Tarleton, the British will be driven from this country very soon. How he became a high-ranking officer I have no idea. If the British keep promoting officers because of who their family is, they will soon be defeated, just like today." I groaned.

"Just to think, if I had not so graciously invited you into The Rangers, you may have been one of those dragoons, blindly charging straight at our guns."

I did not want to even imagine my life if I had stayed with The British.

The battlefield was strewn with the bodies of dead British soldiers. Would someone bury them, or would they become food for the wolves and vultures? I wondered.

I could see some soldiers, and a lot of people from the town, stripping the bodies of anything of value.

'What is the price of a life?' I wondered. I felt a tear run down my cheek.

CHAPTER 23

THE BATTLE OF HAW RIVER

We arrived home on the 1ˢᵗ of February. I am not sure which was more tiring, the fighting or the journey each way. Perhaps we built our headquarters too far away from all the action. What I do know is that all we wanted to do was sleep. Katie and I both slept like a log.

"Are you awake my love?" Whispered Katie. I turned over.

"Kiss me and I'll tell you" I grinned. It might be corny, but it worked.

"What jobs do we have to carry out today?" I asked.

"Two come to mind, the first is to set a date for all the marriages. The other is to list the names of who is responsible for what. For instance, Val was responsible for admin, but the job seems to be Jane's now. And what do her daughters do?" I nodded.

"You have a point. Shall we take one each?" She suddenly lifted her hand. "I think we will also need to build more married quarters for the newlyweds.

I don't plan to share our bedroom with them."

I always loved her sense of humour. We heard the sound of boots approaching our bedroom door. There was a knock.

"Come in." Commanded Katie.

I was sitting on the edge of our bed when the door opened. To my horror, there was a corporal, standing with a message in his hand. I could only bury my face in my hands, with a cry of "Oh no!"

He held out the letter to Katie.

"Are these orders to attend another battle?" She asked the soldier. He nodded. She opened the letter and read it.

"Soldier, today is the 2nd of February. We only arrived home from South Carolina last night. These orders want us to be in North Carolina by the 22nd of the month. It will take about 14 days to ride there. Which will only give my Rangers about three days rest between battles." I could tell by the tone in her voice that she was furious. "Tell your Commander that we will arrive as soon as my Rangers are well rested, and tell them that in the future, we need at least a month between battles." The soldier saluted, and hastily hurried away.

"Damn!" Katie seldom swears, this confirmed how just annoyed she was. "My Rangers have just ridden a journey of four weeks, they fought a battle, now I have to order them off to another battle."

I understood my wife well. I put my arms around her and hugged her.

"Do we have to take all the Rangers with us? Or in fact, do we both have to go?" She pulled away then looked into my eyes.

"So that was why I married you." She grinned. "I thought it was because of your body, but it turned out to be your brain." She was now rushing to get dressed. "You almost found the answer, it just needs my touch to polish our idea off."

It was funny how what I had just suggested, has now become 'our' idea.

"We will send 300 Rangers to this battle, while 200 stay here and rest. By rotating them, they will be kept fresh." I put my hands on her shoulders.

"Wasn't that what I just suggested?" She lifted my hands.

"Almost, where you went wrong was…" There was silence. "You forgot, we are The Dragon and The Eagle."

I had to smile; she was right. When the Rangers get into trouble. It's The Dragon and The Eagle that change the outcome. I hugged her and gave her a kiss.

"You win, you are right as always. We can't send a Dragon *or* an Eagle. They go together."

Katie chose 300 Rangers to go with us. She told them that we would leave in a weeks' time, and to spend the time relaxing and having fun.

"Dafydd, we should sit somewhere and decide what jobs our leaders will be responsible for." I agreed, as I normally do.

"What should we do with Madge?" I asked.

"That's easy, she can join Jen, she will make a good spy."

There was still one man to make a decision about. The former Major John Martin. We may have found him 'not guilty', but the army would not take him back.

"I think that John should be put in charge of the security of the complex. That would be right up his street. He could also decide who should go to fight our battles." She nodded.

"There is one job which I just can't think of a suitable person for." I knew what she was thinking about.

"Maybe we need to ride into the city and check if we can find a suitable candidate." I suggested.

"Ok, let's go after lunch." That sounded good to me, so I agreed.

At 1 o'clock, we left the island to head into the city. Although we were fighting a war, everyday life, including building new homes, continued. It did feel a bit strange. We would ride up to a building site, dismount and watch the builders doing their job. We would make notes, then ride away. More than a few times we were threatened. That made us laugh - if only they knew who they were threatening!

By four o'clock, we felt the need for tea. The logical place to go was a tavern. On the corner of this road, was The Black Ox. The tavern was also not far from a large building site. We entered and found a table to ourselves. I could smell the steaks being fried.

"Katie, shall we have a couple of steaks?"

She had also smelt the steaks and agreed with much eagerness. While we waited, we indeed had a cup of tea. At the next table, sat four builders, most of which had already drunk too much.

"Oi you, don't you softies drink beer?" One of them shouted in my direction. I wanted to avoid a fight, but Katie had different ideas. She shouted back at the drunk.

"I think you should apologise for disturbing us with that remark."

Oh no, I thought. The drunk stood up.

"How about, I will apologise after a quick kiss."

That did it, forget Katie. I moved to the table in a flash. Grabbing hold of the table, I was about to lift one end and hurled it across the room. Then a tall well-built man, who was sitting at the next table, rose and came over to intervene. I was thinking that I was now in for a fight. To my surprise, the big man grabbed my hand and apologised on behalf of the drunk.

"This is his last day working for me, I don't employ trouble makers."

I turned to Katie, and winked. "Please sit here, we would like to talk with you."

He sat down and told us his story. It turned out that his name was Tony Borg. His family immigrated from Norway. After leaving school, he became a mountain man, spending months alone in the forests. One day he was watching the beavers building a dam. He was so impressed that he began to build himself a house in the woods. He enjoyed it so much that he wanted to share his new found skill. He walked out of the wilderness and became a builder. He agreed to come tomorrow, and we would give him a guided tour of our headquarters.

We decided to leave the weddings and the selection of names for officers until we returned from our oncoming battle. Mr Borg arrived the following morning. Katie took him on a guided tour. At the end of the tour, we had lunch together.

"I presume Katie, told you about the new homes we needed to have built." He confirmed that he had, and was very interested in our project.

"There is one other thing," added Katie. "We believe that the war is coming to an end soon. The British are being pressed back towards the Atlantic. Another couple of years should see the end of this bloody encounter." Tony agreed, these were also his thoughts. "Tony, we have a dream which is shared by most of our people. To the west there is a wilderness, which is there for those strong enough to take their share." Tony smiled. "Our Dream is to travel west through the wilderness, coming across strange animals and fierce tribes. Maybe our dream will end at the Pacific Ocean, or on our travels, we just might come across a piece of land that we want to settle on, and carve our slice out of this country. With enough people, travelling with us, we could build a city. How does Katieville sound?"

I laughed. He promised to meet us again when we returned from our journey. Katie also issued another order before we left. She wanted to recruit another 100 Rangers. So, we could have two teams of 300 Rangers.

We left early on Monday morning. We were going to the Haw River, North Carolina.

On February 18th, Cornwallis ordered Tarleton to take a troop of men west of the Haw River. With Cornwallis encamped at nearby Hillsborough, Dr. Pyle gathered 400 troops and sent a request to Cornwallis for an escort. Cornwallis dispatched Tarleton with his Dragoons and infantry.

At the same time, Lee and Pickens were in the area with orders to harass the British. They had sent out scouts to locate Pyle's army.

On the 24th, Lee and Pickens captured two British staff officers. After interrogation, they learned that Tarleton was only a few miles ahead.

In the waning hours of the day, Lee's Legion, who wore short green jackets and plumed helmets, encountered two of Pyle's men, who mistook them for Tarleton's Dragoons, who wore similar uniforms.

On February 25th, Lee had marched a short distance when he met two young farmers on horseback. Cornwallis had sent these lads ahead to locate Tarleton. The lads mistook Lee's men for Tarleton's because they wore similar uniforms. Lee thanked the scouts, and as soon as they had left, he divided his men into several troops and sent them off in different directions.

Lee's troop came into sight of the British a short time later. They were drawn up along the right-hand side of the road in review formation. They were sitting on their saddles with their muskets or rifles slung over their shoulders and their eyes straight ahead. At the end of the line sat Pyle, unaware that the advancing troops were not Tarleton's men.

Riding slowly past the Tories, Lee nodded approvingly and smiled at the British. He reined his horse up in front of Pyle, and they returned the salute. Pyle stretched out his hand in welcome.

Some of the British troops at the far end had spotted Eggleston's men in the woods behind them. This was where we, Katie's Rangers, had been attached. We were witnessing the unbelievable sight of our soldiers riding alongside the British. We couldn't help but laugh. Now we could see all hell breaking out. We charged out of the woods, and hand-to-hand fighting began. Soldiers were slashing at each other with their swords, and some were firing muskets.

Many of the dying loyalists were still ignorant of what had happened. As we led our horses to face our opponents, we would call out "Whose man are you?"

"The King's! The King's!" screamed the British, as we cut them down.

Lee, apparently, had planned to surround Pyle's army and force them to surrender, but the British themselves began the battle.

There wasn't any record of any of our troops being killed or injured, but for the British, it was a slaughter. Ninety were killed and two hundred and fifty soldiers were wounded. None of our Rangers had been harmed. Well, not physically. The picture of helpless soldiers being cut down will forever live in our minds. All because they could not recognise different uniforms.

Katie ordered us all to meet up after the battle. There were many battle-hardened men and women crying.

Was human life so cheap? These young British soldiers, sent from their families to a country far away, were now lying in their own blood, never to return to their loved ones. This could have been me, if things had not changed in my life. Sitting in the light of the campfire, I could feel tears running down my cheeks. I prayed that this war would end soon. Katie sat down beside me. Words were not spoken. We just sat staring into the flames.

Katie gave us the following day to rest. Although our horses needed the rest, all the Rangers wanted to get away from these killing fields as quickly as possible.

"Did you sleep well my love?" I asked Katie. She, as well as most of the camp, were in a sombre mood.

"Sleep?" she moaned. "Twice I faced those young British lads, who were not much older than children. Twice, I asked them 'whose man, are you?'. Twice I received the reply 'The Kings! The Kings!' As I cut them down. They were guilty of giving the wrong answer, which cost them their lives. As the second tumbled off his horse onto the already blood covered road. I turned my horse and galloped back into the woods, where tears ran down my face like a waterfall. How did I sleep? You ask. Dafydd, I may never sleep again. Closing my eyes, just fills my mind with nightmares."

She held me tight as the tears began to flow again. Katie was no different from the rest of us. We were ashamed of our actions. When we go into battle, we expect to fight against well-armed soldiers, who will kill us unless we are better or quicker than they are. Cutting down young lads, without a weapon in their hands, isn't war, it is just a massacre.

I think all Rangers eyes were red, if after being involved in yesterday's slaughter, you hadn't shed a tear, then you couldn't be human, and there was no place in Katies Rangers for you.

During this war, we had ridden home from many battles. This return journey was one unlike any other. We rode in total silence. The silence was only broken when Katie asked for the bridge.

On arriving at headquarters, The Rangers all dismounted. They knew that they had to wait for one of us to give the command for them to retire. Not tonight. They all dismounted and slowly ambled off to their rooms. Neither of us had the heart to say anything or call them back. We wanted to join them, to lay on our bed and let our tears flow again. We all needed time to heal. But when you have accepted a position of leadership, this comes with a responsibility. Many of our friends were running towards us. They wanted us to tell them about the battle.

"Katie, please go and warm our bed. I will deliver the report tonight."

Val was one of the first to arrive. I grabbed hold of her arm.

"Please, go with Katie, help her into bed, and stay with her until I get there. And one more thing, please don't talk unless she speaks with you."

As Katie disappeared from view. I began to deliver the report. Twice I broke down, but somehow I managed to recover. I informed the crowd that it wasn't a battle, it was indeed a massacre. I then gave an order to leave the Rangers who were involved, alone, until they recovered.

"Please direct all questions to me. I am in need of my bed now; I will hold a meeting tomorrow morning."

I ran out of the ability to be able to speak any more., and I ambled off to find Katie.

The following morning, Katie woke up, still feeling down. She looked across at me.

"How you can smile after the other day, beats me." she moaned.

I was lying on the bed with a smile on my face. No, I had not forgotten Haw River, and I never will.

"Katie, what is it that cheers people up?" There was no reply to my question. "The answer, my dear wife, is a wedding." Finally, I had Katies attention.

"Dafydd, you are right! We need to get a date set for all the weddings. Then we can put bunting up and lots of things that can help people push what happened the other day to the back of their minds." She was now also grinning. She ran towards the door. "Last one to meet the vicar is a tortoise!"

The door closed before I could reach it. No problem. I was faster than she was.

Well, I would have beat her, but she got some of her friends to impede me. As I entered the church, I was greeted with.

"Good morning, vicar. I am afraid that Dafydd is a bit slow today." Ok I lost to her abilities to slow me down.

"Have you two agreed on a date? Please."

"Yes, April 13th. Katie, have you got the list?"

She nodded and ran out of the church. This wasn't good, she was overcompensating for the heartbreak of the so-called 'battle'. I finally caught up with her, and held her close to my chest. Eventually she calmed down and tears began to run down her cheeks.

"Yes, I do have the list. Shall we sit somewhere and discuss the list?" She sniffed.

I nodded and guided her to a bench.

"Ok. First Thunder Cloud and Jean. Then White Eagle and Mark. Andy and Lana also want to marry."

"Well, that's three couples at least. How many other couples want to marry?"

"Well, Dafydd, there are another 50 partners who want to marry. Let's put a poster up, say that we are still accepting people who want to marry, so no one feels like they missed out."

I nodded. She continued.

"Next, we need to sort out who will take command of all the various positions. Jane and Val will manage the complex. We will have to create team leaders for the Rangers, who will command under us. Team A will be commanded by Lana and Andy. Team B will be commanded by John and his brother Nick.

Our future detective agency, at present our spy unit, will be managed by Jen and Madge. Gareth and Georgie will manage the tavern. Construction: Tony Borg. Recruitment: Dan and Anne. Future Planning, including developing a route west: Thunder Cloud and Jean as well as White Eagle and Mark."

"Three new roles are needed." I added. "Commander of the Stables. This role is to be responsible for our horses - at present we have about 800 Horses. They are essential for our Rangers. They required food every day, cleaning out and to be kept in good health.

Also, feeding 700 women, men and children, three meals a day was a massive responsibility, which requires managing. At present everyone involved with the kitchen supports each other, with no one really in control. This role will be known as Commander of the Kitchen.

Finally, someone will need to be in total control of the hospital. We can't just have it run by the doctors as it is at present. When we begin our journey west, we won't have a nice building, but we will have people requiring treatment. This role will be the Commander for Health."

We were on the lookout to find people for these jobs. We thought that we should do some research, and see if we could find people with the talent for the three vacant roles.

After all, nearly 800 people were living in this complex. One thing was for sure, we were looking for talent, which had nothing to do with current ranks.

"Katie, shall we begin our search at the stables?"

"After you, my lord." She bowed, giggling.

CHAPTER 24

THE SIEGE OF AUGUSTA

Our stables were massive, all 800 horses required a stall, someone to groom them, and feed them, also at times when we did get a rest from the fighting, they needed to be exercised. We decided to begin searching at one end and work our way up. Eventually we would pass every horse. We hadn't walked far when we heard some shouting, it sounded like an argument.

As we came into sight of the people making all the noise, two teenage girls were challenging one of those who currently had the role of looking after the horses. Five horses were being held by stable lads. These horses had been with us at Haw River. This officer was ordering the lads to exercise these horses. The two girls were challenging this officer. They were arguing they felt that the horse was still recovering, and needed rest, not exercise.

Now when it comes to horses, Katie is an expert. She was taught to ride at the same time as she began to walk.

She quietly moved over to where the horse was being held by the stable lads. It was quite clear that what the girls were saying was true. Katie was almost behind this officer, when they told both girls that they were sacked and raised his hand to strike them. Katie was just in time to grab his hand and with a little help from her leg, she pulled him backwards and he was left lying on his back in dung.

He was furious and got to his feet as soon as he could with plans to remonstrate with the person who attacked him. On coming face to face with Katie, he turned pale.

"Are you in charge of these stables?" Katie asked. He began to stutter.

"Yes ma'am. I was about to order these girls off camp, for disobeying orders."

Katie's face began to turn red.

"You arrogant pig!" She shouted. "It is clear that you have little or no knowledge of horses, these girls were standing up to you, in the interest of my horses."

I decided to interrupt before Katie got carried away.

"You may have heard of me; some people call me The Dragon." He was now panicking. "The way you challenged these girls was commendable. Had it been the correct order. I believe that you should not be trampling in this horse muck all day long. I am moving you to a different unit. What is your name?"

"Sergeant Faraday," he replied.

"Well, Sergeant Faraday. I want you to clean yourself up. then report to John and Nick Baldwin. Tell them that you have been assigned to their team. Tell them that I will catch up with them later."

He saluted and left. I then indicated that Katie should now have a chat with the girls.

"Girls, please, tell me about yourselves." Katie asked.

"My name is April and my sister's name is June. My sister and I are twins, we are both 17. We lost our parents and have worked here for about six months."

"I am sorry, but we had to speak out." Began June. "When we were young our parents had horses. We both learnt to ride when we were young. We have a slogan which we try to keep. 'If you want to ride your horse, then it's you who has to take care of it'."

"You were both very brave standing up to that sergeant." commended Katie. "Would you say that there are more idiots like that officer involved in taking care of our horses?" I asked.

"I am afraid there are many. A few of us try to stand up to them, if we think the horse will suffer, but we are only young and they often reprimand us physically." Replied June. I could feel The Dragon rising again.

"Mind you, there is one older man who we go to, when we are not sure what to do." April added. "I think he is about 45. His name is George."

At that moment, another so-called officer arrived with six men who looked like thugs.

"What are these horses still doing sitting around? Hurry up and get them out exercising!"

"That will not be happening."

"Who are you? Get these troublemakers out of our stables, and teach them a lesson on their way out." He ordered the thugs.

The first one grabbed hold of my arm. That was their first and final mistake. I spun round and punched him so hard that I think I broke his jaw. I then joined Katie who was now standing in front of the girls. To our surprise, we could see more of these thugs running towards us.

Katie and I held hands, gripping each other tightly as we concentrated. Soon, the adrenaline began to flow through our bodies.

All together about twelve of these thugs attacked us. They were soon in dreamland. We called for Rangers to help us remove the rubbish. I had them locked up. My current plan was that bullies should be in the front line of any attack that The Rangers make. If they wanted to fight, then I would let them.

Katie asked the girls to bring everyone who actually cared about the horses to us, including this George fellow.

George reminded me of a man I knew back in our village. The kids could always go to him if they had a problem.

After a nice chat, we ended up making George the Commander of the Stables, with assistance by April and June.

"One down, two to go." Grinned Katie.

"Shall we take a tour of the kitchen now?" I asked.

"Try to stop me." Laughed Katie.

We were soon sitting in the dining hall. It may have been out of normal eating hours; but the cooks were happy to see us. We were both eating a late breakfast, when a stocky, foul-mouthed man entered the room. He seemed oblivious to our presence. The lady who had just served us began to panic and ran out to the back of the serving area. A few minutes later the head cook and all the rest of the staff appeared. He began to inspect them.

"What is he doing?" Asked Katie. I was unable to answer, so we both just watched.

The head cook watched as he inspected her staff. She cringed a bit when he became too familiar with the attractive younger ones. Then they were sent back to continue preparing the dinners.

He called the head cook, a woman in her 40s, over to the nearest table. He then produced sheets of paper.

"Why are you spending all this money?" he demanded.

"Most of our customers are Rangers, they are expected to fight. We need to feed them well." She replied.

"Of course," he replied, "but why give them meals that contain expensive ingredients? Cut your cost down, or you will be replaced!" He groaned.

"Sir, we are given a budget to spend on the meals. I always use just the amount that we are allocated, I never exceed our budget, why do you want me to spend less?" she asked.

He was now getting angry, he seemed not the man to appreciate being challenged.

"The food is not the only item to come out of the budget, I have other expenses to allocate for." He was now showing his anger.

"Such as?" She asked. This woman has a lot of guts, I thought. He suddenly sprung to his feet and slammed his first down on the table.

"I have a running cost; so you must only spend 80% of the budget on food. The remaining 20% will be returned to me." He ordered. Katie had heard enough. She walked over to the table.

"Excuse me sir, what is your role in the kitchen?" She asked.

Apparently, he did not recognise her.

"I am the superintendent. What's it got to do with you?"

Oh no, no blood in the kitchen please, I thought. Thankfully, Katie remained cool.

"My name is Katie Brooks. Colonel Katie Brooks. And you, my friend, are no longer the superintendent. In fact, you are under arrest."

She then called me over to arrest him. I was not sure that this was my role, but I didn't want to stop her in full flow. While I dragged him off to the first Ranger I could find. Katie was having a chat with the head cook. I joined her a bit later. Apparently, the superintendent had been palming off some of the food budget for himself.

"I suspect that you are able to replace him?" I asked the head cook.

"I'm afraid I am far too busy in the kitchen, but I think perhaps Gawain, one of the cooks, would be ideal for the role"

"Can we have a chat with him?" asked Katie. The head cook, who went by the name of Mrs Jones, left the table grinning.

"I wonder why she is grinning?" I muttered.

Eventually Mrs Jones returned with a giant of a man. He wasn't far below 7 feet tall, with muscles everywhere.

"This is Gawain, he is like a lot of your Rangers, a former Mountain man. He, like you, is also from the valleys of South Wales."

Katie asked him to sit with us. We chatted for some time. Apparently, he used to live in the next village over from where I used to live. We began talking about the old times.

"We are here to talk about the kitchen. Not to reminisce about your past!"

Katie had brought us back to the present. It turned out that he knew a lot about the forests, and about what we can live off to survive. Clearly, he would make sure that we always had food to eat.

He was also a good cook. But his extra skill was that he was good at haggling with the suppliers. He seemed a perfect fit for the role. Katie offered him the position and he jumped at the chance.

I looked at Katie.

"Two down, one to go." This time she just winked.

"Hospital next," she ordered.

We decided to pretend to be injured. Katie offered to cut my arm in order for my injury to be more realistic.

"Thanks Katie, but I will give it a miss."

Somehow, we managed to be able to walk around the hospital without being challenged. After talking to many patients and staff. It was agreed that the current holder of the position of coordinator was in fact the best for the job. Also lucky for us she readily agreed. Her name was Gwen Morris.

"Well, my love that all went well. We had better get on with the weddings now, as we never know when we will be ordered to another battle."

When will I learn to keep my mouth shut. No sooner had I finished my sentence, than a rider came into view waving a letter.

"Have you ever been to Georgia?" Katie asked. She knew that I hadn't. She knew everywhere I had been in America from the moment I stepped off the boat. Ok I was running at the time.

"How about you, have you been there?"

She shook her head.

"No, that is one state that I have never visited. Anyway, we have to report to the town of Augusta by the end of April. I understand that last September, Elijah Clarke and Patriot forces set up a four-day siege on the British held Augusta, but retreated on the 18th. American forces re-entered Wilkes County early this month. They joined General Pickens and Major General Henry Lee. They are now heading towards the town's primary fort, Fort Cornwallis. General Andrew Pickens has sent a force of four hundred men to provide a barrier between Augusta and Fort Ninety-Six. Which we are familiar with. This is to prevent the British outpost being reinforced."

"Our Rangers have become famous as the riflemen who never miss." That made her laugh.

"The plan is to surround the fort, and begin a siege as soon as possible. We will have to arrange all the weddings for tomorrow, as we need to leave the morning after."

That would be quick, let's hope they are all ready for their weddings, I thought.

"We will be taking Team B with us this time; they only consist of 200 Rangers, but that shouldn't be a problem. I will inform John and Nick now, while you inform all the would-be marriage partners of the new date."

I had never seen a sight like it. I believe we had about sixty-five couples lined up. I did feel sorry for them, it was their special day. This was nothing like special. But, I had promised them that we would arrange something special at a later date.

The following morning, the newly married members of Team B, left their new wives and joined up with Katie and me. While the members of Team A, were still in bed. That was the luck of the draw.

"Don't worry, I promise to bring all your husbands back." I shouted back to the line of tearful wives, as they waved their good-byes to their husbands.

We arrived a bit late again. It was May the 24th. On May 21st, the stockade house of George Galphin, an Indian agent, which was twelve miles south of Augusta, was captured. Then Fort Grierson, which was only half a mile from Fort Cornwallis, was taken on May the 23rd - as in the day before we arrived.

Three hundred British soldiers defended Fort Cornwallis. They were also assisted in defensive works by about two hundred African Americans.

Our leaders had come with a plan to invade the fort. They constructed a wooden tower, which was about thirty feet high. The tower was high enough to top the walls of Fort Cornwallis.

On June 1st, The Rangers joined others in firing down into the fort. We had other Rangers spread around the fort keeping the fort's defenders below their walls, in fear of being shot. Katie and I were on top of the tower.

That night, a group of British soldiers left the fort under cover of darkness, and engaged with us. They were trying to get close enough to set the tower on fire. But were forced to flee back inside the fort.

I may be of the lower ranks, but I could not understand why they didn't use fire arrows like the Indians did with so much effect.

Next, the British commander then sent out a man who pretended to be a deserter, to try and gain access to the tower, with a view to set it on fire. He almost succeeded, but one of our Rangers became suspicious. I had to hand it to that British soldier. He had a lot of guts.

The cannon which we had dragged to the top of the tower was causing a lot of damage.

On June the 5th, Thomas Brown, the Fort's Commander, offered to negotiate terms of surrender. In order to avoid Grierson's fate, he specified surrendering to a detachment of Continental Army troops from North Carolina, as a number of local militia were interested in seeing him dead over his previous acts of brutality.

Fifty-two British soldiers were killed, and 324 were captured. Only 16 American fighters were killed, none of them being our Rangers, while 35 had been injured. Katie was once again congratulated by General Pickens for the accuracy of her Rangers. She gave orders for a day of rest before we began our return journey. It would take us three weeks to get back home. I was thinking of those new husbands waiting to return to their wives.

Then the unforeseen happened. We were both summoned to meet up with General Pickens. This was not good. He didn't call people to wish them a good rest. He welcomed us with a request to be seated, then personally poured us a glass of wine. I leaned across to Katie and whispered "This doesn't look good." We knew he was going to give us fresh orders.

"My friends, first I have the pleasure to promote you both to the rank of Brigadier General," he said as he shook our hands. "And now, I have more work for you, as well as sewing the new ranks on yourselves. I am aware that you have a three-week journey back to Philadelphia, but I have to ask you for a favour. I thought that we had defeated the Cherokees, but a large war party of at least 300 warriors are burning and killing settlers. Last month, they came across a small unit of Continental soldiers, about fifty, I believe. You can guess the result. They have to be stopped.

I know that you will be travelling through what they believe to be their lands. I want your Rangers to cripple that war party in the name of all the settlers who have died so far. In compensation, I will give you 200 Ferguson rifles and ammunition."

Well, I already had a Ferguson, and I would not be without it. But we had no other choice but to agree.

"Let the Rangers sleep. We will break the bad news tomorrow," pleaded Katie.

The following morning, we called John and Nick to our tent. We told them our new orders. They were as concerned as us about my promise to bring the new husbands home safely.

"How many of your Rangers were married recently?" asked Katie.

Nick told us that there were twenty men and five women who had recently married.

"Maybe we could keep them away from any fighting." Suggested John. This annoyed me.

"Tell me John, are the lives of newly married Rangers more important than the others?"

He apologised.

"The last known place this war party was seen was when they fell upon the fifty members of the Continental Army, and killed them all. This was in North Carolina. We will need to leave as soon as possible, while they are in the same area. They have been raiding over three states. If we take too long to reach them, they will be miles away." Stated Katie.

Nick took control of this discussion.

"We will go now and get the Rangers ready to leave at 10am. We must prevent them from killing any more innocent people." He stated. The two brothers hurried out of the room.

"I think we chose well, for them to be leaders," whispered Katie.

Ten o'clock on the dot. Two hundred Rangers were mounted and ready to depart. We knew it would take us over a day to reach where they were last seen. The only good news was that it was on our way home. After a day's ride, we were a couple of miles short of North Carolina. If only we could get a message to Andy and Lana, asking them to send their three hundred Rangers to meet up with us. Together we could crush this Cherokee war party. But alas, I couldn't think of a way to make that work.

"I think we should be close to the massacre by noon tomorrow."

I don't think many of the Rangers slept that night. Our thoughts were on the soldiers that the Cherokee killed. We were now looking for revenge.

The night before, I had sent out five scouts under cover of darkness. The moon was just a crescent shape which gave out very little light. The scouts wouldn't be able to ride too fast, as their horses wouldn't be able to see very well. They would not want their horses injured due to the lack of light.

It was June and the sun rose early. The scouts stopped by a stream for a few hours to rest their horses and let them drink and graze on the lush grass which was growing. They were about to mount up and move on, when hundreds of horses ridden by Cherokee warriors came into view on the other side of the stream. That was lucky - if they had arrived on this side of the stream, they would all be dead or captured by now. The scouts led their horses through the trees and away from the stream, trying not to alert the Cherokees on the other side.

As the last Ranger mounted his horse. A keen-sighted warrior caught sight of them. It was now a race.

They would either reach us, or get killed in the process. Or worse, captured. No one would wish that on their worst enemy - reports on this war party showed that they were very cruel.

We always tried to provide the Rangers with the best weapons and the best horses we could get. The staff at the stables took really good care of the horses. I know I had to remove the superintendent, but the people under him all loved the horses.

Indian horses, on the other hand, were normally taken from the wild. They worked until they became too old, then they were killed and eaten. So, for those who were chasing our scouts, it's possible that one or two of their horses were really good, but most would quickly fall behind ours.

This was to be proven to be correct. Two riders managed to get close to our scouts. One tried to use a pistol to kill the ranger at the back. Even I could not hit a target while riding a horse at speed. After he missed, he dropped back to the rest of the pursuing Cherokee.

The last one to get close enough to cause any damage, decided to use his bow. This would be more accurate, but he would still have to be an excellent archer.

Maybe he was good, maybe he was lucky; his arrow hit the ranger at the back of the scouts. The arrow stuck into his shoulder. The Ranger was able to hang onto his reins, and keep the horse going without falling off. It was quite a feat of horsemanship and pain tolerance.

Eventually all the Cherokee riders gave up and returned to the stream. By the time the scouts returned to us, it was nearly dark. They were truly exhausted. I gave orders to make camp and all five of the scouts were put into a tent together.

While Katie and I were listening to their reports, a dark-haired woman, who neither I nor Katie recognised, entered the tent.

"I have been looking for these men. This one won't be able to fight anymore. I am aware that The Rangers have to move fast, but you must provide provisions for your wounded." She ordered.

Katie responded by asking who she was and why she was here. She apologised and began to explain.

"I have been sent to take care of these Rangers by Gwen Morris. She is my boss. My name is Dr. Rachell Greenhill. Dr. Morris wanted to know what happens to wounded Rangers. Do they have to wait for treatment whenever they make it back to the hospital? From what I can see, the answer is yes." We were both left speechless. "This man cannot ride a horse. How do you plan to get him home?"

We didn't have a clue.

"Well, you are a doctor, what would you suggest?" I asked.

"There are going to be big changes with the care you give your Rangers. I have been sent to clarify what the state of things are at present. I will be reporting my findings to Dr. Morris when I return. To be honest, I am not impressed." She continued by looking around the tent. "If I was not here, how would you deal with your injured Rangers? Bearing in mind that I understand you will soon be in a battle against a larger war party."

We were now beginning to feel like naughty children, instead of the commanders. Katie finally came to the rescue.

"We are well aware that we have problems with our injured Rangers. This is why we have taken on Gwen and her team or doctors and nurses. So, as she has sent you along, doctor, what do you plan to do so that our injured are able to return home safely?"

"For this patient, I suggest you make a hammock between two horses. This will of course slow you down, as the horses will need to walk, or run, in unison." We asked her if she could arrange this as we needed to prepare for an attack by the Cherokees. I then pulled Katie out of the tent without waiting for Doctor Greenhill's reply.

"Katie, I have a plan, but we must act quickly. The sun was setting fast, it would be dark soon. The Cherokee who were pursuing the scouts have no idea how many Rangers are here. Light a fire in the middle of our camp, then make some beds up outside of our tents. Make them look as if people are sleeping in the beds. I want ten rangers to take our horses away from here, the rest of the Rangers need to conceal themselves around the outskirts of the camp. Then we will wait for the Cherokee to arrive."

They did not take long; some tribes are against fighting at night. They believe that if they get killed, their spirits will wander in the dark forever. Alas, the Cherokee were not one of these tribes. Concealed in the undergrowth around the camp, we could hear and sometimes see the Cherokee warriors as they approached.

Suddenly, a blood curdling scream pierced the night sky. The attack had begun. I fired my rifle as the signal to fire upon the Indians. They were in total shock. They had no idea where the shots were coming from. With the slaughter of those poor soldiers in our minds, we continued to fire down at the Indians.

Slowly we made our way into the camp. Cautious of any Indian who may not be dead, just injured, who may be waiting for their chance to take one of us down.

CHAPTER 25

A SECOND HOME

As we picked our way through the bodies, I noticed that one was still breathing. He looked to be badly injured, but at least he was alive. I had the Rangers carrying the injured man back to Dr. Greenhill.

The final total on the day was 102 Cherokee warriors killed, and 58 injured who were unable to get away. The rest had retreated, I expected that they had returned home. I was so pleased that Dr Greenhill was with us. She had asked for some Rangers to help her, which we gladly did.

Katie and I walked among the wounded. All were Cherokee warriors; not one Ranger with even a scratch. As we walked, I suddenly stopped where the Indian who I had given some help to was lying. As I looked at him, one of the Rangers who was supporting Dr. Greenhill came up to us.

"A few years ago, I fought against the Cherokee. You are currently looking at Grey Wolf. He is the son of the chief of all the Cherokee. If he dies, they will hunt you down until you are killed or captured. When I say you, I mean everyone here." Then he went to attend another patient.

"Katie, he is badly injured, if he dies, it looks like we all will follow him."

We quickly rush off to find Dr Greenhill. I did not take long to find her. She had set up a tent for surgery. She wasn't a surgeon, but she had to do what she could, and most of the injuries were from our bullets. She had indeed come prepared. She was wearing a white coat, and an apron. Both were covered in blood. Her sleeves had been rolled up, leaving us staring at her blood covered arms.

"If you have something to say, you will have to tell me as I work. Your Rangers did a good job. A third of the attackers are dead, and a few of their injured won't make it through the night." I stood in awe of this woman. Katie began to speak.

"Dr Greenhill, we can't find words to thank you. But there is one patient that has to survive, if he dies then we are all as good as dead." She was silent for a few minutes.

"There we are, I knew I would find it." And she tossed a bullet into a bowl next to her. "So which patient are you referring to?" She enquired. Then added, "and you can call me Rachell."

"Let me take you to him." I suggested.

She followed us out of the surgery tent and into the patient care tent, still covered in blood. We pointed Grey Wolf out to her.

She bent over him, then stood up.

"If you wanted to kill him, you did a great job. He has a bullet in his shoulder and in his thigh, which is close to an artery. There are also sword cuts on his side and arm. And to top it all, he has a fever. Maybe we should begin digging a hole in the ground for him now." She said as she wiped some blood off her hands onto the apron.

"I'll make you a deal." She stood with her hands on her hips. "I will remove the bullets, and stitch his wounds. But, unless you can break the fever, he will still die." We had no idea how we would break the fever, but we accepted her offer and agreed to do what we could to break the fever.

Rachell gave orders for Grey Wolf to be carried into the surgery tent. The operations took five hours. She came out with him.

"He has a great desire to survive. I don't think many people would have lived through that operation. Now it's over to the two of you to crack the fever." Rachell nodded and returned to the tent.

We had heard that there were two methods to break a fever. One was to sweat it out, the other was the opposite - plenty of fresh air. In the end we decided to let him sweat it out. If his temperature rose enough then maybe the fever would break. It was late in the day;

the sun was beginning to set. We decided to put our plan into action straight away. We both stripped down to our underwear. Then got into the bed on either side of Grey Wolf. A fire was also lit near us. What a night. Neither of us slept, we just sweated.

At 7am the following morning, Rachell returned. She felt his forehead.

"Well done, his fever has subsided. We just need the wounds to heal now.

Grey Wolf was laying on his side facing Katie. His eyes began to open for the first time since he was captured. He was gazing into Katie's eyes. That was more than enough for me.

"Katie, get up now, wash and get dressed." Katie did what I asked. Grey Wolf was smiling.

"I thought that she was a gift for me." He grinned.

I pulled out my knife, and pointed it at his throat.

"She is my wife, don't even dream of touching her." He got the message.

"I thought that I was going to die, when I was laying in your camp. That was a very good trap that you set for us." He began to roll over onto his back, then realised how much of a bad idea that was. "Yes, I speak english. Who do I owe the thanks for removing the bullets," he then touched his side, "and stitching me up?"

"It was our doctor turned surgeon, she removed both bullets and stitched you up." I replied.

"You are aware that my father is probably on the way here to rescue me, with maybe a thousand warriors. You will need a much more brilliant trap to catch them."

Katie pulled out her knife, and pointed it at Grey Wolf's neck.

"I presume that you understand that your father may find you alive, or dead." She was grinning.

At that moment Rachell arrived.

"You have had intensive surgery. You will need to stay in your bed and rest while your body heals." She ordered. Grey Wolf had not finished yet.

"I think that my father with all his warriors will be here within 24 hours. If he doesn't find me fit and well when he arrives. He may begin killing your Rangers." Rachell stood right next to him. "If I let them move you, you will die. Then you father will kill us all."

A week later, fifty of the wounded warriors were fit to return home, eight had died, their wounds were too severe. Grey Wolf was now up and walking about.

"I don't understand. My father should be here by now."

I was thinking that it was time for him and the other Cherokee warriors to leave, they were making me nervous. Apart from that, it was time for us to be on our way.

"Grey Wolf, I think that you are fit enough to take your healed warriors and return to your father. He may be worried about you." I suggested.

He thought for a few minutes before making his reply.

"You are right, we had better head home, he will be wondering how I lost a hundred warriors. Still, I will make up some kind of reason. Maybe you had five hundred Rangers." A smile came to his face.

The following morning, he left with his warriors. I hoped that this would be the last time that we saw him.

"Katie, I have been talking with Andy. It seems that for every battle that we are sent to, there is at least two weeks' travel. Why don't we build a half-way house? One team can be in Philadelphia and the other in our halfway house. Only until the end of the war, and of course they will be on rota. Lana, have the two of you got any ideas about where we could set up?"

"Well, Pittsburgh is more or less half way." She replied.

"Ok then, we can start to plan for that when we get home." Katie agreed.

We were glad to leave that place. So many corpses. We still had about two weeks of travel to get home though.

"It's nearly July, let's hope we can have a long break before the next battle." Groaned Katie.

We had been riding for a couple of days, when out of the blue, came hundreds of Indians. They arrived so quickly that we were unable to put any plan together, apart from gathering together, ready for a last-minute stand. Eventually we were completely surrounded. Katie ordered everyone to get their horses to lay down, and for the

Rangers also to lay down in the prone position. Smaller targets and better firing position. I was glad that I had given them Ferguson rifles. Katie and I were lying next to each other.

"Somehow, I doubt if even The Dragon and The Eagle will be able to fight their way out of this."

So far, the Indians had not fired a single arrow or bullet. Then a warrior with a large head dress rode forward holding a white flag. I told Katie to stay with the Rangers. We couldn't have both of us killed.

He was sitting and waiting for my arrival. I wondered how many Eagles died to make that war bonnet.

Like Grey Wolf, he also spoke good English.

"Our chief, the great Atta Kul Kulia, had died. The Cherokee have a new chief. You are currently surrounded by a thousand Cherokee warriors." He then continued by saying that he would introduce me to their new chief. As I sat waiting for this new chief to arrive, I was thinking to myself 'when they begin to fire volleys of arrows at the Rangers, I don't think the Battle will be a long one.'

"Oh dear, I did not think that I would have to see you again." I was grinning, as I held my hand out. It was Grey Wolf.

"I told you that the Chief of the Cherokee, would bring a thousand warriors to test your Rangers." Laughed Grey Wolf. I decided to change the tone of the conversation, by expressing our condolences on the death of his father. It was true, his father had been a great chief.

"So, what's your plan, now that you have fulfilled your promise?" I asked.

"Well, I have brought ten horses in exchange for your wife, Katie." I knew he was joking.

"Is that all you think she is worth?" I enquired. He considered his offer. "Well, they are ten of my best horses, and two are breeding mares."

At that point Katie arrived, she saw it was Grey Wolf and knew everything would be ok.

"Katie my love, I have an offer of ten horses for you. Is this a good exchange?" She grinned.

"I think that if he offered six horses for you, bearing in mind that you are strong and can carry lots of wood for his fire. This would be a far better offer. After all, I am just a weak woman."

Weak? Katie? She must be joking! We all sat, and Grey Wolf had some food and drink brought over. We chatted about how he was planning to rule the tribe.

"I am considering refusing to support the British any longer." He gave Katie a special carving. "If you ever meet up with other Cherokees, show them this carving, it will prove that you are my friends."

A couple of hours later we both began our travels back to our homes. It was late July when we eventually reached our island. George and April, met us and had our horses taken to the stables. We dismissed the Rangers and ordered them to get some well earned rest. It was late in the day, and we both wanted to get to bed, but we needed to talk with a couple of people before we made for our bedroom.

I sent Rangers (not the ones who had just returned) to bring Tony Borg and Jane. We explained our thoughts about a half-way house. Tony agreed that building near Pittsburgh would be a good idea. Apparently, the Americans had taken Pittsburgh in 1779. And there was a regiment left in the town. Even Jane saw the advantage of this.

"Well give the idea a thought, we are off to bed." Yawned Katie, she was falling asleep where she was standing. I had to carry her to bed.

We both crashed onto our lovely soft bed, and were soon asleep. I suddenly woke up, I hadn't locked the door, I sprung out of bed and turned the key. I didn't want visitors early in the morning.

I slowly opened my eyes. Through the window I could see blue skies; well, it was summer. I looked at Katie, she was still sound asleep. Then I heard someone knocking on the door to our bedroom.

"Go away, it's too early for us to wake up." I moaned.

"It's 2pm, what do you mean, too early?" It was the voice of Val.

"Don't be silly, we have only been asleep for a few hours." Was my reply, as I closed my eyes again.

Val continued to knock and shout. Eventually she managed to wake Katie up. I think that she must have been still half asleep. She did the unthinkable, she opened the door and let Val into the room.

I opened my eyes again; it looked like my sleep had finished now. No one sleeps when Val is around. She had come to convey a message.

"When you next go in the direction of New York, Jane and Tony will go with you. We can all go into Pittsburgh and check out builders and builders merchants. They should be able to create a plan for a halfway home, and get some idea of the cost." She then looked at Katie "What do you think Katie?"

"Sounds like a great idea. How long do you need in the city?" Katie asked. "A couple of weeks will do. Also, as the war is unlikely going to last more than a couple more years. It doesn't need to be built of long-lasting material. When the war ends, I believe most of us will be heading west." Katie looked towards me, for confirmation. I nodded.

The summer passed and early autumn seemed to fly by. We were all getting bored. Then it came, well, rather *he* came. A rider, looking exhausted, rode into our complex. We all could see the paper carrying our next orders. He dismounted and gave the orders to Katie. We all gathered around her.

"Come on Katie, we are all ready to go." She turned towards me.

"Do you remember Long Island Sound?" I nodded, New York again.

We stopped for a night in Pittsburgh. Escorting Jane and Tony, plus twenty Rangers into the town. The following day, we were off to New York again.

New York overlooked Long Island Sound. We arrived on the 2nd of October. Our plan was to attack and capture a fort named Fort Slongo.

Apparently, The British had contracted George Slongo, of Philadelphia, to construct the fort. In exchange, the fort was named after him. The fort looked to be in a strategic location, overlooking Long Island Sound.

"Taking that fort will be a bit of a challenge, my love. I pray that we don't lose any Rangers in the attempt." I said to Katie.

It appeared the night before, an American reconnaissance force, commanded by Sergeant Elijah Churchill, was sent ahead to plan the attack on the fort. Many of the British officers in charge of the fort were at a party the night before the battle.

After beaching their boats, they made their way to the nearby Nathaniel Skidmore farm. Nathaniel then led the group to the fort to scout out their plan of attack. It was reported that the commanding officer in charge of the fort, Major Valentine, was in New York City on military matters and was not present at the battle.

When we arrived, it was clear that things would kick off at any given moment. A hundred men under the command of Benjamin Tallmadge and led by Major Lemuel Trescott departed from Norwalk, Connecticut in whale boats across Long Island Sound.

Trescott's force was split between fifty men under Captain Richards' company from Edgar's dismounted dragoons, landing in the early hours of October 3rd. Katie's Rangers were already there, waiting for orders.

Captain Edgar's dragoons were ordered to launch a surprise attack on the fort, while Captain Richards' infantry were ordered to surround the fort to prevent any British forces from escaping.

At 3am on October 3rd, Lieutenant Rogers of the 2nd Regiment of Light Dragoons commenced the attack on the fort with his men, with Major Trescott and Captain Edgar's forces in tow. This was the point when Katie's Rangers joined the battle.

A British sentry on duty standing outside the fort saw the American forces attacking and fired his gun to alert the British defenders of an American attack. He then retreated inside the fort, forgetting to shut the gate behind him.

The British put up a lot of resistance once the Americans entered. Katies Rangers were outstanding as a force. Fighting together, they cut their way along the left side of the fort.

The British had 4 soldiers killed and 2 wounded. The only American to be wounded was Elijah Churchill, who later became the first person to receive a Purple Heart. Later, after the Americans left, the fort was burned to the ground.

At last Katie's Rangers had been involved in some fighting! However, we all believed that our Rangers were far better than the other units we had seen. We needed to be challenged with a good battle, where we could show just how good Katie's Rangers were.

"Katie, I often wonder what happened to that sentry who forgot to lock the gates and let us all in." I was smiling.

"Well, I expect the British will hang him. But we would give him a medal." We were both laughing now. "We will find a place to camp overnight, then it's back to Pittsburgh. I hope they have made some good progress." She grinned.

As battles go, with the door to the fort more or less open, this was no more than a skirmish. We all wanted to return home as soon as possible. We knew that we would have to stop at Pittsburgh, but that would be no more than a day. The date was the 4th of October. I was thinking that winter wouldn't be far away.

We arrived in Pittsburgh on the 13th of October 1781. It took a while to find Tony and Jane. The easiest method was to comb the taverns, I was sure that we would find a Ranger or two in one of them. Katie had ordered the rest of her Rangers to camp outside of the town until she called them. We were right, as we approached the bar in one of the taverns, a shout came from the back of the room. Two if the Rangers were playing cards.

"Wait until I get hold of them," whispered Katie. "All Rangers are under orders not to play cards in these places." She was livid. I would not like to be in their boots.

We bought a beer each, then found a couple of chairs near where all the action was. Both the Rangers were almost out of money. The man next to the dealer, who was wearing a smart suit and a stetson, had a pile of money lying on the table in front of them. Katie and I looked at each other and smiled. We both knew what was happening. From where we were sitting, we could see the dealer was messing with the cards.

One of the Rangers began to smile.

"He has got a good hand at last, but he hasn't got enough money left." Katie observed. "This is going to turn nasty. Dafydd, Keep an eye on the man with the rifle on the balcony."

I looked up, I had seen these men before, always ready to shoot someone in the back for money.

Smiling, and looking so happy, the Ranger pushed all the money he had left into the pot, and made his bid.

"What an idiot," claimed Katie, "they all know that he had a very good hand." The gambler smiled and pushed all the money he had to raise the bid. The Ranger may have a better hand, but he did not have the money to bid again. He turned to his friend and asked for a loan, he even offered to share the winnings. His friend was now looking directly at the man with the rifle on the balcony, The rifle was now pointing at him.

"Katie, would you like to say hello to that man?" I asked. She grinned. "I am on my way."

The Ranger who had the good hand, was offering to sell his horse to get enough money to raise the bid. The Gambler smiled.

"I would like to help you; ok you need $2,000 to call my bid. He pulled the money in dollars out of his pocket. There is your money, I will collect the horse later." The Ranger was all smiles now and lent over to collect the winnings. The gambler raised his hand. He got out another wad of money and put it into the pot.

"I think you'll find that I have won the pot."

The Ranger lost his head and nearly his life. He stood up and pulled out his pistol, accusing the man of cheating. The gambler, without looking, pointed up to the balcony.

"Put your pistol down, before my man shoots."

The Ranger looked to where the gambler was pointing. He turned a deathly white. Katie was staring at him. The man with the rifle could only kill him. But this is Katie. While he was distracted by Katie, the gambler picked up his pistol, and fired at the Ranger. I was ready and shot the ranger in the leg causing him to tumble and avoid the bullet from the gambler's pistol. The dealer was now running towards the door. Katie took care of him - it is difficult to run with a bullet in your leg. I now stood beside the gambler at the table.

I turned his cards over, then ordered the other Ranger to turn his friend's hand over. The Ranger had the highest hand. The gambler then argued that he had placed the higher bid. I then picked up the notes he had placed as his higher bid.

"These are British pound notes. This is an American town, and only dollars are legal currency here." I picked up his pounds and threw them at him. "The winner is the Ranger over there. Apart from the money you gave him for the horse that he does not own - which he will return to you now." I stared in his direction.

I turned to shout up to Katie, simultaneously she shouted a warning. I dropped to the floor as a knife flew over my head. As I fell, I grabbed my knife. As I hit the floor, I threw the knife. He was now trying to pick up his pistol, but with my knife protruding from his stomach, it was a bit difficult.

Everything seems to happen at the same time. As he fell to the floor clutching the knife, about ten soldiers ran into the tavern. Lucky we were both still in uniform. The lad in charge was a bit slow. He ordered his men to arrest me. Katie was looking down from the balcony.

"Lieutenant, do you not understand ranks?" He looked at her, then back at me. "Incase you don't understand pips, you have just arrested a major."

I love that woman; she has a great sense of humour. He on the other hand was now petrified. He could be disciplined in many ways. He was very apologetic.

"Ok, just do your work and arrest the man with the knife in his belly, then return it to me. And also, the dealer who is lying over there." I ordered.

He quickly relayed the orders to his men. Then enquired if there was anything else.

"I have one more order. That is for you to clamp down on gambling." He saluted and left with his two prisoners.

Now it was time to watch the fun. Katie was slowly descending the stairs. Katie was loved by every one of her Rangers. They would ride into the jaws of death willingly for her. She took care of her

Rangers and would never send them into a battle that they could not win. She was a fair disciplinarian. But don't break her rules. Ever!

The two Rangers, one limping with blood trickling out of the bullet wound, sheepishly approached Katie. The one with the limp began his explanation by addressing her as Katie. She kicked his good leg and he rolled across the floor.

"My name is Major Brooks."

I shook my head; they were really in for it now. She went through the rules and laws of her regiment.

"What have I given orders for my Rangers *never* to do?"

They both fell to their knees and begged forgiveness. I could see that in this case, there would be no forgiveness, only discipline. Finally, Katie decided on their penalty.

"If I had a group of Rangers with me at this moment, you would both be whipped. Lucky for you, in their absence, I will forgo this. But you have both shown that I cannot trust you both. I therefore banish you from the Rangers, I do not need people like you. Remove your tunics now and leave."

CHAPTER 26

THE BATTLE OF JOHNSTOWN

We both left the tavern with no idea where Jane and Tony were. In the end we decided to check each hotel. This was the next most likely place to find them.

Pittsburgh was a very small town, there weren't that many hotels. Lucky for us, the first hotel we visited was the one they were staying at. They were surprised to see us.

"How many rooms have you booked Jane?" asked Katie. Well one each for Tony and myself. Another four rooms for the Rangers. "If you are staying you can share our rooms." She offered.

"I think that Katie is more concerned about the price of six rooms. Anyway, do you have any information to report?" I asked.

"The news is good. We have found an honest builder. We suggested that the halfway house should be built to hold 400 Rangers. The builder suggested that we would need around 100 buildings to house that many. Also, it would of course require a stockade. He suggested a place to build the half-way house. A river runs past the town to the north, if it was built there, we would get the protection of the town's soldiers. Also, when the war ends, the buildings can be sold to the townspeople." She moved across the room to pour a glass of wine for us. "It's rather a win-win situation for us. A place to stay, a river running by, and protection of the town's soldiers."

"The builder told us that his team could build what in fact was a small fort, in about three months. He then explained that he would

302

begin by building the stockade. Followed by one building at a time. This means that the first building will be completed within a week. With the fence erected, we can set up our tents inside a safe place in no time at all."

Tony and Jane were happy with the plans.

"The important subject is the cost. What are we looking at?" enquired Katie.

Jane was smiling, as expected she had the subject covered.

"He gave us a good price, and will accept payment in gold."

"We won't be able to provide any gold until we get back to Philadelphia." Advised Katie.

Jane was still smiling.

"Do you remember, we bought a wagon with us to carry medical supplies and to carry any injured Rangers?" We both nodded. "Well, under the floor of the wagon you will find enough gold nuggets to finance the project. We waited for the exchange until you arrived with the Rangers to protect the gold."

Katie thanked them both.

"We will stay overnight with you, then collect the Rangers who are camped outside the town. We will then transfer the gold to the builder. The morning after we will be off back home." I confirmed.

We both needed that sleep; we have done a lot of travelling. We sat down to breakfast, the first decent meal for some time. Katie was hoping to get away by noon, and by sunset we would be well on our way back to Philadelphia. What a breakfast, three slices of bacon, four sausages, three eggs, beans, mushrooms. bread and a nice cup of tea. As I was about to bite into my third sausage, the door burst open and in rushed Lana.

The orders for our next battle had been delivered to the complex at Philadelphia. The order was for the Rangers to go to the town of Johnstown, which was somewhere in the Mohawk Valley. We had a lot of memories of our time in the valley.

The problem was that the Rangers had to be there as soon as possible. The letter contained the current information.

British regulars and militia, commanded by Major John Ross of the King's Royal Regiment of New York and Captain Walter Butler's

Rangers, had raided the border area. Local American forces, led by Colonel Marinus Willett, blocked the British advance.

As we already knew from previous experience. New York's Mohawk Valley had been a major area of internecine warfare through the American revolution.

By 1780, raids conducted by British soldiers, mercenaries, Loyalists, and their Mohawk allies, had devastated the valley.

The 1780 fall crops had been destroyed before harvest, and a number of small settlements had been abandoned as settlers sought safety from attacks. In addition to the hundreds of buildings burned, civilian casualties amounted to 197 dead in 1780 alone.

These raids were also threatening the American supply routes to Fort Plain and Fort Stanwix on the frontier. Repeated raids further depleted the ranks of the local militia, already decimated by the Battle of Oriskany, by desertions, abandonment of the valley and occasional casualties.

In response, the Governor of New York, George Clinton, sent Colonel Marinus Willet to take charge of the Militia and organise the defence of the valley.

Willet was well aware of what Katie's Rangers had done in the valley in the past. He sent his fastest riders to Philadelphia, to request the support of the Rangers.

Lana had arrived with thirty Rangers, and told us that Andy said that he would be ready to move in about three days.

"That will be too late. They need us now." Shouted Katie.

"You are right my love, I think it must be us, who depart now, with Andy following." She agreed.

I took a last look at my breakfast, I almost shed a tear, as I followed Katie out of the room. We left Jane and Tony, plus ten rangers behind. They would have to inform Andy that we have gone to fight the battle, and that his men should follow as soon as possible.

We packed as quickly as possible. Katie had wanted to leave at noon and we did. Fighting battles was what we trained for, it was the travelling in between that was so annoying.

We arrived on the 24th of October. Well, I say arrived, we were at the top of the valley, we still had a short ride to reach Johnstown.

To our surprise we somehow bumped into the American force. Katie made herself known to Colonel Willets and he welcomed our arrival. He explained the current situation to her.

"At the beginning of the fall, a large force of British regulars, Loyalists, and Mohawk warriors, entered the Mohawk Valley. They were several hundred strong. They once captured Curry Town, but did not burn it, to prevent the smoke giving us a warning of their whereabouts.

We are following a raiding party, which is made up of British soldiers led by Major John Ross, Loyalists, Militiamen, led by Walter Butler, and Mohawk warriors. We are pursuing them as they travel through this valley on their way to attack Johnstown."

October 25th 1781. We joined up with Willet's soldiers as they continued to pursue the enemy. Finally, we caught up with the enemy just outside Johnstown, in the afternoon.

I so wished that we had Andy's team with us. We were outnumbered, despite the two hundred Rangers. So, Willet decided to divide his forces.

We were ordered to go around the enemy's right flank and attack from the rear. I looked at Katie, she was smiling. Finally Katie's Rangers would be able to use all that training, and show what great fighters they were. Some of the Mohawk warriors had faced us in the past, they were fully aware of how good fighters we were.

Once at the rear, Katie made a short speech.

"We have supported others in many battles, this is maybe our first chance to show just how good we truly are. Are we the best?" That got them all pumped up. Their reply came as a roar.

"Charge!" shouted Katie.

Willet advanced across an open field towards the British, who withdrew into the edge of the forest. There followed intense fighting.

For unknown reasons, the Militia on Willet's right flank, suddenly turned and fled in panic. We were informed about this and Katie led a hundred of her Rangers over to support Willet. Katie and her Rangers attacked the British rear when they were on the verge of capitalising on the collapse of the American right flank.

The battle then broke up into small groups, with both sides fighting each other. Surrounded, the British began retreating to a nearby mountain top.

Over the days following the battle, the British withdrew towards their landings on Lake Oneida. Still pursued by Willet, despite the snow storm. Willet caught up with the British.

We were told later that the unsung hero of the skirmish was Walter Butler, but he has been killed. When Willet's men came upon the enemy, they were drying their clothes by the fire.

Walter Butler was killed by an Indian. The story goes that the Indian shot him, scalped him, then ran off with his red coat.

After this, Willet's forces turned around and headed for their homes. Katie and I decided that this team of 200 Rangers, who had recently fought two battles, should return back to Philadelphia. As soon as Andy, with the other team, arrived we would go to Pittsburgh with them and see how the construction was going.

Twenty-four hours later, team A arrived.

"Andy, you missed the battle! Team B just fought two battles in succession. So, we will be taking a well earned rest until after the winter. Therefore, I would like your support with our halfway house," I told him.

Andy wasn't very happy. I went and found Lana.

"Did I tell him the wrong way? We are friends, I thought he would understand."

"You forget, my husband was a mountain man. He spent months alone in the wilderness, with only the animals and birds to speak with - maybe just the occasional Indian. When he gave this all up, he thought he would be playing an important role in the war for independence. In the beginning, it was happening, there were many battles. Now he spends weeks, months, often bored. He has just missed two battles. Then you ask him to sit and watch the building of a halfway home. Do you understand?"

I stroked my chin.

"The British are on the run; I believe that the war will be over in a year or two. Will Andy go west with us, or return to the mountains? And if he chooses the mountains, will you go with him?"

For a minute or two we both stood taking in what I had just said.

"No, I would not go with him. I was born and brought up on a farm. I will go west with you and Katie. I want to carve a place out for me and my children. Build a farm. Raise cattle. For this I will give blood, get blisters on my hands, and sweat from morning to night. This is my dream. We will travel into the unexplored wilderness. I hope Andy will be beside me, but if the call of the mountain is stronger than his connection to me, then I will wish him well. However, to go west is my dream."

At that point Katie walked into the room.

"I hope I haven't interrupted anything." I shook my head.

"No, it's ok, we were just discussing her dream. Apart from a farm, her dream is the same as ours." Lana said goodbye and left.

"Dafydd, the two of you were not alone. Andy was lurking in the shadows. When I came in, he turned and left, I am fairly sure he had tears in his eyes."

I explained about our discussion.

"I guess that Andy has the call of the wild piercing his heart." I surmised.

"When he married Lana, did he really think that she would want to spend her life living in the wilderness?" Asked Katie.

"I think I had better find him and have a chat."

I found him sitting outside the stables.I sat down beside him.

"Sorry, I did not know that you were listening. That is probably a conversation you two should have had between yourselves. I will tell you a story about a friend of mine, if that's ok?" He just nodded. "This friend of mine, he lived in a small village, not a huge amount of people, but everyone knew each other. His village had three mountains surrounding the village. He used to spend a lot of time up these mountains. When he was at the top looking down on the villages, it was like God looking down at his people from above.

As he grew older, he had a problem finding work. He heard that the army was advertising for soldiers to go to America. He has never had a fight in his life, but he needed the money. He did not want to leave his village, especially the mountains, but in the end he had to go, he needed the money. He put together a plan. His plan was to work and save as much money as possible. He had signed up for two years. After his contract expired, he was going to return home to his village. With money in his pocket, he would be like a king in his village.

Within two hours of landing. My friend met a woman. For him it was love at first sight. His response from this woman was not friendly, but eventually they became closer. Now and then he still thinks of his village. But he knew that he was going to follow this woman wherever she went. Basically, his life had changed too much, no one would be able to recognise him from the lad who arrived from the navy ship."

"That friend was you, Dafydd. Wasn't it?" I nodded.

"I really fell in love with Katie. And I still will do whatever she wants me to. My question to you is, how much do you really love your wife? By the way, I presume that you are aware that most of us are moving west after the war. The west is all the wilderness and adventure you will ever need. Think about it." Then I left.

As I left, he stood up and followed me out of the door.

"Thanks, Dafydd, I am off to see Lana now, I need to make things right with us. I will tell her that I am staying, because I cannot live without her." He grinned. "Then I will report for work on the halfway house." He added as he walked off.

I found Katie with Tony, Jane and a local builder. It turned out that we had two choices. As it was November now, we could expect snow at any time.

Option one: we rush into the forest and cut as many trees as will be needed, then try to continue to work on the buildings during the snow. This may or may not be possible. If we had a bad winter, not only would we have problems with the snow, but there would be hungry wolves roaming, and maybe even the odd Indian after a scalping.

Option two: we simply wait until the spring. We should be able to be building around April. All four of us sat down, slightly depleted. Katie was the first to speak.

"If we choose the first option, I believe many of those involved in the work will suffer, perhaps even die. The second choice is beginning the project in April 1782." She stood shaking her head. "I believe that the British will be in their last throws, and within a year will be driven from our shores." She turned to Tony. "If we begin to build in April, when do you think that complex will be completed?"

Tony picked up a piece of paper and a pen and began to write some notes.

"If everything goes well. It will take six months to complete."

I began to laugh.

"So, you are saying that our halfway house will be ready around this time next year? If we go ahead with the project, it is completed around October/November. Winter will follow, so we won't be wanting to use it until the spring of 1783." I looked at Katie. "I know the idea came from me and if I had come up with this Idea a couple of years ago, it would have been extremely helpful. Now, realistically, we are too late. We should just forget about the project and return as soon as possible to our island. Let's have a vote." I concluded.

Sadly, they all agreed with me, it was too late. Jane was left to sort the builder out, just in case he was out of pocket for any of the planning. Then Tony, Katie and I. went looking for the team leaders.

"I will go find Andy and Lana; I think they will both be pleased."

Katie went looking for John and his brother, they may not be so excited with the decision to cancel the project. While Tony went his own way.

The gold was put back under the floor of the medical wagon. Provisions were bought. Orders were given to be ready to leave first thing the following morning. Most of the Rangers were pleased to know they would be home and spending the winter with their loved ones.

It was now November 25th.

"Hopefully we will be home for Christmas" I whispered into Katie's ear.

We knew that if the snow fell before we reached Philadelphia, it would slow us down drastically. We needed to keep going day and night, but we also knew that we would have to stop, to at least give our horses a rest. Each night we stopped as late as possible, but this was a gamble as riding in the dark, the horses could be injured.

CHAPTER 27

SIEGE OF BRYAN'S STATION

As we lay in our tent, still fully clothed, we could hear the call of the wild. It was wolves.

"They sound hungry, and it hasn't snowed yet. I will go and check that the horses are well secured." Katie said.

The howling of the wolves grew louder. I ran after Katie. There she was, surrounded by about ten wolves.

We both drew on our adrenalin power. As the adrenalin filled our bodies, we became faster, stronger, and were thinking quicker.

One of the wolves noticed me approaching. He ran towards me, hoping for a quick kill. His hope was achieved, but not to its satisfaction - he was on the negative end of the encounter.

I was soon standing back-to-back with Katie as more wolves appeared. We both stood with a sword in one hand and a knife in the other. After we had killed about ten of the wolves, the other Rangers had woken up and were running towards us. This caused the remaining wolves to flee back into the forest.

"Are you ok?" Asked Lana. She and Andy were the first to reach us. We both had a few bites, it's lucky that wolves don't carry swords, I grinned.

"What are you grinning at?" Demanded White Eagle.

"I was just thinking of an old saying. 'You can't put your hand in the fire without getting burnt.'

"That's an old saying. How old are you really Dafydd?" That could only be one woman, Val.

"Age, to us Welshmen, is like fine wine. The older we get, the better we become."

She now had her arm around me.

"I'd say you're more like wine that's been left open too long - past its prime and will only give us a headache in the morning." She joked.

Katie finally came over and saved me.

"Leave him alone, he is defenceless against you! Plus I think he may have lost too much blood"

Then she put her arm around me, and called a Ranger over. I had taken a couple of nasty bites which were gushing blood. I needed to get to the hospital quickly.

"It's ok, I am here." It was Rachell.

She gave orders for me to be kept warm. Then she put on some very tight bandages to stop the bleeding on both bites.

"Ok, take him to the hospital tent now" As I was being led away, I could see her examining Katie's bites.

"Wait!" I ordered the first Ranger that we passed, to find out how the sentries were, then report back to me. Then I fainted.

I came to, lying in a warm clean bed. Rachell had personally taken care of my injuries, and cleaned me up. Both Andy and Lana were sitting next to my bed.

"How are the sentries?" I asked.

They both sat in silence, neither wanted to report the news.

"He is a lot stronger than he looks." Smiled Katie. "Tell him the truth."

Eventually Lana gave me the bad news. All four sentries were killed. The truth was that this was what I had expected to hear. I laid in bed thinking.

"I will send men into the forest and kill every wolf we can find." Shouted Andy, he was wanting revenge.

I shook my head.

"No! They were only hunting to get food for their families. That is not a crime, even if we did become their prey. It is how they must

311

survive." I adjusted my position in the bed, so I could speak more comfortably. "The reason they are dead is not the fault of the Wolves, the fault lies with me. I should have sent a lot more sentries out, heavily armed. When the wolves attacked, they had no chance at all."

"It was not your fault alone; I am as guilty as you."

Katie was now sitting on my bed with her arms around me and tears were flowing down her cheeks. It takes a lot to make my wife cry. As soon as I could, I lifted the sheets and began to get out of my bed. My wounds had been treated and I had had some sleep, I urgently needed to visit the families of the dead sentries.

Katie saw what I was trying to do, and hastily stood in front of me, in order to prevent my embarrassment. Jen and Val were just about to walk into the room.

"Darling, Rachell could not find any night clothes for you to wear after she cleaned you up." I looked down and jumped back into my bed.

"Oh no!"

"It's ok, I have seen it all before." Grinned val.

"Katie, please find me some clothes. I need to visit the families of the dead sentries immediately. They will all be buried with full honours."

"We will have to get back to Philadelphia first." Stated Katie.

It took an hour to find my clothing, then to wash and dress and eat some breakfast, before Rachell would let me be released from the hospital tent.

Then Katie and I made our way out of the Hospital tent to find the families. Two of the Rangers had no family with them. One of the Rangers had only recently got married, and the fourth Ranger had a wife and three children.

"Katie, can we pray before we make our visitations? We will need God with us, as we try to find words of comfort for the families."

She agreed and we found a place where we were alone. We asked the father to give us the compassion to be able to comfort those we will be visiting. We needed his peace, as we shared the grief of the families. After we had prayed, we both felt at peace, knowing that Jesus would be with us.

First, we visited the young woman, who had only recently married her now dead husband. We explained how sorry we were. But words alone cannot mend a broken heart. I explained that we considered her as part of our family, that we would fulfil the role of her husband. I was about to say 'until you find another man to love' but that would be unfeeling for a woman who had only just lost the love of her life. I did say that we would always be here for her, and she would receive a pension. I will need to speak with Jane and Val about that as soon as possible.

Then she more or less collapsed into my arms. Tears were flooding down her face and into my shirt. I looked towards Katie. She nodded her approval. I held onto her while she cried. This was something that she needed to get out by releasing her tears. I became caught up in the emotion. I shed a few tears myself. She cried for maybe twenty or thirty minutes. Then she pulled her face away. Her eyes were a deep red. I felt so sorry for her, I was speechless. I thanked God that Katie came to save me.

Katie and Lana, plus Jen who had joined us, took care of her. Lana and Jen then told Katie to go with me to visit the last woman, a wife and mother of three children. They agreed to look after the woman. After that I was having second thoughts about meeting the next woman, but it had to be done.

We knocked on her front door, it did not take her long to answer. She was older than the previous lady, she looked to be in her early forties. It was her second marriage, but first or second, it makes no difference. She was distraught. Again, we told her how sorry we were.

"Tell me, when will my children and I have to leave?" She sobbed. I looked confused.

"Why do you ask that; you won't have to leave." A smile came to her face. It seemed that when her first husband was killed. She and her children had to leave the married quarters of their regiment. She looked a little bit happier. "But I will need to earn money to feed my children."

"Don't worry about money, you and your children are part of the family. You will receive a pension. We will always be here for you, and your children." Assured Katie.

That was one of the hardest jobs that I have ever had to carry out in my life, I thought. But neither of us were up for any other occupation. Both of us had problems sleeping that night. We were both awake early the following morning.

"Katie, I think we need to take a look at the tavern we own. We will be able to see how my brother and Jane's daughters are getting on." She agreed.

That evening, about 9pm, we both arrived at the tavern. The place was packed.

"With all these people, it should be making a lot of money!" Exclaimed Katie.

We each got a beer, then found a seat at the back of the hall. We thought that we should observe first, before joining them for a chat. Everything seemed to be going well, although I wasn't sure where my brother was. I thought that this was a good time to join the game. I enjoy a game of cards, as long as they are not fixed. I played while Katie observed.

I began to smile; the dealer was dealing as many from the top as he did from the bottom. After a while Katie tried her luck on the roulette. She even won a hundred dollars. It seemed that all the games were straight. This dealer was the only problem. I was not losing any money so I decided to quit the game. After all, I was only making a report. A man in a black suit drew his pistol and ordered me to sit down and draw a card. So that was it - this man and the dealer were playing together. I continued to play.

Suddenly, a man who had lost a lot of money that evening, stood up and drew his pistol.

"Give me my money back, you cheat. While he was watching the dealer, the man in black drew his pistol. He was about to fire when a bullet came from elsewhere. The man in black was no more. The dealer leant across the table and grabbed a handful of notes before running towards the door. My brother shot him.

Georgia ordered the music to play, and six dancing girls appeared. To our surprise, the lead dancer was Anne.

Then, from nowhere, a tall man with blond hair entered. He grabbed hold of Anne and threw her over his shoulder.

"No wife of mine will work in a place like this!" He walked towards the door, with her still over his shoulder.

It was Dan. But why was Anne dancing in the first place? A drunk pulled out his pistol and aimed it at Dan. I had drawn my pistol and shot the drunk before he knew what was happening. I was now heading towards my brother. It was clear that I could not trust him. He saw me coming and was trying to avoid me. Eventually he could not retreat anymore.

"I can't fight you Dafydd. I've heard the stories, I would have no chance."

I punched him as hard as I could. He dropped to the floor as if I had hit him on the head with a hammer. There happened to be about six rangers in the tavern at the time. I ordered two of them to get him back to the island and to lock him up.

Two more were ordered to take Georgia and Anne, with the assistance of Dan, back as well. Then Katie and I, with the assistance of the last two Rangers, began to clear everyone out of the tavern.

It took a while but eventually the place was empty. We nailed a notice on the door. 'Closed until further notice'. We left the two Rangers there, just in case there was any more trouble.

Next, we found the officer in charge for the night and informed him of what had happened. He promised to send troops there to protect the property. I told him that we planned to sell the tavern as soon as possible. He thought that he knew a few people that may be interested. We left things with him and returned back to the island.

By the time we arrived back at our room it was 2am. We went to sleep. Everything else would have to wait until the morning.

We were woken early, six o'clock to be exact, by banging on our boor. Katie opened the door, and there stood Jane. She was furious.

I knew what she was here about, but she was not the only one to be enraged. Katie was in a predicament. Unless the two of us calmed down, there would be a huge argument. How could she calm the fire in at least one of us?

An idea came to her. She got back into bed, and while Jane was left watching. She basically covered me in kisses. Every time I tried to speak; she kissed me. In a short time, I came to my senses and realised that I would have to calm down, after all Jane is a friend.

"Jane, why are you here?" She was staring at me. "My husband is in prison and my daughters have been sent home crying. And you are asking why I'm upset?"

Katie asked Jane to sit down on our bed.

"Let Dafydd tell you what he found when we visited the tavern last night. Jane was beginning to cool down.

"Ok, tell me what happened." She agreed to listen.

"When we entered the Tavern at 9pm. There was no one in charge. I sat at the poker table where the dealer and another card sharp were cheating. Eventually a fight broke out which I had to stop. Later, Gareth turned up and shot both the dealer and the card sharp. Next, Georgie appeared dressed… Well, the only word I could use to describe how she looked was a tart. Then top it all off, dancing girls appeared and who was the lead dancer? Anne." Jane looked shocked. "Before we left, I sent your husband to jail, at least until I have had chance to cool down, then we can discuss what we saw last night."

We sent your daughters back to you, their mother. You can sort them out. The tavern was closed and put up for sale. I can find better use for the money." She was no longer on fire. "If you have nothing else to say, I bid you farewell, as I am now off to have words with my brother."

She sat silently shaking her head.

"Katie, I am off to the jail to find out what was happening last night. I will leave you to answer any questions Jane may have. I would also like to know where Dan Richards is."

The Ranger who was looking after our jail, let me in, then opened the door to Gareth's cell. He was sitting on the floor at the back of the cell. There was a man with 'guilty' written all over him. I sat on the floor of the cell next to my brother.

"So, what's been going on at the tavern?" He took his time preparing his answer.

"I tried to manage the tavern as you requested. But people did not want to come to it. Everyone wanted gambling, girls and music. Generally, a good time. You put me in charge with instructions to make money, and we were not. So, bit by bit I reintroduced gambling. Legal gambling. No cheating. Those two who you saw last night were new. I didn't find out until last night, and dealt with them. It was Georgia and Anne that offered to wear clothes that would attract the customers. Also, Anne has a nice voice and has always wanted to sing and dance on stage." That surprised me, seeing as she had been mute when we first met. "That's everything" he claimed. I called to the Ranger on guard, and told him that my brother could be released.

"Thank you brother, I knew you would understand." He said.

"You are wrong Gareth, I only understand that you're a poor manager, in fact a weak manager. I am transferring you to join Andy and Lana's team. You are now a Ranger, until I find a more suitable job for you." I then left the prison and went back to join Katie.

When I arrived, Jane had left, I told Katie what had taken place and that Gareth was now a Ranger.

"To be honest my love, I do not want to have to rely on him in a battle. He would probably run." I admitted.

We went over to see how Jane had progressed with her girls. As we entered her office, we were greeted by Val.

"Jane will be out in a minute, she has spoken with her girls and wants to discuss things with the two of you."

Val made us both a cup of tea while we waited. Half an hour later Jane appeared. She apologised on behalf of her husband and her daughters, and offered to leave the island. Katie and I were now in shock, Jane was very important to Katie's Rangers.

"Jane, I believe that everyone makes mistakes. If people understand what they have done, and want to change, then I believe that their mistakes should be forgotten." I knew that the girls were in the other room. "Georgia and Anne, will you both please come in."

The girls entered somewhat sheepishly. Katie then began to speak.

"As leaders, we have to put round pegs in round holes, if we try to put a round peg in a square hole, it will not fit. Now Jane is doing an amazing job here. What would the two of you like to do?"

The girls began to talk with each other. Then Anne stood up and began to speak.

"Before, Dan and I were responsible for recruitment. You moved me from that job to the tavern." I was a bit embarrassed now, I had forgotten her original job. "Given a chance, this is what we would like to do. Both of us, with Dan, would like to be responsible for recruitment. But also, as part of this, we were hoping to put together an entertainment group. We can then put on shows to prevent boredom and build morale."

Katie and I looked at each other, and seemed to agree.

"So where does Dan fit into these shows?" I asked.

"Have you ever heard Dan sing?" Anne grinned. I shook my head. "He has an amazing voice!"

"Ok, the past is forgotten and yes all three of you have the ok to deliver what you have suggested."

"And what about my husband?" Asked Jane. "Are you going to put him in the front line at the next battle?"

I grinned. "As we are forgetting the past, I have a special job for my brother. Soon, the war will end, and most of us will be moving west. I think that Gareth's time would be well spent doing research for our journey." Jane thought that would be ideal. "But, I am putting you as his supervisor. If he is irresponsible, you will both have to answer for it." She understood.

Winter came and went. Spring also passed by. Rachell had all the Rangers trained in first aid.

"That way, if your partner gets injured, you are able to help. Perhaps even save their life." She had said.

The Rangers trained to fight, but to them, training was boring, they were all itching for a real fight. It had been a warm dry summer so far, we were now in the middle of July. I was chatting with Katie, when a rider came into view, waving a letter, or at least it looked like a letter.

"Katie, we have orders!" I shouted.

The messenger dismounted. Katie tore the letter out of his hand, and began to read it.

"Does anyone know Bryan's station? It's in Kentucky somewhere."

Everyone was jumping up and down with excitement. Finally we had something to do!

"Who cares where it is, we will find it, and maybe we will get to see our old friend Daniel Boone."

Katie took team A, led by Andy and Lana, as they had missed the last two battles. She insisted that we were away on time - we may have arrived at our location a little bit late on a few too many occasions.

Bryan's station was situated down the Mohawk Valley, an area which we were familiar with, having fought Indians here in the past. We arrived before any action. We met up with our old friend, Captain Daniel Boone, and he set the scene.

"This is a fortified settlement, consisting of forty cabins, which has withstood attacks on many occasions. An army of British Canadian soldiers, led by William Caldwell, along with Renegade Simon Girty and 300 Shawnees and Delaware warriors, is marching towards this fort."

We had plenty of food, but little water. The hostile forces had secretly surrounded the fort, but we were aware of their presence.

As the enemy arrived quickly, we did not have time to collect water from the spring located a short distance from the fort. A daring plan was devised, and some of the women volunteered to collect water from the stream. They believed that the Indians would not attack them, as they were women and it would reveal their presence. It was an outstanding feat of bravery by the women.

The attack on the fort began, known as the Siege of Bryan's Station, on August 15-17th, 1782. When the attackers discovered that relief was on its way in the form of the local militia, they withdrew.

The relief column arrived at the fort, to the excitement of the settlers. They gathered volunteers from the fort, including Daniel Boone, and set off in pursuit of the British and their allies.

Katie was asked to send her Rangers as well, but she took advice from Daniel Boone who believed that they could be riding into an ambush.

His prediction was true. One of the few men who escaped the massacre made his report. It was known as The Battle of Blue Licks - one of the last battles of the American revolutionary war.

After leaving the fort, the Kentucky militia pursued the Shawnee and British forces for 60 miles. The Battle of Blue Licks took place on August 19th 1782, on a hill next to the Licking River in Kentucky. As the Kentuckians reached the river, they spotted a few Indian scouts watching them from across the river. Daniel Boone suspected that the Indians were trying to lure them into an ambush and advised caution, but Hugh McGary urged immediate action.

Despite the warning, McGary mounted his horse and rode across the river, calling out, "Them that aren't cowards, follow me." Most of the men followed him, and Boone reluctantly followed. The Kentuckians dismounted and formed a battle line several rows deep before advancing up the hill. McGary and Benjamin Logan were in the centre, Colonels Stephen Trigg and John Todd were on the right, and Boone was on the left.

Caldwell's forces were waiting on the other side of the hill, concealed in ravines. When the Kentuckians reached the summit, the Indians opened fire with deadly accuracy, at close range. After five minutes, the centre and right of the line fell back, leaving Boone's men on the left to push forward. Todd and Trigg were shot dead. McGary informed Boone that everyone was retreating and that he was surrounded. Boone then ordered his men to retreat, and the battle was lost.

In the end, the Battle of Blue Licks was a decisive victory for the Shawnee and their allies. The Kentuckians suffered significant losses, including the death of many of their leaders. It was the last major engagement of the Revolutionary War fought in Kentucky and the last victory for the Loyalists and Natives. 83 men had been killed or captured, including Boone's son, Israel.

After being told the results of the pursuit, there was a visible sigh of relief that we had listened to Katie, and not joined the others.

CHAPTER 28

SIEGE OF FORT HENRY

While we had been helping to defend Bryan's station. Back on our island, John and Nick had received orders for our next battle, or in this case another siege.

A large force had been spotted on its way to attack Fort Henry. Fort Henry was an outpost in West Virginia. After checking on a map, they found that Fort Henry rested just off the Ohio River, between the south east corner of Ohio and the north west of West Virginia.

George Washington had spies everywhere, as every good general would. News had reached him of a British plan to join up with Indians from four other tribes and attack an outpost in West Virginia.

They sent messengers to Katie and myself, informing us of the situation, and that they were riding to give support to Fort Henry as per the orders.

As Fort Henry was roughly in the middle of both our current positions. They were hoping to meet up there, as soon as we had completed our orders at Bryan's station.

After reading the letter, we both agreed that this was the correct procedure. It also showed the benefit of having two teams. According to Washington's information, the attack was planned for early September around the 10th or 11th.

After the massacre at Blue Licks. We had ridden down and buried our dead, then brought our injured back to the fort. With a sixty mile journey each way, this took time. Clearly team B would arrive at Fort Henry before us, hopefully we would be in time to support them later.

Fort Henry was built for the settlers to retreat into, in case they were attacked. Leaving their cabins subject to the desires of the attackers. As team B approached, they found signs of a very large force just ahead of them. Scouts were sent ahead to check on what they had in front of them. The scouts returned with bad news. There were about fifty British and Loyalist soldiers, as well as about three hundred warriors, from The Wyandot, Shawnee, Seneca, and Delaware tribes.

The scouts also found out that the fort had only forty men and boys, protecting sixty women and children. Nick's idea was that when the sun was almost set, they would surprise the enemy by charging through them and into the fort, hopefully those who were manning the fort would see the American flags, which they intended to fly, and open the gates.

The plan worked like a dream. The attackers were taken by total surprise, and with their flags flying, the gates were opened, and excited settlers welcomed the Rangers inside the fort.

With the Rangers, they were still outnumbered but at least they had more of a chance. Not to mention their more fortified position.

Apparently, Simon Girty, known for his savagery towards settlers, was in charge of the Native Americans. His force joined up with Butler's Rangers and a Loyalist unit from New York. They were all put under the direction of Captain Pratt. This force had participated with Native Americans in the massacre of Patriot prisoners, women and children, early in the war during the 1778 Wyoming and Cherry Valley Massacre.

The Zane family, under the direction of Colonel David Shepherd, was charged with defending the fort.

Girty and Pratt demanded surrender, but Shepherd refused. Stating that they would rather die than surrender. The settlers had two cannons and lots of weapons, they could stand their ground. The first attack failed.

However, the second attack, on the following day, the settlers had a big problem. They were running out of gunpowder. They knew that they would not be able to defend the fort much longer if they lost the use of their cannon and rifles.

One of the women remembered the store of gunpowder in her brother's cabin, outside the fort. She volunteered to retrieve the powder. Apparently she had three reasons for going herself. The first was that she believed that the enemy would be less likely to shoot a woman. The second reason was that she knew exactly where the powder was stored. The third was simply because she was young and strong enough to carry it all.

At noon the second day of the siege, Betty Zane walked the 60 yards and opened the door to her brother's cabin. There was a brief pause in the fighting as she entered the cabin, and she was able to successfully gather the much-needed supplies. However, on her way back to the fort, she was fired upon by the attackers. She ran as fast as she could, managing to make it safely back to the fort with the powder.

With the much needed gunpowder, the defenders were able to hold out until reinforcements arrived the next day.

On September 13th, Captain John Boggs arrived with 70 soldiers to aid in the defence of Fort Henry. The siege had lasted from September 11th to September 13th.

When Nick told me about Betty Zane walking to the cabin and collecting the gunpowder, I remembered the women who had collected the water also in front of the enemy's guns. I also thought of our women, especially my Katie. These frontier women were no ordinary women. They would happily fight alongside their men, and die with them, rather than give way to the Indians, the mountains, the rivers and the deserts which may lay in their way. When it comes to courage, they are filled to the brim with it.

Some people wanted us to chase after the enemy. We outnumbered them, and were skilled Indian fighters. Before Katie could reply to their requests, I shouted a clear "No!"

This was clearly the last major battle in the North. There were some naval battles in The Bahamas, Cuba, Guadeloupe, Cape May, and Martinique. Most of the British and their German allies were returning home, as they had other battles to fight in Europe. If we pursued the enemy, we might lose some of our Rangers needlessly. I, for one, did not want to have to visit any widows or fatherless children ever again. Katie clearly agreed.

All the Rangers set up camp outside the fort. We sat around a large fire, laughing and discussing odd things.

"Just think," said Lana. "If Katie had not taken you in, you might have been one of those British sailors returning to Britain." I sat in silence. "What's wrong with him? Does he miss home?" grinned Lana. I looked up.

"Lana, can you go and get some more beer?" asked Katie. I looked at Lana.

"I do not miss my country." I said loudly before Lana could get up. "As we were waiting to disembark, a stupid, self-opinionated British officer killed my best friend. My friend had helped defeat a shipload of pirates on our way to America. Despite this, he was selected for extra treatment, after which he was killed without mercy. That officer was the first of many British soldiers I have killed. That seems so long ago." I sighed. "So many lives have been wasted in this war. So many young British soldiers have been torn from their mother's arms and sent here to die."

Jen, who had joined us on this adventure, was remembering her family.

"My family were all killed on their farm. They were doing no one any harm, just looking after their animals, when the Indians struck. I had been sent to pick berries - if I was still at home, I would have died with them."

Thunder Cloud stood up.

"My tribe has given their elegance to both the British and the Americans during this war. Many people have died, but my people have suffered greatly. Many have died or are now crippled, but what have my tribe gained? The answer is nothing, in fact much of their land has been taken by the settlers."

White Eagle put her arm around her brother's shoulder as he sat back down. I now stood.

"Many have lost both friends and relatives, but also possessions. We can sit and weep about how badly we have been treated. But we cannot forget that because of this war, many of us have found the love of our lives. I used to spend most days drinking and moaning my life away, but because of this war, I have met the most beautiful, kindest, woman in the world. Now I could not imagine spending a day without her.

Most of us have a dream. If we follow the sun across this land, until it sets, many dreams will be laid out for us to grasp. There will be tribes of strange Indians to fight. Mountains will rise into the sky, rivers will roar, there will be massive deserts to cross, where it seldom rains. We will come across weird and wonderful animals. We can sit here and whine about how the world hates us. Or, join Katie and myself, as we journey west in search of our dream home. We had planned to wait until the official end to this war, and America is truly independent. But Katie and I believe that this war is as good as finished, thanks to people like Katie's Rangers. We are returning to our island now. But this may just be the last time that we will return. The next time, when we head west, there will be no return."

There were a few nods of agreement.

"Let's get some sleep, we will be returning to our island when we awake." Katie said.

"Katie, Dafydd. We have built our wagon; it is all ready for our journey. I just took a look to see if everything was ok in it and found stowaways hiding under our blankets." Informed Lana.

"They are escaped slaves." Andy confirmed. "If we keep them here, then soon we will get a visit from the overseer and his men. It is punishable by death to conceal a slave, and there are six in our wagon."

Katie and I went to visit the escaped slaves. They were all very frightened. The punishment for escaping is also death for a slave. One of the Rangers who was watching, added his point of view.

"If you try to take them with us, the overseer will call in the local law officer. They can hold the wagon train up for ages, and still drag the slaves off Lana's wagon. Katie looked at me.

"What shall we do?" asked Katie. "Slavery, is no way to treat a human being."

A crowd had now gathered. I signalled for the man, who seemed to be the father of the children, to come down. I got him to stand next to me.

"If you look carefully, there is only one difference between us. The colour of our skin. I know that slavery has been going on since the beginning of time. I also am aware that white people have enslaved many black people; black people have also enslaved white people; brown skinned people have made slaves of people all over Asia. Slavery is evil. I for one will not deliver these people into the hands of the overseer and his men."

As I finished my speech, a group of men with guns approached. They were very loud, and the one who appeared to be the leader was giving orders for his men to drag the slaves away. One of his men grabbed hold of the man who had been standing by my side.

I moved like lightning. I punched the man who had taken the lead and was now standing between the escaped slaves, and the men who wanted to take them. The overseer moved forward a couple of feet.

"This is the sheriff. He has a warrant for the arrest of those escaped slaves. As you appear to have captured them, I will give you the reward for their capture."

The sheriff then walked up to me and ordered me to let the overseer take his slaves. I didn't move. The overseers' men pointed their guns at me. I began to smile.

"You have twenty guns pointing at me. Have a look around, you have about six hundred guns pointing at you. Not your men, just you."

He ordered his men to lower their guns. The sheriff then tried to interfere again.

"Sheriff. I am a major in the American army. I am friends with George Washington and John Adams. Tell me, who has the most authority here?" The sheriff gave up and told the overseer that it was a lost cause.

"How much would you say the slaves are worth?" I asked.

The overseer wanted to say that they were not for sale. But he could see his choice was either take the money, or leave without the slaves or the money. He finally made up a price, which I was happy to pay. He took the money and was about to leave, when I called him back.

"Don't forget to leave their papers!"

He reluctantly threw them towards me, and they landed on the ground. That was it, I had had enough of him. I pulled him off his horse, and dragged him over to where the new free people were standing in disbelief. I threw him on the ground and ordered him to apologise to them. The woman, who seemed to be the wife of the family, helped the overseer up.

"We are Christians. We have forgiveness in our hearts. Please, do no more harm to him."

Then two of the family helped him back to his horse. They all rode off as the family picked up their papers off the ground. I was so angry with the slave owners, that I had forgotten that I was a Christian.

"These are our papers; we now belong to you." The woman said, holding the papers out to me.

Katie could see that I was hurt. She again came to my aid. She took the papers from the woman.

"Val, will you write up papers saying our friends here are now free. Then arrange for a wagon for them, and some provisions." She tore the papers up. "None of you are slaves anymore, you are all free people. Please don't think badly of my husband, his heart is in the right place, sometimes he just gets a bit carried away." Explained Katie.

"Not at all, I just wanted things to stop, I am sorry. My name is Mary. My husband is Jake. This is my sister; her name is Carol." She gestured to the other woman in the group. "My son's name is Brian, then we have my oldest daughter, Jasmine, and finally, my youngest is Dawn. Please give my apologies to your husband. It's because of him that we are free. We thank you from the bottom of our hearts."

CHAPTER 29

THE WAY WEST: IN SEARCH OF OUR DREAMS

All five hundred Rangers, or thereabouts returned home on the 1st of November 1782. It was a long, quiet journey.

The war finally ended on September 3rd 1783, when the Treaty of Paris was signed between the United States and Great Britain. This treaty recognized the independence of the United States and set the boundaries of the new nation. The war had lasted for more than eight years, cost countless lives and resources, and fundamentally changed the political landscape of the world. With the signing of the Treaty of Paris, the United States was recognized as a sovereign nation, free to pursue its own destiny. There could finally be peace.

I organised a massive meeting in the town square to decide who would be joining us on our journey west. At the end of the meeting 72 people decided to stay. We agreed that the homes they currently lived in would be given to them to keep. The remaining homes would be sold, to help finance the journey.

Most of us, however, wanted to go west. The Rangers had got used to the adventure, and the fighting. They were not the kind of people who could sit down and live a peaceful life. Yet.

We informed everyone that we were going to meet up with our leaders and put together a management committee, to organise the journey. What was for sure, was that we would need money. And lots of it.

Katie and I went round to see Jane. We explained that we needed as much money as we could get to finance our journey west. She was sitting at her desk grinning at Georgie.

"Do you remember all those pieces of treasure the lads collected off the dead?" she asked. I nodded. "Well, we kept most of that. During the uncertainty of the war, it was difficult to decide what currency to keep. So, we kept the old favourite. Gold. It's finally time to exchange it for dollars, and don't forget the gold which the British gave us.

"I hope that we will have enough. Jane, we are going to offer people to be responsible for certain jobs, will you, Georgie and Val continue look after the finance and administration?"

They agreed. We were so pleased with their decision; it would be so important to have a good administrator.

Later, I sent a messenger to our friend Daniel Boone. I want him to lead us through the Wilderness, and to recommend a leader for our wagon train.

We went to the hospital next, but unfortunately didn't receive the response we had hoped for. Gwen Morris had decided to stay.

She loved the hospital, and wanted to remain as the head. The good news was that Rachell Greenhill did want to go with us. She had more than proven her abilities. It was a pleasure to appoint her.

"Rachell, this is not a job you will be able to deliver on your own. Please choose a team to support you."

She nodded.

"Don't worry Katie, I have a list of names already."

"Where to next, my love?" I asked.

"Dafydd, I have to wait and have a chat with Rachell. You go to the stable, we can meet up at home after." I asked if she was ill, but she said that nothing was wrong, that she just needed to have a chat. I went over to the stables. I had been hoping that everyone who held management positions before, would naturally say yes to joining us. As soon as I reached the stables, there was old George. He knew what I had come to ask and beat me to the punch.

"Sorry Captain. I am too old to travel all that way across deserts and mountains. I will have to decline the offer. But I can put you in contact with two very talented people, who are more than capable of doing the job." George waved to a couple of girls who had been standing around the corner. "Come on, don't be shy now!" he shouted.

Out they came, April and June.

"They have proven themselves to be very talented, with more than enough ability to deliver the job." George assured me.

I turned to the girls.

"If I provide you with all that you need, including a promotion to give you both the authority you will require in this position, will you take the job?" They looked a little worried.

"It will be a lot to handle. To look after the horses, make sure they are healthy, continue to get replacements, and get food for them the whole year. It's a big job."

"You won't have to find food for them, it will all be provided. Also, I will give you 100 % support. Or if you're not up to it perhaps you can recommend someone else?"

That did it. They had been messing with me. They nearly bit my arm off. Job filled.

While I was there, I took advantage of asking Jen if she was going to take care of intelligence, with Madge. They both gladly agreed. Jen then confirmed that they would recruit more help for their department, before we left.

I was back home before Katie arrived. I was tired and laid on the bed, soon I was asleep. I was woken up by Katie pushing me back and forth, and repeating "Dafydd, Dafydd, Dafydd!" excitedly.

Eventually I opened my eyes.

"Hello my love, are you tired the same as me?"

She shook her head.

"Dafydd, the list of names that we made. It is missing a very important position." I tried to think what she might mean, but I had no idea.

"At least one of the wagons should be a creche. And we will need someone in charge."

I nodded in agreement.

"Do you think we will have many mothers or fathers who would need to use it?"

She began to giggle.

"What are you laughing at? Are you laughing at me?"

She was still grinning as she replied.

"I think that you will want to use it my love".

I was trying to work out why I would require a creche. Then the penny dropped. I stared at my Katie.

"So that's why you wanted to chat with Rachell?" I rushed to my feet and held her in my arms. "Ok, no more work for you. You must rest!"

She pushed me off.

"Dafydd, I am not ill, I am just expecting our baby. I am as normal as you are. According to Rachell, our baby is due on May 15th. So, you had better organise a creche quickly, or you will be doing lots of babysitting." she laughed.

"May 15th eh? Ok we will plan to start our journey at the end of May. That's five months to prepare.

The following morning, I could not wait to tell everyone I met that Katie was expecting. I was so excited. I was going to become a father!

I began to wonder what kind of father I would be. Well, to start with, I would keep them safe. Make sure they were never hungry. I began to think back to my childhood. Having no mother, and my father working all hours to put food on the table for me and my brother, I was left on my own a lot. I knew that he loved me but as I seldom saw him, there were times when I felt unloved. I would never let my child feel unloved. The I felt a smack on my back.

"Are you daydreaming again? We still have a lot of things to organise, so get yourself together."

What a woman, she was carrying her first child, but she carried on as though she wasn't.

"Ok my love, let's have a word with Gawain. If we run out of food, we will be in big trouble."

We arrived at the kitchens. As most people now ate at home, and we were not marching off to any battles, it was more like a restaurant. There he was, sitting on his chair in the corner of the hall. Katie was hungry, so decided to go get some food while I talked to Gawain.

"I have been waiting for you to make your visit. You want to know if I am coming with you, and will I still take care of providing the meals?"

"Of course, and you are about to say 'please let me come with you!'" I grinned. Gawain laughed.

"Ok, yes, I will. But. I have asked Thunder Cloud, Mark, John and Nick to take care of the hunting. If you're ok with that, I am in."

"Hang on, what about Jean and White Eagle?" I asked

"Haven't you heard?" he said with a grin. "They are both expecting! Their husbands did not think that they should be out hunting buffalo." I agreed with him. Or rather, them. I could not get back to Katie quick enough.

"Katie, I have been wondering, how many wagons will be required as a creche? Also, I presume that while the babies are in creche, the mums will be working?"

"Don't forget, a creche is not for new born babies."

Now I was not happy - I could lose a lot of mums.

"So even after a mother has given birth, they won't be able to work?" Katie had now realised what I was hedging towards.

"Of course, if you employed some baby nurses, then they could look after the babies most of the time." She grinned.

"How many new born babies can you get into a wagon with a nurse?"

"I am not sure," she replied.

"Could we get three into one wagon?"

She shrugged her shoulders.

"Why three?"

Could be more. Depends on the age of the child.

"Well, I gather that White Eagle and Jean will also be needing a wagon."

Katie picked up the nearest thing and threw it at me.

"Wait till I get you Mr Dragon." She shouted.

I grabbed hold of her gently and hugged her.

"Wait, calm down, remember the baby!"

It took her a while to admit it.

"Ok, you are right. Let's get the rest of the managers signed up."

"We could ask Tony if he would take charge of building the wagons. After all, if he can build houses a wagon should be easy enough."

"Well, he can only say no. I think that the best person to ask about baby care has to be Rachell." Again, I agreed.

After a long tiring day. We ended up having a drink with White Eagle, and Jean, plus their husbands. By that I mean that the men had a beer, while the women had water.

What was I doing? It was two hours of baby talk. White Eagle was expecting in February. Jean was due in April. They had both already begun their knitting. Katie was not a woman to sit and spend hours knitting. I expected that she would either buy our babies clothes or get someone else to do the knitting. That thought made me smile.

"Dafydd, you know that I will have to do a lot of things for our baby when it is born."

I put my arm around her.

"Yes, my love, you will be an amazing mother."

She then wrapped an arm around my waist.

"If I need any help, will you do things for me, my love?"

I gave her a quick kiss.

"Of course I will!"

She then whispered in my ear.

"Will you do some knitting? I need some clothes made."

I felt like a deer who had just lifted its head and seen a hunter with it in its sights.

"I just remembered something; I will see you back at the house." Then I ran out of the door.

I went into a couple of taverns and had a chat with a few elderly people who had been to California on a wagon train. I must admit, talking to them made me want to begin our journey now. It was finally time to return home. Now what am I going to tell Katie? One thing is for sure, I can't tell her a lie.

I then noticed a group of elderly ladies playing a game. They were all sitting on the boardwalk. One of the old ladies was crying, the others were shouting at her.

"I am sorry to butt in, but I can see that something is wrong."

One of those who was doing all the shouting, began to explain.

"This woman owes us four dollars each. But apparently she has stupidly been conned out of the money by some smart talking man. Now she can't pay us."

I pulled some notes out of my pocket.

"There you are ladies, I will give you $5 each to cover any interest." I helped the lady up who had been conned. "There you are, no need to cry. Please introduce me to the man who stole your money."

We did not have far to go. He was propped up against a bar in the nearest tavern, spending the woman's money. I walked in with the lady and asked her to take a seat. I then ordered a beer. I bumped into him, then apologised. I took out a big wad of dollars and offered to pay for his drink to make it up to him. That got his attention, I saw his eye bulge at the big wad of cash.

"I'd be careful with that if I were you, there are a lot of thieves around here." He warned me. "Do you live near here?"

"Not too far away, why?"

"I was thinking that I could escort you home. Come to think of it, I have a few friends here that can help as well."

"That's very kind of you, I will just finish my beer and then I will be ready to go home."

I was having a problem preventing myself from laughing. The bartender knew who I was, and we were quite close. I told him I was going for a walk and asked him to look after the old lady. I finished my beer and walked over to the con man.

"Ok, are you ready to escort me back to my place?" I asked.

They did not know where I lived but were more than happy to help me get there. We had walked about three streets, when two of his friends stood in front of me. That left two behind me, plus this good man who had offered to help me. The con man moved forward, then politely asked me to give him my money.

"I am sorry, I can't hear very well, can you come closer and speak?"

What a fool. He did. I punched him on his nose and broke it. The two at the back and the two in front, came at me at the same time. With Dragon power, I jumped about ten feet into the air over them and the four crashed into each other. They were all soon asleep. I then helped the one with the broken nose to his feet.

"You owe an elderly lady some money. And I doubt if you earnt any of this money. I will take it all and pass it on." He began to protest as I took his coin pouch.

I gave him one more punch, which may have broken his jaw.

"Perhaps now you will consider a change of career. There is no future in this one."

Returning to the tavern, I sat with the old lady. I showed her all the money I took from the thief. She agreed that he must have stolen most, if not all, of it. After taking my money back, we gave the rest to the old people's home, where the old lady who I had helped lived. Her name was Agnes. I was soon surrounded with old ladies who were asking if there was anything they could do to help me.

"I do have a small problem…"

I walked into the house.

"Hi Katie, I'm home. I understand what you were saying about all the hard work you will have to do when the baby is born. And that you wanted me to learn to knit." She knew me well, and was wondering what I had planned to get out of it. "Katie, I would like to introduce you to some friends of mine. They all live at an old folk's home about half a mile away. You will never believe it. But these ladies and their friends *love* to knit."

Now this, she did not expect. She looked at me and burst into tears of laughter.

Katie, Andy, Lana and myself became tavern visitors. We were on the lookout for people who have been to California by wagon train. All of us were looking for information. Sometimes it cost us the price of a few beers, but we got a lot of useful information.

We learnt about the various tribes that we would come across. Also, bits about the geography of the land, we would cross.

It was early days; most of us would be the ones who would make the trails, for others to follow. We were considering the first two tribes we would likely encounter along the wilderness trail. The Cherokee and the Shawnee. The Rangers have fought them many times during the war. Apparently, large herds of buffalo used the trail. If we found ourselves in front of a stampede, we would be in trouble.

Soon, February arrived, along with a baby boy for Jean and Thunder Cloud. It had been a hard winter but it was now coming to an end. Two more messengers were sent off to get Daniel Boone. He finally arrived In the middle of March, at 6am.

I remember it well; White Eagle had given birth to another boy. I had been celebrating with Mark and a few others.

"Good morning, Daniel. Can I offer you breakfast?" I asked.

He gave his approval. Then introduced us to his wife, and the new leader of the wagon train. A man named Ward Bond. He explained that his wife seldom saw him. So, this time, she wanted to come with him. They had got their relatives and neighbours to look after their farm and the children.

At breakfast we were formally introduced to Mr Bond. He was about forty years old. He had taken wagon trains to California and along the Oregon Trail. Lana asked him if they had all gotten there safely.

"My dear, if any had failed to get through, I would be dead, with my scalp hanging in some buck's lodge. Either this wagon train gets through, or none of us will live."

Daniel quickly intervened.

"My friend here, Mr Ward Bond, can be a straight talker. He is just making the point that this is not a game. If we win, we will get the prize of land and a new life somewhere in the West. The Loser pays with their lives. If you don't want to take this gamble, then you should withdraw from this game. Go and find a nice house here, and get a job in Philadelphia."

I knew all the Rangers and their families had made their decision. They would not change now. They knew it may be dangerous.

However, we had gained a lot of other people who wanted a new life for themselves and their families. It would be these who may decide to drop out. They had brought their own wagons and supplies.

We had been having breakfast but ended up listening to a speech. A young man of about 25, smartly dressed, wearing a suit which was better worn in an office, walked to the front of the dining room.

"I am sorry if I am spoiling your breakfasts," he announced to the room, "but I feel I need to respond to Mr Bond's statement. My Name is Edward Jenkins. People call me Teddy. I was brought up at my family's plantation in Virginia. My life has always been easy, everything that I have ever wanted was mine. As a child and then a teenager, I lived in an amazing world. One day, I decided to go for a ride. It was a nice sunny day. I heard some screaming; I rode over to where the noise was coming from. Two black people, who worked on our plantations, a man and a woman, were being flogged. I ordered the flogging to be stopped. I asked why they were being flogged. The reply was that they had not worked hard enough. I looked at the young woman, her back was cut to pieces. I was furious and ordered them both to be cut down and their backs to be treated. The man was cut down first, then as they were about to cut the woman down, the man began to run. One of the men picked up his rifle, and shot the man dead. He then turned to me and told me that it was ok, the dead man was getting old and wasn't worth a lot. At the time I was stunned. I continued my ride absorbing what I could see.

For the first time, it came to me that the good life I had been living was bought with the sweat and blood of these poor people. I stormed into the house and confronted my father. He informed me that this was life, and if I wanted to continue living in a world of luxury, then I would have to accept it. This I could no longer do. At the age of 23, I left my family's mansion. For the past two years I have been doing office jobs. I am well educated and office jobs are easy to get.

However, I heard about this wagon train. To me, this is an opportunity to turn my life round. I will use my education and acquire land. Yes, I may die on the way. But at least I would have tried. Better than just existing here in Philadelphia. If you are happy to accept the life which you have been dealt, please stay in this city. If not, give this wagon train some consideration. Please continue your breakfasts" He then, after all that, went back to his breakfast.

He had been sitting at his table by himself. On return he found Katie sitting at his table eating her breakfast. I had to laugh, I was going to speak with this man, he kept mentioning a good education. He may be of use to us. While I was thinking, Katies was already there.

I bid farewell to Daniel, and told him that I hoped to meet up tonight. I got him to promise that he would tell us a bit about the history of this country.

During the day we checked out how things were going. Tony promised us that the wagons would be ready in two weeks. Food was pretty much sorted already, they did not need hay until later in the year as the horses would be eating the fresh grass.

We met up with Daniel and most of the managers at a local tavern named The Red Dragon. Apparently the first owners were from Wales. Beers and snacks were ordered and we were all seated and waiting for Daniel to begin.

"The first British settlers stayed close to the Atlantic, in order to protect their supply train. At the end of the War of Independence, many more European settlers arrived, and like us, were beginning to move west.

By the 1750s, most of New England had been settled, leaving no other choice than to move west. The Virginia frontier had been pushed as far as the fall line. Some pioneers Have now climbed beyond the fall line, into the Blue Ridge mountains.

Many settlers scurried into Ohio, Tennessee, and Kentucky. Soon these states were transformed from wilderness into a region of farms and towns.

The Pioneers and Immigrants had already torn trails through the wilderness, heading to California and Oregon. They crossed deserts, forded rivers, climbed snow-capped mountains, and fought against many different tribes on their way west. This was all to get a new life for themselves.

"There is so much land to be claimed," Katie said. "Daniel, we have heard of the trail that you and some axemen have cut out, ready for wagons. We were wondering if you would lead the train through your wilderness road. After that, it will be up to our wagon master to decide our route."

"I thought you would ask that question," he grinned. "which is why I brought my wife with me. I will guide the wagons, then I will take my wife back home."

That was brilliant news. Those who were not working rested. We were going to need all our energy to cross the Pacific.

Katie was nearly due. Finally, the day came. It was 2am in the morning when she woke me up, telling me that her waters had broken. I didn't have a clue as to what she was talking about. I ran out of the door trying to find any women who could help. Everyone was asleep. Katie began shouting that the baby was coming. I boiled some water, washed my hands, then knelt down in front of her. I had no idea what to do but I felt like I had to act like I did. After a long time, the baby's head appeared. I felt so useless. Katie was screaming in pain. Finally, I gathered up enough courage to put my hands under our baby's head. Slowly, the head moved forward and the body appeared, then the legs, and our baby was in my hands. It was crying, and Katie was shouting, asking what sex it was. I had become a statue.

Then the thought came that I needed to wrap it up. It must be kept warm. I tore pieces of the sheets when Madge walked into our bedroom.

"I was wondering what all the noise was," she claimed. "Dafydd, you have done well. Now leave everything to me." She found some clean cloth to wrap our baby in, then cut the umbilical cord.

"Madge, Katie wants to know what our baby's sex is?" I whispered. She laughed loudly.

"Dafydd, you were holding your baby. Have you forgotten the difference between boys and girls?" asked Madge as she checked. "Katie, you have a daughter!"

A daughter, I thought, a little baby girl. I was a father.

"Hello Mum, you did so well," I said, walking over to Katie and putting my arm around her. Lucky for me, Rachel appeared with some nurses. They managed to clean Katie and our baby up and change the sheets. Then they left my brilliant wife to sleep. The nurses took the baby and said that they would look after her for tonight.

It was now nearly 7am. Katie was asleep on our bed. I picked up a few blankets and went into the next room and laid down on the floor. To my surprise, I fell asleep.

"Dafydd, get up." was the sweet sound that I received when I woke. It was Val. She had made her way over.

"What is the time?" I asked. Lana replied. "It's 8am on Monday, May 26th, 1784, and we all want to know if you have named your daughter."

There were at least eight women staring at me, waiting for my reply.

"Well, we thought that our baby would be a boy, like the other two, so the name we arrived at was George."

When one is lying on the floor with eight women punching you. It can be very painful. I should not have joked with them.

"Come on, tell us her name already!" Shouted Jane.

"Ok, ok, you win. Her name is Julia."

I then jumped up and while they were discussing her name. I grabbed young Julia, and ran into Katie's room.

"There my love, the product of all our love." I declared as I laid our baby in her arms. Mother and child looking at each other through the eyes of true love.

After a week, Rachell let mother and child out of hospital. I had brought a horse and a small cart. We were soon home. I had built a cot for Julia to sleep in, she was such a good baby.

"My love, a while ago you met up with the lad Edward Jenkins, did he have anything useful to say?"

Katie finished tucking Julia up in her cot.

"He comes from a very rich family. They sent him to the best university in England. I believe it was called 'Oxford'. He studied business and economics. He is a very intelligent man. He has promised to help us. He stated that his dream was to be involved in building a town from scratch."

I thought about what his role could be based upon his experience. "How about our logistics officer?"

Katie seemed impressed. We will talk with him next time we see him.

Jen was working late, trying to complete everything, before she met up with the wagons, and left for her dream home in the west. The door unexpectedly opened.

"Hi, my name is Edward, but my friends call me Teddy. I am glad that I have caught you before you left. I am about to be given the job of logistics officer, which involves helping with the plans to build a new town.

As you run, what I am being told is, a detective agency, I was thinking that you would be able to help me."

Jen thought that this wasn't a good time to talk, but he was a handsome man, and she would like to meet him later.

"Teddy, I am very busy with last minute preparation. I am sure that we can work together. Can we meet up later, when we are on our way."

"I understand, and will make a point to meet up with you in a couple of days. Actually, I have worked in offices in the past. If I can support you in any way, I would be pleased to help."

Jen was going to refuse his offer, but then she looked at all the work she still had to complete.

"Teddy, I have lots to finish in a short time, so I will be happy to accept your kind offer."

Three hours later, they were finished. They bade each other farewell and agreed to meet up later to discuss the town plans.

June 1ˢᵗ arrived. Two hundred waggons were lined up behind us. I was told that everything was ready. Daniel Boone was called over to make a speech.

"We are about to leave Philadelphia. Friends, you are leaving civilization behind you. No more soft bed to lay on. Most of the time the earth we walk on, will also be our bed. There will be no shops to buy your groceries. From now on, you eat and drink what we take from the environment. If you don't, you will starve. This is not a Sunday School picnic, we have a journey of close to 3000 miles. The wilderness trail alone is 200 miles long. The trail is steep, rough and narrow. We will normally travel fifteen miles a day.

Our biggest problem will be the native Americans. At any time, we can be attacked by the Shawnee, or the Cherokee warriors. A lesser problem is that buffalo use this trail, which could actually be to our benefit, as this could provide us with meat. Or death, if we are caught in a stampede. If we survive the journey along the wilderness trail and get through the Cumberland Gap, you will have completed the first stage of your journey to your new life. Before you, there will be snow-capped mountains, deserts, powerful fast flowing rivers, and thousands of Indians, fiercer than the Shawnee or Cherokee warriors.

But my friends, if you survive all these hardships. A new, better life is waiting for you. Some of you may become ranchers, there are miles of lush grass in Oregon. You will all be able to own your own plots of land. These lands are rich in gold. You will have arrived at the end of the rainbow. You will all find your pot of gold.

Anyway, enough talking. Are we all ready?"

If you are then make sure that you have packed all that Ward had advised in your wagons, and are ready to move towards your Dream.

Ingram Content Group UK Ltd.
Milton Keynes UK
UKHW050659200623
423698UK00003BA/8